STONE

By

I. J. Ferrestone

I J FERRESTONE

CONTENTS

Dedicated to all the selfless fighters who made me who I am and in loving memory of my Mum and Nan.

STONE

Chapter 1

Interesting Beginnings

The warm summer breeze blew gently through Eastcote, a suburban area of North London. It was actually a nice day. Well, it wasn't raining, snowing or the first sneeze of a hurricane. That kind of ever-changing weather was what you could expect in the space of a day in the UK, so it was what was seen in England as a pretty good day.

There was a little park in the middle of one the northern neighbourhoods of the city. It was a communal hot-spot, complete with paths that the council hadn't bothered to fix in years, often occupied by joggers and dog-walkers, a playground which was always full of rowdy children and gossiping mothers, and handful of old, tall trees, which swayed in the warm breeze. One of these trees was providing shelter for a young woman, who was sitting under it and looking at the ground and moving dirt aside, absent-mindedly with a stick. She had light brown skin with a reddish undertone, and her full head of dark red curls was pulled up onto the top of her head in a loose bun. Her jeans had dry mud on their cuffs, she just had to remember to knock it all off before she got home, so she didn't get an earful from her parents for tracking in mud again. She had a strange love for old and lost things from another time, and also trying new things and staying busy. The scratching movement was an old habit from her childhood. She'd wanted to be an archaeologist and had caused her parents a lot of trouble at the time, by borrowing her Mum's gardening tools and digging little holes in areas of the park when she couldn't find anything in her back garden. She never found anything beyond an old dessert spoon and mouse bones though.

Someone was watching her, and she knew they were there, but still she continued her absent-minded scratching. The world became strangely still, as if everyone on Earth was holding their breath in suspense.

There was a snarl as something leapt from the tall grass in front of the teenager.

The girl simply sniffed in amusement as a mop of red hair flew towards her. She launched herself into the air effortlessly, turning to see the attacker fly forward and hit its head on the tree she had been sitting under. Then it fell and landed where she had previously been. The girl laughed as she landed gracefully and gently on her feet.

The thing turned, revealing himself to be a freckled child, that looked very much like her. "Aww!", he moaned, "This is so unfair! How do you always see me coming, Tess?"

The girl laughed, her shoulder length black hair catching the wind and turning a little red in the afternoon sun. She bent down, looking her prize in the eye. "Maybe you're too loud, too obvious or too...Billy-ish. But you will never know why.", she answered. And with a smooth movement of her arms, she took him by the ankles, lifted him completely off the ground, swinging the struggling load over her shoulder like a sack. As she started walking, she sighed. "And that's because I don't know myself.", she quietly finished, trying to smile fully, but not succeeding.

Theresa, or Tess, as she was more commonly known, walked calmly down the streets of her hometown of Eastcote. Even though she lived in a large city, she still called her area a town. Her screaming younger brother Bill drew no attention, since her neighbours were so used to seeing Bill being carted, defeated and bound, home by his soon-to-be 18-year-old sister.

As she was heading back to her house, she saw a group of schoolmates from her year, heading towards her, deep in conversation and oblivious to her presence. Once one of them was aware of her, the ring-leader in the front, a pretty and vain girl who was partially convincing at acting like a nice person, fell silent. The other two with her followed her gaze and also fell silent. They knew they were too close to fake not having seen Tess, or to cross to the other side of the street nonchalantly and feign ignorance, so they put on their best smiles and greeted her.

"Hey Tess!" trilled the ringleader, all smiles and brightness, but she couldn't disguise her eyes which leaked annoyance and anger.

"Hi.", mumbled Tess. Their parents were friends, but the relationship hadn't rubbed off on their offspring. "Just heading home with some trouble, I found. How are you?"

"I'm ok.", she sang again. "Oh, congratulation on your medal for that Teen Gymnastics tournament. I heard some scout was even trying to speak to you about doing the Olympics."

Tess shrugged. She heard the venom in her voice and she was about to receive some more.

The girl on the ring-leader's right grinned like a creepy porcelain faced doll. "Talented Tess does is again."

As Tess grimaced at the annoying nickname that had been given to her when she was in Junior School. Her Mum had been bugging her to ask someone, anyone to come to some last-minute birthday plans her parents had put together. But why bother? These guys clearly didn't like her. The boy on the ringleader's left just scanned her up and down and kissed his teeth. Tess closed her mouth, that she hadn't even realised she had opened, stepped around them and said goodbye, continuing her journey homeward.

As if reading her mind, the ringleader suddenly called after her. "Oh, Tess, about your message...." She was referring to a birthday invitation Tess's Mum had sent to her two months ago, unbeknownst to Tess, which she had conveniently misplaced then found and forgot to reply to, just like all the others. "I'm sorry but my Grandma's in town and I haven't seen her in *ages*, so I won't be able to make it. I hope you understand. But we'll do something soon, yeah?"

Tess simply nodded, waved and then kept walking. So, her party attendance list was down to ...zero. More cake for her. And thankfully this rid her of the chore of spending a day socialising with clones and twits. Although she was a little sad, she was grateful for that.

Theresa walked on auto-pilot until she found herself entering her front door. She opened the door to the strong chorus of her mother's loud, assertive tone and her father's patient and quieter voice. She dropped her squealing brother on the hallway floor, adding his voice to the symphony of tumult within the house. She took the stairs two at a time, passing her big brother's room on the way to her own. She smiled at Simeon, as he sat writing his dissertation with Korn blaring from his laptop to his head. She always liked being around him; he always protected her and was the only one in the house who wasn't constantly making noise. Like her, he just listened to it, in the form of intense and odd music, but by choice.

She stepped into her room and closed the door. It was her birthday in two days, and she didn't feel like she had a real future to look forward to. She'd probably just do what every other female who didn't really have a goal seemed to do: finish her A-Levels, go to University, get a job or do something to do with sports, live with her parents until she met a guy who wasn't a complete dunce, eventually marry and then divorce him within a short space of time, have a toy-boy and then spend the rest of her life drinking with her mates and interfering in her kids' lives. She looked in the mirror. She peered at the face she saw every morning but still, something didn't feel right. She saw the eyes, hair and smile of someone who wasn't really content with who and where she was. It just felt wrong. It always had.

She sat on her bed and looked around her room. She saw medals, pictures, newspaper clipping and certificates. Her eyes rested on the online article detailing how, when she was around one-year-old, she had been diagnosed with an unknown biological disorder which meant she had to take regular doses of serum which she injected into her system three times a day. However, she displayed an amazing sense of strength, flexibility and reflexes. She had won diving, judo, gymnastic and karate competitions. She also did dance for a while, but she felt too self-conscious about performing, and stopped after a year. Her parents, Fred and Diane, were proud and saw it as their daughter being given a second chance. Theresa saw it as her being a mystery and a freak, even in her own eyes.

This had made most people in her age range wary or jealous of her. And the ones that *did* like her didn't invite her to anything or talk to hear out of fear of the ones who didn't like her.

Therefore, her birthday would be interesting since everyone her age had other things to do or didn't like her because of her accomplishments. And for these reasons, she would probably spend her birthday with her noisy family. Another blissful day in August. She sighed. At least school was out for the year.

She sat reading a book she had just bought to pass the summer weeks. Since she had no friends to contact, unless you could call her coach a friend, or even cousins, since her parents had no siblings or surviving parents, she had to spend her hours at home as interestingly as possible. She listened to Billy's being picked up by friends to go out for the evening. Lucky devil.

She read for another hour or so. She couldn't tell. Time and her little world fell away when she read.

"TESS!", her mum yelled, her voice shaking the floorboards. "DINNER!"

Tess sighed again. She was doing that a lot lately. "OK. I'm coming!", she answered.

As she descended her staircase, she heard a ringing in her head. She gasped as the sound turned into pain and it steadily increased. She saw flashes, images, a man and woman cowering on the floor, the silhouette of a man holding what looked like a sword and her front door. She cried out as a searing pain hit her chest and a man's scream filled her ears.

Everything went dark and the last thing she felt was air rushing past her ears.

Diane stopped when she heard something heavy tumbling down the stairs. She dropped her kitchen knife and walked unsurely into the hallway. She didn't know how to react when she saw Theresa lying in a pile at the foot of the staircase.

"FREDERICK!!", she screamed. She dove forward and took hold of Tess's shoulder. She turned her over and gasped. Her eyes were wide open and her irises, that were normally brown, were pools of swirling bright colours, like a moving rainbow.

Fred came thundering into the hallway. He came to a stop and groaned. "Oh no.", he mumbled.

Simeon has appeared at the top of the stairs and stood dead still. "Mum!", he cried, "What's going on?"

Diane looked regretfully into her son's eyes. "It's happening.", she announced, sighing. "Help me take her upstairs before Billy gets home. Thank God he had plans."

Simeon rushed down the stairs and lifted his sister one movement, grunting. His parents watched as Simeon slowly carried her back up the stairs and to her room.

Diane eventually managed to move and looked at her husband. Fred looked at the fear and sadness in his wife's eyes. He took her into his arms and kissed her forehead. "It'll be alright, D. We knew this day would come. All we have to do now is to be brave and help her."

Diane tried to answer, but instead she just sobbed. That night, the dinner went untouched, and Theresa slept, as deeply as the dead and did not wake up for quite some time.

Chapter 2

Odd Findings

The sound of rain on the window drummed in the young woman's ears like a marching band. Tess's eyes stung as she opened them. She felt like every hay-fever and hangover horror story she'd overheard in public or at school was happening in one go. Damn it!

She sat up slowly and propped herself up on her arms and looked towards her window, expecting to see the sunset sky she'd walked home under. But it was night. What time was it? What happened with dinner? Why did her head hurt so much?

Suddenly she heard soft footsteps coming to her doorway. Her mum walked in with a mug of coffee. Tess sighed. Either the coffee was for her and her mum had known she was awake, or she'd been out cold for ages and her mum had been watching her.

"Hey, hun. How's my girl?", Diane whispered as she sat down as the foot of the bed. She must have known her head was busting.

"I'm not dead, so I'm good.", Theresa replied, with a grimace disguised as a smile. Even the sound of her own voice made her brain sore.

Diane sighed and attempted an amused laugh. "Wow.", she jested, "What a way to start your birthday celebrations."

Tess tried not to look directly into any light, or any darkness for that matter, for fear of the contents of her skull making an artistic mess on everything in her room. "What do you mean, Mum?", she asked, opening one eye and tilting her head slightly to look at her mother.

"You been asleep for just over twenty-four hours.", Diane revealed, chuckling to disguise how worried she was. "Your birthday is only two hours away."

"What?!", Tess cried, sending her head into a hurting, swaying mass of weight. "Ow."
She scrambled around for her alarm clock. Sure enough, it was three minutes to ten and the moon was glowing like a giant neon sign, letting her know it was, in fact, night-time. She fell back onto her pillow, her head feeling like a waterbed with angry jellyfish inside it.

Diane looked tenderly at her girl, who was clutching her skull and rocking from side to side, grimacing heavily. "I'll go and send Simeon up to chat to you. He's been worrying about you like mad. I had to force him to leave the house and go to work this morning. He was going to call his manager and say he wasn't coming to work due to a family emergency."

Tess grinned, looking up from under her palm. "That's so sweet. OK. Send him up. But no music. My head can't take much tonight."

Diane nodded as she stood slowly and walked quietly out of the bedroom. She knocked her eldest son's bedroom door. There was no reply, so she simply pushed the door and sure enough, Simeon was sat staring out of his window with his headphones on. He loved this form of escapism, but his parents found it annoying. No matter how many times they told him that not being able to hear them would one day lead to a painful demise, he was still walking around, dumb to the world, the next day.

Diane tapped his shoulder. He turned and saw her mouth the word 'Tess'. Diane found it so endearing and amusing as Simeon jumped up instantly, ripping his headphones out of his ears. His dark curls bounced everywhere as he scrambled to his feet.

"She's awake! How is she?", he cried, anxiety colouring his entire face.

Diane put a finger to her lips to silence him. "Shhhh. She wants to

15

see you, but she has a terrible headache. And be gentle with her; no fighting like you usually do, or she may hit you so hard you'll be seeing galaxies for weeks. Do you remember what happened last time you made her mad?"

Simeon looked in the corner of the room at the graffiti-covered cast leaning against his wardrobe that had, in some respects, only just 'cooled'. He turned back to his mother. The slightly annoyed and reminiscent look on his face said it all.

Diane slapped him encouragingly on the back as he made his way to the lion's den. She smiled. They were so close and loved each-other unconditionally. No-one annoyed each-other or stuck up for each-other as much as Tess and Simeon did.

Simeon slid silently into his sister's room. The walls were covered in the usual: trophies, certificates, film posters, and gothic art pieces. Her only real passion was art, fighting and her family, as much as she denied it.

"Hello?", he whispered, looking down at the figure on the bed. She didn't move but she was alert to his presence. He could tell because her eyelids swivelled in his direction like ping-pong balls under her skin. As he leant closer, he almost laughed.

Her eyelids swung open. She was looking right at him. This was normal practice for the pair but this time there was a difference. For a split second, her eyes flashed bright and blood-red.

Simeon's smile fell and he fell backwards, hitting the floor. Tess practically screamed covering her ears and rolling around her bed, scrunched into a tight ball.

"Arrrgh! Simeon! What the hell is *wrong* with you?", she hissed, to avoid further damage to her ears. "My head feels like a firework display right now and you can't keep quiet for *two seconds*?"

Simeon heard his mother tutting as she quietly went down the stairs. "Honestly.", she mumbled shaking her head.

"Well, that would happen after falling headf-!", Simeon began, but he stopped as he saw his sister's eyes flash about ten different shades at once. And she didn't even realise it was happening.

"What?", she whispered, as she saw the frightened look on her brother's face. "What's wrong? Am I bleeding? No? What *happened*, Simeon? Why have I been asleep for so long?"

Simeon slowly sat down on the chair by her, not taking his eyes off his sister's. "You, er... fell down the stairs head-first."

Tess sat bolt upright in surprise. She sat in silence, letting this sink in. "Wow!", she finally mused. "And I'm still alive? That's... pretty cool."

Usually, Simeon was the image of messy playfulness, dressed in black, chains and studs from head to toe, his chin-length black curly hair tucked behind his ears and completing the look. But today his disposition didn't suit his attire. Today he was different. Simeon tried to laugh but all that came out was a quiet, nervous titter. Tess picked up on this.

"What's with you today? You're a bit... distant, like your scared of something.", she asked, pushing her brother playfully. Then she stopped. "Wait a minute."

Simeon felt his skin ripple in fear. Has she figured it out? Had she noticed the change in her? "W-what?", he replied.

"Why didn't you take me to A&E? If I'd fallen down a flight of stairs, shouldn't I be coming round from morphine right about now?", Tess queried, looking at her brother searchingly from a side-angle.

Simeon's tension didn't disappear. "It, er... wasn't safe to move you.", he lied. "Dr Jesser flew right over when Mum called him. He was in the U.S., but he somehow got here really fast. He brought some more of your medication. I gave it to you while you slept."

Tess scrunched up her face in mock disgust at this fact.

Simeon laughed. "Don't worry. I didn't inject you anywhere embarrassing or private.", he reassured. "I'm your brother, not some... other bloke."

Tess smiled. "I know.", she answered. "Were you up all night?"

Now it was Simeon's turn to scrunch up his nose and frown. "Are you mad?! No, I slept like a tranquilised elephant. I've got to sleep, you know, basic human needs."

Tess laughed, ignoring the ringing in her head. She knew he was lying, and she loved him for it. "Hmm.", she said, pretending to think. "That was a pretty apt description of yourself you made just then."

Simeon tipped his head to the side. "What, human?", he offered.

"Nah, the 'elephant' bit. There are people in comas who respond to noise and outside stimulus better than you do.", Tess teased, grinning diabolically.

Simeon started to launch himself forward to squish her with his body weight, but then thought twice. He just laughed and poked her leg. Tess giggled.

He stood and walked out of the room as quietly as he could. "And now...", he whispered, "I'm gonna go catch some more of that sleep I was talking about. See you in the morning."

"Night", she called after him, as quietly as she could. She closed her eyes. She thought it was best if she did the same and without much coercing, her body agreed.

*

A soft humming sound, like a television when it's switched on, rung in Tess' subconscious. It slowly grew, growing so loud and so piercing that it made her wake up with a start. She grabbed her head and shrieked. God! It was like there was a banshee in her room!

She felt around for the side of her bed, unable to open her eyes for the pain, and stood to go downstairs, with a little more caution this time, thanks to the previous days' events. Tess found the sound and pain lessening as she left her room. She stepped towards the stairs and the sound increased again. She turned herself until the whining decreased and found herself heading towards the loft. She didn't know why, but she opened the door and climbed the stairs into it, feeling a little better with every step.

She turned away from the window once she reached the top of the staircase, a soft silvery light illuminating everything in the room. She'd been up in the loft a million times. She used to hide there when things got too loud downstairs, and the case was now the same again, just much stranger.

The relief of the painful headache led her to an old clock, one of those Grandfather's clocks you find in Antique shops.

Tess stood looking at the clock, thinking: 'Now what?'. She felt cold air on her bare feet coming from below the clock. She looked down and saw dust being blown in her direction and more moonlight making the particles cast small shadows on the floor, making the wooden floor look like a Dalmatian's side.

Tess rubbed her hands together and gripped the clock by its sides. She exhaled slightly as she lifted it off the floor and put it aside as quietly as possible. She'd been told off before for doing late-night rummaging and waking everyone up, and she wasn't about to have it happen again.

She stood up straight, turned towards the now vacant space and gasped.

The door that loomed at about 7 feet high looked like something of a mix between a Victorian garderobe and an abandoned garden wall. It had vines and ivy and other intricate details carved into the ebony wood, snaking around the edges of the hinges and doorknob like hungry predators, the eery silver light of the moon making them look like they were moving, but that could only have been Tess's imagination. Couldn't it?

Her hand, entranced and moving of its own accord, stretched forward and gripped the handle, her curiosity and earnest giving her hand the strength and will that her brain would have refused to. The door clicked and glided aside to reveal a dusty room where the moonlight pouring through a tilted window made the dust seem like slow-falling snowflakes. Tess stepped slowly forward.

It was like another world. It was her house but there was... silence.

She walked to the only object in the room: a box. It looked like a small jewellery box, with the same carvings as the ones that were on the door. It rested in a corner where no light could reach it, squashed away, as if hiding from something as hard as it could.

Tess lifted it. She couldn't see it well in enough in its gloomy corner, so she brought it into the light so that she could study it. It seemed to have a lock on the front, but she couldn't see the key anywhere in the room. Maybe it was in the loft. She stepped back. She felt the change on her skin as her hands and the chest touched moonlight.

She heard a tiny click.

She turned and stared wide-eyed at the chest as it opened, by just a fraction, releasing into the room the smell of old musty papers and fabric.

Her eyes widening further with fascination, Tess placed the chest carefully on the floor and crouched down in front of it. She lifted the lid and found three things that she did not expect. One was a small doll, the kind of size that could only be of appropriate size for a very small baby, the other was a letter and the last item was a silver chain on which a pendant hung. It was a nest of silver vines which wrapped around a blue gem the size of a large marble.

The doll's face comforted her nerves and anticipation as it smiled up at her, silently reassuring her that there was nothing to fear. Tess raised it to her nose. It smelled sweet and sort of familiar. She tucked it under her arm as she picked up the letter and unfolded it.

It read thus:

"My dearest child,

If you are reading this, we are not back in Vancouver, you are not aware of who you are but instead you are living with Frederick and Diane. If you are reading this, the headaches and the display of images you do not recall having ever seen before will have started in your head and it is the eve of your 18th birthday. If you are reading this, my beautiful daughter, things did not go as we had hoped they would, and we are no longer with you."

At this point, Tess's eyes were wider than they'd ever been, her breathing was erratic and shaky, and no number of pretty dolls would help her now. Who was this person? Her head warned her to put the letter down and walk away, quickly, but the adventurer in her begged her to read on. And so, she continued, swallowing hard as she read.

"You were born 18 years ago in the mountains of Scotland at our family estate. Ilene Lara McCampbell, 21st August, 6 pounds and 2 ounces. We were so excited. You looked just like your mother. The same dark hair, flashing bright eyes and smile that could win the heart of whoever saw it. But as happy as our lives were that day, troubled times were nearer than we dared to imagine. We were retired members of an organisation, and our job was to protect certain ancient artefacts and people. But one of our close friends was killed by someone in our organisation in order to get to one of the artefacts. One by one, members of our organisation started to disappear. We feared not for our lives, but for yours, so we prepared to flee to London, to leave you with one of our most trusted friends, Frederick. He is probably living in the same house as he is now, with his wife Diane and three-year-old son Simeon. You were only meant to be with them for a while until the traitor was caught or killed, but obviously, it didn't turn out the way we hoped. We were told before we left that the traitor may have caught wind of our plan to flee and planned to chase after us. It seems that he did indeed find us after all.

We have left an incredibly important artefact in your care, since the plan is to lead the traitor away from you, making him believe that we are hiding it back at our family estate.

But now, I need to ask something of you, even though I know you have no reason to do it since you don't know me, but a lot more is at stake than just your safety. I'm asking if you will go to Vancouver and track down Michael Keth, Beatrice Holden and Bob. They will know what to do next. We need to return the artefact to its rightful place where it will be safe. This journey is not only a mission but the opportunity to know about your family and yourself, what you should have known, by right, many years ago.

There is one other thing, and I need you to trust me on this. When you arrive in Vancouver look for McCampbell Manor, our summer home, and the moment you arrive there, stop taking your medication. You will be fine. Whatever they have told you about what will happen if you end your dosage, is a lie. But this is important. Only stop taking the medication after you have reached the manor and don't leave the house until you feel ready to.

Do you look at yourself and see a lie? Do you feel like you're wearing a mask that covers something different, something that you're dying to uncover and see for what it really is? You will finally have an answer to all those questions, feelings of uncertainty, doubt and curiosity that you have been feeling all this time.

If things had been different…. well, you'd know just as well as how I'm about to tell you now: we love you so much. What we wouldn't give to see our darling girl all grown up, every inch the woman we imagined she'd be. I know we can't be with you in body, my precious, but know that we *are* with you. We always will be.

We miss you. We love you.

Your loving parents,

Roger and Sharon McCampbell."

By now, Tess was choking back burning tears that clawed their way from her chest and throat only to be stifled by her shaking hand while she held the letter with the other, staring at it in horror. The tears filling her eyes made the writing in front of her become illegible.

What?! How was this possible? Her…. parents?

*

The sun rained into that room the next morning. The morning of her 18th year. Tess lay on the dusty floor, which was now marked with footprints where she'd stood or stumbled, handprints where she'd tried to steady herself and body prints where she had curled up with her doll in her arms to fall somnolently to sleep, exhausted by her emotional workout.

She had to leave. Today, if possible. Her 'parents' had known the truth all along. But they had been good to her, so she couldn't fault them. If they knew about this, then they would have anticipated the truth revealing itself one day, so it wouldn't be too awkward. It shouldn't be.

She sat slowly up and realised she was still holding the letter. She looked at the handwriting again, the words of love, thinking of the care and preparation in the pen-strokes, and imagined the pain her biological parents must have felt writing that letter with the worst-case scenario in mind. If only she'd known them.

Theresa made up her mind. The trip to Vancouver was happening as soon as possible. Her parents may not be alive, but she'd go to their old home and find out whatever she could about them.

She stood, something that took more effort than she was used to, and pulled herself towards the portal to her present, briefly leaving her past. But this time, the box came with her, tucked under her arm, guarded like the treasure chest it was.

She looked back into the container of secrets, this previously undiscovered room which had now completely changed the course of her life. She had no idea what her future would bring crashing onto her, but that excited her, the chance to discover something new, frightening and perhaps personally monumental.

She had to do it. This wasn't going to be easy, and it scared her but doesn't everything that's never been tried before?

I J FERRESTONE

Chapter 3

Good Morning

Theresa came down the stairs. Her family was getting ready to go to their respective places for the day. Diane's voice could be heard from the kitchen checking with Billy that he had everything for his day trip with more of his friends. Fred was eating his bacon and scrambled eggs and washing it down with his favourite, coffee with two sugars and cream. Simeon was dressed for work, the complete opposite of his home image; hair pulled back, shirt and tie in place and piercings removed for the day. They were all in the same place, which was perfect.

Theresa walked through the kitchen door, feeling like a soloist about to burst into song in front of an unsuspecting audience. She took in a deep breath, feeling pinpricks in her palms and hornets in her stomach. "Hi.", she breathed.

Diane and Simeon looked up and grinned. Fred did eventually but he had to swallow first. Diane headed straight for her and hugged her cautiously, not knowing whether her health was still in a volatile situation. Theresa sighed. So much love and concern. She was going to miss them all so much. The thought made her want to cry.

"Hi, baby. You're up!", Diane chimed, "How are you feeling?"

Theresa sighed again. Here goes nothing. "Actually, I'm feeling completely fine. All better."

Diane and Fred instantly displayed a brief flash of concern and confusion on their faces. They knew considering how bad she'd been feeling, something wasn't right. But Diane masked it perfectly within seconds.

"That's good.", she stated, leading her to the dining table. "Have something to eat. You must be famished. You normally can't go two hours without eating."

Theresa smiled. "Thanks."

As she sat down, leaning forward as she tucked her chair in under her, her silver necklace swung out from inside her t-shirt, the blue gem catching the light, and therefore, Billy's eye.

"WOW!", he exclaimed, instantly reaching for it. "Where did you get that?"

Theresa looked down at it and held it in her hand. Then she looked from Diane to Frederick and stated, "From my loving parents, set aside for my 18th birthday."

Diane went the strangest ashen pale and Fred practically dropped his mug. But Simeon dropped his bowl on the floor, smashing it into fragments. Billy continued to survey the necklace. In such a normally noisy house, a bowl smashing wasn't going to break his concentration even for a second. "That's so wicked. Mum, Dad, am I going to get something like this on my 18th?"

Diane put her hand on a chair to steady herself. "We'll see." Her lips moved but the voice didn't sound like hers. This time it was like a slight breeze, empty, devoid of life and almost inaudible.

Billy seemed satisfied and turned to his sister, smiling. "So, Tess, how does it feel to be an adult?"

Theresa sighed and smiled. "It feels....different. But it also feels like a new beginning."

Simeon groaned. He knew what was coming next, so he turned and stooped down to pick up the shattered bowl. Not just because it needed doing but because he couldn't let anyone chance seeing the tears he was fighting back. She knew the truth, which would practically guarantee another course of action.

Theresa took a deep breath in. "Which leads me to an announcement. I'm going to Vancouver. I feel like travelling and I've always wanted to go there."

When she said Vancouver, Fred jumped slightly like he'd been hit by a bullet. The look was all over his face, a frown asking plain and loud how the devil she knew to pick Vancouver. He was stunned but his face settled when he probably reasoned that she knew about it the same way she'd found the necklace.

Simeon spoke quietly from his low position in a voice that didn't really want to come out, but curiosity and despair forced it out. "When are you leaving?", he breathed.

Tess turned and looked at his face. The way he phrased the question wouldn't have made anyone else's ears prick up but the way he said leaving made it clear that the gravity of the situation was known to him and that in leaving she might be leaving everything behind, never to return. He could be losing his sister forever.

"As soon as possible.", Theresa said softly, as if saying it quieter would make it easier.

Simeon exhaled in such a shaky way that Diane thought he'd collapse. Instead, he did the opposite and got up, heading to the front door without another word. As he left the house and the door closed, Tess felt her knees disappear. She'd never seen him that upset in all the years they'd been together. She hated that he felt hurt by plan to leave, but she needed this.

Diane simply looked at the sad look on her face. As she was about to speak, Billy's friends arrived to walk with him to school. Diane waved him off and then walked to Tess' side. She put a hand on her

29

shoulder.

"Come on. I'll help you pack after you eat something. And we have a lot to arrange."

And so they walked upstairs and found her suitcases and bags while Fred agreed to book her a last minute ticket on a flight to Vancouver for lunch-time a week that day.

This was happening and there was no going back on it.

STONE

I J FERRESTONE

Chapter 4.

Goodbye, London. Hello, Vancouver

Theresa stood at the entrance to Heathrow airport flanked by her suitcase and hand luggage. Her flight was in four hours. And she was terrified. What if she got there and found nothing? What if she had no-where to stay? And what point would she feel it right to come back? Was this the right thing to do?

She turned around and exhaled shakily, smiling nervously at her family. They had all made their arrangements with work or school to come and see her off. "Well, this is it. I'm here. Thank you for helping me. I don't know if I could have done this on my own.", she admitted.

Diane and Fred smiled. They'd come to terms with what was going to happen that day and it felt a lot easier than they'd pictured it would over the years.

"What do you hope to find in Vancouver?", Fred asked, looking for a sign of confidence to ease his worrying for his adopted daughter.

"Answers.", Theresa said, well aware she couldn't say 'pieces of my past' in front of Billy, especially since Diane had told her Billy didn't know anything about this and shouldn't be made aware of it, fearing what effect this would have on him in the future. "A future. Something I can use to complete myself."

The last sentence sounded so strange to Tess when it finally came out of her mouth, but it was simply her years of dissatisfaction with herself finally voicing itself. She simply giggled and shrugged.

Diane smiled and stepped forward. "I know you'll be fine.", she stated, smiling. "You've always been the kind of person that, once you've decided on a goal, you reach it, no matter what it takes."

Theresa was so glad for her adoptive mother's confidence in her, especially on perhaps the scariest day in her life, when success seemed to be something she felt she'd be lucky to reach.

She hugged each of them in turn, hugging her mum the longest and picking up her brother to sling him over her shoulder one more time. She would remember this day, especially since she didn't know if or when she'd come back or see them again. She had a job to do and things to discover, and she knew it wouldn't be just something you could do in a few weeks.

Simeon was still pouting about it but he'd come to terms with it too. Saying goodbye to him was going to be the hardest. So, they stepped away from the rest of the family to have some privacy.

"Are you scared?", he asked, searching her eyes.

Tess sighed, thankful to not have to keep the pretence going any longer. "Terrified! I've never been on a plane completely on my own before and I have no idea what will happen once I get there!"

Simeon shrugged and punched her shoulder. "Meh, you'll be fine. Just don't give up and be careful. People over there can be a bit nuts.", he advised, trying to look serious. "And remember that the three people you just hugged love you very, very much."

Tess smiled so hard; her cheeks reached their limit of elasticity. "And what about you?", she probed.

Simeon shrugged again, attempting to look nonchalant but not pulling it off, since Tess could read him all too easily. "Hmm,... I'll get there."

Tess felt her lip begin to tremble. She wanted this goodbye to be happy and couldn't risk him seeing her all bleary-eyed and emotional.

She dove forward and wrapped her arms around him, so quickly and with such force that it took him by surprise. But soon he was hugging her too, resting his chin on the top of her head.

"You will *always* be my sis, Tess.", Simeon assured her. "And no matter where you go and what you find... we'll always be here for you. OK?"

He squeezed her hard, lifting her off the floor slightly. "Don't let this be goodbye forever, alright?", he whispered, so quietly she barely heard it. He was trying to make sure no-one else heard it either.

Ilene nodded, burying her face into his shoulder. "I promise I won't. Keep an eye on your emails and stuff."

Simeon placed her down, his eyes puffy and slightly red. He simply nodded. He wasn't brave enough to let himself speak again right now.

Tess smiled at them all again and then turned towards the security area. Every step she took felt heavy and sounded like an elephant's feet to her.

Tess suddenly found that tears were spilling right down her face and dripping onto the floor, and she couldn't stop them. The only thing that stopped her sobbing out loud in the middle of Heathrow airport was the fact that she was biting her bottom lip as hard as she could to keep her mouth closed.

She walked forward and put everything into the security boxes and removed her shoes, jewellery and jacket. Once she's gotten through the checks and had got all her things, she stole one last glance back at her family.

And there they were, faithful as ever, as they had been for as long as she could remember, watching over her for as long as was possible. She smiled and nodded. Simeon responded with the same, and for that brief and last moment, there wasn't a feeling of sadness. It was hope, excitement, pride and deep love.

And with a deep inhale, Tess straightened herself up and strode towards her new life.

*

Tess didn't remember what happened on the flight. All she remembered was going onto the plane, sitting down and trying to figure out what she was going to do first when she arrived.

She'd need to go to a City Hall of some kind and show the copy of her birth certificate which her dad, meaning Fred, gave to her before she left and also the letter as proof of who she was along with the original Canadian citizenship paperwork that her parents left with Fred and Diane. Then she'd need to get to this summer home, then check out job vacancies, and then maybe......

She didn't remember everything going dark. But the next thing she saw was the images she'd seen almost a week ago. The images were clearer this time. There was more to them. Was someone trying to tell her something? She heard a male, raspy voice say something about the necklace. Then another deep voice replying, almost angrily. Was that her father? But then it ended the same way, with a man's cut-off scream filling her ears and her mind.

Tess woke with a start, gasping and sweating slightly. She looked to her left and right. Past the amused and slightly startled faces of the passengers near to her, she saw through the windows that the plane was on the ground.

Tess sat up properly and looked around. Had they not taken off yet? Then she saw people removing their baggage from the overhead compartments. They were already *there*! She'd been asleep for the whole 10 *hours*?!

Slightly embarrassed and shocked, Tess scrambled to her feet, got hold of her hand-luggage and shimmied her way off the plane. She must have looked awful. She quickly tamed any possible signs of bedhead before being greeted by staff at the airport, welcoming her to Canada.

She took a look around. She was definitely not in the UK anymore, although the weather pretty much felt the same. She walked to collect her baggage, got through security checks again and customs. Once she made it through to the shops and tourist information areas, she bought herself some lunch. She was absolutely starving.

Now Tess had time to properly gather her thoughts and decide on the next course of action. First, get a taxi.

Getting used to dollars was going to be interesting. She had to have someone explain the money and coin system in Canada to her. 'Pitiful,' she thought. 'I *so* look like a dumb tourist right now.'

She made her way through the city to the Registration Offices at City Hall. She spoke to staff, explained her situation, queued for hours, filled in paperwork, had her original birth certificate, provided by Fred and Diane, and passport copied, took a picture of herself in a booth and sorted most of it out. By the time she was outside, it was night. Her paperwork would be ready the next day, especially since after mentioning her parents' names, the staff were more than willing to help and the manager there explained that they were important figures in government work in Vancouver.

She thought it was best to check into the nearest hotel and come back first thing the next morning for her paperwork. What with the time difference, Vancouver being nine hours behind London, she should already have been asleep, so she was exhausted, despite her 'little snooze' on the plane. Tess found a hotel, sleep-walked up to her room and collapsed, fully clothed, onto the bed.

And once again, the world went black.

STONE

I J FERRESTONE

Chapter 5

Introducing Miss Ilene McCampbell!

Tess sat during breakfast thinking about the night before. The jetlag was going to take ages to get over. She'd had the dream again, which was beginning to annoy her. At this rate, if her night-time ritual continued as normal, she could say goodbye to her subconscious nocturnal fantasies about Richard Armitage.

Oh well.

Tess wiped her mouth and knocked back her coffee. She stood and headed for the hotel's main entrance with her suitcase in tow. She got a taxi to the Registration Offices to pick up her paperwork and asked the driver to wait outside.

The manager came out and personally handed them to her, checking that each document was in place and signed by the appropriate people. He was a white male possibly in his early 50s. His greying brown hair was parted and styled to perfection and his pin-striped, black suit was well fitted with not a crease or gape in sight. You could tell this man strove for organisation and perfection, and if you wanted him to do something for you, he'd do it well. He introduced himself as Mr Thompkins. "Welcome to Vancouver, Miss McCampbell."

Tess smiled. "Thank you.", she said, shaking his hand as she stood up. As she turned to leave, she stopped. "Excuse me, what work did you say my parents did? You said yesterday it was something to do with the government."

The manager smiled broadly, bringing creases to the corners of his eyes, and stared off into the past. "I'm not sure what they did, to be quite frank. I think it was to do with the historical works at the Vancouver Museum. They were very respected in this city and no-one knew the artifacts or looked after them better than the McCampbells. I had just started working here as a junior advisor when I first saw them, but I remember the Director at the time always 'moved mountains' for them and gave them special treatment, and I sensed it wasn't simply that they were protecting cultures and heritages. There was something more to what they did, but nevertheless, I followed the last Director's example. I know this isn't a professional comment to make, but your parents had a certain way about them. They were always neatly and impeccably dressed. Friendly too. Your mother had a smile that just made everyone bow to her wishes. And your father was friendly but strong and focused. It was like magic whenever they spoke to you."

"Wow!", Tess whispered, her eyes wide. "They sound amazing." It was nice to finally have some kind of mental picture of them both. But it also meant she had a little something to live up to.

The manager smiled. "They were. I've worked here for almost 25 years and of all the people who have come through those door, they were two of the most pleasant, beautiful and memorable."

Tess grinned. "Well, hopefully, I can keep the family in a good light with this city and the people who knew my family."

The manager reached forward to shake her hand again. "I have no doubt you will. Already I see your mother's smile and you father's determination in you. You will always be welcome here. Good luck with everything, Miss McCampbell."

Tess felt proud to hear that and a touch stronger too. "Thank you, sir. I'll remember that.", she said.

She walked out of the building with her head held high, smiling from her head to her toes.

Well, that was a good start. She got into the taxi, which was, thankfully, still waiting for her, and gave the driver her new address. As she was driven through and out of the city, she took in the beautiful buildings, the colourful market, the bustling port and historical structures which she would have to learn her way around and maybe call 'home'.

The taxi sped out of Vancouver and then through a place called Whistler's Village. Tess began to dread the end of this journey simply for the revealing of the size of the taxi fare and the confusion in figuring out what she'd do next. She saw mountains and breath-taking natural landscapes and found herself gazing out the taxi with her head out of the window like an excited puppy.

Suddenly the taxi came to a halt.

Tess looked around, woken from her dreamy haze. She saw a tiny path leading off into the trees and a sign stating the address she had been given. She saw also that the path up to the address was almost inaccessible for vehicles.

"Here you go.", the taxi driver announced.

Tess almost laughed until she realised what was coming next. "I have to walk into those trees?"

All she saw was the driver's eyes in the rear-view mirror looking at her impatiently and expectantly. She rolled her eyes and handed him the money. Then she clambered out and got her luggage. She'd only just closed the car boot when the taxi sped off.

Tess just shook her head as it disappeared. "Theresa, my dear,", she said aloud to her new self, starting to make her way up the path. "You're on your own. You've read enough R.L.Stine during your childhood and King and Crichton recently to know if a local practically runs away from an old property, it's either got a tragedy linked to it, or it's haunted."

'Well, I know which story is linked to this house, in part, anyway.' Tess thought.

The path seemed to go on forever. There were stones all the way up it. It looked like a drained river and as Tess entered the trees her worries grew. This mini forest almost blocked out the sun, she had no idea where she was going and she thought she'd heard one of the wheels on her suitcase break. Great. All that needed to happen now was for the signal on her phone to completely go and some deranged old woman to run in the other direction babbling warnings and she'd be right in the perfect typical horror movie setting.

Soon, though, the stones became pebbles, and the forest began to clear. Tess found herself walking into a pebbled driveway, flanked with fir trees and beautifully maintained hedges. And when she came round the last of the trees and looked to her left, she dropped her hand-luggage in shock.

In front her stood a stunning Edwardian age mini mansion, about 4 floors high which included the basement below. Through the windows Tess could see out the back a large almost endless garden with a flawless lawn, a fountain and a garage big enough for at least six cars. The front door was probably eight feet high, and made of exquisite dark mahogany, with a large shiny doorknob and the most grand and imposing-looking door knocker she'd ever seen shaped like a stag's head. She'd have to enter the place by a side-door. This door was *far* too big for her to open on her own.

Just as she was musing about how she would go about knocking the front door without finding herself swinging from the knocker and if she'd got the right house, a voice broke her thoughts.

"Excuse me! Can I help you?"

Tess turned towards the sound. Standing by the right corner of the house was a young man, probably around the age of twenty-two. He was medium height, well built, with deep brown wavy hair, strong jaw and defined cheekbones. He wore jeans, green wellington boots and a powder blue t-shirt, each dusted with mud. He looked like an underwear model, except for the fact that he was clothed. The only thing that didn't fit the image of the person in front of her was the fluorescent pink gardening gloves he was taking off as he stepped towards her.

"Are you lost?", he asked.

Tess shook the thought about his gloves from her mind. "No. I'm trying to find my way in here."

At the sound of Tess's voice, the man almost laughed. "Man, you *are* lost. What are you doing here of all places? Shouldn't you be strolling through the Aquarium with one of those 'I Love Vancouver' T-shirts on?", he japed.

Tess found herself turning to face this man with a slightly aggressive posture. "Excuse me?! I'm not a tourist. Well, I can guess why you think I'm-! Never mind. I'm going to live here.", Tess flushed.

"That's impossible. No-one lived here for years. I'm just paid to maintain it. And it's not for sale.", the man explained, bristling a bit.

"Alone? All this? That explains why you feel you can get away with wearing those gloves, since no-one would see you.", Ilene returned, with a cheeky grin and another directional glance at the offensive attire. "Let me guess, it says the words 'Where my hoes at?' on the back, doesn't it."

The man blushed and tried to hide them behind his back. "They aren't mine. They're my mother's."

Tess raised an eyebrow. "Oh, *really*? That's one I haven't heard before. That's even worse than 'the dog ate my homework'.", she jeered.

The man exhaled through his nose, irritably. "Actually, it's Jason. My mother is the person who maintains this place, not me. I'm just helping her today."

And almost as if on cue, a female voice called out. "Hey, J! Where *are* you? I need you help moving these..." A woman came storming round the corner, and then slowed when she saw Ilene. She had obviously been a stunning blonde in her youth, and although some years had passed, it hadn't had much effect on her, leaving the girl she had been still visible. She had long, slightly faded blonde hair with small touches of grey to it, a smooth strong jawline and the same sharp questioning blue eyes her son had.

"Hello. Can we help you?", she asked.

"Hello. I'm sorry to barge in like this....", Ilene began.

"Oh no, it's fine! It's just odd to see someone here, so I'm just a bit curious.", the woman laughed. "I'm Amanda Dunney and this is my son Jason. We maintain this property."

"Hello.", Tess greeted. "I'm sorry, but why do you maintain this? Your son said no-one's lived here for years."

Amanda shrugged. "Over 18 years ago, I was hired by the owners when Jason was a toddler, and they told me they'd be away for a while and they'd set up regular payments to me as long I maintained this place until they got back. Well weeks turned into months, months to years and the payments kept coming but no-one came back. Jason thinks I'm crazy to still bother with this place."

"Well, it's been almost nineteen years, Mom. They're not coming back. Just talk to the bank about stopping the payments and get another job- one that there's sense in doing.", Jason explained, with tired gestures. Ilene had a feeling he'd said this over and over to his mother hoping to make her see sense.

"I wouldn't be so sure about that.", Ilene mumbled.

Jason gave her a puzzled look but before he could ask what she'd meant his mother spoke again.

"Hey, boy, don't knock that money, it paid for your upbringing and education. And give me back my *gloves*! They don't suit you!", she cried, snatching her gardening gloves from behind her son's back and smacking him on the back of the head with them. "Oh my god! I'm rambling like this, and I forgot to ask your name, honey!"

Tess took the hand she'd just been using to stifle her laughter and extended it to Amanda. "I'm Ilene McCampbell. It's nice to meet you.", she greeted. "And I can definitely say I'd love you to keep maintaining this property and I'd like to help you do it."

Amanda and Jason both stood staring at her for a few seconds. It took a while for them to move and when they did, they looked at each-other. Amanda let out a nervous giggle. "I'm sorry but that's not possible. As far as anyone knows there wasn't a child. How old are you?"

"I turned 18 just over 2 weeks ago.", Ilene stated.

Amanda shrugged and nodded. It was possible. "What happened to your parents? I mean, why did they never come back? And why didn't you come back sooner?"

Tess thought it best not to regale them with her 'visions'. They'd commit her instantly and then how would she achieve what she'd set out to do?

"They left me with friends in London for safe keeping. It was only meant to be for a few days. But they died shortly after, so I was with their friends for longer than they planned. And on my 18th birthday, I was told about my real parents.", Tess explained. It was the first time she was telling anyone this. And it sounded so odd, coming from her own mouth. It sounded like she was talking about someone else's life, not hers.

Amanda's face was suddenly full of sympathy. Now realising what this girl was going through, maybe asking questions about her family was something she shouldn't do again. "Oh, you poor thing."

Tess hated pity. Even Jason was showing a little in his eyes, mixed with a little discomfort from not quite knowing what to say. She just smiled and shrugged. "I'm not suffering or anything. I'm curious though. So, I'm here to find out what I can and pick up the pieces, so to speak. I just came from the Registration Office after showing ID, letters and proof of who I'm related to. The house and grounds were left to me, but I had no idea it was be this...big!"

Tess was trying hard to keep smiling. Of course, in reality she was scared, intimidated a bit and a touch lonely. But she wasn't going to let that show. If her parents had been described as friendly, strong and focused, she wanted to prove that she could carry on their memory. First, she'd have to work on her memories of them.

Amanda smiled, gently. It reminded Ilene of Diane, and it made her suddenly miss her unbearably. "Everything must seem big right about now. A big discovery, big changes, a big new country and a new home."

Tess looked at the house again. The word 'big' didn't really do it justice. To her a four-bedroom detached house seemed big. She was from north London, so this place was frigging huge! Too much for one person.

"Yes. A lot of big things going on.", Tess stated, with a weak chuckle.

Amanda walked up to her and put a hand on her shoulder. "Well, then. How about we take these big changes down a pace?"

Tess felt more confused than ever.

Amanda winked and turned towards her son. "Jason, go and change your clothes, have a shower and get the keys. We don't want you sprinkling mud inside the house. In the meantime, Ilene and I will sit near the old Oak and have some scones and tea. They like that in England, don't they?"

Tess suddenly found herself laughing out loud out of sheer delight. "Yeah, it is a nice little treat that people have sometimes. With clotted cream normally."

Jason nodded and ran off before shooting a strange look at Ilene. Was it annoyance or curiosity? She couldn't read him well.

Amanda took Tess's suitcase and motioned to Tess to follow her round to the back. As Tess rounded the corner, she saw a smaller stone path leading up a vast lawn and to the left of it all was the largest oak tree she'd ever seen, which sheltered a table and three chairs. The branches grew out so far that it created a circular shadow roughly twenty metres out from the base of the tree on all sides. Tied to one of the lowest branches was a swing.

A searing pain hit Tess's head as she saw a foggy image of a woman with long, thick black hair and a wide smile, sat in a white dress on that exact same swing. The vision was different though. The angle from which she was seeing this was right down on the floor. Could this have been an image from her past?

"Are you alright, Ilene?", Amanda asked.

Tess opened her eyes and saw Amanda walking hurriedly up to her carrying a tray. It's like she'd blacked out whilst standing under the tree. Tess suddenly realised she was clutching her head with one

49

hand. She lowered it and laughed.

"It's nothing.", she assured. "Just a headache. They come on every now and then."

Amanda looked like she wasn't entirely convinced but she nodded and anyway. She set the tray down on the table. She watched Ilene a little longer and smiled. "There's hot water in the teapot. I didn't know what kind you like, so I bought Green Tea, Darjeeling, plain tea and Earl Grey."

Tess smiled at her thoughtfulness. "I'm an Earl Grey girl."

Amanda grinned. "Excellent!"

As Tess put the mug to her lips and savoured the flavour, the thought passed through her mind that she never thought that a small taste of home could feel so comforting, right now when everything was unsettled and thrown up in the air. Amanda was her Canadian version of Diane. It must be a mum thing. She knew just what she needed at that exact moment.

They sat looking at the Manor, taking in the weather and their beautiful surroundings.
"This house is so beautiful. And so huge.", Tess mused aloud. "Mum and Dad must have had lots of visitors and friends. Or they were planning a big family."

Amanda and Tess laughed at this thought. But Tess found her last sentence sad. They had never got to live the life they intended, and she felt sorry for her parents for that, more than she could feel sorry for herself for not knowing them at that moment. Just as she finished her second scone, Amanda sat up, focusing on the back door of the house. Tess looked too and noticed Jason stood there looking fresh and clean and waving to get their attention.

Amanda smiled. "I think it's time to take your luggage in and get you home."

Tess smiled back and found her breathing was shaky. This thought was suddenly scaring her. It was like the first day at a new school.

They stood up and walked to the house taking the tray and dishes with them. The lawn was so big it felt like it took forever to reach Jason. But he was stood looking quite patient.

For the first time, he smiled at Tess. That was slightly more unnerving than anything else. Maybe his shower had washed the grumpy off him.

"Right. Let's get you inside. I'll take you round the front.", Jason announced, motioning to the left.

"Oh. Ok.", Tess said, feeling a little deserted as Amanda walked off elsewhere carrying the tray.

They went round the right side of the house and ended up right where they'd first met. Jason walked up to the front door and pulled out some keys. As he found the correct one, Tess had a thought that made her giggle.

'I wonder if he will be able to open the front door on his own.'

But to her surprise, he pushed it as if it was no more than a screen door. 'Impressive. ', Tess caught herself thinking.

Jason turned around and held out his hand. He smiled again. This cheerfulness was truly beginning to freak Tess out.

"Come on in.", he invited.

Tess took in deep breath and climbed the small amount of sandstone steps before stepping hesitantly through the front door.

She had to stop for a few minutes to take in her surroundings while she gazed about, mouth open.

The hallway was wide, with tiled floors. It had two large doorways coming off each wall on the left and right. In front and centre leading up to the upper back wall was a long staircase, made of dark wood and carpeted, wide enough to have seven people walk down it side by side. At the first floor's back wall, it split in half and continued up the sides of the left and right walls. There were vases as tall as the average person, two full suits of armour stood by the upstairs back wall, side tables and cabinets....and this was just what she could see from standing in the hallway. It looked every inch an ancestral home and lived up to the name Manor entirely.

Tess stepped to her left and pushed the first door open. The curtains were drawn but she could see a sliver of light. She walked to it and pulled. The sun poured into the room. She could suddenly see it was previously a drawing room, now modernised with twenty-first century things to have fun with. All the walls were dark wood, possibly mahogany again. There was a fireplace opposite the door, and a pool table next to it. A leather sofa in the middle of the room, facing the fireplace, with an end-table on either side decked with a table lamp each. A television, the largest Tess had ever seen, was on the wall to the right of the door and directly opposite the large window. And finally, by the window a black Steinway grand piano.

Tess took it all in, not even realising that Jason was standing in the doorway watching the excitement build in her face. She half-walked, half-ran out of the room and into the next room. It was an exquisite dining room with a lovely long oak table. Beautiful, varnished dining chairs sat waiting on all sides of the table. There were probably thirty seats at this table. At the other end of the dining room, it turned into a conservatory, with glass panels from ceiling to floor, probably perfect for a quick drink under the stars with your guests after dinner. Against one of the walls were three dining carts.

As Tess ran back into the hallway to investigate the other side of the ground floor, she grabbed Jason by the arm and pulled him along with her. "It all looks brand new!", she squealed, "I've only ever seen places like this in films. How come everything isn't covered over with sheets?"

"Well, I did some dusting yesterday anyway, and while you were having 'tea with mother'," Jason imitated, dropping into her accent, "I quickly ran around and removed the sheets again."

Tess stopped with her hand on the next door. She turned back and looked at him. "Thanks, Jason."

Jason flustered suddenly and went red. He cleared his throat and ran his hand through his hair. "Well, erm... you're welcome."

She almost squealed as she stepped into a beautiful large kitchen. It was almost industrial in size. Tess imagined people running around making meals and entrées for the house parties and important dinners. The family must have had a tonne of history and a substantial income for historians. At least Tess's love of antiques and history made sense now.

Tess inspected the China, cookware and crystal glasses. An impressive wine collection was stacked from ceiling to floor in one part of the kitchen. Tess made a mental note to try one, now she was old enough to legally enjoy a drink. And then she reminded herself she wasn't in the UK anymore.

"Jason?", she called, not turning around as she was still surveying every cabinet and surface. "What's the legal drinking age in this country?"

Jason was sat on a stool next to the cooking island in the centre of the kitchen. Tess noticed his silence and looked up to see an evil smile. She groaned. "Please don't say it's 21."

Jason chuckled and shook his head. "No. It varies from province to province. In this area, British Columbia, the age is 19."

Tess cursed under her breath. "Oh well.", she sighed, she started heading out of the kitchen to the fourth room. "But that's for buying outside the home. Since this is my place, I can crack open a bottle or two." She flashed a cheeky grin to Jason before turning the corner.

Jason was quickly growing to like this girl. She was excitable, impulsive, curious and a little rebellious. It would never be boring in this house again.

He heard another excited squeal.

He walked in to see her scanning through the shelves in the last room which was a library. In keeping with the mahogany theme, the shelves and stairs to them were polished and beautiful. There were different kinds of chairs in the centre of the room, and of course, a fireplace opposite the door, with a glass panel in front of it, to protect the books. A beautiful desk faced into the centre of the room with the back of its chair facing the window. Jason had read some of the books here. Most of them were historical non-fiction but there was a fair amount of fiction and more genres than he ever knew existed.

Tess was in heaven.

She'd read her local library dry at home and spent most of her pocket money at the London bookshops from a young age. She couldn't describe her excitement at the prospect of having all this new reading to do. She spotted a couple of empty shelves and made a mental note to put the books she brought with them in there, depending on how long she'd be staying.

Jason just bathed in her excitement. It was so tangible She almost hopped from spot to spot.

54

She left the room at a surprising pace and sporting a huge grin as she headed for the stairs.

Jason called after her trying to keep up with her. "Slow down!", he shouted, "You don't know where you're going."

He found her on the first floor. She'd discovered the home gym, archive room, which was locked as he explained, watching her attempting to wrench the door open, another office room which took up one side of the house, and had walls line with glass cabinets filled with antiques and trinkets.

Jason and Tess walked up to the 2nd floor. Jason could see the running around taking its toll and her energy levels dropping a little.

Jason led Tess into a dojo. Weapons lined its walls, but they weren't protected by glass. Tess was very surprised. There was wear and dents in the floor and walls. This room and its equipment clearly had been used often. Once again, the walls were mahogany. And in the corner of the room was a small shallow pool decorated with pebbles on its edge, with a waterfall feature than ran down a solid rock wall. Maybe this room would be a good place to work out and do her gymnastic routines, but she was unsure about the pool. She'd rather shower. Tess touched the water. It was quite cool. Not ideal for a dip at all.

But the room was incredible. Tess knew she'd never be bored in this house. She wondered of she'd ever feel the need to bother with going out.

"Jason... do you sleep here sometimes?", Tess asked as she kept analysing every corner of the room.

"Yeah, when we don't need to urgently go back to the city. The loft was converted into bedrooms. One half is open plan and the other is a suite.", Jason explained.

"Cool. It's nice to know I won't always be in a huge old house completely alone.", Tess said, laughing to herself, thinking of every horror film she'd ever seen.

Jason signalled to follow him. "Do you want to see your room?"

Tess was almost afraid to respond. Instead, she just walked nervously towards him.

Jason checked Tess was behind him before he pushed the bedroom door.

Tess stepped gingerly into a larger and warm room. It was decorated with modern vases. There was a bay window opposite the door with a curved ottoman fitting perfectly into it.

To the left of the door, against an unused chimney breast was a queen-sized four-poster bed made of intricately carved elm wood, like one she'd seen in a castle she'd visited on Isle of Wight. There was a cushioned bench at the foot of it. The bed was made and adorned with lots of pillows and cushions. Opposite the bed were two dressing tables. One was made from blackened mahogany, with a matching stool and the other was white painted oak. Both had perfumes, combs and brushes, watches, jewels laid out on them and to the extreme right and left of each table, was a door. Tess headed for the one on the right, opened the door and found the light switch. She gasped as two conjoined walk-in closets lined with every kind of clothing and accessory was illuminated. She could see coats, dresses, shoes, bags and drawers filled with goodness knows what.

Tess stepped out and closed the door. Her head was starting to spin. There was so much to absorb. Jason was in front of her asking if she was alright, but she was so lost in thought she could barely hear him. Something wasn't right. And then it hit her. "Photos.", Tess whispered.

"What?", said Jason.

"There are no photos here. Of them, of me or their relatives.", Tess declared heading out of the room and scanning the corridor walls. "Don't you find it odd that we're in an ancestral home with no evidence of ancestry?"

Jason was also stumped by this observation. He'd never thought of it himself.

Tess could see she freaked him out. So, she sighed and smiled. She didn't want to scare him off with anything suspicious or weird. She needed his help. "Oh well I'm sure I'll find something. There's lots to look through here. I'll find something."

As she walked past the door to a room that was evidently smaller, she froze. This felt familiar. Something was pulling her to this room. Jason was only just exiting her parents' room, now *her* room, when she was pushing the door open.

Tess looked around and felt her eyes brim with tears. In front of her stood the most beautiful nursery, fashioned to look as though it belonged more within the late 19th century. Chiffon was draped over the curtain poles, letting a gentler light into this room compared to any room in the house. Every surface was trimmed with white lace. There was not a speck of pink anywhere, as if her parents hadn't known what gender their baby would be. The lace looked handmade. This ground was the only floor on the second floor that was carpeted. It was the softest carpet Tess had ever felt when she bent down to touch it. The smell of the room was making her feel a level of belonging she didn't understand but didn't attempt to fight. Fluffy teddies and beautiful dolls covered every shelf, windowsill and chair in the room. There were a few books of varying levels of age-appropriateness. Reminders of the future her parents thought they would get to see.

A little chest of drawers and wardrobe made of solid oak stood to the right of the door. In them every item of clothing a newborn to toddler could wear. Dresses, bonnet, stockings, shoes, booties, coats and mittens.

The crib next to the window was beautiful and sturdy with a little tennis ball sized dent in its top bar. As Tess ran her hand over the dent, an image entered her mind. The sounds of a baby crying and of a blow to a hard item were in her ears. And then the image of a woman running into this nursery and picking her, a smaller version of her, up.

Tess started as if she had been stung. What did that image mean? Maybe something fell onto the crib and dented it, almost hitting her. Or it was damaged while her parents were building it? Tess was starting to feel a bit frazzled mentally. So, she focused on the room again.

The familiar scents made her want to cry. But Jason, a relative stranger, was in the room. So, she just smiled and walked out.

Jason stood slightly stunned for a moment, at how, out of all the little doors, laundry chutes and airing cupboards, she'd known which was the nursery on that floor. She really was the child of the previous owners. However young she was when she left the house, she still remembered parts of it.

Jason could feel his guard dropping, and his trust growing, which was usually a feeling he guarded himself against. He followed Tess into the hallway. He found her rubbing her temples.

He kept his voice low in case. "You feeling OK?"

Tess looked up towards the sound of his voice and smiled sheepishly "Yeah. Just a little headache."

Jason started walking to the stairs "Well, I'll bring the tour to a close. I show you the basement and garage, then we'll do something about dinner. OK?"

Tess felt guilty for just walking off and complaining about a headache. Today had been a dream, something she'd never have imagined in a million years. The clock in the hallway chimed saying it was two p.m. She turned looking for a further set of stairs when she reached the hallway on the ground floor again. Jason grinned as she turned towards him and shrugged. "So where do we go, Batman? Behind the grandfather's clock in the study?"

Jason cocked an eyebrow. "Why Batman? I'm the help. Shouldn't I be Mr Pennyworth?"

Tess laughed. "Alfred would never give up Wayne Manor's secrets. *Bruce* is more likely to do that."

"Or Dick.", interjected Jason, walking towards the left-hand side of the staircase.

"Ah yes. Trying to impress some girl.", Tess finished, laughing again.

Jason pushed what looked like a wooden panel on the wall at the base of the staircase It swung open with a click and the sound cut Tess's laughter short. She tiptoed forward as if expecting something to leap out. A set of lights came on revealing a flight of tiled stairs.

Tess's face stretched to its limits with a gleeful grin. She turned to Jason and raised her eyebrows. "Holy secret staircase, Batman!" Then she leapt down the stairs with a triumphant yell as Jason followed.

He heard a shriek followed by a person sized splash. She'd found the pool.

As he ran in, he found Tess floating on her back fully clothed, eyes closed, laughing to herself.

Jason crouched down. "So, I take it you like the bat-cave?"

Tess didn't open her eyes. "Oh yes, Alfred."

"I'll vocally finish our tour then. To my left, you'll see the sauna, steam room and shower room, stocked with fresh towels and dressing gowns. The laundry room is to my right. All chutes feed into there. Straight in front of me is the door leading to the stairs which take you to the six-car ground level garage and machine shop. Are there any further questions or any feedback you wish to share?", Jason concluded.

Tess opened her eyes and looked over at Jason. "Yes. Thank you, Jason. I feel like I've won the lottery. Feel free to use every single facility in this house, if you weren't already."

Jason laughed and stood up from his squatting position. "OK. Feel free to clean up, then. There's shower gel, loofas, sponges and soap already in there."

"OK. I'll see you in a few.", Tess called back to Jason as he walked back up the tiled stairs. She stayed floating on her back as his footsteps faded.

Tess floated for a few more minutes before pondering what to do next. She decided to shower and then take another walk around the house. She'd have to check if the finances really were covered for the house and utilities. Of course, she'd worked before, but she couldn't hope to land a job at her age and level of experience to be able to pay for a place like this. Not a legal one anyway.

Tess chuckled to herself as she climbed out of the pool, drenching the tiled floor. Thank goodness her phone and passport were in her hand luggage and not in her pockets. It was gone two p.m. already. Time sure flew when you were having fun in a dream house you had no idea was even in your name until just over a week ago.

After a refreshing shower, Tess dried and lotioned her skin. She found the nearest dressing gown and let it drift onto her body. It was so soft, she stood hugging herself for a minute or two, enjoying the softness and warmth. She smiled. Any second now, her eyelids would flicker open, and she'd be back in London, putting this adventure down to a vivid and wonderful dream. But when she blinked, she was still stood in the basement of her new lavish home.

Tess strolled up the stairs to the hallway. She could hear Jason whistling in the back garden and intermittently calling out questions or information to his mother.

It wasn't as loud as her previous home, but Tess was incredibly thankful for the sounds of family interaction. The thought of being in this manor by herself in silence, was terrifying.

She walked to the dojo on the second floor and stopped in the hallway in front of a large sandstone statue. Tess wondered why on earth a statue made of this material would be indoors rather than at the entrance of an outside path or in the middle of a fountain. It was a man who was dressed except for his torso. He wore a kilt, boots, and a large shield across his back. His two hands were resting, overlapped on the hilt of a sword which, from his elevated ground level, stood at about shoulder height. His stance was strong and defensive, as if he was guarding something. But what stood out was his face.; the strong features, framed by long wavy hair. And his eyes. The look of calm determination and vigilance. The firm set of his lips. Tess felt strangely safe in the shadow of this figure, which suddenly made her realise she been a lot more terrified of this trip than she'd let on, even to herself. She smiled and put a hand on his foot, since it was the nearest thing within reach. She knew where to come and sit now if she felt afraid, which was an odd decision to make, but still reassuring. This eight-foot statue *was* a protector, that was for certain. She might as well give it something to protect.

Tess switched on the lights in the dojo. In true dojo style, the door was a sliding one, but in keeping with the style of the house, it was a solid mahogany one. The floors were wooden except a section on the right which was marble. Its purpose was unclear, but Tess's eyes grew wide when she noticed a long thin crack in it, near the centre. What on earth could have made a dent, let alone a large crack, in a marble floor? It was like an anvil had been dropped from several hundred feet up. Tess looked up to test the idea. The roof was old, intact and showed no signs of recent repair, so that couldn't be it.

Tess walked over to the weapons on the left-hand wall. Some she'd seen before, various styles of katana, spiked balls on chain, clubs and small throwing blades, but some she'd never known existed. There were some oversized axes and bows. Tess had loved archery when she was in school. She told herself she'd try these out one day soon. It was strange to see a family home with a collection of weapons this diverse, but when she remembered that her parents had been historians working for the government, Tess didn't find it so strange. She tried lifting one of the swords herself and the weight of the thing tipped her forward as its end crashed to the floor, almost sending her flying over it with a shriek. She looked around a little, embarrassed, blood rushing to her cheeks and used both hands to carefully position it back on the wall with a laboured grunt.

She brushed her hands on her jeans, to subconsciously be done with that part of the room and crossed over to the right side. The whole wall was stone with a waterfall function over it, the kind she'd seen in a few restaurants, but this had much more water cascading down into the long shallow pool below. She understood the calming side of the water in this room, for instance, if you wanted to meditate rather than exercise. 'But honestly', she mused, 'Why have that inside the house? My parents seem to have got indoor and outdoor décor mixed up.' She shook her head and walked out of this confusing room, sliding the door closed behind her.

She walked straight and turned into her parents' room. The sun was starting to as it was late autumn. She sat down on the bed and closed her eyes. Her mind was desperately trying to keep up with all the things she'd been seeing. She was trying to memorise the layout of the house and grounds. She hadn't visited the garage yet. She'd passed her driving test a year ago. She'd have to do that again here so she wouldn't have to be constantly shelling out for taxi fare.

Tess laid back and closed her eyes for a moment. Or so she thought. She reopened her eyes and instantly noticed it was darker. She groaned. She didn't need to check the time; she had nowhere that she needed to be. She turned her head anyway. The clock on the bedside table said it was a few minutes before four.
Tess rolled onto her side and sat up. She might as well start unpacking. She walked to the window and opened it a little to get some fresh air circulating in the room, and hoped this would help her wake up a bit.

She strode across the room and grabbed her suitcase which was stood against the wall by the door. She walked to the closet and tried to find an empty drawer or two and try not to feel unaccomplished and frumpy simultaneously as she inspected her mother's clothing.

She walked back into the bedroom to put her toiletries in the ensuite bathroom. She looked at her tousled auburn and brown mess of a head. She'd brush it out later. Wasn't the whole upside of being home that you could look dishevelled and gross without judgement?

Tess changed into a pair of cotton joggers and a vest. She walked over to the ivory dressing table put some of her jewellery and makeup away. She saw a beautiful horsehair brush. The soft bristles were set in an extravagant decorative sterling silver handle. 'How much did this set you back?', Tess mentally asked her mum. She spotted a strand and pinched it between her thumb and forefinger before pulling on it. The strand that came away was long and black, thick and coiled. So, her mother had been black, like Fred. How on earth had *Tess* ended up with auburn hair then? Maybe her father had been a redhead.

Tess looped the hair and rested it on a little China dish that was probably for placing down the rings and earrings that had been worn during the day by her mother when it came to an end.

At that moment, her thoughts of a faceless mother were interrupted by urgent beeping. Her phone's medication alarm had adjusted to the time zone and was setting off the reminder to take her four-thirty set of pills, or injection, if she was unconscious. But then she remembered her father's letter.

Tess took her medication out of her bag and walked to the bin she'd spotted by the window.

It'd be odd not having these as part of her daily routine. All this change was bewildering. It would take a lot of time to adjust. She looked at the two green capsules in her palm and sighed.

At that moment, the last sliver of sunlight dipped below the landscape of her new back garden. Tess's skin subconsciously registered the change in temperature in seconds, goose-pimples lifting on her skin.

In the same heartbeat, the hand that held the pills began to tremble.

Tess looked at her hand, wondering if this was her nerves and anxiety from the day manifesting themselves finally. That thought vanished as both hands started to tremble and then began to shake more violently. She tried to regain control of herself. It didn't work. Her head started to spin, and her stomach lurched inside her.

Tess felt her legs give way beneath her. She instantly put her hand out to catch herself as she hit the bedroom floor. She heard herself groan from the impact and her pills bounce off the floor quietly. But a third sound reached her ears, one she didn't expect. It was the protest, creak and then yielding of wood. Her head turned to source this sound and what her eyes found made her completely still.

STONE

Chapter 6

The True Sickness

Tess blinked. She wasn't even sure if she was breathing still.

Attached to her right forearm was a hand unlike anything she'd seen with her eyes. But it wasn't hers. It couldn't have been.

The skin looked thicker and where painted cuticles should have been, dark flint-like claws protruded from the digits. And they were digging deep into what was until twenty seconds ago, a beautiful, unmarked windowsill. The trembling returned, but not quite so unexplainably this time.

Tess leapt onto her feet gasping in air as if she was drowning. She felt as though she was. She began to panic more openly. She watched in horror and disbelief as her limbs went through more changes at random, from hard scales and sharkskin to more claws appearing on her other hand.

Her pills! She dropped back to the floor, scrambling blindly for them, but she couldn't find them. All she was achieving was destroying and etching rough grooves into the flooring. The floor was slippery now. She realised she was sobbing, and screams were stinging as they ripped from her throat and lungs.

These hallucinations *had* to be side effects of withdrawal, and right now she'd give anything to find her pills again. They had been her last remaining dose. Why had she trusted the instructions in the letter so blindly? Why hadn't she just stayed in London?

All she was feeling was fear and regret.

She called out for Diane and tried to climb up to get into her bed. As she sat back in defeat, something hit her back. She instinctively spun but moved further than expected, whirling herself to the middle of the room. Something heavy was hanging off her back. The fear of it was making her feel she would vomit at any moment. She reached back and felt what seemed like bone covered in skin jutting from her shoulder blades. She started screaming again.

She could hear Jason calling and running up the stairs. She felt relief and gratefulness from being reminded she wasn't alone. She'd get him to take her to the hospital and it could all be sorted.

That thought stopped as she stepped out into front of her mother's dressing table mirror on her way towards the sound of Jason's approaching footsteps. In the fading light, she could see what her hands had found behind her. A pair of large leathery wings were hanging down to floor. As she gasped again, one of them flexed and extended slightly. It was huge, looking like a bat's wing. She could see it, feel the weight, the movement and the air it stirred when it moved. Also, there was something else. Her eyes, specifically her irises, were changing to bright luminous colours, changing from the colour of the sun to fire, to emeralds, to a tropical ocean.

It suddenly occurred to her that this may be no hallucination.

Jason's footsteps were almost outside her door.

Suddenly true dread filled Tess's whole body, new parts included. He couldn't see her like this!

In a fraction of a second, she saw in her mind's eye her being dragged away to a remote location to be experimented on, caged and vivisected, never to be seen again. It was a wild mental scenario, but nothing was insane in her mind. She had *friggin' wings*!

However, any course of action to be chosen was too late. Jason appeared in the door and fresh tears appeared in her eyes. All Tess had time to do was back up and press herself again on the posts on her bed. She closed her eyes and held her breath.

Jason called Ilene again, but he wasn't looking *at* her. He was looking in her direction... but looking *past* her. He spun, his eyes scanning wildly. They landed on the floor and windowsill. Then he saw the window open and gasped. He ran past her and looked outside for a moment, before running into the closet, still calling for her, and then the en-suite bathroom. He then ran back out of the room, calling for his mother. Now she was heading up the stairs. They were talking loudly in panicked voices, but Tess couldn't hear any of the words. And she realised that her back had become normal again, as she could feel the weight of those wings any more.

What the bloody hell had just happened? Why couldn't Jason see her?

She turned to the mirror and squealed again. There was no one there.

She looked down and froze. "What....?", she breathed.

Her skin was there, and it looked like the wall and bedpost behind her. As she started to breathe a little slower, her normal skin tone returned. She looked up in time, to see her skin normalise in patches until she was staring at herself in the mirror like always. But her eyes were still bright flashes of random colour.

Now two sets of feet were racing along the corridor.

Tess turned to the window and stepped onto the damaged windowsill. It was highly unlikely she'd be lucky twice.

She looked at the drop below and suddenly really wanted those monstrous wings back. Her back became heavy again in response. She silently thanked whatever brought them back.

"You'd better work.", she mumbled to them. She closed her eyes and groaned. "This is *nuts!*"

She held her breath and jumped....and soon connected with the garden path, face-first, with a loud thud accompanied by a muffled scream of pain and a few choice words.

Thankfully years of martial arts and gymnastics meant falling on her face was normal. But she'd never done it from two or three storeys up.

She could hear Amanda and Jason in her room now. She immediately started to run towards the treeline across the garden. She knew she wouldn't make it in time. In the next instant, the thought occurred to her if she had four legs, she'd be able to move a lot faster. There was a pop sound and Tess soon felt her spine and frame change, so she followed the sensation and bent forward. She focused on moving as fast as possible and cleared the two hundred metres of lawn in around 10 seconds, maybe less. By the time Amanda reached her bedroom window she was almost in the trees and covered by darkness.

As Tess stopped to catch her breath and come down from the adrenaline. She was somehow able to hear the conversation going on in her bedroom.

"Look at the floor!", Jason gasped. "Looks like a wolf got in here."

"Oh my god!", Amanda almost whispered. But she sounded too calm. Tess put it down to motherly instinct and ability to remain calm for others' sake. "Jason, get the car. We'll check every room one more time and then we'll go looking around the area for her."

"Shouldn't we call the police?", Jason asked, his voice shaking a little.

Tess felt her breath catch in her throat.

"Not yet.", Amanda stated, the ring of decisiveness and authority in her tone. "If we can't find her by tomorrow, then we call them."

Jason sighed. "I hope she's OK."

Tess smiled and felt a little warm sensation in her chest at the caring sound in the voice of a man she'd only met this morning.

"I'll check this floor and then meet you downstairs.", Amanda informed.

There were no other words exchanged after that. Tess heard Jason leave the room and head downstairs. Amanda turned back out to look out of the open window.

Tess froze, because Amanda's head wasn't turning and scanning the area. It was facing straight at the treeline. At her.

She stepped back and away from the stare even though she couldn't really see it. Then Amanda disappeared from view.

Tess slumped against a tree in relief. And then she looked down. Her shins were distorted, her bones bent into a lupine shape which explained the pop sound and the speed she'd achieved.

Tess nodded, in understanding.

Then, finally, she turned and vomited violently into the bushes.

*

It had been hours since the weird events in her bedroom and Tess was freaking out. She was sitting hugging her legs to her body, on the ground and scared to move, in case something else happened. As she sat in the dark, terrified of all the sounds in the night, she went over the evening's events in her mind. It had been better she'd thought it was a hallucination. What in the hell was she? Is that why she'd been on medication all her life? To stop this insanity?

'Hello?', a deep male voice called.

Tess leapt to her feet again. Her heart was pounding. There was no one there. The moon was out now and she had a clear view of everything.

'Who are you?', the voice asked.

Tess thought both of her names before she could speak, and the voice answered.

'McCampbell? That's not possible.', the shock in the voice was undisguised.

A new voice joined. A female.

'Who's this? Never heard this one before. She sounds young.' She was well spoken with a slight accent that Tess couldn't place.

Tess groaned. 'Oh my god. I'm going insane. Maybe the meds were for mental health issues.'

'Believe me, you're not insane.', the first voice answered.

Tess stopped breathing. 'Really?', she thought, 'This coming from a voice that responded to something I never actually said *out loud*?'

'Stay calm, my dear.', the woman soothed.

'Ahhhh. Someone else has been drummed into the ranks, huh?', a third voice added. It was male, higher in pitch than the first and it dripped with sarcasm and bitterness.

'Oh, cut it out.', spat back the female.

'You'll scare her.', the first voice warned.

There was a dry laugh from the third voice. 'She's hearing voices in her head in the middle of the night. I doubt I could make it worse.'

'For the love of god, don't attempt it.', advised the second voice, in a sweet but slightly threatening tone.

Tess's breathing became erratic again. She couldn't take any more of this weirdness.

'So what's your name?', asked the second voice. 'Where are you?'

'How old are you?', the first voice questioned more urgently.

That was the last straw and Tess's mental 'back' broke. "Shut up, shut up, SHUT UP!", she screamed, aloud this time.

They must have heard it in her head too because for about 30 seconds, the only sound was the echo of her cry bouncing of the trees.

'Enough.', decided a fourth voice. It sounded deeper than all of the others, older, more tired, or calm. Tess couldn't decide.

There was a sigh from the first voice. 'He's right. Let's give her some peace. Besides why should she give out information about herself when she doesn't know us?'

'Looks like I wasn't needed to freak her out.', the third voice teased quietly.

'So help me, if you say one more word-!', the second voice clipped. Her calm was breaking too.

But the first voice, the Leader, cut them both off. 'Quiet, you two.'

'Ok.', the second and third thought in unison.

'Get some sleep, young lady. We'll find you. Don't worry. Everything is going to be fine.', the first voice assured.

The comforting tone to his voice relaxed Tess more than anything she'd ever heard. She felt she could trust this stranger.

'Goodnight Ilene.'

And then there was silence.

Tess stood, with nothing but the sound of her mind and woodland life around her now. Instead of feeling a bewildered mess, she suddenly was calm and strengthened. She smiled. If she was losing her mind, at least she wasn't going to do it alone.

I J FERRESTONE

Chapter 7

What In The Hell...?

The deep whirring of a nearby lawn mower shook Tess awake. She had no idea where she was for a moment then she realised she was sitting where she'd decided would be the safest place to sleep, in a large tree about ten feet in the air, so no large and threatening unknown local wildlife could reach her. She looked forward and saw the branch she had her legs stretched along. Somehow a pair of branches had grown parallel to each other, with only a one-inch gap between them and the base of the tree leaned away from their direction of growth, like a reclining chair. It had been the perfect sleeping spot. But now Tess had to get down.

She looked for the nearest branch and started to move. There were a couple of near misses, but she eventually made it to ground level.

Her feet were bare, her vest was torn at the back and lord knows what her face and hair looked like.

Tess groaned and walked out of the tree-line towards the house. She hoped Amanda and Jason hadn't been up searching all night for her. She wanted to her to apologise but then she'd have to explain what she was apologising for. And she was in no place to explain something so confusing that she didn't understand it herself.

The sun was up. It could have been any time past nine. Not that she had anywhere to be.

The sound of the lawn mower ceased and running footsteps approached hurriedly from her left. "Ilene! Oh, thank *god*!" Jason's face was a picture of both anxiety and relief at the same time. Tess took a few seconds to collect herself before she looked him in the eye. She was so embarrassed but frightened also. Something that had never happened to her, or possibly anyone, before had happened on day two of her new life and day one in her new home in front of her new acquaintances. Her situation, body and health were unpredictable and she couldn't afford to be around people too much in case it happened again.

She gave him a sheepish lop-sided smile. 'Morning.', she greeted quickly.

'Are you feeling OK?', Jason asked standing in front of her. 'I can't believe you were out here all night. You must be freezing.'

Jason reached his hand out to touch her arm and check, but a terrified Tess dodged it quickly and started heading towards the house. He couldn't touch her. Her skin was reactional and did things without warning, consent or control. She had to get inside and clean up.

Jason turned to follow her. "Ilene?", he called. "What's wrong? I won't hurt you."

Tess didn't look back as she walked into the kitchen side entrance of the house. It was the nearest way in. "I'm sorry.", she stammered. It's all she could say. If she explained why she recoiled from contact, it would lead to more questions she didn't want to answer.

"Mum told me what's wrong.", Jason announced, hesitantly, as they entered the hallway.

Tess stumbled slightly as this caught her off guard but kept moving. She wanted to laugh. This should be good. How could she know?

Jason tried to catch up with her, but she kept increasing her speed when he did. "Sleepwalking is nothing to be ashamed of. My grandfather had it too, apparently."

Tess stopped this time. That cover story was genius. And she would thank Amanda later, as well as question her. She didn't answer but she did look over her shoulder briefly. He was stood on the staircase, and she was on the first floor. He had this look of understanding and almost pity in his eyes. And that look of pity riled Tess up a little. She wasn't used to charity, assistance or pity. Especially not pity. It made her feel small and weak. Tess clenched her jaw and exhaled through her nostrils before continuing on to her bedroom.

Jason followed and decided to change the subject. She was clearly embarrassed about it. Not many people sleepwalk to such an extent that they wake up in the garden after climbing out of window twenty feet off the ground.

Her clothes were dirt-covered and torn. She had leaves and feathers in her hair. At any other time that would have been a sign of a wild and fun night out.

"What happened to your shirt?", Jason quizzed as she reached the second floor.

Tess huffed but answered anyway. "I fell out of a tree."

It was Jason's turn to stumble now, "Wow!", he gasped, "You're not hurt anywhere, are you?"

As Tess entered her room and closed the door behind her, Jason saw a glimpse of a sad look on her face.

"I'm fine, Jason. I'm...gonna shower. I'll see you later.", Tess answered, her voice muffled by the door between them.

Jason nodded. The poor thing. Alone, freaked out and coping with a sleeping disorder. It would *definitely* never be boring again here.

"Call me or find me if you need anything, OK?", he said.

There was a brief silence.

"OK.", her little voice replied.

Jason nodded again. He'd head downstairs to continue working until Tess felt comfortable enough to come out and talk.

Tess heaved a sigh of relief and headed to her bathroom. She almost laughed. She looked like she'd been rescued from a desert island. Her hair was full of twigs and leaves, there was mud everywhere and her clothes were torn in different places.

She shook her head, turning and opening the taps to fill up a hot bath. She brushed her teeth, trying to spot any differences. As the room steamed up, she tried startling herself subconsciously by jumping and snarling at her reflection. It didn't work and all it achieved was to make her look more ridiculous.

She discarded her destroyed make-shift pyjamas and lowered herself gingerly into the bath. She relaxed for a while and shut her eyes. She let the quiet and the warmth wash over her. Tess sat up after a while and reached for her loofa. She could still feel the dirt on her skin, so she began to scrub. Her skin looked the same as ever. Nothing seemed to have changed, but everything had. Her simple mission of discovering more about her biological family would have to go on the back burner for a while.

She had to figure herself out first. Tess put her head in her hands and groaned again. This was like some twisted gap year. She was far from home, trying to experience the world and find herself, and it was all going incredibly wrong.

Tess dried and applied lotion like normal and decided to keep testing herself. She found a blank notebook in her father's office on the floor below and stole it away to her room.

Over the next few days, she spent her time jumping from items and testing her strength. She seemed back to normal; flexible but feeble.

Then the sun began to set again, and she remembered that the changes had happened around this time. As the sun vanished fully from sight she felt the goose-pimples again.

Then she recommenced her testing. And it worked. She lifted the ottoman with one hand, grew wings at the thought, and discovered a few other new traits, like clinging to the ceiling with her hand and cat-like flexibility.

She snuck to the kitchen for food the next morning and to return the plate Amanda had left her from dinner the night before.

She was starting to figure it out. Her changes were time limited, between sunset and sunrise. She had to concentrate on things she'd already experienced and put herself in danger to discover new abilities, like attempting to jump from her bedroom window again. Her changes were all biological and mimicking animals. The clues were in the changes in her skin- shark, snake and chameleon were the ones she knew so far.

This was going to be interesting. So, she knew her limits. She still wasn't in control, but she knew now to disappear at about 4:30, 3:00 to be safe as the winter drew in and the days got shorter.

Another thing she was beginning to understand was the voices in her head that could only be heard when she left the house, though she didn't know why.

She'd nicknamed the voices now, although she concentrated on not thinking them. The first male voice she called him the Leader. He was clearly in control, despite the second male's protests. This person she called the Suspicious Whiner. He was bitter, sarcastic and pessimistic, but intelligent. Tess guessed this because he would lose focus during conversations and start doing calculations 'aloud'. The third male voice, deep and ancient, she nicknamed Mono, for his reluctance to give anything but one-worded answers or comments. The fourth and only female voice, she called the Tactician. This woman was very careful of what she said and how she phrased things. She continued to attempt to gain information from Tess, but it didn't work. Tess didn't trust either of them. She remembered the advice in her father's letter, which she re-read daily, and trusted no-one. And her caution was showing- even Amanda and Jason noticed her quiet and more distant behaviour.

It had been three full days since the night of Tess's first transformation. Tess had risen feeling a little more positive and ready to face a new day. Today she would start analysing her father's library for clues about his life and what kind of person he was.

She was so lost in thought; she almost forgot her tray of empty dishes from the night before. She snapped her fingers and ran back up to her bedroom to get them. Once she had taken it downstairs, sauntering past Jason sitting, relaxed, at the breakfast bar, she found an apple in the fruit bowl and started eating it.

"Good morning!", Jason muttered, from his stool in the kitchen. "Glad to see you've emerged from your crypt, Madame Dracula."

Tess snorted a laugh in response. "That would have been a clever and amusing comment, but vampires come out at *night*!"

Jason grabbed a banana and started peeling it. "You could be a day-walker."

"Really?", Tess retorted, holding up her breakfast, "A Day-walking vampire that sucks the life-force from dairy, meat, pulses, fruits and vegetables."

Jason winked. "That's how you fool us and walk among us."

Tess laughed. "Plans for the day?"

"I have a couple of classes at University.", Jason explained. He was studying Architecture and Engineering. "We have a class today on Eastern palaces."

Tess breathed in a playfully jealous hiss.

"And you?", Jason asked. He was standing now, gathering up his jacket and car keys.

"The library.", Tess informed, leaning her head in the room's direction. "I want to do some digging before I take life seriously and start job hunting."

"And then back to the crypt?", Jason teased.

Tess nodded. "Back to the crypt. To prepare for my next hunt for hapless vegetables...and pizza."

Jason laughed, heading for the front door. "See you later."

"Bye.", Tess called, watching him leave.

As the door closed with an echoing bang and click, Tess finished her last couple of bites of her apple and threw it in the little compost bin sat next to the side exit of the house, the kitchen's other door. Then as she started to head to the library, she realised she'd left her notebook in her room. She clicked her fingers again as the thought hit her. She turned and headed towards the stairs. Amanda walked out of the dining room at that moment, heading for the kitchen.

"Morning Ilene!", she chirped brightly.

"Morning Amanda.", Tess responded, starting to climb the stairs. "Jason just left."

"Yes, I heard him. He's such a hard worker.", she answered, a loving smile playing on her lips as she stared off wistfully into thoughts of her son.

Tess smiled and turned to climb the next flight of stairs.

The door knocked.

Maybe Jason was as absent-minded as she was and had forgotten something. Tess heard Amanda walk to the door and open it.

"Oh my god!", Amanda exclaimed. "Well, *hello*! I haven't seen you in forever. I didn't think you still lived in the area. How are you?"

This excited tone in Amanda's voice peaked Tess's curiosity. She pivoted on her foot she'd just placed down and headed back down the stairs.

Before the mysterious person could speak, Amanda piped up again.

"Come in, come *in*!"

There were footsteps, slow, cautious and they belonged to someone sounding heavier than either Amanda *or* Jason.

"Hello, Amanda. Are you alone?", a male voice asked, in a slightly hushed voice.

Tess was really curious now. Was Amanda dating? Who was this guy? Before she realised it Tess had gone from simply poking her head around the stair banister to stepping out.

As Amanda went to answer him, she froze and looked past her guest. Tess could see him only from behind, but he looked impressive. He was in a well-tailored pair of black suit trousers and loafers, wearing a mustard jumper over a shirt. She could see its white collar poking out over the jumper collar. His back was broad and muscular, and he was tall, more than average height. And his short dark brown hair was combed and styled to sweep backwards and cross at the nape of his neck.

He turned to follow Amanda's gaze and froze also. His face was handsome and chiselled, his jaw and neck strong and angular, showing an almost Scandinavian bone structure. But what surprised Tess most was the look on his face. His mouth fell open and his eyes began to mist over and then well with small tears of recognition.

"My god!", he breathed. "Siobhan?"

Tess knew his voice in that moment. It was the Leader. He said he'd find her, and there he was, gaping at her in her hallway. But the sound of her mother's name made her feel less wary towards him.

"No, I'm sorry.", Tess apologised. "How do you know my mother?"

The man blinked and started as she said that last word. "You...you're her daughter?", he questioned. "You *can't* be. That's impossible!"

Tess's eyebrows furrowed. The dismissal of her existence ticked her off slightly. Why was it impossible? She shook her head and folder her arms. "Clearly not. I'm standing right here."

Amanda stepped up behind the man, who was still staring up at Tess dumbfounded. "Is it-?", she started to ask.

"You know the laws as well as I, Amanda.", he interrupted, barely audible.

What the hell, were they talking about? It's like she was being left out of some private joke. He was so tight-lipped when they spoke after sunset, she knew he'd never tell her anything.

"Well, I'll leave you two to catch up.", Tess said, waving her hand dismissively and turning to go back up the stairs.

"Wait!", the man called. "I'm sorry!"

Tess did pause. She glowered over her shoulder at him.

"I didn't mean to offend you. It's just...we never knew...", he began. He was walking up towards her.

Tess turned to face him as he reached her. Suddenly he started laughing and the sound grew louder, tears forming in his eyes.

"I must apologise again. I'm not laughing at you.", he managed to say, wiping his eyes, as Tess looked up at him questioningly. "It's just I haven't seen Roger or Siobhan in almost twenty years, and I thought I never would. And yet, here is Siobhan's face, scowling at me the same as ever."

Then his eyes turned sad, even though he was still smiling.

"Forgive me. I have so much to ask you...and tell you. Will you please walk about the grounds with me so we can talk?", he pleaded.

Tess looked at Amanda, unsure, to see that she too was looking emotional. This man must be linked to her parents as Amanda was. And he spoke like someone out of a Jane Austen novel, which she hadn't noticed before.

Tess nodded. "I will.", she agreed, and put out her left hand. "I'm Ilene McCampbell. It's nice to meet you."

The man grinned and took her hand firmly, shaking it. "And I am Mek'el Keth, at your service. But you can call me Mike."

*

Tess was running over today's turn of events and the upheaval of her research plans. One moment she was heading upstairs to fetch her notebook, now she was walking with a half-stranger along the grounds of her parents' home. He was just in his shirt now, and has rolled the sleeves up, as he had removed his jumper and put it in his car. And he was staring at her. It was freaking her out even though she knew why. She had to break the silence.

Tess turned towards her visitor. "So...Mek'el, was it? That's an interesting name. I've never heard one like it."

Mek'el blinked and snapped out of whatever memory he was in, his blue-green eyes losing their haziness. They now looked at Tess with focus. "That's because it's a very old name that has been lost with time."

Tess furrowed her eyebrows. "Well clearly not. Your parents knew the name enough to give it to you forty-something years ago."

Mek'el laughed and looked ahead. "A little longer ago than that."

"Is your name European? It doesn't seem like a name from this side of the pond.", Tess asked.

"You're right. It's a very old Scandinavian name."

Tess nodded. She had no idea what to say next. She was a chatterbox but for the first time she was stumped. What do you talk about with the man who'd been inside your head for over three days? Thankfully Mek'el had it covered.

"Ilene...I'm sorry I was so dismissive about your relation to Roger and Siobhan. It's just that... no-one knew Siobhan was pregnant. She made excuses not to socialise and your father...well, he had a very focused mind, so we never heard anything about it from him. Then the next thing we all heard, the two of them had died in England on their way to Roger's ancestral home in Scotland. So, you can understand my confusion."

85

Tess stopped and spun to look at his face. He looked sad but composed. She felt annoyed that she didn't have memories, or such sadness linked to the death of her own parents.

Tess's eyes dropped and then she sighed. "Actually, they were murdered."

Now Mek'el looked confused. "You were there?"

Tess waved a hand. "No, no! They'd dropped me off in London with friends for safe keeping."

Mek'el nodded and relaxed a little. This girl didn't need any more horror in her past.

"I keep seeing it when I sleep. Clearer each time. I first saw it on the night before my birthday, almost three weeks ago."

"You can *see* it? Not *hear* it like you do with my voice?", Mek'el questioned, stepping closer to scrutinise her face. "And which birthday was it?"

Tess felt his confusion and urgency. "Yes, I see it. Why is that a shock? And it was my eighteenth birthday."

"Of course!", Mek'el breathed, nodding. His eyes hazed again as he became lost in thought.

"You didn't answer my question! Why is seeing a big deal? Why can't I hear your voice when I'm inside the house? And what do you mean 'Of course'?", Tess demanded grabbing him by the arm.

Mek'el looked her in the eye with a determined look that froze her.

"Seeing someone's mind is a rare skill that usually comes with centuries of practice among our kind. The eighteenth year is when your abilities kick in...if you're born to two individuals of our kind.

And you can't hear me in the house for the same reason, I'm guessing, as to why your existence was never discovered while you grew up in England: there's a protective barrier placed over the house."

Tess suddenly couldn't feel her legs. She was a part of a group of telepaths. And how could anyone practice anything for centuries? And how was she never able to see this barrier? She had so many questions, but she only asked one.

"Mek'el... why did my parents keep my conception *and* birth a secret?"

Mek'el sighed. "To answer that question, I'd have to tell you a long story."

Tess was about to ask for all the details but then she realised what the time was. She looked to the horizon, and the sun was setting.

Tess cursed.

Her phone was still on her mother's dressing table, so she hadn't heard her normal four o'clock alarm.

Tess smiled and started to turn herself to suggest walking back to the house. "Well, unfortunately that story will have to wait until next time, I have to get back inside."

Mek'el smirked and took her left forearm in his large left hand and gripped it firmly. "Why? Do you have plans?", he asked, watching her closely.

"No, no!" Tess countered laughing weakly. "I still have jetlag, so I still go to sleep on UK time. Also, it's getting dark and the dark scares me a little."

Mek'el was unaffected by these revelations at all. "It's ok. I have a torch on my phone."

Tess's heart was starting to pound. "I-I'm afraid that little light won't be enough. It's more like a medically deemed phobia. I really...really have to get into the house."

At that moment, the new garden lights Jason had installed switched on in response to the increasing darkness. In that moment, Tess cursed Jason's hard-working nature. It felt like the sun was setting faster than ever. She was finding it hard to breathe. She could feel beads of sweat forming on her forehead. Any protection the shadows would have provided was now gone. He would see everything...and so would Amanda!

"It's ok.", Mek'el cooed darkly. "Stay here with me. There's so much to talk about."

"No! NO!", Tess gasped as she tried to wrench herself away from his tightening grip. Why wouldn't he let her go? Why was he acting like this? This questions in her mind drowned by the voice of her subconscious screaming one word only: hide.

"*Let me GO!*", she shrieked. She was pulling until her shoulder started to ache. As she saw the sun dip for good and the last speck of light vanish, she screamed and started to cry. As the goose-pimples started to work her way up her body, she went back to basics and sank her teeth into Mek'el's arm as hard as she could, but he didn't flinch, and she tasted no blood. He just stared down at her tear-stained face.

She closed her eyes and screamed again in protest as she felt her body changing instinctively. The next thing she knew, she was clawing at his arm and hovering in the air, her body jerking back and forth wildly as she flapped her wings desperately, hoping the momentum would break her free. But Mek'el planted his feet and didn't move. Tess raised her free claw to swipe at his forearm. In the seconds before her claw contacted his skin, something happened.

And her claw bounced off thick scales, sending up a couple of sparks. Tess stopped moving and dropped, landing on the ground.

Mek'el let go of her arm, but Tess did not run. He raised his arm up in front of her face and as he flexed his fingers, his skin thickened and claws, even longer than hers, sprang into existence. He stepped back and crouched on all fours, his legs changing to a lupine shape before he ran around her at such speed that she almost didn't see him. Then he leaned backwards, crouched slightly and leapt about fifteen feet into the air. He did a neat forward flip and unfurled feathered wings, hovering.

Tess suddenly realised she was laughing with joy. New tears were running down her face now as she stared at this glorious man. She was not alone. The words 'our kind' suddenly made sense. Hope radiated through her body and the fear she'd felt over the last three days was gone.

Mek'el smiled and lowered himself to the ground, performing a gentle landing he had clearly perfected with time.

His eyes glowing a pale pink colour. He bowed low. And then he spoke, his mouth still closed.

'I'm sorry I scared you like that. I had to show you that we're the same. Allow me to reintroduce myself. I am Mek'el Keth, second General of the Verndarar army. I was your father's best friend. I was born in the Netherlands and raised in England. And I am seven hundred and fifty-two years old.'

Mek'el smiled and then his shoulders shook slightly as he reached his hand out to Tess again, making his wings disappear. She took it and began standing up. Mek'el's laughter rang in the air as Tess stood shaking her head with her mouth hanging open.

I J FERRESTONE

Chapter 8

Mek'el's History Lesson

Two dark figures floated through the light of dusk and began descending into the trees at the same time. Mek'el and Tess landed in a forest clearing a few hundred miles North of Tess's home, somewhere near Mackenzie, after taking flight following Mek'el's revelation in the back garden.

Tess could smell water nearby, possibly a lake because she couldn't hear the water rushing. She was noticing things she hadn't before. And now she'd be able to explore more, without worrying about fuel costs or being crammed in hot vehicles with sweaty, coughing or crying strangers. As strange as this situation was, it had some perks.

She looked for Mek'el and found him, sitting down on a fallen tree. She walked towards him. He had "put away" his wings and looked like a normal man just enjoying the night air.

Mek'el smiled at her. "You look so much like your mother. Except for the hair colour of course. Neither of your parents had red hair. Roger's was brown and Siobhan's was ebony, but the kind of ebony that caught and reflected light. She was so stunning. As accomplished as Roger was, he still couldn't believe his luck at having earned her love."

Mek'el was staring into the recent past, lost in the memory of their faces. Tess sat in front of him, cross-legged on the grass.

'Do you want to have this conversation aloud or this way?', he asked, looking down into her face.

'Won't someone else be able to hear us?', Tess asked, her brow furrowing.

Mek'el shook his head. 'We're too far away for anyone of our kind to eavesdrop. There's no-one around for miles, so we can talk normally.'

Tess grinned. "Aloud it is then. So, Mr Keth...what *are* you?"

"You mean what are *we*?", Mek'el corrected, his left hand gesturing back and forth between them.

"Yes.", Tess confirmed.

Mek'el thought for a moment. "Sorry, I haven't had to explain this to anyone before. You see, we're a secret."

Tess eyes widened and she leaned in slightly. This was only making her more curious and excited.

Mek'el sat up straighter and cleared his throat. "Imagine a body, and this body gets sick. The virus feeds off the body, body parts and the good bacteria, damaging the body. The body creates antibodies to fight the virus and keep the body from dying. We are that antibody. The body is the Earth and its people. We are the embodiment of this planet and all it provides, agents of life itself. We had a few names in the past. Humans called us Gods, angels, saint and things. And we each called ourselves different words from our own lands. But we eventually decided on an old Icelandic word that we felt sounded right for who we are and what we do. We are the Verndarar, entrusted with the protection and preservation of the Human World."

"Verndarar?", Tess repeated. The word sound strange but strong. It sounded old like it had legacy and lore attached to it. She loved it and could see why they'd chosen it.

"Yes."

"What do we fight? And who created us? God? A mad scientist?"

The last question made Mek'el chuckle, but he shook his head.

"We are individuals who proved to be brave, selfless and strong in our human lives and died saving many people. We are brought back to fight for human life once more. And we are brought back by... some call her Mother Nature. Others call her Gaia. She is the spirit of this world, as old as time. Over the course of history and especially in the last three hundred years, with the creation of technology, the use of fossil fuels, she has become sicker, and she left us to protect this world for the monsters created by the malice and harm done to this world. We call them the Tainted, because they're elemental substances poisoned by the evil and greed in this world. It builds and gives them more life and power than they should have, and they go on a destructive rampage."

Tess sat silent for a moment as Mek'el waited for her to form her next question. "Gaia...", she muttered to herself. "You said that we're the embodiment of what this earth provides. Is that why we can imitate the physical traits of animals?"

"Yes. All those legends of humanoid creatures? Selkies, mermaids, werewolves, centaurs, satyrs, fawns...that's us. The more animals you know about, the more you can do. We try and not to be spotted while we fight but we used to get seen. Now we're just legends and ghosts. No-one takes us seriously, which is good. But every time a species goes extinct, we lose that ability forever."

"So, where do we come from? Do we just live among humans the whole time?", Tess quizzed.

Mek'el smiled. She adapted to the information so quickly. "No, we have our own realm. It's another dimension that only we can get to. It's lush and green, the way this world used to be. But we can't get back there anymore."

Tess pictured it. A green paradise full of people training to fight monsters, changing forms over and over and not having to hide. "I hope I can go there one day.", Tess said absent-mindedly. "Is everything about us for the purpose of fighting?"

"That's right. The camouflage, the speed, the flight, even the telepathy helps us work as a more efficient unit while destroying the monsters. One person sees something and feeds it back to the others. It shortens the fight and reduces injuries. We don't die but we can be hurt. We heal quite quickly though.", Mek'el explained.

Tess rubbed her head. It was starting to ache. There was so much to take in, but she still had questions. So, she kept asking. "Are we, you, me and the other three, the only ones?"

"No, there are hundreds of us. But we are disappearing.", Mek'el stated, his features looking full of sadness and frustration.

Tess could see the pain in his face. He was thinking of comrades and friends lost. So, she changed the subject.

"Why did you say it was impossible for my parents to have had a child when I met you?", Tess asked. "Last question for tonight, I promise."

Mek'el's face became serious again. "Because about five hundred years ago, coupling and breeding among Verndarar was forbidden and I never imagined that of all people, your parents would break the rules."

"I'm an illegal *child*?! But why was it made illegal?"

Mek'el got up and started to walk around. Tess took his original seat on the fallen tree.

"Several hundred years ago, Verndarar realised they could create children. They would be human through childhood and on the day of their eighteenth birthday, their Verndari traits would kick in. It was a proud moment for Verndarar parents. It would mean they would be able to train and fight together. But the elders later decreed that because their powers were strongest at eighteen, that all Verndari-born would join them at their temple for the rest of their lives to be bridge between the human world, Gaia and the warriors. This is how we'd be informed of missions. The celebration of eighteen years became a proud but a sad moment for all parents."

Tess grimaced. "Is this why they banned producing children? To spare parents that pain of never seeing their children again?"

"No that's not the reason. And the parents would still get to talk to and see their children, although they could never leave the temple. Water is our gateway. It's the way that we used to get to our realm, into the human world and get direct messages from Gaia. The reason it became forbidden was because of an event that changed everything. There were four elders, and unbeknownst to the other three, the wife of one had borne a son. They named him Velohnen. They kept his birth a secret and raised him in secret also. Just after the son's eighteenth birthday, the other three elders discovered the son. There is a sword the elders have called Mwisho, which is the only thing capable of killing one of our kind, in case of law-breaking. The name is Swahili for last, because it's our last death and the last thing we would feel. The elders brought it in case the family fought back when they came to take Velohnen. Somehow the boy got hold of the sword and struck down his own parents. He resented them for keeping him prisoner for his entire life. He took the green gem from one of the elders and fled into the human world. He was unrestrained and at the height of his power. The elders announced that young Verndari-born were too dangerous and unstable, so they banned relationships and children among our kind. Despite that, people still fell in love, but no children were born for five hundred years... until you."

Tess shivered. Was she capable of something like that? Could she lose her mind and kill someone? Or be unable to control her strength and do it accidentally?

"I don't want to be like him.", Tess breathed.

Mek'el walked to Tess and dropped to one knee, placing a hand on top of her head. "You won't be. I promise to keep you safe. I will teach you everything I know. But most importantly, I will teach you control and restraint, so you can live a good life, unrestrained, unafraid and free."

Tess nodded and sighed as Mek'el leaned forward and wrapped his arms around her.

STONE

Chapter 9

Rookie

Tess rolled over as the morning sun broke into her bedroom window. She was going to have a busy day. Mek'el was coming over just before lunch to discuss training.

She brushed her teeth and had a shower before heading downstairs for breakfast. She was so lost in thought that she didn't hear Jason greet her as she poured herself a bowl of cereal.

Her head snapped up as he called her a second time. "Oh, hi.", Tess replied.

Jason shook his head. "Wake up, Ilene.", he muttered, grabbing his normal morning banana.

"I *am* awake, cheeky.", Tess answered, sticking out her tongue. He reminded her so much of Simeon. She would check her emails later on to see if he had replied to the message that she'd sent yesterday. She missed her family, but she had so much to do and learn. So many adjustments to make and she couldn't tell them about any of it.

"How have things been going in the crypt over the last few days? Were any pulses or vegetables lured into your lair yet?"

Tess jutted her bottom lip out and shook her head in mock sadness. "Not yet. And I'm getting really peckish. This cereal will be villager number five for now until I hunt again."

They both laughed. At that moment, the front door was knocked. Jason was surprised by the speed at which Tess put down her bowl and ran into the hallway. What had gotten her so excited?

He followed in the same direction, moving much slower than Tess had. He stepped out to see Tess hugging a tall middle-aged man. Jason felt disgusted for a split second before seeing the almost paternal affection in his eyes. But there was still something unsettling about the man.

Tess turned towards Jason and was sporting the biggest grin he'd ever seen on her face. Perhaps he was an old friend from her childhood.

"Jason, this is Mek'el. Or Mike if you can't pronounce that.", Tess introduced, still beaming. "He's an old friend of my parents. He's been telling me about them."

Jason stepped up, disposing of the banana skin in his hand before extending it towards the stranger. "Oh, that's good. Jason Dunney. Nice to meet you."

The man smiled and nodded, almost crushing Jason's knuckles against each other with his grip. "Amanda's boy! Nice to meet you too."

Jason's forehead creased. "You know my mom?"

Mek'el nodded again. "Yes, the McCampbells, your mother and I were friends with each other for about twenty-five years."

Jason squinted slightly at him, giving him an accusing stare. "How well... did you know mom?"

Mek'el smiled a knowing smile. "She's been a helpful and good friend. She's like a sister to me, the same as Tess's- I mean Ilene's mom was. We were an odd but tight circle of friends. More like a makeshift family, actually."

Tess saw Jason's shoulders lower and his breathing slow down. Then she heard Mek'el's voice without the echo of the room. She knew he was speaking just to her.

'He's wondering if I'm his father.', Mek'el explained.

'Well, you're clearly not or I'd have heard you think it by now.', Tess responded.

'Not if I concentrate on something else.', Mek'el corrected.

'Or on thinking of nothing. I hear men are good at that.' Tess jabbed.

Mek'el continued to smile as he let go of Jason's hand. 'You heard right. Even among our kind, you'd be amazed how much silence there can be.'

"I'll catch up with Amanda later. Right now, I'm here to see this little lady and fill her in on some history.", Mek'el boomed, placing his hand on Tess's shoulder.

Jason shrugged and moved aside as Mek'el and Tess walked towards the staircase. "O.K Well I'm going into the city to meet some friends.", he called as he grabbed his jacket and keys from the table against the wall. "Have fun!"

"Bye!", Tess called back. She turned back to Mek'el as the door boomed closed. "So... what do you want to do first?"

Mek'el tapped his leather shoulder bag. He'd probably had it for decades, or longer. It was well made and equally well-worn. 'I brought photos.', he thought aloud. 'We can be ourselves, by the way. Amanda's car was gone when I arrived, so we have the place to ourselves. No need to hide.'

Almost as proof of this, Mek'el rolled his sleeves up and thick scales appeared on his left arm and fur on his right. Tess jumped back and almost fell down the stairs. "Woah!", she asked. "How'd you do that?

The sun's still up!"

Mek'el smiled, started walking up the stairs and motioned her to follow as he returned his arms to normal again. 'Apparently when we first gain our abilities, because we're naturals at hiding, our subconscious tricks our bodies into only transforming at night. I personally think it's something in sunlight that prohibits us from changing easily in the beginning. Don't worry. With time and training, you'll be able to transform, day or night, at will.'

Tess smiled and heaved an audible sigh of relief. It'd be nice to be unafraid when she was around normal people. Especially once she started working.

As they reached her father's office, Mek'el spoke mentally again. 'Exactly. It helps to be able to assimilate with society, in case of lengthy missions, or... being trapped in this world.'

Tess followed as he opened the door. 'You miss it? The... Verndari realm?' She was still getting her head around the new terminology.

Mek'el stopped and turned, giving her the chills. His green eyes were sad and serious again. 'Of course. It's been my home for over six hundred years and some of my friends are there.'

'I'm sorry. I can't imagine what that's like.', Tess answered, her mental voice soft and sympathetic.

Mek'el turned, walking towards her father's desk. 'So much like Siobhan. Good Gaia, I miss her.', he thought. He sat at the desk and rested his bag on it. Tess found a stool nearby and brought it to the desk. Mek'el reached into the bag and pulled out a laptop and thick leatherbound photo albums. Tess's breathing quickened. She was suddenly nervous. Now she would be able to put faces to her dreams, and the figures in her visions. Now she would be able to picture what their lives would have been. Final parts of the puzzle would come together in her mind.

Mek'el noticed her hesitation and opened the album. On the first page was a face she recognised.

"The statue.", she whispered.

Mek'el nodded. "Yes. The statue outside the dojo. It was a gift created on his thirtieth birthday and placed in his ancestral home centuries ago. He moved it here because he didn't want it to be accidentally destroyed or taken by some museum. It's one of the only things from his past still left."

"This is him? My father?", Tess asked, almost standing in excitement.

Mek'el smiled. "Yes. The kindest man and a natural born leader."

It was the same face Tess had passed in the hallway. The wavy locks, shorter in this picture and brown with a hint of auburn, the strong jaw, the stature, the eyes, which she could now see were hazel. He had a gentle smile on his face, a welcoming and trustworthy one. Now the things Tess had felt on seeing the face made sense. No wonder she felt safe looking into those eyes, because she had already seen them, trusted them and loved them. She felt so touched by the realisation, but she didn't let herself get carried away by her emotions. She couldn't break down looking at only one picture, otherwise she'd never manage the rest.

She reached for the next page, as a sign of strength to herself, and smiled.

The woman on the next page was her, only a bit older with jet black, thick and long hair and gleaming deep brown eyes, her skin smooth and dark, catching and reflecting the light. She wore a wide toothy grin and was stood with her arms gently folded. Tess could almost hear her laugh, or was she remembering it? She wanted to leap into the picture and run into the woman's arms.

She didn't realise she'd been staring silently for quite a while until Mek'el spoke again.

'Want to take a guess at who this is?', Mek'el asked, his voice soft, but eagerness still noticeable.

Tess couldn't help it this time. She swallowed a few times, but it only made it harder to breathe and strained her voice when she did eventually speak. 'Mum.', she confirmed, 'I....I know her face.'

Tess smiled and then she felt tears run silently down her cheeks. She cried, quietly, for the faces she would never get to see again, the confusion of the bond she felt with these faces, for the life she'd never had and for all the hell she was going through without them. She sniffled but didn't allow herself to even whimper. She didn't even realise her face was against Mek'el's chest until she felt his hand squeeze her shoulder, his breathing shudder and a warm droplet land on her t-shirt and soak through to her skin.

Hearing the girl mentally call for her mother and the longing to know her in her "voice" suddenly unleashed all the pain he'd held in for over seventeen years, against his will. He suddenly felt all of it, wash over him like a dam had broken. He hadn't really had to see the effects of their loss for a long time, and now here it was, sitting in front of him. Siobhan was gone and so was Roger, and their daughter needed him. She was lost, scared, sad and from what he could glean from her mind, she had always been that way. He didn't know how much he'd be able to do for this girl, but he'd do his best... for the sake and memory of his best friends. He listened to her mind as she cried. He heard her pain, her fear and voices he recognised as belonging to his two dead friends. He was angry. Angry for having been robbed of them and the years lost with their daughter. But there was nothing more he could do about the past. Mek'el made a vow, he wasn't sure how silent, to protect Tess as best he could. He would train her to survive, know her heritage and, if she wished it, fight as her parents had.

Tess looked up and saw Mek'el's eyes. They looked sad and drained, the saddest eyes she'd ever seen, filled with such deep pain. His irises glowed a deep blue, like the ocean under the moon, glowing so brightly that the light almost drowned out his pupils. And that light illuminated the rare tears streaming down his face. He looked down at Tess and started slightly. He wiped his face with his free hand, which was made difficult by the new wave of emotion that hit him as Tess suddenly moved and hugged him tightly around his middle.

"I'm sorry, Tess. I shouldn't cry in front of you. I miss them. They were my dearest friends and fighting beside them was the greatest time and honour of my life.", Mek'el apologised, steadying himself as Tess sat up and away from him again. He turned the pages of the album again and smiled.

Tess was now looking at a group picture. She didn't recognise the other faces, but there was Mek'el, standing next to her father, looking dutiful but a smile creeping through his serious expression. His eyes looked completely different to now. In this colour picture, his irises were pinkish-yellow. She recognised the room as the house's conservatory.

Mek'el smiled as he heard the recognition in her mind. 'This house was almost like Headquarters for our kind. It was used for celebrations, battle planning, exits and entrances, training and... sleepovers, as juvenile as those sounds. Everyone was always welcome here. Siobhan refused to allow anyone to stay at a hotel if they were staying in the area. The front door never seemed to close.'

Tess's mind was flooded with images of smiling faces, dinner, the dojo with weapons missing, and the library and office with maps strewn across the desks. 'Looks like it was fun.'

Mek'el's brow furrowed. But Tess thought before he could speak again.

'What did you mean when you said: "exits and entrances"?'

'I'll show you in the dojo later.', Mek'el responded. There was something about one of the words Tess had used earlier that was bugging him. But he would observe and ask later if it happened again.

"Wow!", Tess exclaimed as she turned a page. The pictures were getting older. The last picture was full of perms, this new one was her parents, Mek'el and a few others in forties clothing. The image was black and white and frayed at the edges with age. Her mother sported pin-curls, a sequinned dress and elbow length gloves, while her father and the other men looked elegant but menacing in pinstriped suits and side-parted slicked hair. It looked like a mob photo. Tess wandered why no-one was smiling in this picture. Perhaps it wasn't the style at the time.

She turned another page and saw a polaroid of a painting containing the same group of people but in late nineteenth century clothing.

Mek'el spoke again. 'This was in Spain. There had been a massive battle, and we'd just won. It was our tradition to take a group photo picture after a successful major mission. The next was nineteen forty-six in New York. Our earliest is somewhere in this house; seventeen hundreds after the 'black plague'. That was mainly caused by a huge demon outbreak and the infection spreading from the bodies caused more death. Your mother always complained about fighting in corsets. She hated how restricting they were.' Mek'el laughed again. ' "You boys don't know how lucky you are! I'm wrapped in metal and carrying steel!" ', he pulled a face as he imitated her.

'Her elegance, speed and ferocity... I've never known anyone to dispatch fifty monsters in a gown and without messing up her hair.'

Tess laughed aloud and hard. She could picture the annoyance of fighting in that kind of outfit. 'I bet she celebrated when Queen Victoria died, and corsets were out.'

Mek'el belly laughed. 'She had to wait another ten years. But she celebrated it in style. She tore it off, threw it about thirty metres in the air, leapt after it and shredded it with her favourite sword.'

Tess almost squealed with laughter. 'Genius!', she cried mentally. 'She sounds like a wild child.'

Mek'el laughed again. 'She was. She did exactly what she wanted. That wild nature made Roger love her all the more. He was more "follow the rules" and calm. They balanced each-other out. His calm and her fire. What a mix. You should have seen them spar. When Siobhan fought, she had no morals, rules or scruples. She won almost every time.'

'She fought dirty, then.', Tess asked, turning away from the album to listen to Mek'el properly.

'Yes. She was like a feline. Flexible, graceful and ferocious. Your father was more like a bull. Once he got moving you couldn't stop him. His strength was something to see. If he lost his weapons in battle, it wasn't a set-back. He'd simply grab, slam or punch.'

Tess's mouth dropped open again as she saw her father through Mek'el's descriptions.

"I wish I could be like that.", Tess sighed. She didn't realise she'd thought it let alone said it.

Mek'el nodded. "Come with me.", he encouraged. Tess followed him up the stairs as he carried on speaking. "I'll train you, guide and teach you everything you want to know."

As they entered the dojo, Tess looked at the crack in the marble floor completely differently. The apprehension was replaced with a bursting sense of pride. One of her parents had probably done that.

Mek'el was stood next to the water feature by the right wall. Tess walked to him, and he pointed to the pool. "Place your hand in the water but keep your eyes up."

Tess looked nervous again. What was going to happen?

She sat on the edge of the pool-pond and did as he asked. But nothing happened. She looked at Mek'el with one eyebrow raised. "Now I have a cold wet hand. Was this an obedience test?"

Mek'el chuckled slightly. "No. Now say this aloud: Obstende nobis in domum suam."

Tess nodded and obeyed. As the last word left her lips, she felt a tingle in her right arm, which was dipped in the water. She noticed a bright blue glow coming from her chest. She looked down to see the pendant her father gave her, glowing and trembling of its own accord. The pool started to glow also, and the light travelled up the running indoor waterfall. The light glowed brighter and brighter until it was a blinding white light. As Tess shielded her eyes, she noticed in her peripheral vision that Mek'el was staring directly into the light, like there was something he didn't want to miss.

Then the light dimmed a bit and Tess gasped. She was staring at a live image. It looked like a clearing in a large forest full of the tallest, thickest trees, at least twenty metres wide. Everything was green or lush with vines, flowers and fruits. Sunlight streamed through the boughs and leaves on the trees and reflected dazzlingly from the river nearby. This place was paradise, unlike anything ever seen or painted, untouched and healthy. Tess had never known a place so beautiful. It hardly looked real. There were people of every ethnicity all dressed in brightly coloured flowing thin fabric which looked influenced by all cultural styles. There were homes made of stone and wood, on the ground and in the trees, reachable by vines, ladders and knots on the trees, used like a climbing wall. They looked like they were growing out of the ground and trees themselves. People were training, sparring and practising stances and katas or testing their strength. Then one of them, a woman, did something that gave away exactly what she was looking at.

She wore a backless dress, secured by belt and weapon holsters, and her long red hair was pulled up. She had a basket of fruit under of her arm. She sprouted leathery wings and drifted effortlessly off the floor to one of the homes growing out of one of the trees. She stepped onto the house's porch-like doorstep and entered, simply as if she'd walked off a level street.

'This is the Verndari realm?' Tess asked, unable to look away to confirm it using Mek'el's face.

'Yes.', Mek'el answered, his mental voice thick with emotion.

'Can we...?', Tess began, not realising she was walking through the shallow pool with her hand outstretched.

Mek'el sighed. 'Sadly, no. Although the gem around your neck can become a gateway through bodies of water that bear the Verndari marker, it takes immense practise and power. We're a long way from being able to cross through it.'

"What marker?", Tess asked aloud. She found her answer as she said the second word. The vines climbed up the wall connected at the top and twisted around each other. To the untrained eye the twisted vines looped around itself leaving a small gap. But she could see they wrapped themselves around a stone which now was glowing just like the water.

Tess lifted her arm out of the water and watched the image and light fade as she stood. Her mood dropped a little as this happened. She turned to Mek'el and faced him squarely. "We'd better get training then.", she suggested.

Mek'el shook his head. 'Not until you know what you're training for. When you practise something there's usually a reason or a goal, right?'

Tess nodded. She was a little anxious to get started.

Mek'el let out a slightly bitter laugh. 'Well, we'll see if you feel the same way after sunset.'

He started walking out of the room and towards the stairs, with Tess still in tow. 'Let's keep looking at photos until it's time to eat.'

*

Amanda had arrived at the house at about 2pm. She'd done a huge grocery shopping spree. She found Mek'el and Tess in the library talking. Mek'el hugged her tight and greeted her with a gleaming smile. Tess could feel the years of fondness between them. Mek'el and Tess helped Amanda bring all her purchases. Mek'el carried lots of heavy bags at once, which Tess didn't dare attempt before sun-down. But what surprised Tess was the lack of reaction from Amanda when this happened. She didn't even appraise the situation, not even with a second glance.

Tess began to wonder if Amanda was one of them, but as she wondered this while trailing behind Mek'el and Amanda towards the kitchen, Mek'el looked over his shoulder slightly and shook his head. So, she was human after all.

Tess rolled her eyes. She kept forgetting that her thoughts were no longer private. It saved time but it was a little invasive.

They enjoyed a heavy lunch together, a team effort done by Mek'el and Tess. Tess caught him thinking that it showed they worked well together. He laughed mentally every time Tess reminded herself speak out loud so it wouldn't seem to weird when they handed ingredients and implements to each-other like a well-practised kitchen ballet. Tess was only just handling the weirdness herself. It might send Amanda over the deep end.

'Give her a little credit!', Mek'el chuckled. 'She's stronger than you realise.'

Tess smiled at Amanda as they ate. This comment then made her wonder what Amanda had been through to warrant such commendation from a warrior. Maybe she would ask her someday when she knew she could trust her.

They cleaned up as Amanda prepared dinner and talked. Tess expressed her wish to start job hunting in a couple of weeks' time, so Amanda started writing down list of good companies to work for in the city. She was always so helpful. Almost too helpful. Tess wanted to trust her but eighteen years of bad experiences and her most recent discoveries simply reaffirmed her knowledge that nothing and no-one was who or what they seemed to be.

At about 4pm, Mek'el put his jacket on. "We'll see you later, Amanda. We're just going into the city for a bit.", he called, as he put on his boots.

Tess was ready before him and waiting at the door.

"D'accord!", Amanda shouted from somewhere downstairs.

Mek'el walked to his car, a beautiful black Jaguar. "We'll take the car. It won't be good to leave it here when we've made it known we're going into the city.", he stated. "We'll also act human for the night. Nothing weird, OK?"

Tess nodded. "OK. Agreed.", she acknowledged aloud.

They drove in silence for a few minutes. Tess watched the mountains and greenery whizz past them and marvelled at how her life had turned out so far, going from terrifying to exciting. She relaxed and studied the car's interiors. It really was a very nice car.

"Mek'el?", Tess piped up, still hypnotised by the dashboard.

"Hmmm?", he responded, not taking his eyes away from the approaching hills.

"What is it you do? How do you afford this car?"

Mek'el gave a lopsided cheeky smile. "In this lifetime? I'm a brain surgeon, for the last twenty years. Five hundred years of knowledge helps too. I'm going to have to start greying my hair soon. I can get away with looking a youthful forty-five but soon people will ask questions."

"Will I have to do that too? Do Verndari-born not age either?", Tess asked. Her voice was suddenly high-pitched. This wasn't something she factored into her life. She'd forgotten about this trait in her genes. She had thought she'd simply carry on ageing as normal but maybe it would be different for her.

Mek'el sighed. "From what I remember, Verndari-borns don't age once they reach their mid to late twenties. It will be something you'll have to do as well. It's not too stressful. Once you get used to it, it's a bit of giggle, actually, creating new identities and faking your own death."

"What about the humans you become friends with?" Tess was staring blankly forward, the horror clear on her face.

"Try not to. Sadly death and... loss is a part of life. For everyone."

"Amanda... Jason....My parents, Simeon, Billy...Oh my god...", Tess was muttering with her head in her hands. All she was picturing now was a circle of gravestones, engraved with the names of her loves ones and friends while she stood in black, with stone cold eyes, not looking much older than she did now.

She suddenly was fully cursing her genes and what she was. She was now wishing she'd never found the letter and that she was still with her family in London. But wouldn't that be worse? Thinking she was human and not ageing while everyone crumbled and died around her?

Tess shook the thoughts from her mind. She couldn't think about it anymore. She'd go crazy. She'd deal with it later. She cranked the radio up as loud as she could and found a song she could sing along to. She continued to sing as they zoomed forward into the heart of the city. They parked in a multi-storey car park and started an aimless amble through the streets of Vancouver.

Mek'el put one of his arms around Tess and kept it there. Maybe he should take her home. She was already taking in and dealing with so much. Seeing what he had to show her would probably break her.

Tess was lost in her surroundings focusing on the present and forbidding herself from thinking of the future. "So...", she started, breaking the partial silence. "Fighting must keep you very busy along with all the surgeries you probably do."

Mek'el looked at her and smiled. She was smiling too but her eyes were desperate and wild. Tonight, was make or break. Either she'd accept what she was, or she'd freak out and demand not to see him again, living life as a closet Verndari. "Yes. It doesn't happen often. Just the odd attack here and there. There are Verndarar stationed in every city and town around the world. We can tell there's an attack happening, and we get there as quick as we can, dispatch the monster and hopefully save the human."

"What happens if they see something? Or catch us on film?", Tess asked. They were walking into a park now, away from the streetlights.

"We have a clean-up crew. We're all taught to remain 'invisible', but if we fail at that, which is rare, we erase devises and memories."

Tess cocked an eyebrow. "Memories? How? With a rock?"

Mek'el laughed, his shoulders bouncing visibly. "No. We check first if doubt can be sewn into their minds, because if they can't convince themselves, they won't convince anyone else. But if they're adamant... we have to use airborne hallucinogens or call one of our leaders to wipe their memories. It helps if they're already drunk or high because their statement will have no validity."

"But wouldn't the police notice a pattern if stories start hearing a recurring theme?", Tess probed.

"Well, I hate to say this, but usually we arrive during the initial attack, so the only witness is normally already dead."

"Oh!", Tess was shocked by how calmly he said this. But then six centuries as a soldier would do that to you.

"We just stop the monster before it can attack someone else."

Tess realised they were in the centre of the park. It was dark, secluded and creepy. At that moment, she heard a shout. It was a man protesting. She automatically headed toward the noise. As she rounded the corner of the path ahead, she saw two men in each-other's grip. One was wearing a hoodie with the hood obstructing any clear view of his face, trying to rob the other, a gun in his hand. The victim, a middle-aged Asian man in a suit, was trying to fight back. The air was thick with confrontation...and something else. Tess had always hated confrontation growing up. It made her nauseous and an easy target for bullies.

As her head began to spin, she heard the cracking and splintering of wood. Her eyes picked up movement behind the two struggling men and followed it.

Shards of bark and broken tree limbs were moving and falling to the ground. It was windy, and what with the noise of their fighting, they must not have heard it. The attacker hit his victim across the temple, knocking him unconscious and letting his limp body flop to the floor. He crouched down to search the unconscious victim's pockets. She started to step forward, but something was stopping her. Mek'el had a tight grip on her upper arm.

"We have to help.", Tess rasped, trying to break free.

"Normally, I would but the innocent person isn't in danger yet.", Mek'el explained. "Just watch."

Tess clutched her stomach. "I feel sick. I don't know why."

"I'll explain later. Look there."

Tess watched as the splinters of wood started rolling themselves towards the thief, before stopping behind him and arranging itself into a humanoid shape and standing, crouching over him slightly. It was huge, maybe nine feet tall. The man noticed the noise and turned, but it was too late. He didn't have time to scream fully. The thing lunged itself forward and pierced the thief's body with its splintered appendages, cutting his cry off. The sound of his voice faded with a gurgle.

Tess suddenly felt angry. The nausea was completely gone. The man was no angel, but he didn't deserve this death. No-one would be able to be brought to justice for it. Someone would mourn him, but what explanation would be given to his family and friends? How *dare* this thing invade her world and kill people!

The creature turned itself to the unconscious man and took a step towards him. Tess suddenly realised nothing was holding her back anymore. At that moment, the creature let out a shriek, like creaking wood in a hurricane. Tess could just make out a shape falling from a height, a blade in its hand. Mek'el became visible as he landed underneath it. The demon swiped, turning, towards the source of the pain, it's featureless 'face' coming into Tess's line of vision, but it's movement was in vain. Mek'el spun and in one move sliced off its leg and leapt on its chest as it fell backwards. He spun his blade, readjusting it heading for a downwards stabbing motion and drove the metal through the creature's head.

The form was disassembled into splinters and pieces once more, from the point of impact outwards, and the world became still again as the splinters did.

Tess eventually convinced herself to walk around the splinters and stood as Mek'el assessed the dead body. Tess's skin went cold as she set eyes on it. It was just skin and bones, drunk dry by the monster that attacked it. She could see the blood glistening on some of the wood lying motionless beside him. The way it had been broken up, it looked as if a tree had broken near the roots, fallen and killed the thief accidentally in the process. The thief lay, holes gored in him from head to toe, his face fixed in his last terrified expression. The smell of tree sap and the almost metallic scent of blood was all that filled Tess's nostrils.

Tess couldn't move. This was what her parents had fought, what they had protected humans from for centuries. This is what they put themselves at risk of, if the monsters could even do this to them. This was the real world that the average Joe knew nothing about and would never have to face. But was Tess ready to?

'I know I said we wouldn't do anything weird, be human for the night, but that plan's scuppered now. Do you ever feel ill when there are negative things happening around you? Do you feel your guts turn during confrontations? That's the Verndari in you sensing energy. That energy: hate, greed, jealousy, evil, it mixes with what already exists within things or elements, animals and people. They change into the Tainted and attack people over and over. They never stop until they're stopped... by us.'

Tess was starting to wobble. She wobbled over to the unconscious man. Mek'el kept talking.

'Don't touch him, Tess. Your fingerprints...remember?'

Tess stepped back. He was breathing. Thank God.

'Deforestation to make way for roads, cities and factories angered the forests and jungles. Dumping and littering angers the water and gives sediments and oils life. That anger resides in all of them. And when that anger and other evil mixes it gives the vegetation extra energy and... life. Humans use wood to build and feed their greed, so... the trees use humans to feed themselves. Like some kind of twisted tit for tat. I would say that's justified but once the trees awaken, they go on a rampage. They need to be reminded of who they are and calmed down or destroyed.'

Tess finally spoke. Her voice was tiny and shaking. 'I didn't see much talking going on when you approached it.'

'There was no time for that. It was almost upon the second man.'

Ilene suddenly found she was shaking. Her body was now hot, and her fingers and ears were tingling. She stepped over the debris and the unconscious man and stood right in front of Mek'el, looking him dead in his eyes. *"Why*? Why did you let the *first* man die?!"*, Tess suddenly screamed. Anger exploded out of her. It made the wind seem quiet in comparison.

Mek'el froze and then panicked as he saw her glowing red eyes facing him. He could hear a couple of nearby trees awakening. He had to calm her down.

'Tess, you needed to see... it's true I could have gotten to him in time. But he was attacking that other man. He could have shot me or the other man. He could have *seen* us! I don't know any leaders in the area that would have been able to wipe that from his memory.'

"So, because all humans die, what's *one more untimely casualty*?",

Tess roared. The nausea was rising in her stomach again, but she didn't care. "Has living for centuries made you that disinterested in humans that you let one die tonight? I know you can't save everyone, but Jesus Christ, man! *You're* the monster! If living forever and fighting these things means I have to become like you, numb and unaffected, then I don't want any part of it."

Tess took off her jacket and felt her wings tear though her t-shirt. She flew straight for home as fast as possible before her would-be teacher could even reply.

*

Mek'el started to go after her as she disappeared from view, bringing his wings out too late. She had her mother's rage and her father's intolerance of injustice. And she was right.

Mek'el clench his jaw fighting the sinking feeling in his stomach, listening as the trees fell asleep again. He probably wouldn't hear from her for a while.

He disposed of his wings and turned back towards the edge of the park and walked back to his car. He was disgusted at himself for allowing that man's death. But merely seeing the demon would not have driven home the dangers and risks fast or effectively enough.

Mek'el wasn't a superstitious man anymore, despite all he had seen in his many years, but for the first time in over five hundred years, he crossed his fingers.

"Please, Ilene... forgive me. And understand.", he pleaded into the silence.

As Mek'el unlocked his car, he heard the moving of heavy stone that made him alert. He changed his hand a claw as he searched quickly

117

for the source of the sound. He heard and saw nothing, so he turned back to normal before climbing into his car and driving to his apartment.

*

Tess landed a few metres down the drive. She was in a haze. She couldn't get that body, the blood and the monster out of her mind. Anger burned in every inch of her skin. Mek'el's inaction was part of it but the fact that this was happening all over the world was bugging her. She couldn't bear it. Mek'el was right to make her see it. She knew he didn't really want to hold back from saving the thief. She could hear his quiet thoughts under her own racing ones, but she was distracted at the time. However, she was still mad at him. She needed time. She had so much to think about and decide on. She needed sleep.

She put her jack back on. It was only about nine at night. Amanda and Jason were cleaning the kitchen as she entered the front door. They were all smiles, but Tess couldn't fake it. She couldn't reciprocate.

She mumbled something about being tired and headed up the stairs without another word.

She didn't see the concerned looks that passed between Jason and his mother. She was already in her room and safely locked in before either of them even reached the foot of the stairs.

She left a trail of clothes on her floor and fell into bed. For the first time, she really wished her parent were there. She needed a hug, an explanation and an apology...something! Anything to help her mind accept this and keep from melting.

She let her eyes close, and the evening air soothe her skin, as she fell into sleep filled with dream-like memories of her mother. And this Siobhan sung Tess comfortably into the darkness of much needed rest.

Chapter 10

Downtime

Morning broke over the Manor as it always did, gentle and cool. Jason rolled and fell out of his bed, his eyes still closed. He damn-near broke his neck coming down the loft stairs. He managed to navigate the main flights of stairs, dragging his feet towards the kitchen, and then found a piece of fruit to munch on. He didn't realise he'd made a cup of coffee until he was drinking it. His mum walking briskly into the kitchen and greeted him. He groaned a reply.

"My god! Put some clothes on, boy! We have female company now.", Amanda cried, stopping when she could see him fully.

"Wha-?", Jason began, looking down. He was in boxers and socks. He laughed.

"Ilene's eighteen, Mom. I think she's seen a male body or two by now."

Amanda rolled her eyes. "Well don't blame me if she suddenly starts avoiding you after catching you like that. How would you feel if you saw her similarly dressed?"

Suddenly Jason went silent. Amanda turned in time to see the back of him but the flaming pink blush at the top of his ears was unmissable. It was cute how he was always so shy around women, especially if he got on with them.

"Go and check if she's awake, will you? I'm worried about her.", Amanda ordered, flourishing her hand dismissively while she fixed them both some breakfast.

Jason nodded and ran, glad to be out of the room. He still couldn't shake the mental image that was intruding in his brain thanks to his mother's line of reasoning. He grabbed a t-shirt first and then headed upstairs. He moved towards Tess's bedroom to find the door open and the room empty. It was warm and humid. Tess was up and she'd showered. He could smell the toothpaste and body wash she used. He was already getting used to having another person around and she hadn't even been there a month.

He heard a grunt down the hall. As he followed the sound, more grunts sounded. He poked his head into the dojo and found Tess having a little match with a punch bag. But she looked she knew what she was doing. Her form was excellent, like something from the matches he watched with his friends, and her strikes moved the bag much more than he expected. Her hair was pulled up, which was not usual because she tended to wear her long curls down. She was in tight-fitting gym clothes, sweat covering her back and forehead. Jason thought she was just working out but then he saw her face. Her jaw was clenched, and her eyes were focused. She looked furious, like she was picturing someone. Then all at once, with one last strike, she kicked with a loud shout and something broke through her anger. Jason was stumped as he watched her wipe her eye with one of her gloved hands.

Jason stepped forward as she caught her breath. "Wow! And that's what you can do on an empty stomach?"

Tess looked up and smiled. "Morning, Jason. Nah, I ate hours ago. I couldn't really sleep last night."

Jason couldn't take his eyes off her as she walked over to the water feature and splashed some water on her face. He'd never properly seen her figure. It was athletic but with obvious curves. A mix of power and beauty. The mental image he'd just fought suddenly returned with a vengeance.

"Is everything alright?", he asked, leaning against the nearby wall.

121

"Yeah...well, no, actually.", Tess admitted. She turned to face him. "I... I saw a man getting beaten up and mugged at gunpoint last night.

Jason walked over immediately. "What?! What part of the city were you in? That Mike guy took you there? What was he thinking?" Questions and exclamations flew out of his mouth in rapid succession.

Tess almost laughed at his disapproval and outrage. "It's OK. North London is the same. You get rough areas all over cities to be fair. I'll be careful next time.", she assured. "But still... I wish I could have helped or done something." Tess felt a little guilty for only telling half of the truth, but Jason couldn't know the full story and she certainly was not ready to talk about it.

"You? Do something? Don't be dumb. Even *I'd* leave it alone and I'm taller and stronger than you.", Jason laughed.

Tess felt her temper flaring slightly. "I'm stronger than I look. Don't judge so quickly."

"Really?", Jason queried, cockiness and doubt dripping from his voice.

Tess turned and walked to him, smiling in a way that unnerved him. She almost laughed aloud as his face dropped on her approach.

He put his hands up, but it was too late. She had struck him in his shoulder and then knocked the opposite foot from under him, throwing her remaining strength into her palm which was on his chest, helping him to the ground.

The bang with which he hit the floorboards knocked the air out of him.

Jason was suddenly angry, his pride wounded. He brought himself upright, grabbing Tess by her braid. He reached out to suppress her free arms that immediately flew towards her hair. He wrapped his arm around her, pinning her arm. This worked for a moment, until she lifted her legs and kicked off the front of his legs, throwing their combined weight backwards. He flailed his arms, but she was holding him up and behind him before he even realised it, pinning his arms. She knocked one his legs so that it buckled, and he was forced to take a knee.

They both stayed like that for a moment, panting.

Jason laughed eventually. "Where and why did you learn that?"

Tess let go and fell backwards onto the floor. "Six years of Judo and Karate. The reason? I got bullied a lot in school. Everything from beatings to burning my homework. But I only used it to block. The one time I fought back it didn't go well."

"Wow! Why would *you* get bullied? And what happened to the person you fought?", Jason asked, wobbling a little as he stood.

Tess didn't answer at first. She crossed her legs and folded her arms. "I got bullied because I was different. I did lots of sports and won lots of stuff, which was odd from a sick kid on lots of medication. People spread rumours I was doping and when the tests came up negative, they lashed out. And as for the bully I snapped and... three broken ribs, a snapped collarbone and an obliterated tibia later, he never bothered me again. Neither did anyone else."

Jason just stared at her. He did not expect this explanation from the chatty, perky, energetic girl who was sitting on the floor in front of him.

"I made a promise never to fight again. But you can't always avoid confrontation forever, can you?"

Jason shook his head. Her disposition was a front. An ill, bullied, adopted girl sat in front of him smiling. Her life had been unpleasant from the start and now it had been turned even further upside-down.

"Right...", Jason said, reaching for her hand and helping her up. "You, young lady, need a day off to let your hair down. I have no big jobs to do here today, so we're going out. Get showered, get dressed and I'll meet you downstairs."

He pulled Tess to her bedroom as he spoke, feeling her drag behind him, pushed her through her doorway and shut the door behind her. Tess stood in silent shock, turning to look at the closed bedroom door.

After a brief moment, Jason called out again. "I don't hear any movement in there. Chop, chop!"

Tess smiled and shook her head, heading to her bathroom. Outside of her parents and some of her coaches and teachers, she didn't normally let anyone tell her what to do. He was a bit stubborn, but his heart was in the right place. She did need a day to relax. She desperately needed a distraction, and he'd handed it to her on a silver platter.

Tess walked downstairs, dressed in skinny jeans, platformed military style boots, a jumper and jacket. She was a little anxious preparing to go out again, after what happened last time. But she was going out with a normal human, so she'd be ok. It seemed that trouble followed the Verndarar wherever they went. Tess was hoping she would break that trend.

Jason was dressed similarly, a yellow beanie hat covering his dark short hair. Tess's critical look at the hat was met with a preventative warning. "Not a word. You're not the fashion police, Ilene. Stop commenting on what I wear."

Tess just walked past him smirking. "I didn't say anything.", she replied, trying not to laugh.

"You didn't need to.", Jason mumbled, almost inaudibly. Then he called out. "OK, Mom. We're off into the city."

Amanda walked out from under the stairs sporting her usual cleaning gear. "OK. Remember to be careful.", she called back, but only looking at Tess. Her eyes stayed fixed on her as they exited the door.

Jason spotted this as well. He laughed as they headed to the garage. "She clearly doesn't think you can handle yourself out there either."

Tess feigned another attack and Jason's giggles got worse.

"I don't need reminding that I was wrong!" he shouted, running away from her.

Tess gave chase, catching up easily.

They opened the doors of the garage and climbed into the Mini Cooper. They sang all the way through Whistler's village and reached the city in no time. They parked up in the centre of the city. It was very active with bustle and energy the way a city should be, but Vancouver was different. The sunlight glistened off the beautiful silver skyscrapers coupled with the smell of the sea made it unlike any city Tess had ever been to. There weren't the same limestone old buildings, churches and museums that London had, since the city wasn't as old.

Jason led her from shop to shop, stopping at maps of the city to pick their next destination. Tess took that opportunity to learn the city. They looked through all of the nearest attractions and decided on the Aquarium. On the way there, Tess stopped almost in the middle of a busy street when a familiar smell reached her nose.

She ran towards it with a smile on her face before she knew what she was doing. On the corner of the next street over, completely in the opposite direction of the Vancouver Aquarium, was a Fish and Chips shop. She almost squealed when she saw it.

"So, the stereotype is true about Brits and fish and chips?", Jason observed, catching his breath and coming to a stop next to her.

"Yup. Sometimes, nothing beats a good fish and chips. Especially when you're missing home.", Tess answered, her eyes scanning her options through the heated glass cover.

The vendor's eyes lit up. "A fellow Brit! It's a bit rare to hear that accent so from home.", he boomed. He was a jolly round man in his fifties probably, his short strawberry blonde hair greying at the sideburns and hairline. Tess recognised his accents as being from the Midlands. It wasn't quite northern but not north or central London either.

"Hi! I just moved here. What's it like in this city, from one immigrant to another?", Tess quizzed leaning forward and smiling invitingly at him.

The vendor collected himself. This girl's friendliness and bright smile caught him by surprise a bit. Well, that and her direct gaze. "It's beautiful. The weather is very similar to the U.K. It's a collection of many cultures just like all cities in the West. It's lively. There are always things to do, and being a coastal city, it has some of the freshest fish you'll ever taste."

Tess winked and made the man blush all over again. "Ah, you've twisted my arm now. Can we have a large cod and a large portion of chips with mushy peas and curry sauce? Oh, and two cokes please?"

As they paid and turned to walk away, Jason couldn't help but feel relieved. Tess was smiling again, really smiling and powerfully so. His plan had worked. He texted his mother with an update. She replied with a smiling face and thumbs up emoji.

They found a bench to perch on. By the time they sat down, Tess had finished all of her chips and half of her half of the battered cod. She was revelling in the flavour and gesturing soundlessly towards her meal with her wooden mermaid fork.

"He wasn't kidding about the fish. I lived near a huge indoor market with a sizeable fishmonger's stall, so I know fish. I wonder if the boats are looking for recruits.", Tess wondered aloud, looking into the direction of the docks.

"You? A fisher...woman?", Jason questioned tipping, his head as he tried to picture it. He shrugged. "I suppose it's possible."

Tess and Jason finished the lunch and started back on their original route to the Aquarium. Jason suddenly had a thought and laughed a loud belly laugh.

"What?", Tess asked. "Share the joke."

Jason managed to stop himself, his laugh becoming maniacal and borderline evil towards the end, as they walked into the entrance to buy their tickets. "Don't you think our lunch was in bad taste considering where we are?"

Tess realised the joke and laughed so loud, it echoed in the lobby and made people turn around. Both her and Jason struggled to suppress their laughter after receiving some disapproving glares. What was their problem? This wasn't a library.

They looked at the maps and programmes. They couldn't do any of the shows, as you had to pre-book, so they decided to just stroll around.

As they entered the walkways, Tess nudged Jason and handed him a mint, which made them laugh all over again. It was an evil thing to be entertained by. It would upset some Green Peace people and vegans, but it was the joke she needed. Childish silliness was a welcome rescue. As they both threw their mints into their mouth, Jason leaned in and whispered, "I won't tell them if you don't."

Tess calmed herself down a bit. "How much do you want to bet that at least fifty percent of the cafe menu is seafood?"

Jason's eyes almost flew out of his head. "No! They wouldn't!"

Tess shrugged. "It's a coastal city. What do you think they'd cook?"

They kept laughing, talking and walking as they went from tank to tank. The jelly fish were beautiful. Tess couldn't stop staring at them. "I heard somewhere that jellyfish are technically immortal.", Jason informed.

Tess jumped at the last word as if she'd been stung and the conversation from the night before returned just as painfully.

Jason sighed. "I don't know if I envy them or not. But I guess it's not so bad when you don't have a brain."

Ilene just stared blankly through the tank realising she was the same as these gelatin-based creatures, except she would be perfectly conscious through her eternity. She wanted to suddenly crawl back into her bed and take a couple of sleeping pills. Her brain was never going to shut up now.

Jason noticed the change in her eyes, the sadness. He didn't know what had triggered this, but he needed to stop it. He started moving to another section. They were in the penguin's enclosure.

"Penguins are one of the very few animals that mate for life.", Jason read from the description board.

Tess suddenly thought of her biological parents. "That sounds like my parents. They went through a lot and broke some rules just to be together."

She noticed the questioning look out of the corner of her eye. "Mike told me.", she answered. "They were together at the end too. They always had each-other's backs."

"Mom said it was an accident in the U.K.", Jason continued. "They'd left you with friends while they were out during a business trip or something. Your adoptive parents are amazing for just... adding you to their family like that."

Tess smiled gently. "Yes. Fred and Diane were awesome. Are awesome. I miss them...and my brothers."

"You have brothers? Did they know about...everything.", Jason asked.

"Two. Simeon, he's twenty-one. He would have been three when I was dropped off. Billy is ten. He doesn't know. He just thinks I upped and decided to travel the world because I'm an adult now.", Tess sighed. "I think he's too young to know. I'll wait till he's old enough to handle it, that's if Mum and Dad- I mean Fred and Diane- don't beat me to it."

Jason stared off at two penguins huddled together and nuzzling beaks as the male protected a shiny grey egg. "I envy you. My family doesn't have a good track record for... fidelity or monogamy. My mom's parents broke up when she was the same age Billy is. She left home as soon as she could and settled here. And then she had me pretty young. I'd be happy for any sort of family, even an adopted one."

Now Jason's suspicion of Mek'el's familiarity towards his mother was starting to make more sense. And the slight strain in Jason's relationship with Amanda would be more pronounced to Tess, as she now knew it definitely existed.

"Well, you aren't your predecessors. You can have a life that's different to theirs. Someone else's choices don't have to define yours.", Tess mused, not sure if she was reassuring Jason alone.

He nodded anyway. And they moved to the sea-lion tank. They were dancing through the water leaving beautiful bubble trails. Tess smiled as one swam towards her and hovered in the water right in front of her.

"How cute!", Tess exclaimed. "He likes me. Hello, there!"

Jason smiled. "Maybe he can smell your lunch."

Tess laughed. Then things got a little weird, as slowly, every single sea-lion turned and looked at her. Not just looked but stared. Jason was laughing and started to take pictures. Tess thought she heard him make a comment along the lines of 'lion tamer', but her mind was racing, and her stomach plummeted. This was the awful truth; even if she never fought, she couldn't fight what she was. Wildlife could sense what she was. They knew their relationship, that this thing that stood before them that wasn't quite a human but not quite one of them either.

Tess walked away, picking up speed as the sea-lions continued to follow her around the tank. She was hoping if she laughed it off Jason would forget it soon. But the same thing happened when she reached the shark tank, even though she stood well back behind the crowd of children that were marvelling at these predators. The sharks ignored the hunk of meat thrown into the tank and bored their black abyss-like eyes into her. Thankfully Jason was in front of her, reading information and geeking out.

Tess was starting to hyperventilate. She headed for the exit as fast as she could go. Was this what her future held? No trips to zoos, aquariums, farms or sanctuaries before closing time? It wasn't fair. First, she was being robbed of blissful ignorance, then the ability to even die and now no public outings near animals? This was bullshit!

She wished she'd never found that damned box. She just wanted to go home.

Jason found her thirty minutes later. She just lied and said she'd walked ahead without realising. Jason was buzzing with information. He revealed on the drive home, that his mum used to take him there when he was little. He'd always loved animals, but sea-life was his favourite. He started running off facts the whole way home, talking about the white shark's life span of seventy years and bioluminescence.

As they pulled into the driveway, the chatter stopped. Tess's mind was still spinning but she knew she had to say something. "Thanks, Jason. I needed today."

She lifted his hat and ruffled his hair. He didn't even protest. He was just smiling at her. For a few errant seconds, Tess began to think about having relationships, dates, children... a normal life. Her mind wondered if it would be possible with someone like Jason. But the cold truth hit her like an icicle to the heart: it could never be.

Tess smiled as best as she could and handed him his hat. "I'll see you inside. I need to make a phone call."

Tess practically ran into the house, although to her it felt as though she couldn't move fast enough. She ran up the stairs, heading for her father's office. As she was about to close the door, she heard an exchange between mother and son that now made sense. Amanda spoke first, as always.

"You're back. How was your day out?"

Jason's voice was calm and emotionless. "It was good. We did some shopping and went to the Aquarium."

"Aquarium?", Amanda repeated a note of horror in her voice. There was a heartbeat of silence that anyone, but Tess would have missed.

Tess heard a smile return to Amanda's voice, but it still sounded shaken. "You haven't been there since you were... I don't know, maybe six?"

Jason smiled and replied. "Yeah."

Then a longer silence hung in the air. So Amanda broke it as she always did. "I'll have dinner ready in about thirty minutes."

Jason left the room and headed for the Games Room, calling back another monosyllabic answer. "Sure." The Games Room door closed and all that could be heard was muffled sounds of the TV and kitchenware from two different directions.

Tess closed the door of her father's office and moved towards his desk. She stared at the vintage phone that sat on the right. It was about eighty years old and had been updated to be used in the twenty-first century. Tess had a choice to make, but she felt like it had already been made. She was fighting for some form of control but there was none left.

She picked up the phone and dialled Mekel's office number, which she'd discovered he'd left on the desk as they left on their last visit. He must have known she'd need to contact him sooner or later.

It rang three times and then a chirpy female voice spoke. "Portman's Neurosurgical Consultants. How can I help you?"

Tess smiled. The company sounded impressive. She'd expect nothing less from someone who had lived so long. "Hi, I'd like to speak to Dr Michael Keth please? It's Ilene."

"One moment, please.", the receptionist replied and then the line went over to classical musical with a slight click. Tess didn't have to wait long.

"Ilene?", Mek'el sounded pleased but surprised.

"Yeah, it's me. Are you free to talk?"

"Of course. But let me apologise. You were right. I should have done something sooner. I'm-"

Tess cut him off. She was shaking her head even though he couldn't see it. "I needed to understand. It wouldn't have sunk in otherwise. I need to...talk to you. Give me five minutes. I'll step out of the house grounds.", Tess interrupted.

"OK. Thank you. Talk to you in five.", Mek'el acknowledged. He ended the call immediately. Probably working out a way to get outside or alone for a good amount of time.

Tess leapt out of her bedroom window a few minutes later and ran to the treeline. Neither Amanda nor Jason had left their rooms. As she reached the shadows, she felt her mind slip free of the barrier. She felt Mek'el's mind almost immediately.

'Hello.', he greeted. 'Have trouble getting away?'

Tess smiled despite herself. His voice was so warm, so comforting. 'No. It was no problem. How was about you? Why can I see the heart of the city?'

'You can see what I'm seeing now? You really are amazing. I'm on the balcony at my office. Surgeons work crazy hours. I just did three operations today. Thank goodness I don't really need sleep.'

'Wow! How do you manage your schedule and all this?'

'Years of practice.', Mek'el admitted.

Tess smiled. 'I-I've made a decision. I made it for myself, but I have a feeling you will be happy about it but first I have a question.'

'Fire away!', Mek'el responded, patiently.

'Is there no way to get back onto my medication and go back to the way life was?'

Mek'el sighed. 'I can't say for certain. Your medication was made to mask Verndari abilities. Because you hadn't come into your abilities yet, it suppressed it completely. But now you have your abilities and are over eighteen... I know that for normal Verndarar that it can take a long time to take effect and is very painful as it makes your body fight against its own instincts and make-up on a cellular level. This medication has never been used in your type of situation, or on a Verndari-born, before. So, ... who knows.'

Tess scanned his mind. He was telling the truth. She could see his memories. His conversations with people walking with crutches and in ice baths who were taking her same green tablets, their irises changing colour when they felt pain. The grimaces on their faces and weak smiles, which didn't reach their eyes, stuck with her. It was too great a risk. There really was no going back.

'OK. Then my decision still stands. I realise now that I can't change what I've become. I mean, what I've always been. I can't run away from it, no matter how I try. I want to do what I was born to do. I want to protect, to fight. At least I'll be putting my temper to good use.'

Mek'el laughed. 'Are you sure about this? Even if you aren't, you can step away at any time.'

'Thank you for that option, but I'm stubborn. I'm very unlikely to step away now.' Tess sighed and looked back at her home. Everything would change now. There would be more secrets and she wouldn't be able to truly be close to anyone, except her own kind. She couldn't go back to London for a very long time. Simeon would be able to tell she was different and hiding things straight away, even without this decision.

Tess nodded. 'I want you to train me, Mek'el. Teach me to fight. Teach me my ancestry, how to blend in, set up a life, fake my death and then do it all over again. And then after all that, teach me to find this Velhonen so we can save our people and our world.'

Mek'el was silent for a minute. When she spoke, his dutiful voice was coloured with emotion. 'Alright. When do you want to start?'

'Tomorrow, please.', Tess answered.

'OK. I'll come around lunchtime. I have a surgery in the morning.'

'OK. See you tomorrow, sensei. I have to go. It smells like dinner's ready. Goodnight.'

'Goodnight, Ilene.'

Tess caught the edge of Mek'el's thoughts as she turned and headed back within the safety of the barrier. The feelings of pride but also fear. They both knew the kind of world she would now be involved with. Maybe he was scared that he couldn't keep her safe. After all, there were Verndarar older, wiser and more skilled than her who were disappearing while on missions. All she could do, all any of them could do was their best.

Tess made sure she wasn't seen, before leaping up in a simple motion to her bedroom window. She peeked into the room to make sure there were no surprises waiting for her, but her room was empty, so she climbed in, changed her clothes and descended the staircase as if she'd never left the house.

Dinner was delicious. A Sunday roast, English style, complete with Yorkshire puddings. It seemed everyone's mission today was to make Tess feel better. But she just got reminded more of home and the change in her life. But now she'd made her decision to stay and learn, the thoughts of her past didn't make her heart ache as much.

Conversation was light-hearted and positive. Tess announced she was going to being job hunting. This was met with excitement on Jason's part and the usual thinly veiled concern played off as enthusiasm by Amanda.

After Jason and Tess cleaned the kitchen, they decided to have a game of pool to burn the hours before Amanda and Jason were due to go home. Jason beat Tess, which healed his damaged ego from that morning. Tess didn't mind. She spent the game wondering what she would do in thirty years' time when he would start to notice the lack of wrinkles and crow's feet on her face. She couldn't fire him. Hopefully he'd find other work before that. Amanda would be retired and enjoying her time travelling the world by then. Either way, either she would need to leave, or he would. Tess could hear something like a radio on low, so when Jason was putting everything away at the end of the night, Tess reminded him to turn it off. She didn't see the concerned and confused look on Jason's face in response to this request.

Tess waved them off and locked the front door. She walked around the house and drank in the calm and the quiet, enjoying her last night of semi-normality. When she realised how wide awake, she was, she went to her bedroom and found her MP3 player. She felt like staring at the stars for some reason. Tess found one of her mother's fur coats and put it on. She danced around in it, watching herself in the mirror, comfortable in the knowledge that no-one would walk in and see her. She put her music on shuffle and placed her player in her pocket. She then opened her bedroom window again, climbed out and scaled the walls until she was on the roof.

She looked out over the landscape and sighed. The world was still. There was a slight glow to the south-west from the city but other than that there was no artificial light in sight. The sky was dark and glistening with jewel-like stars and a waning autumn moon. It was beautiful, and it was hers.

Tess decided to herself to make this her other place on the grounds to go for a touch of peace when things got too crazy. And they would.

Tomorrow, she was getting off the bench and would hit the ground running.

Chapter 11

The Other Three Voices

Mek'el arrived just after lunch as he said he would. Jason was out and Amanda was busy so again they had the place to themselves. He seemed anxious but excited at the same time.

He had a gym bag with him. He was in a suit as he had just come from the local hospital. His surgery had gone well and with no complications, thank goodness.

Tess didn't mean to intrude in his mind, but she couldn't ignore the sounds coming from it.

Tess was stood in her normal place, at the foot of the staircase, as he walked in. He stood in front of her, smiling. Before he could speak, Tess leaned forward and wrapped her arms around his shoulders. He dropped his bag and responded with a stronger squeeze. He was still apologising mentally for the events of two nights ago, and Tess had a feeling he would never stop.

Tess broke the hug and gave him a comforting smile. It was odd that she was the one reassuring him when she was the one who should be scared. But today she felt strong.

Mek'el heaved a big sigh of relief at the strength he saw in her eyes. "Are you ready?", he asked.

Tess grinned. "Yes I am."

Mek'el grinned back. "Then in that case, to the dojo!"

They ran up the stairs as quick as their ever-changing legs could carry them. Tess was getting better at changing her physicality outside of sunrise. But now her control would really begin to be tested. Tess suddenly realised something. Mek'el answered her realisation aloud.

"Yes, I have a change of clothes. I was hoping your decision would be to accept what we are. What you are."

As he spoke, he started to remove his jacket and top. Tess just stared. He was an impressive size and shape, kept in tune through years of fighting and training.

Mek'el turned and cocked an eyebrow. "You're not embarrassed?", he questioned. It sounded like the question was intended to be just a thought.

Tess smiled and shrugged. "My adopted mum is an NHS nurse in the A&E, I was a gymnast and artist during my school years. I have seen more naked and injured bodies than most people."

Mek'el's eyebrows were both raised now.

"Plus, with the internet, nudity is no longer shocking anymore.", Tess added, "So what are we learning first?"

Mek'el turned back around and took a vest from his bag. "First, I will see what you're fighting abilities are like."

Tess didn't have any time to answer. Mek'el was suddenly ploughing towards her, throwing his vest on in a movement so fast she didn't see it fully. She planted her feet, panicking and wondering how on earth she was going to handle what was coming. He swung his right arm with a haymaker, and Tess countered with her left forearm, the strength of the blow knocking her slightly sideways. Something in her lower peripheral vision moved and Tess jumped just in time as Mek'el's left leg swung to knock her over.

She thought she was safe, but he spun fast and grabbed her by the throat. She felt her back slam against the weapon wall. She would not lose. She hated to lose. Suddenly her sensei's voice was in her head. She had spotted a scar on his left side and swung for it, hard. Mek'el exhaled and his grip loosened. Tess's previous training took over and she put both forearms between his arms and pushed outwards quickly. She struck his chest and heard him exhale again, but he caught her ankle mid-air and threw her against the opposite wall again, where she dropped down in a heap, winded. Tess's temper was kicking back in, even though her rational brain told her she was crazy to be attempting to take down a seasoned warrior who was over half a millennium in age.

As she turned towards him and prepared to charge, he raised his hand. He was lit up with a grin. His brain was repeating only one phrase: 'I wish your parents could see this.'

"You're good. You were thinking about karate training from your childhood. How strange that things rooted in and necessary for learning Verndari combat forms are hobbies you took on instinctively in your youth. Did Fred and Diane make you do those activities?"

"No.", Tess answered, standing. That had hurt. "I insisted on joining those classes myself. It is an odd coincidence, huh?"

Mek'el nodded. "You're stronger than I thought. Your natural genetics have definitely *fully* formed. Not many people could knock me back, especially not one so young. But you need to control your emotions. It's true Verndarar children tend to be very in touch with their emotions and it can make them a little... hard to control."

"How do I control it then?", Tess asked, dread filling her as the story of Velhonen's murdering spree sprung back into her mind.

"Training, practice and meditation.", Mek'el answered, surprised by Tess's answering groan. She wasn't a naturally calm person. "Improving your combat skills is one good reason for getting a handle on your emotions, but not the main one. When you were, justifiably, losing your rag in the park the other night, ... you almost woke five other trees."

Tess stopped moving and breathing. If that had gotten out of hand. Mek'el wouldn't have been able to stop all of them in time before they killed more people, all alone. She'd left him all alone.

Mek'el placed his hand on her shoulder. "Your emotions are powerful and dangerous if they are allowed to run riot. This is true whether you're human or not. But if you learn to channel them...", he stated, stepping to the weapons wall and taking off a double-headed axe and wielding it expertly. He then spun and swung, stopping it, millimetres away from the floor. "...it can be powerful and dangerous to the creatures that harm this world."

Tess suddenly understood. This is why Mek'el was so reserved, even in the face of violence, death and year upon year of unpleasant memories. He couldn't lose control. He had a job to do, and making things worse didn't help.

Mek'el nodded at everything he heard. "This is why I can mourn inside this house. The barrier prevents our thoughts or extreme emotions being detected by the Tainted, Velhonen or anyone who could sense it. It's the only place I can let go without adverse effects. And also why this is the best place to train you without danger of the consequences."

Tess exhaled, uneasily. Self-control on an emotional level was going to be tough. She'd spent eighteen years becoming the absolute master of her body and had been forced to relearn it and was still learning. Now she'd have a bigger hill to climb. This was going to suck.

"Next time we do combat training, and you manage well, I'll start doing my attacks using my Verndari abilities.", Mek'el announced, seeing a brief flash of yellow in her irises. "Wouldn't want to make it too easy for you at any point, would we. Besides, the Tainted won't go easy. Why should I? Do you have a swimming costume?"

The end question threw Tess off, and she wrinkled her nose. Mek'el burst into a muffled fit of giggles. She could hear her mother's name bouncing around his head again.

"Yeah, in my room.", Tess answered, straightening her face quickly.

"OK. Grab it. We're off to the pool downstairs.", Mek'el instructed.

Tess bowed, instinctively. Her karate class habits were coming back. But she could hear the pleasure and gratitude in his mind, so she decided to keep doing it as she was about to stop it for good.

Tess changed quickly and threw on her slippers and dressing gown before sliding the staircase banister. She descended the stairs to the swimming pool and found Mek'el stood near the doorway in trunks. Thank God, no budgie smugglers. He didn't seem narcissistic enough to wear them.

'Maybe next time.', he thought, with a smirk. He laughed again at Tess's clearly disgusted expression. 'No problem with nudity but one with spandex? I'll wear that during training to help you learn to concentrate.'

"Oh god.", Tess groaned. She stepped forward, dropping into the pool. Mek'el was next to her in seconds. He took her arm and started mentally apologising again. Tess panicked. What now? She didn't bother trying to break his grip. She doubted heavily that she could. But she did try pulling herself to the surface. She was running out of air and her heart was hammering in her chest. Then she heard two words.

'Think FISH.', Meke'l commanded.

Tess's mind took herself back to the aquarium...and suddenly the pain in her chest was gone. Her skin was cool from the inside. Mek'el's grip was released. She opened her eyes and the lights in the pool seemed brighter than before. And Mek'el, a new version of him, floated in front of her. His fingers and feet were webbed. He had gills showing along the contours of his ribs, and when he moved his arms as he slowly tread water, shiny scaled shimmered against the lower lights.

Tess looked at herself. Her hands were similar, and her feet were longer, more like fins, as if snorkelling fins had grown as part of her body. She grinned. She felt for her gills. They were on her back, which made sense as her costume was backless. She could taste the chlorine and salt in the water. It was a little gross.

'This is incredible! I always wished I was a mermaid when I was little.', Tess gushed. 'So, are we the reason for those legends?'

'Yup.', Mek'el answered, 'Come with me to the bottom of the deep end. Roger had this pool built to be thirty metres deep. Most pools are only ten feet.'

Tess glided forward effortlessly and faster than she had pictured. 'Why can we do this? Are there water versions of the Tainted?'

'Yeah. We call them Aquatis. Caused by oil spills, dolphin hunting, garbage and toxin dumping, to name just a few things. The ocean is furious. It feels like its angrier than the vegetation most days. We called those ones the Viridis. And then there's the tree ones, Aboris, the rock and earth ones, Tertis, the fire and magma ones, the Ignis and the ones made from dead things, the Mortis. We clean it as much as we can despite our busy lives. But it got more difficult with the increase of non-degradable materials like plastics, and the

143

dwindling in our numbers.'

'Yikes.' It was all Tess could say. She tried to picture a sea demon but couldn't.

'Can you notice any changes?', Mek'el asked.

Tess suddenly realised the difference. 'I can't feel the pressure change!'

Mek'el nodded. 'Our bones automatically become denser to handle the pressure changes. We're able to go where only sea creatures can go. I've been to the deep sea a few times. It's incredible.'

'Really? Will you take me some day? Do you realise how amazing that it? We...*humans* have been trying to explore there for centuries!', Tess blabbered, excitement making her words form at speed. To think that she'd be able to see a place less explored than her own galaxy made the adventurer in her wild with curiosity.

'Yes. One day.', Mek'el nodded again, making the movement look easy despite the pressure.

Tess swam off to show her happiness and test her abilities at the same time. She was fast and she loved it. She changed direction easily. She struck at nothing above her and watched surface become disturbed, bubbles spreading across the surface after the splash. She swung her arms, and her movement was barely hindered by the liquid around her.

Mek'el was practising as well. Most of his missions were on land but he had done a few in water.

At that moment, both their heads raised at the sound of a key in the front door. Jason was back.

Mek'el heard something that he wasn't expecting: a sad sigh from

Tess. 'Time to human.', she acknowledged, swimming quickly to the surface.

Mek'el couldn't believe it. She was embracing and enjoying her abilities. There was hope. Plus, this would make her learn faster. People learn things better when they're enjoying it.

They both climbed out and dried off. Tess put on her dressing gown and flashed Mek'el a quick smile before heading up to the front door.

'Meet you upstairs.', Tess called mentally.

'OK. By the way, we're going out for dinner tonight.', Mek'el replied.

'OK.', Tess responded.

Jason was already in the Game Room when she had reached the hallway. He smiled when he saw Tess, his eyes flitting down briefly at the dressing gown. "How have you been?"

"Yeah, I've been good. Mike is here. We were catching up and making up.", Tess informed, sitting on the arm of the sofa while Jason switched on the TV and sat down on the seat of the sofa.

"And swimming?", Jason queried.

"Naturally.", Tess replied. "What's the point of having the pool if we don't use it?"

Jason thought and then shrugged. "Makes sense...strangely enough. Where is he?"

"Downstairs showering, I think. I have to go and do the same. Gotta get the taste of chlorine out.", Tess said, standing and heading for the stairs.

"Don't you mean smell?", Jason questioned, turning in her direction.

Crap!

"Yeah, that's what I meant.", Tess agreed, laughing it off but cringing inside.

"Well, I'm clean the pool in a few days.", Jason said, shrugging again.

"OK. Mike and I going out later, so I'll see you when I get back.", Tess shouted back.

Jason shook his head and changed the channel. "That girl already has a more active social life than me, and I was *born* here.", he muttered.

*

Tess texted Amanda and told her she didn't need dinner today. She felt bad having people do anything for her anyway. So, she took over cooking and cleaning duties of the first floor as often as possible.

Mek'el had called ahead to a Korean restaurant at the east side of the city and was dressed in his usual smart-casual clothing. Tess wondered if she would ever see him sloppily dressed. She doubted it.

They entered the restaurant car park and stopped. Tess was wearing one of her mother's trench coats and heels but wore a simple purple blouse with jeans. Comfortable and neat. No need to go overboard. As they reached the door, Mek'el 'spoke'.

'I have some people I'd like you to meet... properly. Now, remember, make small talk aloud, and we'll order three large courses so we can really talk. Try not to let your face give away what's happening.', he advised.

Tess panicked. She was about to meet more Verndarar! She suddenly found herself wishing she had put more effort into her outfit.

Mek'el chuckled. 'You look fine. They're all just looking forward to seeing you.'

He approached the woman at the reception desk and smiled broadly. "Hello, Mrs Park. Reservation under Mr Keth?"

The little Korean lady, probably mid-forties, returned the smile, her skin creasing at the corners of her eyes being the only sign of her age amongst the rest of her smooth creamy skin. She signalled towards their table. "Yes, sir. Your friends are already here."

"Thanks!", Mek'el replied, as the two of them followed her extended arms direction. "Same booth as usual?"

"Of course, Mike.", she replied, winking.

Tess smiled. 'Ooooh. She likes you.', she teased.

Mek'el nudged Tess playfully. 'Maybe, if she was younger.'

Tess almost laughed aloud. 'You mean "maybe if *you* were younger", grandpa.'

She heard Mek'el take in a mock breath of injury through his teeth as they reached, they're destination. It was a dimly lit booth, probably perfect for hushed and clandestine meetings or conversations of a non-human nature. There were ancient paintings on the walls of landscapes and women in Hanbok playing ehrus and such. But the décor wasn't what was holding Tess's attention. It was what was in front of it. In the circular booth sat three people.

One was a woman in her mid-thirties. She was pale, slender and beautiful. Her eyelashes were thick and long, framing her big blue eyes, which flanked her straight nose. Her hair was brown and wavy, pulled back into a knot at the nape of her neck. She wore a t-shirt dress but still looked regal. She grinned at Mek'el in a way that almost shone, a look of familiarity in her eyes so deep that had Tess

147

not known the nature of it, it would have puzzled her for hours before she gave up and let it go.

The man next to her was early forties. He was a little taller, and not as muscular as Mek'el. His skin had an olive tan to it and his face had softer features than Mek'el, not as angular except for a strong straight lightly hooked nose. His face was framed by curly black hair, slicked somewhat with gel to control it. His pin-striped suit and immaculate tie screamed perfectionist and control-freak. Even his fingernails were trimmed and manicured to perfection and clean. And his facial expression was a little off-putting. It was just a slight frown and never changed no matter what seemed to happen.

On the far right sat an Indigenous American. He was the most muscular and tall man Tess had ever seen. Like the man sat in the centre, his face was composed but his eyes were gentle and interested. His jawline was strong, and his nose was broader than the others. His borderline brown skin caught the minimal light in the room in a warm way. He smiled at Mek'el too, though his lips never parted. His long dark hair was hanging down his back, shiny and thick. He wore a black t-shirt that somehow managed not to tear as it enveloped his form.

Tess was starting to guess who they all were. The woman took no detective work. The central man was the suspicious tactician, and the Indigenous man was Mono.

"Mek'el! Good to see you, my friend.", the woman welcomed, a slight French accent in her clear bright voice.

The other two nodded. "General.", they greeted in unison.

"Hello, my friends. I'm glad you've come. I'd like to introduce someone to you.", he greeted, happily, signalling towards Tess with his arm.

Tess swallowed, nervously. "H-hi! I'm Ilene McCampbell.", she announced as she sat down.

"Hello, Ilene.", the woman greeted. "My name is Beatrice Holden. McCampbell? That sounds... familiar."

Tess nodded and switched to her mental voice. 'I'm the daughter of Roger and Siobhan McCampbell. We've talked before.'

The change made the three blinks noticeably and at the same time.

"I get that a lot.", Tess said out loud to cover the silence.

'Wow!', the man in the centre commented. He seemed genuinely impressed. He spoke up. "I'm Marcus Romano. Nice to meet you."

The man on the right bowed slightly. "And I'm Bob.", he greeted.

Tess grinned. She really wasn't alone. This was fantastic.

"I'm starving!", Mek'el announced, clapping his hands and then reaching for a menu. "Let's order."

They all ordered little dishes to share. Thankfully Tess loved all food and had no allergies, so she was excited to try everything. When everything arrived, they began eating immediately.

'So, Mek'el,', Beatrice began, 'What have you told our young friend?'

'As much as she can handle, Charlotte.', Mek'el answered, as he took more noodles.

'Which, knowing you, means everything at once. He's so hands on and always goes in at the deep end.', Marcus added, dryly.

'Hang on! ... Charlotte? I thought you were Beatrice.', Tess countered, remembering to keep her face pleasant and keep chewing.

She didn't turn her head. 'That's my alias this lifetime. My real name is Charlotte Grayson. I'm almost six hundred years old. In this alias, I'm a receptionist for a law firm, even though I could run that place.'

Marcus looked up from his plate. 'I am Marcellus, a Roman soldier from the year 300 A.D. I'm over six hundred years old. And this fellow is Kuruk, a Chipewa chief from the 1650s. So, he's four hundred. In this lifetime, I'm an accountant for many high-end businesses. I don't do inconspicuous. I like money and comfortable living.'

Bob looked at Tess and smiled. 'I'm a Bouncer.', his thoughts revealed.

Tess was amazed. They had adapted and survived while carrying out their dangerous missions, mostly undetected. She couldn't wait to learn from them.

'So how long have you been in Vancouver.', Tess asked, tucking into her rice, chicken and kimchi.

'We haven't left Vancouver in over twenty years.', Marcus answered, 'but it's not as if we had a choice.'

Tess couldn't help creasing her face as the questions formed. 'Why?'

Marcus suddenly let out a bitter and audible laugh, causing a couple at the other table to turn around. 'You haven't told her?', he asked Mek'el, looking straight at him. 'That's the first thing a Verndari should know.'

Mek'el's head dropped a little and his face had a look of guilt across it. He turned to Tess. 'You remember I explained we couldn't go home, so we're stuck in this world? And that we are disappearing?'

'Yes.', Tess answered.

'Well, that's not the only problem we have. If we try to fly away from our areas by plane, train or even using our wings, somehow our movements are tracked, and we disappear. I don't know who is doing this or why, but the person must be powerful within the world and the human world.'

'Then why don't you look into it and try and stop this person?', Tess asked. 'I'd like to be able to visit England at some point.'

'We have been. But anyone who has come close to figuring out who is behind it goes missing too. However, I'm not giving up. We are nobody's prisoner.', Mek'el said, setting his jaw.

There was a minute of silence. Tess could hear anger coming from Marcus and sadness coming from the other three.

'When we lost your father, we didn't just lose a friend, a brother, and a leader, we lost our way home.', Charlotte mused, her voice breaking. 'He was the only one outside our realm powerful enough to use the gem. He would fly to portals all over the world and grant us passage to our home. Also, the gem healed serious wounds, so we could go back to our human lives without arousing suspicion. We still heal much faster than humans, but if something goes wrong on a mission, there's only so much sick leave you can take, you know? Now we just bandage ourselves up, dose up on damn-near illegal painkillers and try to limit movement. Thankfully I'm female, so I can lie and say it's cramps.'

Mek'el laughed. 'It can make concentrating difficult. Remember that rock demon six months ago? I was popping Co-codamol like smarties for weeks!'

'Yeah, you get injured so rarely that it stumped me for a second. Your poor back.', Charlotte shook her head, eating another dumpling.

Tess tried to keep still, even though this conversation interested her.

'But you have no *scar!*'

Marcus chuckled. 'Stripping off in front young girls, Mek'el? You should be ashamed of yourself. I hope you didn't upset her. Lord knows how she'll feel when she sees the old uniforms.'

Tess cocked an eyebrow, but Mek'el spoke before she could ask anything. 'She doesn't shock easily about human stuff. Like Charlotte said, we heal very fast, even without Roger's help.'

They finished their courses and Tess listened to Charlotte, Bob and Mek'el swap stories aloud while she drank her green tea. So many memories and images were 'shown' to her, unknowingly. She marvelled at their adventurous and long lives. She learnt a lot about their previous lives. Charlotte was a French noblewoman who was raised in England for most of her human life. She had been executed for sneaking medicine to the poor and falling in love with a tradesman.

Bob's name was Kuruk and he had been his tribe's strongest warrior. He had died of bayonet stab wounds and gunshots to the body fighting off the British while his tribe escaped on boats.

Marcellus was a Roman who had defected from the tyrannical rule of an evil leader. He freed a group of slaves who were sentenced to the arena for being uncooperative to their new masters. For his 'crime', he was drawn and quartered in the arena they would have died in.

All brave, with a strong sense of justice. They had all died to protect people who weren't close to them, so to speak, but were in need. They refused to sit by and allow these horrific events to take place, disregarding the displeasure of their families, friends and superiors. Gaia had seen this and given them a second chance. She had given them stronger bodies and the abilities to save everyone, literally everyone, and live through it.

And Tess had been *born* this way. She felt so undeserving of what she been given. Maybe, in time, she would have done enough to earn her life, as they had.

At that moment, Tess's head spun, and her stomach churned. The other four turned their heads in the same direction.

'A demon.', Charlotte confirmed.

Marcus kept drinking and pulled out his phone. 'Not our problem anymore.'

'How can you say that? It's what we were brought back to do!', Charlotte spat, scowling at Marcus in a way that would melt steel, had her eyes been fire.

'Attacks, death and violence happen every day, perpetrated by humans and demons alike. Are we supposed to stop all of them?', Marcus retorted, not looking up from his phone.

'The ones that pertain to our purpose? Yes.', Charlotte said, standing and throwing down her share of the bill. 'You're such a grouch. I hate that some of our kind see being stranded here as some kind of betrayal.'

'Why bother? We don't owe her anymore! We've done plenty! No-one's heard from her directly in almost five hundred years, or from anyone else at home. No-one else has come through. We have been abandoned, Charlotte! When will you understand that?', Marcus shouted mentally.

'*I* will do what I can. This is still our earth, our world. We have to protect it.'

'Yes.', Kuruk boomed.

Charlotte turned to Tess and smiled. "Let's go, honey. I'm gonna show you a thing or two."

Mek'el stood and paid also, heading for the door at a pace, after respectfully bidding his two friends goodnight.

That night, Tess observed while two seasoned Verndarar dispatched a rock demon, another form of earth monster, in a matter of moments. The victim, a woman, had been knocked unconscious by a blow and would have been crushed to a pulp if they had landed any later. It had been awakened during an argument with a contractor who couldn't continue drilling and construction. Ilene had heard the fight as soon as they 'winged up' and took off. They surveyed the area as they approached and landing, a construction site with three cranes, temporary high steel walls and thick steel supports inside a hole in the earth probably about two hundred metres wide. Charlotte had revealed two daggers on the inside of each boot. Mek'el had the same sword he'd used before, although Tess didn't know where he had hidden it. They struck as one, using their telepathy to stay out of each-other's path as they fought. It was seamless, efficient and deadly.

Tess was impressed. Suddenly, getting to their level was all she wanted. She would train as long and as hard she could.

As the gravel tumbled to the ground, Charlotte turned and gave Tess a thumbs up. Tess laughed. It didn't have to be terrifying after all, as long as they were together.

'Why didn't Bob come?' she suddenly thought.

"Because he thought three Verndarar would be too many for one demon.", Mek'el answered aloud, walking towards her. Charlotte and Mek'el sprouted feathered wings, and Tess produced her leathery ones. They left the scene and headed for Mek'el's car again. Maybe the woman would simply think it was a gas pocket that had ignited and exploded. There had been no sign she had seen the demon, so there would be no clean-up needed. A lucky escape, really.

They went for some ice-cream and crepes, while Charlotte shared advice and stories. She gave Tess a big hug when they parted. They didn't exchange phone numbers because they didn't need to. She could talk to her whenever she liked.

And with a successful and eventful night behind them, they went their separate ways.

I J FERRESTONE

Chapter 12

New Life

It had been two months since Tess had met the other three Verndarar. In that time, things had changed and settled surprisingly well.

Tess had increased her training and could now transform in any way outside of night hours. She had made her first demon "kill" seven weeks ago, after which they had gone out for drinks to celebrate, even though legally, Tess couldn't yet. But Marcus was friends with every club manager, so there was never an issue.

Tess had been watching nature documentaries to learn more defensive techniques she could hopefully mimic. She normally did this in her room, which was as a good idea because at the beginning there had been a couple of mishaps involving being unable to switch back from changing her eyes to an eagle's and electricity that she couldn't stop producing from her hand when she studied eels. She had called Mek'el and Charlotte in tears and they had rushed over and helped her out, thank goodness.

Tess had found work in the Mail Room of a major cooperation's Head Office in the centre of the city, which she reached daily on her father's vintage motorcycle. She'd had to retake her test for the Canadian licence, but it went smoothly. The company she worked for was called Hillman Co. It had its hand in many areas; agriculture, art, medicine and engineering were its main veins. Tess enjoyed having money to call her own and having something to do. She was pleasant to people but kept her distance, not volunteering much more than basic information about herself. She helped out at the Manor as often as she could. Amanda and Jason took her on as part of the team for work around the house, and soon it felt as though she'd always been there.

Mek'el came for dinner weekly, which made Amanda happy and Jason slightly less suspicious of him with each visit. Tess could feel an effortless closeness with these three as each day passed which made her less and less upset that she was unable to go back to the U.K. She had never found it easy to get close to people as everyone always seemed to push her away, due to her being accidentally and naturally good at whatever she tried, but Amanda and Jason saw her as a person, not her abilities, although they had made her show them some of her gymnastic skills after Amanda had found some pictures online. And as for Mek'el, Tess had never felt so close to anyone in her life, not even Simeon. He was like a second father, or technically third, considering the fathers she'd already had. He was a teacher, friend, guru and her biggest fan. She was encouraged to be herself more than anyone had ever wanted her to be. Even Fred and Diane had asked her to tone down aspects of herself, but for her own good, to hopefully decrease the bullying and ostracization. They had been there for every time her injuries or loneliness had left her crying by herself in her room. But that was Tess; Ilene had a different set of fears now and loneliness would *never* be one of them ever again.

Ilene had been calling and emailing her family in London as often as she could. Simeon had tonnes of questions. They would Zoom whenever it wasn't too late for them. Billy had been there for a few of the conversations. He was missing his big sister now she was gone, but Simeon was the one who took the longest to sign or log off any conversations. Ilene's heart ached looking at his forced brave face. She promised him she'd visit as soon as she could which wasn't a lie, but she wondered if he could see the panic in her eyes as she wasn't sure when that would be.

Ilene had taken to wearing shades or contact lenses while she learned to control her emotions. Mek'el didn't make it easy. He threw images her way during meditation to test her. He showed her parents, battles they'd fought, their graves, the bodies of people they'd failed to save, and the faces of the Verndarar who had disappeared. Pain, conflict, guilt, fury, in waves over and over. But Ilene had learnt to picture something else or somewhere else and controlling her breathing. She had found a new place she'd enjoyed, a mountaintop a few hundred miles away that she liked to watch the sunrise on. She had also found the key to a locked room on the first floor and Mek'el and Charlotte had been there for the unveiling. It had been an emotional day. It was full of mementos from their Verndari missions. Horns of rare demons, half-destroyed armour, snapped weapons and in a glass cabinet in the corner, two uniforms. Ilene's jaw fell open. They were nothing more than a series of leather straps, buckles and holsters. Charlotte laughed at Ilene's unfettered disgust.

'It made transformations easier if less clothes were in the way.', Charlotte explained. 'Mine's locked in a trunk in my apartment.'

'I ain't wearing that.... *ever*!' Ilene protested. 'I'd rather fight naked. In fact, it would be just like fighting naked. Good god! You guys fought in these over the last five hundred years?!'

Mek'el and Charlotte nodded in unison, still smiling. Ilene scoffed out loud.

'You guys were afraid of human's discovering our kind, but you weren't afraid of being seen in these things back when the most women showed was shoulder and two inches of cleavage!'

'So, you'll stick to what you've been doing? Backless vests and capris?', Charlotte asked.

'Yep.', Ilene responded, marching away from the cabinets as a sign that the uniform discussion was over.

There was a large safe in the corner of the room, hidden under a wall table. Mek'el tried using his strength on the door, but it seemed Verndari proof. It was funny watching the frustration and powerlessness on his face. They figured out the solution within two seconds thanks to their telepathy. Charlotte 'asked' for Ilene's birthdate and Ilene provided it instantaneously. The safe clicked open on the next try.

Ilene recoiled as she recognised the aroma locked in there. It smelt like the inside of the little chest she had found only four months ago. Mek'el reached in and pulled out photo albums with ivory leather covers.

They all sat down together on the floor, Ilene in the middle with the other two looking over her shoulders.

A shuddered sigh escaped Mek'el as Ilene opened the first album. There, on page one, was a smiling Siobhan, sat in the nursery windowsill, holding her round stomach. She was looking past the camera at Roger, who was no doubt taking the picture. The next few pictures were Siobhan around the house, in the bedroom, the kitchen but a lot in the library. One of Ilene's favourites was Siobhan doing pullups in workout clothes, very heavily pregnant. The concentration on her face was bewitching. The caption, handwritten under the image made Ilene smile. It was the same cursive writing from her father's letter, so she knew it was by him. It said 'My warrior queen still at it. Nothing stops her from training.' It was dated two months before Ilene's birth date. What a woman!

The next album was dated three months from the last date. The pictures were of both Roger and Siobhan. In the first, Siobhan was sporting the biggest smile yet and breast feeding a tiny baby with sparse dark hair on its head. Each picture was sweeter than the last. Some of them were of Roger dozing with the baby in his arms, Siobhan washing bottles, bath time, Roger holding a crying baby slightly away from him with a bewildered look on his face. It wasn't until a picture labelled 'Ilene 5 months', that Ilene connected herself fully to these images. She recognised herself. She was holding herself upright and reaching forward, her blue irises sparkling with infant joy, two baby canines protruding from her gums and a bow clip in her hair. It *was* her. The same nose, the same smile. She could see her parents features in her face now.

The pictures got happier and happier. Roger in the dojo with Ilene showing her the weapons on the walls as she reached forward to them. Siobhan on the piano with Ilene on her lap.

Mek'el was starting to well up again. 'I wish we could have shared in this happiness with them. That stupid law! If only this hadn't needed to be a secret.'

Charlotte nodded, swallowing tears. 'Only one of them would come on missions at a time after you were born. They both had such mental discipline, that none of us even knew or guessed about you. There was no clue.'

"How did they hide the pregnancy?", Ilene breathed, still absorbed in these forgotten images.

"For the first three months, they did missions as normal.", Mek'el answered aloud. "Roger was very dedicated to keeping up the guise of our human lives. He told us Siobhan had been sent on sabbatical to an archaeological centre in Japan for 6 months. I guess she was hiding at the house the whole time. She *loved* fighting. That must have given her crazy cabin fever."

"No.", Charlotte answered. "When you're pregnant, it supersedes everything. The excitement and love you feel... You while your days away picturing what life will be like on their arrival and preparing."

Ilene's head snapped up. She could see the slight hint of indigo in Charlotte's pupils.

Charlotte smiled. "I had a child when I was human, but it didn't survive beyond a few months. Medicine wasn't great back then. So many preventable deaths...."

Ilene didn't know what to say. But she could hear Charlotte's thoughts as she looked at the pictures, the sadness, the envy. She also thought of Ilene as the daughter she had lost hundreds of years ago. Ilene was glad her existence could bring someone peace as well as save lives, even though it had already cost two.

They had spent the rest of the day going through Roger's notes and photo album. The last entry was from when Ilene would have been ten months old. Ilene felt guilty as a daughter that she as a person had just moved on and completely forgotten her parents so easily. But Mek'el had reminded her that she was so young when it had happened and that it wasn't her fault.

Ilene had begun to notice a change in her appearance; not only were her muscles even more toned but her hair was changing. It was turning black from the roots at a rate faster than normal hair growth. So, Ilene had taken to wrapping up her hair before buying dye to cover the change. Apparently, the medication she'd been taking had been altering her appearance on a cellular level, changing the colour of her hair to make her fit in with her adopted family and not arouse as much suspicion. How people had accepted and never questioned Fred and Diane's addition to the family, Ilene would never know.

Ilene and Jason had been spending more time in the city to get a break from being in the Manor so much. Jason had introduced Ilene to his University friends, and they had asked a lot about her home in England and what it was like living with Grumpy, as they had nicknamed Jason. Ilene was learning her way around the city. She already had five favourite eating spots. She had learnt the whereabouts of all the good parking areas. Amanda still warned her to be safe a lot, which was really starting to intrigue her. It was something about the way she said it, as if she wasn't entirely worried about Ilene's safety. As if she was worried about someone else, probably Jason. Ilene promised herself she would uncover the mystery of Amanda at some point soon. What did she know? Why was there this tangible wall of tension around her and Jason? They were both extremely suspicious and distrusting people.

Ilene began to realise that the number of attacks were dropping lately. Either there was less anger in the city, or the demons were being awakened and moving elsewhere. There were still bodies of unconscious and sometimes, not so unconscious people at the scenes. But the chances of facing a demon were becoming fewer and fewer. It was like they had something better to do. There was only the initial victim but no trail of further victims.

Even Mek'el was confused by it. He mentioned it at the next meet-up with Charlotte, Marcellus and Kuruk. Marcellus just laughed and joked that Mek'el was becoming obsolete.

But Ilene was really worried. If the demons weren't hanging around to do more damage, where were they? This was building up to something, like the quiet before the storm. It scared her.

Mek'el was concerned too, but about Ilene's safety. He recommended that Ilene use her adopted name everywhere, not just at work. This would protect her from whoever attacked her family. Also, if she's unknown to the community, she would hopefully be able to flee the country if something did happen.

This was a comfort to Ilene but the thought of leaving the six new people in her life to face *anything* without her made her feel sick.

So, life went on. She carried on with the mundane activities of each week. She worked, she shopped, she cleaned, she trained, and she rested.

One day, at clock-out time, she was saying goodbye to her colleagues and emptying her locker as usual. As she was walking to the staff exit, she was slammed in the head by a voice she'd never heard. And it was angry.

She saw a book. And then a blaze of red light. It was an angry Verndari.

'This is ridiculous! It's not *working*! We've questioned everybody we have! What's it going to take-?', the man bellowed. Silence suddenly rang. 'Who's there? Who are you?'

Ilene panicked but managed not to answer mentally. She had to leave. She ran to the nearest alley and made sure she wasn't visible. She removed her top, winged up and flew away as fast as she could, heading straight for home. She landed in the treeline she had spent her first Verndari night in. Once she crossed the back lawn and was safely within the barrier, she pulled out her phone and called Mek'el.

He answered almost immediately. "Ilene? Are you ok? I felt your mind briefly a few minutes ago. You were freaking out. What's wrong?"

"I think my cover's blown. There's another Verndari in the city and I heard him! He's angry and I think he felt me listening. I was able to run before I accidentally answered any of his questions."

Mek'el was quiet for a moment. Then he exhaled.

"I'm coming over. Don't worry. You did good. We'll do some more mental training so you can keep yourself closed off from other Verndarar. See you soon."

And the line went dead.

Mek'el was trying to sound calm, but he had spoken a tad too fast which had given away his real feelings.

Ilene waited in the library until the doorbell sounded.

When the door opened, he didn't speak, he just hugged her, which actually helped. All Ilene could think about was the Verndarar that had disappeared never to be seen again. What had happened to them? Imprisonment? Torture? Or the same thing that happened to her parents? Then she began wondering if there was an afterlife for the Verndarar and Verndari-born, especially seeing as most of them had already had some form of afterlife.

Mek'el placed one of his large hands on her shoulder and turned her towards the staircase. 'Come on.', he beckoned, 'We're going to train but first, we'll meditate.'

Normally she hated that word but after what she'd heard, she needed a quiet mind. And she knew what she needed to see before she meditated. Mek'el went to make some tea and said he would see her in the dojo. When he arrived, he found Ilene already cross-legged on her usual spot, in front the waterfall feature, except this time the waterfall was more active. He could see the Verndari realm again. The feelings of belonging and calm he and the others associated with their home must have stuck with her, conjuring up similar feelings when she thought of it. He tended to forget Ilene's ability to take more than just sounds from other minds.

And so, they practised and talked into the night until Ilene was visibly and mentally calmer. He made certain of this before she announced she was going to bed. He saw her to her bedroom door and waited downstairs until he couldn't hear her stirring anymore.

He left the house of his friends and steadied himself as well before driving home. What had he gotten her into?

*

Ilene felt rejuvenated the next morning as she entered the city. She closed her mind and ignored any quiet, lingering sounds.

As she reached her office building, she noticed a change in the atmosphere. There was anxiety and excitement. She couldn't think what was causing such a ruckus, so she asked the nearest colleague, who was Telissa, a university student, also from England, who was doing her gap year in the city.

"The big boss is doing a surprise visit today!", she announced, her voice low. "It's super rare. Apparently, the last time he came to anything other than a board meeting and the odd Christmas ball for a few minutes was *twenty years* ago!"

Ilene huffed in derision. She hated those bosses that didn't really get involved with their company, but instead spent their time at fancy lunches and pointless fully catered meetings. This guy sounded no different to every CEO she'd ever seen or met. Her mother, father and brother had given her plenty of opportunities to get a peek into the working world, through visits and daily feedback, not to mention the work she'd done during her school years.

So, the morning was spent arranging the mail room to look like an efficient, spotless machine rather than the centre of mayhem it normally was. In the meantime, Ilene listened to the women gossip about the CEO. Apparently, he was absolutely loaded, received the company from his father, which was created by his great-grandfather. Also, he'd never been married despite being 'completely dreamy'. Yikes! If these numbskulls all agreed he was dreamy, he probably looked completely manufactured. After all he did have access to the best clothing and personal care money could buy. Besides, she'd seen an large salary make an average man look like an Adonis to other people. It was ridiculous.

Ilene had looked up the company's history and the CEO's life-story when she's been offered a job at Hillman Co. He was a philanthropist, engineer and art dealer specialising in rare painting and gargoyles. Half of the important buildings in the country were decorated with his creations and items from his collection.

About two hours later, a strange stillness came over the ground floor, and everyone became busy after some non-verbal communications were shared from the one person to the next.

Ilene could hear voices travelling down the corridor, and almost looked out in curiosity. He wouldn't bother coming into the Mail Room. It was a very unimportant room.

But then the noise suddenly grew and didn't pass. Ilene turned and saw an impressive entourage entering through the double doors. There was an assistant, hair cut into a pristine bob, in a well-tailored skirt suit to the right. A tall, broad man stood on the left in a black suit with an ear-piece on, looking like an Agent. He was scowling at and scrutinizing everyone in the room. The other men, dressed similarly, stood at the back of the group, their eyes never leaving the man in the centre. He was something to behold. The boss was shaking hands with her manager. His skin was slightly tanned, mostly likely from the many holidays he treated to himself to as a break from doing...nothing. He was average height, about the same height as Mek'el, maybe a little shorter. His eyes were shocking ice-blue and grey, and his hair was a dirty blonde colour, making it harder to see greys. His build was athletic, and he held himself like a soldier. He was looking around the room with keen interest, listening attentively to every word her manager was saying. His suit was fancy, sure and his shoes were no doubt worth over £400 but this was no spoilt rich boy. Something in his eyes made that clear.

The men beamed and the women, along with some of the men, faltered as he met all of them individually.

When he finally reached her, she smiled but not too much.

"Hi. I'm Victor. It's nice to meet you.", he greeted in a deep silken voice. "And you are?"

"Theresa Blackman.", she answered, finding it all too easy to use her old name.

"Ah! English!", he exclaimed, "I love going there. Which county are you from?"

"Just London.", Ilene answered, still smiling. She didn't like the way his eyes probed a little harder than normal into every inflection of her face.

"Enjoying yourself here?", he asked.

"Yes, sir. Your company is incredible.", Ilene answered, honestly. The company *was* immense, and the building's facilities and benefits were unlike anything she'd heard of or seen.

"Why, thank you.", he answered, bowing slightly. "But I can't take much credit. It's all thanks to Great Grandpa that we're all even here."

At that moment, his assistant skuttled up like a restless puppy and reminded him of his schedule, after which he bid the office goodbye, leaving with his surrounding 'people cloud', as Ilene decided to call them. Although 'moon cluster' sounded more appropriate.

There was maybe a minute of silence before the excitement burst out of the seams for everyone in the room, especially the ones who had just developed a new crush.

While everyone else was letting out their excitement, Ilene was releasing her anxiety. That had been intense and more uncomfortable than she had anticipated. Why did he make her feel so on edge? Was it no coincidence that she had heard a voice the day before and then this rich recluse shows up? She tried to lift the pitch and volume of the voice she had heard when Victor spoke. But she couldn't quite get it to match what she'd heard the night before.

She relaxed for the rest of the day and went home as usual. Then her guard was brought up again when she received an official email from Victor to every member of staff inviting them all to a party to celebrate the company's ninetieth anniversary. Ilene didn't really like parties anyway, but this one was one she was too curious to miss. It would, of course, be fully catered, accommodation was free for anyone who wanted to spend the night and the party after the meal would be headlined by one of the most famous DJs in the world. Even she would be fool not to go.

The next day at lunch, she caught up with Telissa again. They talked about home as usual. She was from Yorkshire, not a city girl at all, and was still not used to the lack of greenery and how crowded everywhere was. Then Telissa dropped her voice, just as she had the day before.

"You'll never believe what happened to me, Tess.", she whispered, her eyes widening a little. "Guess who got into the lift with me and started flirting with me."

"David from I.T?", Ilene guess, chewing on her bento. "You've been staring at him for over a month."

Telissa recoiled slightly, blushing. "Y-you noticed that?!". She shook her head eventually and waved a dismissive hand, her short curly hair bouncing with the movement. "No! Not him! VICTOR!"

Ilene's mouth fell open. Oh god. There was that sinking feeling again.

"We got talking. He was subtle at first but then he suddenly asked if I wanted to have coffee with him some time."

"What did you say?", Ilene asked, trying not to look worried or horrified.

"YES, of course! Have you *seen* him? He's gorgeous! It took me a few seconds to answer though as I thought he might the type to do the cliché CEO thing."

"Bang his assistant.", they whispered in unison, before bursting into a fit of girly giggles.

"I mean, who's to say if he is not or hasn't.", Ilene mused. "Just be careful, T."

"I will. But could you imagine if it *became* something?", Telissa gushed.

"Now *that's* a rags-to-riches article worth reading. Hang on, how's he going to reach you?", Ilene asked, her brow wrinkling as a million thoughts buzzed through her head.

"He*llo*! He owns the company! You think he can't just pull my phone number from H. R's records?"

Ilene cocked an eyebrow. "Well, that's a little unethical, isn't it?"

"Tess, he's not a telemarketing agent.", Telissa joked, shaking her head.

"Just be careful. Trust me. Don't let his handsome face and bottomless pocket make you forget that he's just a bloke, like the rest of them.", Ilene cautioned.

Telissa hugged Ilene and then bounced back to her office, visibly happy, even if you couldn't see her face.

Ilene never understood the whole infatuation thing, as most people didn't appeal to her or affect her. She was never able to get too close to most people anyway. Maybe one day she'd find it, the person that made her giddy but right now, she had bigger things to worry about. Like surviving.

So, life went on as normal for a few days. One day, less than a week after Ilene and Telissa's lunch time catch up, Ilene had been finishing her rounds and was heading back to the Mail Room, with the morning mail to be shipped filling the trolley. She turned a corner slightly too quickly and a bundle of envelopes slipped from the top tray, tumbling to the floor. She was trying to be clumsy and human. If her reflexes were too good too often, people would notice her. She didn't want them to. As Charlotte liked to remind her, there was more than one way to be invisible which didn't involve changing her skin tone.

But there was no thud. A hand was there, a well-made watch just above it.

"Careful. All communication is important and meaningful here.", Victor warned, placing it back on the trolley. "Can't have the wrong stuff going to the wrong place or anything."

Ilene started breathing again. "Sorry, sir. I'll make sure these get out to the right people."

Victor smiled. "I know you will. Information and knowledge are everything. That's something my father told me. Whether it's omitted, shared or revealed accidentally, it can have profound effects."

Ilene was fighting to keep her mind clear. Victor's Head of Security was stood a few feet away, which was not comforting at all. "Words move mountains, Theresa.", Victor advised. He smiled as she jumped at the sound of her name. "Yes, Tess. I'm good at remembering names, faces.... voices."

Ilene could feel her heart hammering in her chest. Where was his 'people cloud'? Why was his muscle dog stood so far away? Was he protecting Victor or watching her? This was wrong.

Victor laughed and took a step closer. "Sorry if I freaked you out a little. Tell you what: I'll make it up to you. How would you like to have coffee with me? Saturday evening? I know this little Italian bistro that makes the best biscotti."

Ilene smirked internally. He *was* a spoilt rich boy after all. He seemed to have a thing for girls with accents. No wonder his Head of Security was giving him space. Allowing his boss room to flirt, as was his usual practice, probably. He had several buildings full of women who weren't going to turn down the chance to date the owner of a huge conglomerate. Not if they were smart anyway. The man was hot and had the power to hire and fire. So, this was going to be interesting.

"I'm so sorry. I'm at a party that night.", Ilene apologised, as convincingly as possible, while feeling disgust welling up in her.

Victor blinked rapidly but then eventually spoke. "O.K. I understand. Another time then.". His smile wasn't as wide now. Also, that last part didn't sound like a question.

Ilene nodded, smiled and took off as fast as she could without looking like she was running off. There was something about him, aside from his spoilt rich boy act that turned her insides in the worst possible way. The way his eyes scanned everything didn't match his face, the careless Batchelor in his forties. Was he human? Even if he wasn't, Ilene got the feeling she couldn't trust him.

She'd never been happier to clock out as she was that night.

*

That evening, Victor sat in his office texting Telissa, amused by her forced nonchalance and occasional spills of emotion into her messages. He would figure out who the voice was he'd heard the other night was. He was currently investigating all new staff that started within the company over the last six months. It was a lengthy but interesting task. He thoroughly check and tested all staff every year or so, to keep the upper hand. His Head of Security walked in and coughed quietly for his attention.

"Anything on Theresa Blackman, David?", Victor asked, not even looking up from his phone.

"Nothing. She was born and raised in England and came over on a work Visa just over three months ago. She has a small apartment on the edge of the city. Not many friends in her past or presently.", David replied.

"Alright. Telissa?", Victor probed.

"Born and raised in England. Travels a lot. Currently on a Gap Year from Leicester University. Seemingly a big fan of social media. Be careful with her.", David reported, shaking his head and sighing at her typical youthful behaviours and tastes.

"O.K. Good work but keep digging. I want to know absolutely everything. There's another of the Verndarar in this building, and the mind felt young. And that much power is something I need for what's coming.", Victor ordered, sitting back in his chair.

"Of course, sir.", the wall of muscle replied.

Chapter 13

Digging Deeper

Ilene was relaxing at the edge of her garden in the tree which she had dubbed her sleeping tree from that terrifying first night of her new, strange life. She was looking forward to the company anniversary party tomorrow. She'd been training and working so much she felt like she hadn't had enough time to relax and let her hair down. Tomorrow night would be a good chance.

'Hey there.', Mek'el greeted. He was in his apartment again. Ilene could see it through his eyes.

'Hi. You ok?', she replied.

'Pretty good. And you?', he answered.

'Burnt out and exhausted. Feeling pretty human right now.', Ilene rolled her eyes as she thought those words.

They couldn't help but laugh together. 'Well, I would apologise but the training is necessary. It's feeling increasingly dangerous here. We haven't had a demon attack in days. It's freaking me out. Also, another Verndari disappeared in the next town over yesterday.', Mek'el explained.

Ilene tried not to think about how much that scared her too, but she was sure Mek'el had heard it already. 'Oh, by the way, thank you for the idea of getting that apartment in the city. You're right, the last thing we need is for whoever is taking us to discover this house.'

'No problem. It's an apartment I bought over a century ago. Glad it could come in handy. I used to use it as a safehouse or lend it out if your parents were away.'

Ilene shook her head. Contingency plans left and right. Years of wisdom in action. Hopefully she would learn to think ahead in the same way.

'I have a couple of questions.', Ilene announced.

'O.K.', Mek'el responded, preparing his mind.

'How long do you think it'll be until I'm able to use the stone around my neck the way my father did? And how come no-one else can use it?'

Ilene felt Mek'el picking phrases from his memories and composing them into an adequate answer. His mind was clear and pleasant to be in.

'It's hard to say, as you're Verndari-born, which makes you more powerful than ordinary Verndari. As for the other question, stones are assigned to members of the Varlharar in positions of power and trust by Gaia herself. Since we can't get to the Verndarar realm right now, it can't be... reassigned. And in the event of the death of a gem's guardian, its used to be passed over to the next of kin. If it hadn't been for you showing up, we would have no hope of using the healing gem at all, as the Verndarar don't usually have another Verndari relative.'

Ilene nodded. She really needed to get stronger then. But just the thought of that made her feel even more tired. 'O.K. Next question.'

'I thought you said you had two.', Mek'el protested, trying to sound grumpy, but the joking tone in his voice slipped through.

Ilene giggled and continued. 'So, Velhonen took the gem that gets you into the human world. Can it do anything else? I mean, you said mine heals the Verndarar. Also, what happens if the gems are near each other?'

Mek'el's voice livened up. 'Actually, there's three gems. You have the healing and home gem. Velhonen has the green gem, which influences demons and allows you into the Human world, which explains the increase in attacks in the last five hundred years because it's with an angry young man. Who knows what he's used it to do. The elders have the third stone, a red gem, which opens a direct path to Gaia. If all three are brought together, the individual holding them can control or destroy all demons, become impervious to harm, and the undisputed leader of the Verndarar.'

This made Ilene afraid of the possibilities available just because of the three gems. At the same time, she felt proud that this level of power was entrusted to her father. She pictured him now, leading battles, the gem around his neck and power coming off him in waves.

'Who were my parents in their human lives?', Ilene asked unintentionally.

'Their names were the same or similar at least. Your father is from so long ago, there's no written record of his human life. Roger was a Scottish soldier named Ruairidh de Cambel. His village was attacked by the English in the 13th century. He gave his life to save his people and buy them time enough to get hold of weapons and evacuate the vulnerable. He held off sixty Englishmen in armour before succumbing to his wounds.' Mekel paused while he remembered Roger telling him the story. 'When he opened his eyes again, he was lying in the grass in the Verndari realm. He was one of the first.'

Ilene shuddered. The weight of his history was now in her mind. 'And Mum?'

'Her name was Efua Obeng. She was the daughter of Tribe chief in what is now known as Ghana. Then the Portuguese came to their shores and occupied it, killing her people and taking her lands. They were looking for gold. She led a battle that held them off, interrupting a public execution and freeing her father and siblings. She died doing this in the 15th century.'

Ilene was feeling more and more inadequate with every Verndari origin story she heard. She imagined the other Verndari-born being entertained with the same stories and feeling inspired. Ilene mentally shook herself. She shouldn't be put down by these stories. She was part of this incredible legacy. She should train harder. She would have her chance to prove herself.

'They fell in love over the space of three to four hundred years they were with each-other. Siobhan's agility and fearlessness impressed Roger, and his compassion and natural abilities as a leader impressed Siobhan.', Mek'el continued.

'Well, if they came back once again, why didn't they do it twice?', Ilene asked, sifting through Mek'el's mental images.

'You remember the sword I told you about? The one that can kill our kind?'

Ilene immediately saw her visions again, seeing the silhouette of it in the moonlight, falling to silence her parents' cries. 'Yes.', she replied quickly. 'The one Velhonen took. That's why?'

'Ilene, promise me.... *promise* me, if you ever meet or find Velhonen, just run. Don't fight, don't talk to him. Just come home. Find me.'

Ilene shuddered again, the fear of death sending tremors through her entire body.

'I promise.', she vowed. She wouldn't risk it. She needed to live to get through the Verndarar portal where she'd be safe or get reinforcements if things went bad. She had to live.

Mek'el's relief radiated from his mind. They bid each other goodnight and Ilene climbed back into her bedroom window. The night felt that much colder considering the dangers that were out there. She was scared but thankfully not alone. They would figure this out and fight it together. And even if she was alone, like her parents, she'd fight tooth and nail. McCampbells didn't quit.

I J FERRESTONE

Chapter 14

Party Time

It was one of the biggest parties the city had ever seen. Victor had rented out the entirety of the Van Dusen Botanical Garden, including Heron Lake and the Floral Hall. There were two huge marquees near the Hall, one for dining and the other for bathrooms, cloakrooms and powder rooms. It looked like a fairy tale, with the fairy lights, chandeliers and waiters in pristine uniforms. They had transferred the company's security to the party, where staff used their employee passes to get themselves and their plus-ones in. Ilene had brought Jason as hers. She'd explained that she was using her English adopted name at work. When he asked why, she told him the truth: that her name hadn't been legally changed yet, but she could use both. She ignored his suspicious stares, feigning excitement at the event. She was wearing a simple coat with a fur trim collar. Jason was in a rented tuxedo and was looking dapper. It made a huge changed from jeans, torn t-shirts and compost marks. He was driving which stopped him from talking and probing too much. He wasn't used to big parties. He kept his groups small, so this was well out of his comfort zone.

They parked up and walked towards the cloakroom marquee. Ilene signed them in and removed her coat.

Jason almost stopped breathing when he saw Ilene properly for the first time that night. Her ebony hair was swept to one side, beautiful jewellery hanging from her ears, neck and wrists. She wore an ombre blue strapless dress that started sky blue and then became midnight blue at her knees. It floated like vapour when she walked.

Ilene suddenly realised she was walking alone, so she looked around.

Jason was still stood by the cloakroom exit, looking at her with his mouth open. Ilene laughed and that snapped him out of his stupor. She reached out her hand.

"Come on. I can't party alone.", she called.

Jason walked up, smiling and held out his bent arm, which she took.

As they walked in, heads turned. Everyone was staring. Oh no! Why were they looking? Ilene was trying to be invisible. This was the most inconspicuous dress she'd found in the closet. Was a boob showing? She checked. Nope.

It was Jason's turn to laugh. "Have you seen yourself tonight? Do you even know...er.... how pretty you are?", Jason whispered, leaning in. "Besides, you don't exactly carry yourself like the girl from the Mail Room."

Ilene stopped walking. No unrelated man had ever said that to her before. She didn't know what to say. When she had finished blushing, she squeezed his arm and smiled sheepishly. They went to the photo wall, decorated with flowers and the company's logo. That photo was printed for them, and Ilene smiled again. It was her first picture of her in her new life. They looked comfortable in each-other's company. Ilene wondered what people would say if they knew she and Jason effectively lived together. It probably wouldn't be of note. That's good.

They walked through to the other marquee and found their seats, which took a while as there were so many tables. She never realised there was this many people in her building. It was unbelievable.

Within minutes of being sat down, Telissa found them and planted herself next to Ilene. She was introduced to Jason, which solicited an unmasked look of attraction and approval from flirtatious little Telissa. She was wearing a form-fitting green dress, with a neckline that was dangerously low. But knowing Telissa it was done completely intentionally, so as to catch Victor's eye.

They went through their normal greetings, complimenting each-other's hair and make-up. Then Telissa's voice became low, and her voice became low and her tone anxious.
"You won't believe what happened in my flat last night. I got home and the place had been *trashed*!", she whispered.

"You were burgled?!", Jason whispered back, leaning in.

"That's just it: nothing was taken. I still called the police and reported the break-in.", Telissa responded, shrugging.

Ilene felt her stomach drop. It was too coincidental. Victor shows up after she hears a voice, asks out the only two Brits on her floor and one of their apartments are searched. She turned to look for him and found him socialising and drinking with some celebrities he'd invited. But that wasn't what caught her eye. It was the fact that his Head of Security was staring straight over at Telissa. This place wasn't safe. But Ilene had to get Victor to expose himself once and for all. She had to know what he was. But how would she do it without informing the world of her people's existence? She wasn't going to be the one to blow the lid off the secret after almost a thousand years of successful stealth.

Ilene decided to do some slight sleuthing. "On a more positive note, how are things going with Victor?", Ilene quizzed, resting her chin on her hand, her arm balancing on the table in an act of casual conversation.

Telissa lit up; the 'burglary' completely forgotten. "It's great! We go out to dinner, he buys me gifts and we text each-other, like, a hundred times a day."

Ilene had not expected that answer. Her eyes popped open, wide with shock. "Wow! That sounds like a fairy tale.... and serious.", she commented.

Telissa sighed and stared off into the distance. "Yeah. He's amazing. He's intelligent, funny, knowledgeable of the world..."

"...Rich.", Jason muttered bitterly under his breath as he sipped his mocktail, receiving an elbow to the ribs from Ilene, although she was thinking the same thing.

"I really care about him.", Telissa suddenly turned to Ilene and grabbed her hands so tight, that it would have hurt, had she been human. "I'm going to tell him how I feel...*tonight*!"

Before Ilene could move her lips to tell her what a bad idea this was, so soon after simply meeting him, she was prattling on some more.

"I'll text him to meet me in the toilets in five minutes. I've been thinking about telling him for weeks. And it's now or never.", Telissa jumped up and headed towards the first marquee.

The two sat at the table in stunned silence. Ilene hadn't moved, but Jason carried on drinking. "Are all British girls like that?", he asked, amused.

Ilene sighed. "I think it doesn't matter where on this planet you're from, most women act like that. The rest of us have our heads screwed on and our wits about us."

"Oh really?", Jason asked. "So, you wouldn't succumb to girlish ways if a rich handsome man paid you attention?"

"No.", Ilene answered, "I have other things on my mind."

"Like...?", Jason probed.

"My new family, my new home, going through every memory from before my eighteenth birthday and remembering that there's a lie under all of them. Trying to figure out who I am and where I belong in this world."

Jason went silent. He hadn't realised how much she had going on in her mind. How was she not a wreck?

"So, romance and all that are for people who are settled in their lives.", Ilene stated shrugging.

Jason immediately shook his head. "Wrong."

"What?", Ilene countered, turning to look at him.

"You're wrong.", Jason explained, "People find love during wars, struggles and whilst finding themselves. Sometimes that person helps you figure out or build who you are."

Ilene blinked at this deep and mature version of Jason. "You... sound like you know this subject well. Did it happen to you?"

"No."

"Your parents?"

Jason froze. His forehead creased and his jaw set. "I don't know who my dad is. I don't think my mom does either."

They both sat in silence and just as the length of the silence was getting uncomfortable, their starters arrived. They smiled a quick and slightly awkward smile at each-other, and Ilene squeezed Jason's arm again briefly before they started eating.

The food was exquisite, but Ilene was watching Victor. Telissa had probably chickened out. He hadn't left for the toilet all evening. Now they'd had all the porcelain, cutlery and crystal taken away by the waiters.

Telissa was sat at her table still. She probably was nervous and was eating so she wouldn't faint, mid-confession. This surprised Ilene as nerves before something huge made her lose her appetite, not load up on every carb that she could get her shaking hands on.

Just after dessert, Ilene saw Telissa reach for her phone. She could hear her heart hammering from across the room. It slowed slightly as she watched Telissa take in and release a large steadying breath. Her thumbs suddenly moved furiously and after a brief pause, one last tap sent the message. In a matter of seconds, Ilene heard a vibration from the direction in which Victor was sitting.

Telissa was now standing and walking towards the toilets. Ilene stood as well and smiled as she excused herself, taking her bag with her. Telissa had just walked into the Ladies' toilets when Ilene rounded the corner. How would she get Victor to show himself without endangering Telissa? Almost as if in answer, she bumped into a sandstone carving fixed firmly to the ground. Ilene groaned. It was a good idea, but she'd need to be invisible. She saw the disabled toilets and dove in, locking the door behind her. She took off everything, putting all the essentials into her bag, before stepping into the hallway again, after checking it was empty. She wrapped her dress around her bag and tucked the bundle under the marquee wall, hoping no-one saw it and took it.

She focused and emptied her mind as she blended in with her surroundings. If she was wrong, she will have attempted to kill her boss, and Telissa would sail into the sunset with a handsome rich man who doted on her. Plus, they'd have an interesting story to giggle over in the future. But if she was right.... Ilene shook the thought from her mind. She'd cross that bridge when she came to it.

About a minute later, Victor appeared. Ilene's heart rate increased. She stood by the statue and placed her hands on it. His Head of Security was waiting at the end of the corridor, giving him space to socialise, yet again. Good. She could do this unhindered. As he walked nearer, Ilene drew in a breath as she tightened her grip on her impromptu weapon. She pushed and heard its fixing break loose. Victor was sending one last text, so his head was down. But as he noticed a decrease in light his head snapped up. He cried out as several hundred kilos of stone landed on his left side, pushing him down, but only onto his knees.

Ilene gasped. The statue hadn't fallen completely. It was leaning, supported by an arm... but not a human one. It was large, scaly and clawed. It looked like an armadillo hybrid. Victor's Head of Security ran as fast as he was able to his boss' side but didn't react when he saw the arm. Victor pushed the statue aside and it shook the ground with its landing. His eyes gleamed red with unhidden fury.

"I need the toilets sealing off immediately!", Victor growled. "There's a Verndari here!"

"What makes you think that?", the Head of Security asked, reaching to his earpiece.

"That statue was nailed into the ground. No human could have moved it. I was right. There's one within the company."

Ilene suddenly felt her stomach fold in on itself in fear. Could this be who she thought? She had to know. She cleared her mind again. She thought only of one word.

'Velhonen.', she called.

Victor's breath caught and his face drained of colour. His eyes had the slightest hint of yellow in them.

"David, they know who I am.", he whispered. "And they're still here."

Seeing Victor's fear, David stepped into action. "We need a team here now! Seal off the bathrooms, take the girl for questioning. Someone just attacked Mr Hillman."

In seconds, men in suits were in the corridor. Ilene heard Telissa's protests as some of them entered the toilets, followed by a muffled scream. The next moment, the same men exited the toilets, carrying her unconscious body. David was muttering orders, and a long dining cart appeared. The laid her on the bottom shelf on her back, her wrist zip-tied together. They draped a linen tablecloth over the cart, completely concealing her body. Two members of the security team changed their black jackets into white catering smocks and took the cart down the corridor, disappearing around the corner.

The whole time Ilene stood transfixed, and terrified, fighting to keep her mind clear in front of the man who had terrorized the Verndarar for centuries and murdered her parents. She was unarmed and defenceless. But she couldn't think about that. She had to leave.

Once everyone was preoccupied, she ducked under the marquee wall and found her bundle and bag. Thankfully, it was still there, and the outdoors had been on the other side of the wall. She sent a quick text to Jason before throwing her bag into the darkness. People would notice a floating handbag.

She stood against the hanging wall until no-one was walking by. Then she ran in the direction of where she'd flung her bag. She had just enough time to put on her dress. She found her shoes and underwear and put them on once she was near the exit, passing a few couples who were too preoccupied with their mischief with each-other to hear her tiptoe past.

It took about seven minutes for Jason to drive out and pull over. He climbed out and wandered over to the treeline.

"Ilene?!", Jason called.

"Who?", Ilene called back. What was the point of telling him about using her adopted name unless he was actually going to use it? She could have punched him, but she needed him.

"For god's sake, just come out here! What's going on?"

"Did you get my coat?", Ilene responded.

"No. You said you had an emergency, so I got out here as fast as I could. Come out!"

Jason cursed under his breath. What was going on with her? Then he heard a twig snap from the tree line and Ilene stepped out, her hair was a mess, and her dress was creased badly, all over.

"We need to go home.", Ilene urged, climbing into the passenger seat, not daring to look at Jason's face.

After a moment which felt like an eternity, Jason climbed into the driver's seat and started the car.

The drive home was silent as the grave, except for the radio. Ilene reached forward to drown out the near silence, but the stereo wasn't responding.

Jason let out an annoyed sigh. "What are you doing?"

Ilene frowned. "Your controls are busted on the radio. It won't turn up or down."

"The radio isn't even on, you nut job.", Jason muttered. His tone was bitter.

Ilene could feel her temper rising again.

"So, what happened to your clothes?", Jason pried.

Ilene opened her mouth and closed it. What could she say? The truth was insane and any lie she came up with would seem equally ridiculous.

"So, the girl who just told me romance is off the table for her, sneaks off for an eventful toilet break?", Jason growled. "You keep secrets, and you *constantly* contradict yourself. What is going *on* with you?"

Ilene shook her head. "You wouldn't believe me if I told you."

Jason's jaw was clenched and so were his hands. "I honestly thought you were different. No wonder you and mum are thick as thieves. You're just like each-other: Untrustworthy, secretive and common."

He heard Ilene's mouth open with a pop, but he couldn't stop his own mouth. He was too angry. "Just do me a favour. If a kid results from tonight, at least have the decency to remember the father's name and tell him."

Ilene went numb. Why would these words from a man she'd only known for a few months hurt so much? The why didn't matter. She knew she couldn't be around him for another minute without completely losing her temper and self-control.

"Stop the car.", Ilene ordered, so quietly even she barely heard it. "Now."

Jason pulled over. He turned to look at her and saw the shine of a teardrop on her chin in the dashboard lights.

Years of anger towards his mother had been thrown at a girl he'd not long been friends with and now he'd ruined it. She hadn't deserved that. Her personal life wasn't really any of his business. As he thought this, Ilene opened the door and stepped out of the car.

She took off her shoes and began to run. At first on two legs, ignoring Jason's calls and then on four when she could no longer hear him. And once her legs got tired, she took off her dress and flew to the nearest mountain top.

She hated being accused of things she hadn't done, like cheating in competitions. It always made her cry. But this was so malicious. It hurt more than anything before. The hatred in his voice was unbearable. As if she didn't have enough to worry about. Maybe Jason's comments had been the last straw and the tears that now flowed from her eyes were due to the fear from earlier, the anger of meeting her parents' killer and the worry for Telissa all bubbling to the surface. She couldn't go home. She was terrified and alone, the way she'd felt those few months ago when she'd turned eighteen.

*

Amanda put down the book she was reading as she heard the front door open and close. Her excited smile vanished as she stepped into the hallway and saw only Jason. There was grass and mud on the hem of his trousers.

"Where's Ilene?", Amanda asked.

Jason shrugged and waved a hand as he walked to the stairs.

Amanda smiled. "She met someone at the party?"

Jason stopped. He spun on the spot and faced his mother. "She wouldn't tell me. But I guess so, yeah. Of course, you'd know all about that."

Amanda saw his clenched fists and heard his tone. She stepped towards him. "What's that supposed to mean?"

"Well, you two are so alike. She is just like you were, right?", Jason quizzed, a dark smile on his face, and anger burning in his eyes.

Amanda took a calming breath. "Choose your next words carefully, young man. What I do or did is none of your business. And neither is what Ilene does. She's her own person and so was I. Until I had to think for two, not just one."

Jason laughed, a dry humourless laugh. "You should have been more careful then. Too much casual fun can become serious all too easily."

Amanda's breathing stopped. Her eyes began to brim but she blinked the tears back.

The sight of another woman about to cry because of him froze Jason again. He felt the disgust he'd thrown at his mother bounce back and stick to him.

"Mom... I'm sorry.", he whispered.

"That's what you've though of me... all these years?", she asked so quietly that it was lighter than a whisper.

"You never spoke about who he was, so I assumed...", Jason answered shrugging. He'd been such an idiot! If only he'd spoken sooner. "It doesn't matter if you remember who he was or not. Just tell me this: is it something you regret?", Jason asked, walking towards his mother and standing in front of her.

Amanda smiled. "I loved your Dad. And no, I don't regret a moment of it."

She wrapped her arms around her son. "It's just complicated and it's simpler for you not to know everything, so I didn't talk about it." Amanda stood back and took her son's sad face in her hands. "Look, I know you're worried about Ilene. She'll be OK. She's stronger than you know."

Jason sighed, squeezing his mother to him again, feeling the arms that had kept him safe and content for over twenty years. "I'd feel so awful if anything happened to her. I said some horrible things and she ran off. She looked rattled."

Amanda smiled, the slight wrinkles in the corners of her eyes showing again. "You and your mouth. It has no filter. This is her home. Don't worry, she'll come back."

Chapter 15

Acceleration

Mek'el arrived at the McCampbell estate the next morning, screeching to a halt right at the front door. He knocked the door, remembering to not use all of his strength.

Amanda awoke at the sound of the front door. She was laying on the sofa in the Games Room. She felt a weight on her chest and stomach. She laughed as she looked down. Jason was laid across her with his arms around her just as he had up until the age of seven, mouth slightly open and a little drool escaping onto her top. She squeezed him and kissed his forehead one more time. After all these years, he was still the wide-eyes boy she sang to, finger-painted with and who felt the most at peace in her arms.

Amanda slipped out of Jason's grip and replaced herself with one of the cushions they had exiled from the sofa last night. She scooped her hair back as the door was knocked again.

She opened the front door with both arms as usual.

Mek'el stood there smiling. Amanda smiled back but she could see his eyes were a little unsettled.

"Hi Mannie. How are you?", he greeted.

"Hi Mike. I'm O.K. Just woke up. Come on in.", she replied.

"Thanks.", Mek'el answered, stepping in and hanging up his jacket. "I'm here to see Ilene."

"She's not here.", Jason answered, shuffling towards the pair, stretching and yawning.

"She didn't come home last night.", Amanda explained, motioning towards the Games Room. "We've been waiting for her or for word from her all night."

Mek'el's eyes looked at the Games Room but turned back to Amanda. But before they reached her, they rested for the briefest second on Jason's face, giving a quick look of protective anger so strong it made Jason's blood run cold. Had Ilene told him? Had his mom called him? Is that why he was here? He decided to come clean anyway.

Jason sighed. "I hurt her last night and she... ran off."

Mek'el nodded, not looking at him. "Yes, I know. She sounded pretty upset when I spoke to her this morning.", he answered coolly.

Jason's eyes lit up. He stepped towards Mek'el until he was right next to him. He grabbed his arm. "Is she hurt? I mean, physically? Where did she sleep? Is she alright? Is she coming home again? Did she seem-?"

At that moment, something struck the side of his head. Jason picked it up from the ground and recognised Ilene's bag from the night before. Dread knotted his stomach as he turned slowly towards the direction which the missile came from.

Ilene was stood halfway down the stairs, arms folded. He couldn't quite see her face, as the rays of morning sun poured in behind her, making her just a silhouette.

Jason sighed. "Oh, thank *God*! You're dressed."

Mek'el's head whipped towards the young man, horrified and furious. His protective side was becoming stronger. At his side, Amanda turned away trying to stifle a fit of giggles and failing.

Jason looked down at the ground looking confused. "I have no idea why I said that. I guess I thought...with the dress and...you not coming home....I mean, you ran into a forest in a gown, I thought it'd be torn up again like that time...in the garden.... You know what I'm trying to say right?"

Amanda shook her head. "I don't even think *you* know what you're trying to say.", she muttered.

Ilene strode down the stairs and towards Mek'el. Her eyes looked duller than usual. She was still fuming, which was evident as she walked past Jason without even glancing at him, but instead mentally bombarding him with curses and expletives like cannon fire.

It was Mek'el's turn to attempt not to laugh aloud. 'Come now. You were raised better than that.', he scolded.

Ilene's eyes didn't change. 'He deserves it. We need to talk. Outside.'

Mek'el put his hand on Ilene's shoulder after she put on her coat. "How are you doing, missy?", he asked, for the advantage of the humans within earshot.

Ilene simply grunted and shrugged.

Mek'el stretched out one hand and pulled the front door open again without so much as a heavy exhale.

They stepped through to the outside. As the door closed, Jason sighed sadly. "I've lost a friend."

Amanda ruffled his already messy hair as she headed to the swimming pool bathroom to freshen up.

"Don't give up. I don't think she'll be furious for long.", Amanda advised.

"And you?", Jason called.

Amanda stopped and shrugged. "Meh. I'll ground you later."

Jason smiled, the guilt still pinching at his lungs and stomach. It would get better. He would work hard until it did.

*

Mek'el sat down on Siobhan's swing and watched Ilene staring at nothing.

"So why aren't you dressed for work?", Mek'el asked, relaxing and kicking his legs.

Ilene wanted to laugh, watching this great warrior swinging, content as could be. "I'm not feeling very well, besides..."

Ilene focused as she explained the events of last night mentally and as fast as possible. As she knew he couldn't see memories, she replayed the audio in her memories.

Mek'el was suddenly on his feet, the swing still moving. He didn't speak for a while.

"Of *course*. He's powerful enough to be him.", he mumbled to himself. He spun towards Ilene, visibly rattled, pointing at her. "Don't go to work. I'll get one of my medical friends to sign you off sick for a while. I'll do some more investigating and come up with a plan."

"Won't that look a little fishy? Right after an event where someone clearly attempted to attack him?", Ilene queried, secretly grateful not to have to go.

Mek'el winked. "No-one questions the doctor's note.", he assured, starting to pace excitedly and anxiously at the same time. "If you're right, it will be too dangerous for you to be anywhere near him."

Ilene was standing now. "But what about Telissa? An innocent human was abducted because of *me*!", she cried.

Mek'el stood in front of her and placed his large hands on her shoulder in an unspoken message that urged her to calm down.

"I'll find out about the girl. But you have to understand that hundreds of us have gone missing in the last five hundred years. Who's more important, Ilene? One human or what remains of our race?"

Ilene's irises started to glow red. She stepped back quickly, wrenching herself free of his hand with a jerk. "Everyone- *everyone* is important! Isn't that our *job*? Protecting *everyone*? Why are we putting our own before the humans we protect?"

"Because if there are none of us left, we can't protect them."

"And without *them*, we have no PURPOSE! No reason to have been reborn in the first place!", Ilene found herself yelling at the top of her lungs. "Velhonen killed my parents, seasoned warriors, without a *second thought*! How long do you think any human will last?"

Mek'el took a step back. "I'll look into it and get back to you with what I find. Stay....*out* of this. Stay here.", he commanded in a voice so calm it just infuriated Ilene further.

Ilene growled and bristled, stomping back towards the house.

"Don't even think about leaving the house or grounds. If I feel so much as a *hint* of your mind, I'll come back and chain you up in the attic. Or weigh you down in the bottom of the pool."

Ilene briefly changed her voice box and roared at Mek'el as he climbed into his car.

She walked to her room and ran a bath. She was fuming again. Eighteen years old and grounded. What bullshit.

She pulled out her phone.

*

Ilene took in the city lights and sounds as she walked around, still wondering how the hell she was going to stop Velhonen and save Telissa and both realms all in one. It was making her head hurt.

She heard the music of a familiar mind. A figure jumped calculatedly from a nearby rooftop and off the wall fixtures in a nearby alley.

"Shouldn't you be at home, sick as a dog?", Charlotte teased, stepping out in a casual but smart ensemble, topped off with a long leather jacket.

Ilene smiled. "Got any chains in that jacket?", she asked.

Charlotte stuck out her tongue and then grinned. "Yep. But not for you."

Ilene raised her hands and closed her eyes. "I don't wanna know. Pretend I never asked."

They both laughed and hugged each-other, Charlotte cradling Ilene's head like a child in her embrace.

"I'm glad you're safe. I was surprised when you called me. You don't even have my number. How'd you get it?", Charlotte asked.

Ilene giggled. "Stole it from Mek'el's mind earlier today."

"Wow!", Charlotte responded, nodding. "I've never heard of any of the Vendarar being able to do that before."

"I hope it comes in handy in a battle someday soon.", Ilene said, lost in her thoughts.

Charlotte could hear her thinking about Velhonen but reining in her inner anxiety. "Maybe.", she agreed. "Hey, are you hungry?"

Ilene grinned. "Always."

Charlotte linked her arm with Ilene's, and they strode off to a nearby café.

As Ilene tucked into her toasted sandwich, punctuating with sips of cappuccino, Charlotte watched her and listened to her mind. She was so young and yet her mind was swarming with things no eighteen-year-old should have to handle. Mek'el name kept resurfacing amongst the mental din.

Charlotte sighed. "I know Mek'el's being hard on you, but you have to understand why he's so terrified of anything happening to you."

Ilene listened but never stopped eating. Hot fries wait for no-one.

"When he lost your parents, it was the straw that broke the camel's back. Five hundred years of friendship, just...over. And then one day the only evidence of their existence strolls into the city.", Charlotte explained, looking pointedly at her during the last sentence. "He

200

won't lose you too. None of us will."

A heavy silence lay between the two of them.

"So... if my parents were the last straw, who were the previous 'straws'?", Ilene asked to cut the tension.

"Well, dozens of our comrades vanished or were injured. Some turned to Velhonen's side after becoming bitter and dissatisfied with our task, our way of life. I'm surprised Gaia didn't do something to those traitors. But the disappearance that hit him hardest was Gierozzo's. He, Mek'el and your dad were the Three Musketeers or the Marauders. And boy, did they manage to get up to mischief."

Charlotte laughed as Ilene saw images of pranks, hugs and general ruckus with three faces starring in most of the memories. The first two she knew but the third was a man with hair as dark as her mother's. He had a handsome face accented by a scar along his left jawbone. This led Ilene to wonder if there were any average or hideous looking people among the Verndarar. Everyone looked like Gods.

"Those three kept us light-hearted no matter what we dealt with or saw. But just a few years before your parents were murdered, Gierozzo disappeared. It shook us all. He was so strong and wouldn't be the type to be captured by anyone. He must have been ambushed by a large group of traitorous Verndarar and demons alike. Mek'el searched and mourned every night for almost a year. It was hard to watch. But then when Roger and Siobhan... It took all the hope he had left out of him. These few months are the most hopeful I've ever seen him. He can't lose you, Ilene, for more reasons than you could ever realise."

Ilene had never felt like she was truly important to anyone. She had simply taken Mek'el's nature for being his constant personality and a reaction to being with the child of his lost friends. He was more mentally disciplined that she'd ever realised, as she'd never sensed an inkling of this information when she was with him. She was certain more than ever that he was the master of self-control. Training with him would make her more than just a warrior.

Ilene and Charlotte paid and left. They walked the city until both their bodies were hit with a large sinking sensation. They followed the feeling and then the screams into a network of alleys.

There were four demons, Tertis, eyes glowing with light of the earth's core, lumbering towards a group of homeless people. They must have fed on their despair and woke from the walls, because they looked like they were mostly made of red brick and sandstone.

Ilene looked around and saw empty bottles on the floor. The homeless people were inebriated. Good. Sadly, no-one ever believed the word of someone drunk anyway. The ones she'd seen in England usually slept a lot, said nothing or babbled incoherently to themselves. As depressing as this was, it would work to their advantage.

Ilene ran forward. 'Sword!', she called and raised her hand, feeling the hilt of Charlotte's favourite sword land in her palm. She swung forwards and slid on her knees, swiping at where the nearest Tainted's knees would be. She heard a grinding sound that seemed like it was trying to simulate pain or anger.

She stood and groaned. "My jeans!", she whined, looking at the tears in the knees and the dripping unnamed liquid stains. The homeless group looked at her in shock. She mentally regretted her first-world whingeing. "Sorry."

The other three Tertis turned to face her, allowing the potential victims to flee.

Ilene heard rubble tumble to the ground as Charlotte landed behind her, another sword in her hand. She grinned, terrifyingly. "Christmas has come early, Ilene.", she announced.

202

"Let's do some wrapping. Your special ribbon, please.", Ilene asked, holding her hand out.

Charlotte removed her bracelet and snapped it in two. She handed one half to Ilene, stretching a serrated steel cable between them.

They ran forward, leaping for the opposite walls in the same moment. They ran and jumped, swinging themselves around, under and between the demons, as it caught on their rock bodies.

Ilene landed in front of the creature and something about its semblance of a face made her feel sad. Ilene called out to the demons mentally. They always looked so lost and unfocused. 'This isn't you. Please, pay no attention to the despair and anger of this world. There is still hope for humankind.'

Charlotte gasped as she saw Ilene standing in front of the Tainted, the gem on her chest glowing like she hadn't seen it do in years. Not since Roger last used it.

Ilene didn't feel anger or sadness. She felt calm and a cool sensation spreading through her body as she reached up to them. But one of their arms broke free and struck Charlotte. Ilene felt her pain as her arm broke... and saw her land in a heap on the floor.

'You're doing well, sweetheart.', Charlotte acknowledged. 'But we can't save them yet. You're not quite strong enough. You know what we have to do.'

Ilene nodded as the demon started to raise its arm again. She took the cable and tied it around a thick pole embedded in the ground. She picked up Charlotte's sword again.

It was a choice: save Charlotte and destroy the Tainted or keep trying to cleanse them and allow Charlotte's body to be almost obliterated.

She stepped forward. "I'm sorry.", she whispered.

Ilene jumped up with lupine legs and swung for the first one's head. It came off in one swing. Ilene cleared her mind and continued. Within moments they were all dispatched. And the only evidence of the struggle was shattered bricks on the ground. Thankfully the hole in the wall they'd come from was part of an abandoned building, so no repairs or evacuations needed.

Ilene sighed again. 'Why did it feel so different this time? I could sense... what the Tainted were before the despair crept in. I had to try...'

Charlotte stood and wrapped her good arm around Ilene, cradling the back of her head in her palm.

'I heard your dad describe something like that once. You're getting stronger. Mek'el will be proud when we tell him.'. Charlotte encouraged.

Almost as if on cue, they heard Mek'el's voice but in a way, they'd never heard it before. It was a strangled cry of pain.

Ilene screamed and grabbed at her head. She fell to the floor clawing at her legs, her powers going into spasms as Charlotte called out to her in panic.

Ilene gasped as she saw through Mek'el's eyes. She saw Victor in front of her, angry, frustrated, one of his hands raised offensively. She felt pain spreading up her body. Charlotte watched Ilene's distress helplessly, only able to crouch next to her and hold her. Her irises were glowing yellow, and tears spilled almost golden as she stopped moving. Ilene just kept screaming that it hurt, and repeatedly calling Mek'el's name. Her vision finally went dark from the outside in. The pain reached its peak and then subsided. Ilene went limp. Her eyes were still open.

STONE

The world was still and silent, for one heartbeat.

Charlotte was frozen in horror. They had to move. Charlotte stood and slung Ilene's body over her good shoulder. She was fighting to keep her mind clear. Her emotions were about to betray her.

She sprouted her wings and flew straight to the McCampbell's. They had to get inside the barrier.

*

Ilene groaned and turned her head. She opened her eyes, somehow, without moving her eyelids. She looked around. She was back in her room. Charlotte was sat next to her.

'Charlotte.', she called.

Charlotte immediately started sobbing and crushed her in a one-armed hug.

"Thank Gaia!", she cried aloud.

Ilene started to struggle out of Charlotte's embrace and head to the window. "We have to save Mek'el. Velhonen has him and had done something... awful to him."

Charlotte beat her to the window and grabbed her by the arm. "You can't. Mek'el told you to stay out of it, and you've already disobeyed him once today. It could have been you this happened to. You have to stay safe and say here!"

Ilene balled her fists. "Well, he's not my father, and he's not here. And if we don't act now, he's never coming back.", she countered through gritted teeth. "Move!"

Charlotte could feel herself reaching for her weapon instinctively. Ilene was fuming and the mood coming off her in waves was

205

murderous.

"I won't let you. You can try and fight me if you wish, but it'll only result in broken bones.", Charlotte advised.

Ilene took a step back, recoiled by the casual voice in which the threat was given. Maybe she was no nonchalant about it because she knew Ilene would heal in a couple of days. Just enough time for Charlotte to act without interference. But knowing that didn't make it any less disturbing.

Charlotte was visibly taking deep breaths to keep her composure. "There are more of the Tainted popping up ever since the party. The others have been contacting me about it. The numbers are alarming. They're looking for the Verndarar, drawing us out harder than ever before."

Ilene heard her words but as contained as Charlotte was trying to keep her heart, Ilene heard it thrumming in her chest. And then she got a glimpse of what was really bothering her. Charlotte's concentration slipped just long enough to show her most prominent thought. She saw herself, screaming and jerking on the floor of the alley they had just been in. But what was jarring more than the image was the sudden flow of intense emotion that went with it. Such fear and sadness that it knocked the air from her.

Charlotte heard Ilene's breathing stop and swallowed. Damn. She sighed and hung her head.

"Please... please don't make me go through that again."

Ilene couldn't get that feeling to leave her. It weighed her heart down. She was still finding it hard to breath. Maybe it was her British upbringing, but she didn't know what to say. So, she took Charlotte's hand.

"You won't. I'll stay. But we need help. We need the others. They're not drawing us all out. They're only looking for one of us.", Ilene reassured. She realised that the last sentence wasn't terribly reassuring but it was the truth. Charlotte would pick it up mentally.

"I was afraid that was the case. You're right. Maybe the thinking is if they take enough of us, you'll either have to come or will be less defended." Charlotte raised a hand and stroked Ilene's cheek. "I keep forgetting that we're allowed to feel in this house. I'm so used to holding back.", she admitted, fresh tears falling down her ivory cheeks. "I've never been so scared. I hate feeling helpless after several centuries of power."

Ilene got annoyed at powerlessness after only a few months of having strength and power. She could only imagine Charlotte's frustration. They both had restlessness and anxiety coming off them in waves.

Charlotte's brow creased, her eyes never leaving Ilene's face. "What happened to you? What did you see? Your rare gift sadly isn't something I can tap into."

Ilene explained everything, a hint of yellow appearing in her irises again as she recounted the sight.

Charlotte's mouth was open and didn't close. Her mind was in shocked silence.

Ilene was unsettled by it. "Charlotte?"

"This book.... what did it look like?", Charlotte asked slowly. It was as if she was afraid of the answer.

"It was a leatherbound book. The leather was red and worn, and the book was about A5 size but thick. I think there was a symbol on the front. A wiggly circle, I couldn't quite see it clearly."

"Oh god!", Charlotte lamented. "The sword wasn't the only thing he stole. Why didn't they tell us? It looks like he took the Book of Calling."

"Calling?", Ilene asked, sitting on the edge of her bed.

"Well, that's a loose translation of the book's original name. With it you can call on the elements, calm them or aim them on people..."

"Control elemental demons, perhaps?", Ilene suggested, pointing at Charlotte.

"Oh dear! Maybe... but you'd need to be powerful enough to use it and have time to master it."

"Well, he's the only heir to one of the Elders and has had five hundred years to brush up on his skills." Ilene responded.

"What you described seeing and feeling, it sounded like an old punishment that was used on wayward Verndari a long time ago. Sometimes falling at the hands of the corrupt and powerful and then reawakening with powers you never imagined possible would poison the minds of even the most righteous person. Stone imprisonment was used for the most dangerous ones, so they couldn't escape or hurt anyone while final punishment was decided upon. No wonder no-one ever come back! They *physically* couldn't!"

Ilene's mind was ticking over and processing all this new information and a stray thought made Charlotte's eyes bulge.

"What was that?", she demanded.

Ilene shrugged. "I was thinking about his career: CEO, City Council board member, party animal and art dealer...."

Charlotte's jaw set and clenched. There was a tinge of red deep in her blue irises. "...who specialised in sculptures, chiefly Gargoyles."

Ilene wanted to vomit. This man was getting more twisted by the minute.

Charlotte growled and ran from the room at such speed, Ilene blinked a couple of times before she realised that she was gone. She followed sounds of crashing and heavy thuds to the dojo where Charlotte was destroying two of the dummies, the silicone torso and the wooden Wing Chun one. She could hear her screaming in her head. Fury, rage, faces of hundreds of friends, picturing the transactions as they lined the walls, corridors and cathedral ledges. They were now decorations and talismans for the wealthy, instead of the respected warriors they truly were. The light coming from her eyes was leaving streaks and blurs in the air, lines of red and blue, she was moving so quickly.

'Monster!', Charlotte kept screaming. 'Belittling us. Torturing us. Selling us like vases to the HIGHEST BIDDER!"

Charlotte eventually collapsed to the floor, sobbing amongst a cloud of splintered wood and dust. All Ilene could hear was her mumbling the words 'my friends' over and over. She'd never seen her like this. And she couldn't imagine what this felt like for her, to live so long and suffer more and more with each year.

Ilene sat down in front of her. "This is good. It means we can find them- all of them. They're not dead. I'll get stronger so we can take them home and the elders can bring them back. I promise."

Charlotte lifted her puffy, red eyes to her face. "How could he turn us into trinkets?", she asked to no-one in particular. "Why does he hate his own kind so much?"

"I don't know. Maybe if I can get close enough to him..."

"NO!", Charlotte bellowed. "You'll do nothing of the sort. I refuse to look a building one day and see you and Mek'el posed there, mid transformation."

That was another thing Ilene had picked up from Charlotte's memory. That's why Gargoyles looked like humanoid animals, because it was a Vendari reacting to the pain of the Calling, unable to control themselves. And that's how they were frozen when it was finally over.

Ilene would never forget that feeling as long as she lived. The feeling of being slowly dipped into acid or hot oil, burning from the outside in, and then going numb afterwards while the feeling spread upwards. She'd do everything in her power to avoid such a torturous imprisonment.

"Why would he sell us though? It makes no sense. He seems proud. That kind of man would normally display his victories somewhere instead of selling them off." Ilene explored, absent-mindedly.

Charlotte didn't respond. She just sat motionless, weapons next to her on the floor and her will having left her. But her mind still answered the question, venom and anger giving her thoughts power. Shipping frozen Verndarar around the world meant that no matter where he travelled to, he would never be more than a few hundred miles from proof of his power. He was still gloating and proud, but the whole world was his gallery.

"Unless....", Ilene continued muttering to herself. "We're painful reminder of his past, what he did to his parents. So, he sends them from him sight. But why sell them? He's already rich."

"Money is power in this world.". Charlotte whispered. "He's probably bought the police and most security companies, which is probably why we can't leave the country without being intercepted."

Ilene found a broom in the corner cupboard and began cleaning the wreckage. She didn't want to have to give explanations to Amanda and Jason, especially when they realised that the person that did all this had one broken arm. "So, if you go against him as a human, the legal system wouldn't give you any justice and if you do it as one of the Verndarar, you're imprisoned or killed. Great. He's impossible to defeat. All our abilities are useless. Without this.... we're defenceless and there's no hope."

Ilene touched her father's pendant.

Charlotte slowly stood, every century showing in her eyes. 'We need to meet with the others, so we can decide what to do.', she mentally announced, looking a little stronger with every word. 'I'm sorry to say this to you again but please stay put. Don't do anything without consulting myself, Bob and Marcus first.'

Ilene wanted to argue, but she simply nodded. She was so fed up with everyone telling her what to do but thanks to the telepathy she understood the reasoning.

Ilene picked up a weapon and started training to keep herself occupied as Charlotte left the room without hugging her. It was scary to think that despite having powerful Verndarar mentors, she still had to worry about losing them, sitting at home this time wondering if the last sight she had of them would actually be the final time they were together. It made her feel positively mortal... and she hated it.

And so, Ilene waited, amidst the echoes and creaks of an ancient house for her new family to return.

Chapter 16

Revelations

It had been several days since Charlotte had started contacting other Verndarar and searching for Mek'el. The feeling of terror and loss were beginning to swallow Ilene up inside. It was true what they said about not knowing what you had until it was gone, and now it was all she could think about. Every time the front door moved, she strained her ears hoping it was Mek'el. She missed his training, his reassurance and his strength. She missed his strength most of all; she needed that now more than ever.

Ilene kept having nightmares about cities on fire, every person living encased in stone, her house burned to the ground and demons roaming the streets feeding on survivors. Fire, blood and stone. Every night, over and over. Just like her visions of her parents' murder, clearer every night. Fire, blood and stone.

No more humans. No more Verndarar. Just Velhonen laughing over the corpses of his victims whose only sin was being unfortunate enough to be alive the day his plan was fully executable or being one of the Verndarar.

There had been a few close calls with some demons. Even the media had noticed the increase in violence and disappearances. They thought it was kidnappers or human trafficking, and police were engaged in fruitless investigations. Some bodies weren't found because the demons had chewed them up and walked off. But no mention of any mysterious humanoids battling anything. The Verndarar really were the world's best kept secret. There wasn't a blog or a single video with solid evidence, just the usual conspiracy theories and ramblings about myths and legends from different cultures maybe having some validity.

Ilene was sick of being stuck in the house with the only thing that could possibly calm the demons. All she could see was the towering monsters and their glowing eyes advancing and blinded with unfocused rage. She had tried to escape once but didn't even make it to the city limits before Bob landed in front of her like a falling boulder and took her home forcefully. That was the day Charlotte broke several bones and Marcellus lost an eye. Taking Bob from the fight to manage her had been costly. So, she didn't attempt it again.

While Charlotte healed, Ilene reminded her what happened to the last three people who were hell-bent on protecting her above everything. Charlotte simply smiled and said was their choice and they would all do it over exactly the same way if they had another chance.

Ilene's power as Verndarar and importance to taking Velhonen out was getting on her nerves. She didn't ask to be different in a race of super-humans but here she was. She couldn't wait until they had the numbers they needed and a strategy so she could finally have a crack at this psycho and end this nightmare, for everyone's sakes.

Once both Charlotte and Marcellus were healed, they restocked on weapons from the old archive room and left. Each time they left, Ilene became more fearful. All this was too much to take. It was like waiting at home for your cousins and brothers to return from war, fearing that dreaded delivery of the yellow telegram. The demons were stronger than ever and more elusive. Every time they tried to follow them, they'd disappear into the elements and probably reappear somewhere else in the city. Without extensive knowledge of the Callings, they'd never be able to track them at this rate.

Ilene had taken to sitting in her sleeping tree, to keep a mental eye on her friends and listen out for any sign of Mek'el. But all it did was reduce her to tears and give her migraines. And the Varlhari migraines, full of pain from several different minds, were on another level. It felt similar to the night Mek'el had been taken and caused a nosebleed or two. Charlotte was worried that she was straining herself too much, but she had to try. She had to do something.

The sound of the back door of the house closing broke her concentration from that night's efforts. She drew in a slow breath through her nostrils. It was Jason. She knew his scent as well as she knew her own. Even if she hadn't used her nose, her other senses took in so much that she'd have been able to tell by his gait, the weight in the sound of his steps and the unique sound of his breath passing through his bronchus and out of his nose or mouth, which changed depending on how hard he was working or how anxious he was.

Ilene was learning to trust and read her new body. She wondered how she ever lived without all the accurate senses before. She couldn't even remember now.

"Hey, Ilene.", he greeted, as he reached the treeline. "How are things today? I swear, you barely spend any time in the house anymore."

Ilene smiled and huffed a little. Was *everyone* monitoring her now? Or was she just acting that weird? "I'm OK. Feeling a bit better. I don't think I'm ready to go back to work yet though. But I am sick of being stuck indoors."

Jason nodded, pulling a leaf off a bush and fiddling with it absent-mindedly. "So, where's your friend Mike? I haven't seen him in a while. Did you and your sugar daddy have a fight?", he laughed, the way Simeon did when he was teasing. "What is the deal with you two anyway? You know, it isn't romantic, but the way he looks at you... it's protective. Super protective. Like parenting on steroids. And he pulls weird faces sometimes, when he thinks no-one's looking. He's a bit loopy. Or maybe he's running future surgeries over in his mind. You did say that he was a surgeon, right?"

An awkward silence followed this barrage of questions.

215

"No, we didn't fall out. He's... gone missing.", Ilene answered, her voice quivering just a little.

Jason's stunned silence let Ilene know a tonne more questions were on their way. She was right.

"*What*?! How come you didn't say anything? The police, have they got any information? I can't believe you've been dealing with this on your own! Does Mom know?"

"I didn't think I needed to say anything. No, the police aren't involved yet. Too soon. Beatrice already told Amanda. I do things better on my own."

Jason's face was mixture of concern and anger. "That's not healthy. I don't know what your life was like back in the UK, but while you're here, you don't have to shut everyone out. I know you don't really want to."

Ilene clenched her jaw. It was so annoying how observant he was, and the fact that he did it without telepathy made it more impressive *and* irksome.

"We'll find him. We'll be fine.", Ilene answered, but she didn't truly believe it. Jason didn't buy it either.

"No. Come down and look me in the eye. You can fake an even tone all you want. I can still hear the cracks."

There was the sound of brief rustling and the thud of a heavy thing hitting the floor. Jason started to walk forward, wondering if Ilene had fallen, but he saw her coming towards him and stopped, not because she was fine but because she clearly wasn't. She was smiling but her eyes were red from crying or trying not to cry. And they were unfocused too. She was looking at him... but she wasn't.

"Ilene... when are you going to involve the police?", Jason asked slowly. "It's been a few *weeks*!"

Ilene's bottom lip started to tremble. "We can't.", she all but whispered. "We believe he was taken by someone very powerful who had paid off the police."

Jason hugged her immediately before he knew he was doing it. This couldn't be real. She must be terrified. "What can we do?", he asked.

Ilene couldn't hug him back. If she did, her brain would register the sign of weakness, and the tears would flow again. "I've been told to stay put. It's too dangerous. And I can't involve you. Amanda would never forgive me."

Jason stepped back, brow furrowed and bent his head to find her eyes as she was still refusing to look at him.

"First of all, what I do is my choice. Secondly, you're a grown woman. You can do whatever you wish. Now, true, we can't really go arresting or fighting people, but we can sneak around and do some digging. I know you already. You've never done something you didn't completely want to do or given an explanation if you didn't feel it was owed, nor should you start to."

Jason took Ilene's chin in his palm and raised her face to his.

"He means a lot to you. That kind of fast connection is rare. And I know his disappearance is eating you up inside. You think I haven't noticed you pacing along every inch of the grounds?", he quizzed, his brow furrowing more. "I'm going to get the bikes. You get your jacket and helmet. We're going out."

Ilene sighed. He was right. The other three would have to forgive her later. And if they didn't, at least she wouldn't feel so useless.

She must have been just on the edge of the barrier, because as she went inside to pick up her helmet, her phone vibrated. It was a message from Charlotte.

'Observation and sneaking only. No fights. Keep a low profile. Be careful. xx'

Two hours later, Jason and Ilene were driving through the city. They checked at Mek'el's favourite restaurants. Mrs Park was concerned about him as well. The head librarian at the University knew him too and hadn't seen him either. He tended to give biology lectures from time to time. At least he did.

Ilene was feeling better for being able to take part in trying to find him. She wanted to storm into Victor's office, but the security would be all over them and would blow Mek'el's cover story for her.

Ilene scowled every time she saw a monument to Velhonen and his fake legacy. He had been pretending to be his own ancestor for over one hundred years and building his power and reputation. That was the reasons why he was so well protected by the police. She hadn't needed to lie about that. She wondered if there were some Varlharar defectors in the police force backing him up, telling a similar lie about their lineage, faking their deaths and rebirths.

Ilene secretly did her digging regarding Velhonen, in person and on social media. Apparently, no-one had seen him in the city or even in the province for almost a month. She'd need to find out where he was when Jason wasn't with her. She kept her mind clear so it couldn't be heard by unwanted 'ears'.

She and Jason had stopped to get a snack so they would have strength and brainpower to continue their work. Jason could see the unrest behind Ilene's eyes, as she bit into her burger, not really looking at anything, but simultaneously looking through everything.

Ilene sighed. It was getting late. Places would be closing now, everyone would be heading home, and unless they were prepared to do some light stalking, they wouldn't be able to ask anyone any further questions. Plus, she was tired. So tired, she wouldn't be able to do much for long. As if on cue, Jason yawned so wide, the hinge of his jaw clicked, sending them into a quiet fit of giggles.

"You ready to head home?", Ilene asked. He must have been more knackered that her. He was human, after all.

He shrugged and threw his napkin in the nearest bin. "I could go on for a couple more hours.", he lied.

Ilene smiled. He was trying so hard. Why was he being so helpful? "Well, I might have an hour max before you have to drape me over the back of your bike and drive home hoping I don't roll off.", she admitted.

Jason tried to laugh at the mental image. But the thought of that happening made his stomach tight. He noticed a different in Ilene and spoke before he could stop. "I notice you always wear that necklace. It looks old. Did it always glow like that? Or is it because the lighting is different out here?"

Ilene reached for it calmly. If she moved too fast and freaked out, he'd notice.

"It's a gift from my dad, my real one. It's been in the family for years. And yeah, it's probably the lighting out here."

As Jason opened his mouth and started replying and Ilene was wondering why on earth her pendant was glowing when she wasn't even using her powers, she heard something. It sounded like stone rubbing on stone above her. Just when she was about to dismiss it, there was a noise like a boulder cracking in half, deafening to her but barely noticeable to anyone else. And soon she felt what seemed like slight increases in air pressure coming towards her head. There was no more breeze. Something was about to fall on them.

No time to be safe or subtle.

Ilene turned to Jason, stunning him into puzzled silence and placed her hands on his chest. She shoved him into the empty street as hard as she could just before she was crushed by almost a tonne of cement and limestone.

The shops were shut. Barely anything stirred for a good thirty seconds. A couple of lights switched on in the apartments above as disturbed occupants tried to locate the source of the sound.

In that time, Jason had found himself on his side in the centre of a street, his arm scuffed and bleeding from falling and sliding on one side. His jacket was torn. He could have sworn he was pushed... by Ilene. But that was impossible. He was a good fifteen metres from where they had been standing. His chest hurt from where he was pushed. It would definitely bruise later. Jason suddenly remembered the sound he heard before he landed and realised, he couldn't see or hear Ilene.

His breath caught and his skin went cold, as he saw the pile of rubble where Ilene had last been standing. He stumbled forward, calling out to her.

"*Ilene*! Can you hear me? Oh *god*!", he cried. "HELP!! SOMEBODY HELP!"

"What the hell's going on down there?", a man shouted from one of the windows above.

"I- I think part of the building broke off! It fell!! It fell on my friend! Please call an ambulance!", Jason begged.

STONE

His hands were clammy as he stepped over a statue and a fallen streetlight to reach the rubble. As he took a piece of it in his hand to try and lift it, he heard a groan behind him.

He was going to ignore the sound and start digging for Ilene until he remembered he hadn't passed anyone or seen anyone on the street. Just the... Oh my god!!

He turned slowly feeling bile rise to his throat as he watched the statue start to move from the head down, the surface of it turning less and less grey. She was a black woman with smooth dark skin, slim and toned, with shoulder length thick hair. Her beauty only added to how bizarre this situation was. He wanted to scream, he wanted to run but he couldn't move. His legs were like water.

As he stared at the woman coughing and staring at her hands, he heard the rubble shifting behind him, but he still couldn't quite get himself to move. He managed to turn his head and see Ilene push herself out of the humongous mound of rock. He could have sworn her arms looked different but the next time he blinked they looked the same as ever.

Ilene walked straight to him, covered in dust and sediment, not a drop of blood on her. She grabbed his face. "Are you OK, Jason? You're not hurt, are you?", she quizzed, running her eyes and hurried hands over him to check for injuries.

Jason just looked at her, dazed.

Ilene shook her head. "I think you may have knocked your head. I hope it's not too bad."

Jason just pointed in front of him. "The... the statue.", he whispered. His hand was trembling.

Ilene looked at the woman and the woman looked from her hands straight into Ilene's face. Jason saw a weird, intense stare pass between them for a few seconds.

Ilene walked forward and took her hand.

"Jason, we're getting to the bikes and we're heading home. She's coming with us.", she instructed, grabbing his arm. Ilene gave the woman her jacket, as she was dressed in next to nothing. Just a series of leather straps covered in empty holsters.

"OK.", was the only answer Jason could muster.

They left the block just as an ambulance pulled around the corner.

The stranger climbed onto the back of Ilene's bike after shooting a perplexed look at the vehicle. But Ilene gave her a reassuring smile and she simply conceded. It was completely confusing to Jason, but he was so dazed and bruised that he didn't want to ask any questions. He felt like he was going crazy.

He did the whole journey home on autopilot, like he was in the backseat of his own body. He barely remembered arriving home. It was hearing his mom's voice that woke him out of mini hypnosis.

"Guys! Where have you been? Who is this woman? And what happened to you? Was there an accident?"

Ilene had headed straight to the library with the woman and sat her down. She ran into the kitchen to make a cup of tea and something to eat. Who know how long this woman had imprisoned. She wasn't listening to anyone. She was on the phone to Charlotte, who had caught the tail end of what had happened from Ilene's mind. She was on her way over.

Amanda stood listening to Jason's story watching him rubbing his head. He sounded out of his mind, especially when he mentioned superhuman strength and a statue turning into a woman.

When she looked for Ilene as she reassured Jason, she saw her reassuring the stranger. Everyone was freaked out, some more than others, although the stranger didn't seem uncomfortable with her surroundings. First Mek'el went missing, now this... Amanda had a feeling this wouldn't be the end of it. There wouldn't be peace and quiet for quite some time. But it wasn't completely alien to her.

Jason sat in the Games Room to gather his thoughts. He wasn't sure how long he'd been sat there when the front door and Beatrice ran in. She stopped short in the hallway, her head turning straight towards the library in half a second.

The stranger stood and ran straight into her arms sobbing, as they hugged and kissed each other, memories poured back and forth in waves in the one place where emotions could be let loose without detection.

Ilene tried to focus through the buzz and found what she needed. The woman's alias was Celeste, she was an Ethiopian merchant's daughter who was murdered by Spanish soldiers hundreds of years ago and had been one of Charlotte's closest friends until she was captured by Velhonen and turned to stone over thirty years ago. Ilene realised she recognised her face from Charlotte's breakdown in the dojo a few days ago.

'I can't believe it really happened. I don't know how you did it, maybe your emotional state amplified your abilities, but statues have been moving all over the city tonight.', Charlotte informed.

Ilene's mouth briefly opened with a pop, but she was aware other eyes might be watching.

'*What*?! Oh my god! How is that possible?! I haven't even been meditating or training to improve my abilities as much as when Mek'el...'

Charlotte closed her eyes. 'I know, Ilene. Kuruk and Marcellus are looking after them. There is at least a dozen. They'll mentally call out to any they've missed but they'll be careful, so no defectors manage to sneak in.'

'O.K. That's great. We could use the reinforcements. Maybe then we can come up with a plan and take action now. But if there were so many survivors found, why did you come here?'

'Because aside from your mother, Celeste was closest to me. Like a sister. When she disappeared it nearly destroyed me.'

Ilene saw the memory in Charlotte's, her crying like she had done a few days before.

Celeste just sat slightly dazed. Almost as if her telepathy had switched off and she couldn't really hear the conversation. Maybe she couldn't. Had she been mentally conscious while she was encased in her solid, unyielding case cage? Had she gone mad like a prisoner sentenced to decades in solitary confinement? Her thoughts seemed to come in waves, in bursts of noise and then silence. She was traumatized. Her freedom hadn't sunk in yet.

Charlotte continued to comfort her friend, and they hugged each-other and cried more.

Amanda strode, trying to maintain control of her emotions, to get some form of explanation. A half-naked stranger had arrived and her son and possibly Ilene had been hurt. She wanted answers.

"Ilene!", Amanda called in whisper, not wanting to disturb the very emotional reunion. Ilene turned at the sound of her name, but Amanda never took her eyes off the two women, who cried and just stared at each-other. "Who is this woman?"

"She's...a friend of my family, like Beatrice and Mike. We found her. She was held by the same man who we think has Mike. I hope once she's calmed down, she can tell us what happened, so we can get Mike back.", Ilene answered in one breath, and with such confidence it surprised Amanda.

"How did she get out? Won't he be looking for her? He might come to take her back.", Amanda asked, butterflies developing in her stomach. "And isn't this enough evidence to go to the police."

"She got free somehow. I don't think he's realised she's gone yet.", Ilene answered, making sure every word she spoke was the truth. "Also, we need to assess her mental state. Even if the kidnapper hadn't bought the police, what would be the point of bring forward a material witness who is half out of her mind? She seems frazzled!"

Amanda raised an eyebrow. "What do you mean? How long has she been captive for?", she quizzed grabbing Ilene's arm.

Ilene still wanted to be honest. She couldn't answer with the full length of time without freaking Amanda out and thinking they'd kidnapped a child. So, she simply looked over at Celeste and said, "Years."

Ilene seemed to be thinking about something as she left the library and subconsciously went to sit at the foot of the staircase. She was so busy processing the night's events and deciding on her next move, she barely heard Jason walking up to her.

"Ilene, what the hell is going on? I think I'm going crazy! I've seen things tonight that... Never mind, why did you bring that woman...thing or whatever she is here without so much as a word?", he hissed.

Ilene recoiled and felt her temper flare at the use of the word 'thing'. She didn't like the idea of someone dehumanising her or people like her, although she was probably the most dehumanised creature he would ever meet, in every sense.

"We did speak, Jason. You hit your head, maybe you blacked out for a second and missed the conversation.", Ilene was angry already, and now she was furious for having to tell the second lie of the night to the same person, the person who was concerned about her without even knowing the full story. Maybe alienating him would be safer.

Jason took in a large breath and held it while he looked at Ilene's tired but stubborn face. She clearly wasn't going to offer more information. The look in her eyes said: 'That's that' and it really wound him up. He wanted to shout, scream or scare the full story out of her. Even a little.

"I know this isn't my house or anything, but isn't it a bad idea to have a stranger here who looks like an escaped bondage victim? What if she slits your throat? How much do you know about her?"

"Enough to know my parents trusted her.", Ilene answered in a level voice, fighting to keep her own temper at bay.

Jason growled. "Yeah, and that equates to the full amount you know about your *own parents*. You're pinning a lot on two people you NEVER MET!", he was getting closer and slowly louder now. "No-one should be content with half the information about their own history. Or not being able to go to the police when their friend is kidnapped. But *you* clearly are! You sit here trusting strangers, not asking for help to find your friend, for all we know is *dead*, and allowing yourself to be put under house arrest for some bizarre and unknown reason. Why won't you fight? Why won't you react or investigate when there are holes in explanations? Why won't you act like a normal person?!"

Ilene had her head down during this tirade of confusion and fury. Charlotte, Celeste and Amanda had come out of the library. Ilene's fists were clenched, and she could hear Celeste and Charlotte shouting inside her head to stay calm and leave. But her own mental voice along with the others and her own frustration and grief had mixed together and reached the boiling point. So, she exploded.

"Because I'm *not normal*! And it's too dangerous, especially for you.",

226

she screamed, in a voice that shook the hallway. Now everyone was silent.

"But not for *you*?", Jason asked, suddenly concerned and sad again. Ilene just nodded, but other than that she didn't move.

Jason breathed again but more shakily as if he was afraid of what was coming next, but he knew because he was going to do it. In a voice, so quiet only the Verndarar heard it, he asked, "You're not human, are you."

No-one moved and the only ones now breathing were the two actual humans.

Jason kept his voice low, although it shook as he spoke. He knew how he sounded. "I know what I saw. You pushed me almost twenty metres away with one arm and survived...what should have *killed* anybody else. And I think... I saw your arm. I still can't believe what I saw. But I know...I know I saw it."

She could feel the tears coming and she didn't want anyone to see them. The cracks in her defences were turning into fissures. This was getting out of hand. She stood at human speed and moved upstairs before Jason could query her more.

Once she was of human fields of vision, she wolf-ran to her room and locked the door. She didn't care who heard what. She cried and screamed, like she'd been wanting to for days. She was a fool. Jason was right. She was trusting people based on her parents' past. For all she knew, Mek'el was dead, but she couldn't get the police involved to help. She was alone, confused, exhausted and frustrated. As she cried, she could hear Charlotte and Celeste hearing her pain and crying also. Celeste cried because she was just learning of her parents' death for the first time and Charlotte cried because she hated hearing her in pain.

She heard Jason deciding to sleep in the games room and finding the spare blankets and sheets in the basement laundry room. He was still concerned even though he was clearly puzzled and disappointed by her.

Once she'd worn herself out, Ilene climbed into her parents' bed and just lay listening to the sounds of the house. She could hear Jason tossing and turning. Was he still angry or still curious? Either way, it would either end with him acting on his own, going to the police and maybe ending up the same as Mek'el.

Ilene was at war with her own mind. What should she do?

Jason was somewhere between half awake and nightmares. He wasn't sure if Beatrice and her friend were still in the house. When he closed his eyes, he saw scaly demons and destruction. It was clear he wasn't going to sleep tonight.

He got up and looked in the other room. His mum was fast asleep on another sofa, but this one was in the library. This room was all about organisation and comfort. Stiff leather couches and leather-bound ten-pound books don't go together, although that traditional library look would match the house.

Jason decided to go to the dojo. The water feature always gave him a feeling of peace.

As he walked past Ilene's room, he felt his annoyance grow a bit. If what he saw was real, could her trust her? Should he report her? Would the government take her away? Also, if it *was* true, no wonder she was stressed and distracted, to have that to handle on top of everything else: the adoption bomb, her dad's friend going missing and adjusting to a new life.

Jason got a few large cushions out from the dojo storage cupboard, the ones he saw Ilene meditate on sometimes when the stone floor got too uncomfortable. She'd outgrown them. She was tougher now. Maybe that's why she could handle everything that was going on, as she'd already conditioned her mind and body.

As he laid down and down his eyes, he listened to the water. He felt sleep start to engulf him, but he was less afraid now. He smiled. Maybe he was a little strong too.

Tak!

Jason's finger twitched, still content and relaxed at last.

Plink!

His brow furrowed. Nooooooo! Just as he was rested, too. He heard a hinge moving but refused to open his eyes. Whoever it was could just get lost. Then he remembered that the dojo had a Japanese sliding door as did everything in the room except the window.

BOP!

Jason cried out as a sudden pain struck him in his temple. He opened his eyes to see a pebble spinning on the polished wooden floor.

His skin goose-pimpled with fear and also the cold breeze from outside. He lifted his head and eyes hesitantly.

Hovering just past the window was a winged figure. It was so dark Jason couldn't see clearly, but he could suddenly hear his own breathing filling his terrified ears. He thought he'd escaped his nightmares for the day. The only difference was the figure's eyes were changing from beams or dots of light blue to yellow instead of maintaining a bloodthirsty glow of red.

If he just closed his eyes and reminded himself it wasn't real, so he could break himself out of this part of the dream. He laid his head back onto the cushion.

"I've gotta stop eating fast food before bed.", he grumbled, "My dreams get so weird when I do."

Ilene huffed and threw another pebble, remembering to be gentle. "Oi!"

Jason cried out and woke up fully this time. He leapt up a little, moving himself onto his knees, eyes wide, trying to speak.

Ilene groaned internally. Oh well. No going back now. Charlotte might break her legs for this, but she was trying to do the right thing. Thankfully she was away with Celeste meeting with the other rescues. This was the only time she could do this without someone older, wiser and faster stopping her.

She just prayed Jason wouldn't run. She lowered herself onto the windowsill and folded her wings down, but she didn't get rid of them. He had to adapt to what was physically in front of him before she started showing him her ability to change herself.

She leaned a little forward into the light.

Jason took it all in. He wasn't sure if she was breathing now. He couldn't hear anything, not even the waterfall next to him.

Ilene's arms were the same as ever except her skin looked thicker and was partially covered in thin dark scales. Her nails were long, thicker and pointed like claws. Her feet were similar. And there were a pair of wings neatly folded behind her slender back. He was sure they were hanging past the windowsill. If this had been anyone else, he'd have been terrified but because he knew her, he had the calmness of mind to take in everything. Three words kept bouncing around his mind: powerful, mystical and... beautiful. Despite all these attributes, despite Ilene's tangible nervousness, the way she looked and how she held herself was breath-taking.

Jason smiled, taking in a deep breath to steady the shaking of his hands as he stood up.

Ilene grinned back and the yellow in her irises vanished into a bright crisp blue, and slowly stepped down and walked forward a few steps.

"So, ... you aren't human?", Jason asked, walking, taking slow, small steps around her and appraising her. His fear was turning into curiosity. He couldn't contain it, which surprised even him. All his life, he'd hoped to see something beyond his world and there it was. Here *she* was.

Ilene laughed a little and shook her head, keeping her eyes on his every move. "No. Not since I got here. Actually, now that I think about it, I've never been fully human."

"Wow! You have *wings*!" Jason gasped, part of him wanting to touch them. All of a sudden, he couldn't stop talking. "I can't deny it, I'm jealous. Is Mike one too?".

Any sane person wouldn't be stepping near and asking questions.

"Yes.", Ilene answered. She was scared this calm and light-hearted behaviour would suddenly vanish. This was going almost too well.

"Is this like a werewolf thing? Does it happen at certain times or when the moon's up? Is that why I've found you outside in the trees sometimes?", Jason quizzed, checking Ilene's legs now.

"It was kind of to start with. I apologise that you had to see that.", Ilene replied, embarrassment filling her whole body, including the extra parts. "But I can control it now."

Ilene raised her clawed hand in front of Jason's face so he could watch and accept what he was about to see. Baby steps. She slowly and gently changed just that hand back to normal. His jaw dropped and then it lifted slightly into a child-like grin, like a little boy at a magic show.

"Amazing! Does it hurt?", he asked.

Ilene shrugged, hearing her wings brushing against the floor. Jason leaned to look at them again. "No. Just felt really weird the first few times. But now... I can't believe I've gotten used to it." Ilene was now staring into space, taken a back at how something this bizarre could ever become normal to someone.

"What's your wingspan like?", Jason asked, suddenly serious, as if he was taking notes.

Ilene laughed. "Do you have a yard stick? I don't know, frankly. Want to see?"

Jason nodded wildly and started walking, almost jogging, backwards.

Ilene kept her movements slow, and unfurled her wings, feeling the strain on her shoulder blades and dorsal muscles increase. She looked to her left and right and looked at her wings properly for the first time. They were gigantic. They had to be big to carry her weight and any additions she made to herself.

She heard Jason let out a little squeak. He was bouncing on the spot like someone who really needed to pee. His hands were over his mouth like a pageant winner, and his eyes creased as he smiled.

Ilene smiled a devilish smile as she suggested something dangerous. She didn't know what possessed her to ask this. She was a little nuts tonight. "Want to take them for a test drive?"

Jason's smile dropped slowly. "How? I'm a little afraid of heights-"

"As is any rational person.", Ilene interjected, nodding.

"-but I can't climb on your back.", Jason explained. "How would I hold on?"

Ilene looked around her. There had to be something. She was the curtain tiebacks, thick as mooring rope, and she had an idea. "Jason, grab the armchair from the hallway.", she instructed, turning towards him, eyes bright with excitement.

He was back in seconds and handed it to Ilene with a slight nostril exhale. Ilene lifted it and tested its firmness like it was nothing. She then took the tiebacks, which she'd already removed and began tying them under the seat, wrapping it around the top of the legs for extra security. She hovered off the ground slightly holding the ropes to make sure the chair stayed level, setting back down when she was happy with it.

Ilene ran and opened the windows wide. She lifted the chair and put it on the ground floor outside, away from any windows. If she tried taking off holding the chair with Jason in it, she'd have to jump and then unfurl her wings. The sudden jerk might shake him from the chair, and there goes the good first impression.

Instead, Ilene stood on the windowsill, her back to the outside, started to flutter a little and reached her hand out to Jason.

He was keyed up already from watching the preparations. He stepped up to the windowsill.

"First you throw stones at my window, now you're going to carry me to a chair as if we're crossing the threshold. I feel like I'm in a romantic comedy.", Jason commented, taking her hand.

Jason's face clouded with a sceptical expression. "I swear, if you start singing 'A Whole New World', I'm going back to sleep.", he grumbled, faking a pouty expression.

Ilene laughed, because of the similarity in their current and impending situation. "No. No singing, I promise. It's not a superpower of mine anyway. I still suck at it."

She took Jason off the window easily holding his waist, smiling to keep him at ease. They drifted gently down, Jason securely in her arms, and placed him gently in the chair.

Jason heard Ilene cry out "Ooh!" and in a gust of air, she vanished. By the time he turned, she was gone. In a few seconds, she reappeared with a winter coat that belonged to her father, simply jumping from the dojo window this time and landing with a scattering of gravel. She handed it to Jason. "You'll need this. It gets chilly up there."

Jason was already half inside it once she finished speaking.

"You ready?", Ilene asked, taking the ropes in her grip.

"Let's do this!", Jason almost shouted, before suddenly remembering the fact that they were sneaking off in the early hours and grimacing. They both shushed each-other and giggled like naughty children.

"O.K. If you need anything, just say. Even against the wind, my hearing is very good.", Ilene urged, with a wink.

Jason nodded and settled back into the chair, gripping its arms. His heart began to pound in his chest, and he began to wonder how much Ilene could actually hear, and in an inexplicable response, he blushed.

Ilene fluttered her wings slowly, picking up speed once she felt the chair start to lift. She lifted Jason gently until he was higher than the house.

She heard Jason take in a long breath. She waited for him to exhale, and nothing came.

"Are you alright?", she called, looking down.

He wasn't moving, all she could see was the top of his head, the brown fur coat and the paleness of his knuckles as he gripped the arms of his seat.

He didn't seem to have heard her. But then she heard him speak. It was barely a whisper, but the tone put Ilene at ease immediately.

"Just look at it.", he breathed, an audible smile in his voice.

Ilene looked forward at what he was seeing. He saw the edge of the city and the nearby village. She was so used to flying now that she didn't truly pay attention to what it looked like. She forgot what it was like to see it all for the first time. The stars accented the deep darkness of the night's sky, the moon threw silver on everything it could reach, peeking out from behind small clouds. The mountains stood tall like guards over the world she already guarded, and the trees gave the breeze a voice. The city light brought a strange pale orange glow to one section of the horizon.

Ilene turned around slowly. They weren't heading that way. It was unsafe. She had to head North as fast as her wings could take her and keep her mind clear, so Charlotte and all her friends didn't suddenly come after her. She didn't know how forbidden it was to let a human know of their existence. Although Mek'el had instilled of these fears in her about it, she know she could trust Jason. And she didn't normally trust anyone. Every part of her brain reeled against trusting anyone but herself.

She kept them close to the ground, but not too close to hit trees or be seen. She could hear where people were, even feel the heat from their bodies, so she steered clear of them.

They flew over Mamquam mountain and through Garibaldi Provincial Park, all the nocturnal wildlife stopping in their tracks to watch them fly overhead. Then Ilene reached Lilloet Lake and flew low enough to skim Jason's feet along its surface, right along its full curve. By now he was laughing clearly, having the time of his life and completely relaxed. Ilene was happy to not to feel like a freak to someone outside of her family. Even when she was just a human teen, people around her reacted to any sort of difference or skill with anger, bitterness, cruelty and distance. All those trophies, all those hobbies, all those worlds she was part of, but she had no close friends. And here was this perfectly ordinary human guy who knew who she was *and* what she was but wasn't repulsed. Well...not for now anyway.

"THE BIRDS!"

Jason's gleeful voice shook her out of her thoughts, and she looked to their right, following her other senses and seeing a flock of birds in a V formation. She smiled and looked down.

"Want to join them?", she asked.

Jason turned his head up to face her. His smile was wide, he'd got the deepest crinkles at the corner of his eyes. Ilene had never seen him like this, and it was infectious. "Aren't we already?", he said in his normal volume. His grin somehow grew when he saw Ilene's reaction to what normal people could never have heard. Ilene grinned back and started nodding eventually as she considered his question. He was right. They were already there.

Ilene had also decoded his expression, the look of joy and incredulity bursting from his eyes and smile.

They stayed near to the flock until they turned and headed elsewhere. Ilene started to look for a place to set down. She spotted a relatively flat mountaintop that wasn't too high but still provided a great view of the surrounding scenery.

"Time to touch down!", she called, laughing when she heard Jason's disappointed whine from below.

Ilene was extra gentle lowering the chair and its contents in case Jason's adrenaline high gave way to nausea.

Ilene touched her feet back to the earth and sat on the floor at the right of Jason's chair and then gazed at the world before them, their beautiful, damaged and surprising world, busy even in the dark.

The sun would start rising soon.

They sat in a silence for a quite a while, Ilene in just her jeans and a T-shirt watching absolutely everything around her. Jason was watching Ilene and wondering two things. First, how she wasn't blue already from the cold and how to break the silence. What was worth saying after being given an experience like the one he just had? His mom had always told him to keep things simple, so he started with the first thing in his mind.

"Thanks, Ilene.", he said, smiling and looking out in front of him. "This...is beyond anything I could have imagined seeing. And so are you."

Ilene just smiled.

"Also, beyond just my 'magic carpet' experience, thank you for changing the way I see this world. I was feeling so depressed lately, thinking that University, working, retirement and death was all there was to everyone's life here. I thought everything was just monotonous, doomed and boring. But now that I know that there's more to this world, I feel happier. Honestly, I'm still slightly terrified but I'm happy. So, what are you?"

Ilene smirked. Now it was her turn. She turned toward him and filled him in with the basic: Gaia, the other realm, the demons, her parents and how she ended up spending 17 years in England.

Jason just leant nearer, his feet curled up under the coat, hanging on every syllable. "So, ... how many of you are stuck here?", he quizzed. "How many have you met?"

"I don't know and six, one of them being the psycho who offed my parents."

Jason gulped and some of his facial muscles twitched nervously. So, there were not only cool and good ones but demons and bad people from her realm? Geez. How was she not breaking down constantly knowing this? It would freak him out. He knew there was something odd about her, but he would never imagine it'd be something along the lines of saving the day, nightly.

"Do you think my mom knows about this or do you think she's just insanely calm about everything in general?", Jason quizzed, looking out into the sky.

Ilene tipped her head back a bit as she thought. "I'm not sure. I get the feeling she has some clue. It's impossible to know how she knows."

"Well, it's a shame you can't read human minds...which is super cool by the way and explains a lot."

Ilene huffed a quick laugh. "I can't believe anyone in this day and age uses the word 'cool'."

Jason went to playfully swipe at her, but her wing lifted to block it before he'd reached her. He smiled again. It was like having a live-in guardian angel.

"Don't you experience any...overly private or gross thoughts?", Jason wondered, looking again to the horizon.

Ilene realised the answer and was pleasantly surprised. And grateful. She'd been around predominantly Verndarar men and had escaped any embarrassment.

"No. Only unexpected painful memories from the last few centuries.".

"...centuries...", Jason whimpered, astonishment and disbelief filling every syllable.

"They've developed incredible mental control. I can't believe I've never noticed. I've never felt or heard... *that,* even a whisper, in any of their minds. I guess after
five-hundred or so years after losing friends and family, surviving death and looking the embodiments of the greatest of the Seven Sins in the eye, basic human needs aren't important."

Jason could feel himself blushing at his next thought. He tried to keep his heart rate and temperature down, urging himself, violently, to calm down and stop feeling so embarrassed around someone younger than him.

Ilene kept her face as still as stone. She could hear and feel all his changes. She wanted to smile but he might literally die of embarrassment, and she want him to still talk to her.

"We're not all like that though. I'm still a red-blooded woman. Must run in the family. Or else I couldn't be here.", she admitted.

That thought made her chuckle, picturing two respected warriors from a proud and composed people throwing caution and restraint to the wind. It didn't even gross her out; knowing that they loved each-other so deeply that they defied the laws of their superiors made her oddly proud. Judging by what Mek'el and Charlotte had told her about her mother, she was most likely the lead troublemaker.

Thinking Mek'el's name suddenly wiped the smile off her face.

"Come on. It's dawn.", Ilene announced, indicating towards the growing light at the horizon with a jerk of her head, as she stood.

"Let's get home before your Mum finds us both missing and freaks out."

Jason nodded but didn't move. He didn't even hold the chair's arms. Progress: he trusted her.

In a matter of seconds, they were aloft and trying to beat the rays of the morning sun to the manor. They didn't quite manage it, but Amanda was still asleep. Ilene let Jason out of the chair into the dojo window. If he went through the back or front door, Amanda would wake. She soon followed and put everything back in its place.

She met Jason in the hallway, and they smiled mischievously at each-other before returning to their last humanly known locations.

Ilene lay still and listened to Jason creep into the Games room and settle back into his blanket on the sofa. Amanda didn't even sigh, let alone stir.

Jason started to drift off and jolted at the near-sleep feeling of falling. He'd settled so well in his original spot that he remembered his flying experience and instantly wondered if he'd dreamt it. But then he looked down and saw that the hem of jeans was still damp with lake water and he grinned. It has all been real. And with that knowledge he sighed and settled again, sleeping soundly and dreamt of armoured angels protecting him and his mother from towering monsters.

STONE

I J FERRESTONE

Chapter 17

After All This Time

In the weeks that followed, Ilene and Jason spent evenings and weekends searching for more imprisoned Verndarar around the country and bringing them back. Jason's knowledge of the city and local areas, and strangely accurate memory of the locations of all the statues really helped. Sometimes it was just a statue but at the other times, they got lucky.

The news started covering the story of art thief groups and vandals to try and explain how heavy sculptures placed metres off the ground could go missing with a trace. This made them chuckle but at the same time it meant they had to do things even more carefully.

Ilene had to shut down nearby cameras with help from Charlotte who surprisingly had some skills with computers that went far beyond calendars, spreadsheets and meeting bookings.

Ilene had been surprised at her lack of anger with her decision to tell Jason the truth. In a mental conversation shared the day they arrived home with another rescue; Charlotte had let her know that they had formed alliances with a select few trusted humans in the past. Hence how things little things like mood rings to big things like marine exploration and flight has come into creation with their help. Also, after seeing Ilene's thought process, Charlotte agreed that allowing Jason's anger and curiosity to go unchecked would have likely ended with him being killed, which went against their mission of preserving human life.

Of course, having to strip and drop her body temperature to be 'invisible' to avoid any security measures they had missed was embarrassing at first, but Jason turned his back every time, like a gentleman, and held her clothes until she got back. If she found no-one, she came back, but if she found someone, she contacted him with a specific sound to signal to meet him at home, as she was carrying or accompanying the person.

Soon the Manor was filling up and the air was full of happiness. Amanda was going along with it. She recognised a few of the new arrivals, which only made Ilene more suspicious.

She had to be in on it all. Maybe Amanda was one of those few trusted humans Charlotte had spoken of. How could her parents hire a human woman to take care of a house which was essentially the Verndarar's Canadian Headquarters and *not* have told her or had her question things at some point? Ilene had the odd feeling Jason's ire at being kept out of the loop of suspicious activity was a learnt trait.

Ilene had spent evenings when she wasn't out searching, chatting with Jason, sneaking out to his and Amanda's apartment to discuss their next step. It was on these nights Jason would suggest other activities, not only to get Ilene used to the city and have good cover story to keep Amanda off their backs, but to have some balance in their lives. It couldn't be demons, deaths and missions all the time or they'd both go crazy, especially Ilene, who had a direct line to every Verndari thought in a ten-mile radius, depending on how strong she was feeling. They did everything from galleries to the cinema, although Jason complained that he'd been annoyed by someone talking throughout the whole film. Ilene hadn't heard anything above the snacking, but she shrugged it off.

Their last rescue had involved two very stubborn and angry water demons at the pier which Ilene managed to subdue before using her connection to her father's pendant to return the element to its correct docile state, which had been a big deal. The others were very happy to hear this. Charlotte was brimming with pride, and they did a big celebratory dinner. The other Verndarar couldn't contain their hope at this news. They were all thinking the same thing: they could go home. Despite the pressure of this collective thought, Ilene was excited by it too.

During one of the down-time nights, Jason had taken Ilene to a music festival to let her dance off some steam.

Ilene quickly found them a booth. She was getting more comfortable in herself. When Jason first saw her, her hair was always pulled back and her clothing was baggy. But now she was capable of hunting the world's unknown terrors without backup, she wore her hair down more, curls full and healthy, but always kept a hairband on her wrist, in case something happened. Hair tended to get in the way when you were fighting. Her clothes were form-fitting, even outside the dojo. She was wearing more black items with metal on them. Ilene smiled when she noticed Jason looking at her outfit. She leaned over, having to shout above the rumbling beat. "You like?"

Jason nodded. "Looks cool."

Ilene face formed an expression to show she was touched. "Thanks. It's because I miss my brother Simeon, to be honest."

She pulled out her phone and, for the first time, showed Jason her pictures and memories. She hadn't had anyone to share anything with at home. And she'd shared memories since she got to Canada, but by accident. Not like this. Not in a way that felt so...human. It was nice and funnily enough didn't make her feel sad at all.

Jason smiled at each picture of Ilene's old life, taking note of Ilene's sweeter, more innocent face, and then he excused himself to get them some shots. Ilene sent a quick email and selfie to Fred and Diane in reply to their message from the day before. She was grateful that she'd remembered to leave her sword at home, as you got patted down at the venue's entrance. Thankfully, Charlotte had lent her a variation of her belt, so she was covered in case of any incidents.

As she watched Jason shimmying his way back over, she smiled at how well he carried all this new information. She only told Jason her Verndari friends' aliases, partially because she didn't want him to slip and say their real names in front of the wrong person. But also, it was because he had enough to remember. She was worried if she gave him too much information, the scales would tip, and it'd send him over the edge.

They downed their drinks in rapid succession, laughing at each-other's uncontrollable expressions when the taste hit the wrong spot. Theresa had never been one for drinking, but Ilene was stronger and had a higher metabolism.

Ilene leapt onto the dancefloor once her glasses were empty and started to move with a confidence and fluidity that had to be due to her training. She was not a confident anything before, let alone a dancer, even when she'd done her gymnastic routines.

Jason hadn't gotten up yet. He just watched her, and he wasn't the only one looking. Everything she did was unearthly and fascinating from the way she handled weapons, like they were part of her, the way she flew and now the way she danced. In the dim hive of movement, he swore he could see her irises glowing sky blue every time she looked up.

Jason felt himself tense up as he noticed two men, taller and older than him, heading towards her from opposite sides of the floor. He got and started heading for Ilene, all new information and her inhuman strength forgotten, but the crowd made moving tough. He wasn't going to reach her in time. But he needn't have worried. The one behind her got their first, and although he couldn't see the guy's hands, he knew where they'd gone as he saw Ilene start for a moment. Her eyes changed colour in a flash. Yellow for the briefest moment, and then a smouldering red, like the dying glow of coals. She turned to him, grinning. Jason was suddenly moving much faster, the object of his fear unexpectedly changing. If he didn't get there first, he'd end the night giving a police statement that even he couldn't explain without sounding like he was high.

Ilene simply reached up and placed her hand at the base of his neck to pull his head to hers. Jason saw her face disappear to the side of the brute's, probably by his ear. Suddenly the man's whole body tensed. When he pulled back, he recoiled, looked over her at the other man with wild panic in his eyes and shoved his way through the crowd in the opposite direction with force and brute strength that proved he would have been a problem for a human woman. Ilene turned toward the other man, and his knees buckled. Ilene was already heading back to the booth as the man tumbled backwards, escaping the chaos this caused. Jason could have sworn before she lowered her head, to walk towards, she'd been sporting longer and different teeth than he was used to seeing in her smile.

Ilene sat down getting her face under control. She was somewhere between anger and elation. She just triumphed in a situation the old her would have lost in. Sure, she could have broken a few fingers to teach a lesson but how would that help? The last thing she needed was to make it easier for Velhonen to find her.

Jason sat next to her, unsure of what to do. Did he even need to bother to check if she was ok? She'd clearly had the upper hand. But she looked up and he saw a faint glimmer of yellow in her eyes. She *had* been scared. After all, even with her new abilities, her old human nature kicked in when normal human situations came up.

Jason put his arm around her shoulder and gave her a squeeze. Even against the din, his ears picked up her voice. "That was scary.", she whispered.

Ilene looked up at Jason and pulled off a smile. "I could hear you rushing to help me despite...", she began. What could she end that with? Being only human? It being an uneven match? Being smaller than even *one* of the men heading for her? "How are you so brave?",

Ilene asked, her brow furrowed.

Jason shrugged, looking off into nothing. "I've had good examples.", he stated.

Ilene nodded. "Your mum."

Jason nodded in answer and looked back down at her face. "You too."

For the first time in months, Ilene blushed. Like, really blushed. Jason felt her freeze and felt her skin temperature jump up under his arm. Then she exhaled and her irises started to glow a cotton candy pink. Jason had never seen this colour in her eyes before, and he wondered what it meant.

She rested her head on his shoulder for a moment. This felt nice...and new. Maybe it was the alcohol in her system that was making her relax so much. She didn't know when she'd get a day like this again.

Suddenly she was angry. She was tired of being always on edge, always afraid and having to tip-toe around a whole country. How would they ever be able to come up with a plan to bring all this misery to an end? "Know thine enemy.", she whispered, her brow furrowed with concentration.

She sat and put her hand on Jason's shoulder, looking him dead in the eye in a way that startled him, as she'd been leaning on him a second before.

"I'll meet you at home. I have to do something dangerous.", she announced.

Jason was stumped by the change in mood. He managed to follow her out of the venue. She was heading to the centre of the city, towards the tallest building. He recognised it.

"What the hell, Ilene?", he gasped, trying to keep up with her determined march.

"I've got to do some surveillance. You can't come. You could get caught or arrested."

"But-"

"No buts. You're human. You can't do anything to help me.", Ilene states, her focus on her mission weakening her mental filter.

Jason pursed his lips together and let out an angry breath through his nostrils. "Well, this weak little human couldn't really help you all those *other* times either. But you let me come along."

Ilene spun around on the spot so suddenly, he almost collided with her. Usually their tempers matched each-other but the look on her face was pained.

"I could handle those situations. One or two demons? No problem. Four or five? Might need some support, but not yours. Having you with me for your knowledge of the city is useful...and also the way to keep an eye on you so you didn't run off and do something...bloke-ish and stupid."

Jason's shoulders raised as he inhaled and held his breath to keep his temper under control. The way she said "bloke-ish" and "stupid" made it sound synonymous. It pissed him off. Yes, there wasn't much he could do, and it was all terrifying, but he wanted to help, just like her.

Ilene stepped closer and spoke softer than he was used to.

"But this is the man who controls most of the demons I've fought, who has imprisoned hundreds of my kind and took away the two people who loved me most in this world."

Jason heard her voice grow more frantic as she spoke and break as she mentioned her parents. On instinct, he took hold of her hand.

"I'm going to watch him, get some information, track his movements, maybe figure out where his base of operations is so we can take to him and *end this!*", Ilene hissed, gripping Jason's hand tight. "But if he sees me or catches both of us together, he'll lithify me, kill you and get away with it scot-free. It'll kill Amanda and break me. I won't let it happen."

They walked into a nearby alley and Ilene took off her jacket ready to sprout her wings.

"O.K, you don't have to take me with you all the way. Just put me on a nearby rooftop so if anything happens, I can climb down and get help. Also, if you're gonna break into a historical building I can help. You know my degree is in architecture and engineering, right?"

Ilene sprouted wings and formed an expression of sarcastic surprise and fascination. "Wow.", she muttered. She sighed and shook her head, turned to Jason and held out her left arm as he got closer and put his arm around her waist, mirroring the action, like they always had been doing lately. He felt that being scooped up in her arm was emasculating. He tensed as Ilene bent her legs and sprung upwards with a neat and powerful jump.

The night was a little cloudy which would give good cover on the way home. Ilene found a slightly lower rooftop nearby that Jason could stay on, concealed, and broke the door to the stairwell so Jason could escape easily if things went bad.

Then she climbed into the clouds and glided down silently to the glass roof of the Hillman Consolidated towering building. She dropped her temperature to be undetectable to any infra-red cameras and landed noiselessly on the steel roof. It looked so old, like something from Prohibition times, maybe older. She was careful not dislodge any old fittings and give herself away. The roof had a glass panel in the centre pointing up into a pyramid shape, making the building look like the pyramids when they were first built, with light at its peak.

She craned her neck, peeping into the skyline. She could hear footsteps. In a matter of seconds, the man she was looking for walked into view. He was on the phone, dressed in another finely tailored suit, and he was clearly rattled. David stood, unmoving nearby and awaiting instruction as normal.

"Yes....Yes, Yamamoto-san, I understand. I don't know how this keeps happening. Yes, of course! We will catch those responsible."

Velhonen hung up the call silently, lowering his hand. Before spinning round to face David, the whole of both of his eyes glowing a hypnotic bright red. He swung out and smashed a nearby table, sending paperwork and splinters cascading to the floor. He was shaking with rage, the colour in his eyes looking like leaking beams of light. He was struggling to contain himself.

"That was the *THIRD CALL TODAY*!", he exploded. "My customers have noticed a link between them missing statues. They're all *mine*! *My* prizes! *My* captures! They're demanding refunds, which I can't do. These rich fools never think to insure some of the art they buy."

David answered evenly and coolly. "Well, you wouldn't think you'd have to insure two tonnes of stone. It's meant to be physically impossible to steal them."

"Why would those stupid Verndarar steal them? They can't do anything with them."

"Well, after examination, the sites of the, ahem, "thefts", I've noticed the stone around and under the figures were still there, sometimes on the floor in pieces, as if they took the figures but left the mounting base.", David advised, swiping through images gathered on his tablet, the one that ran both of their lives.

Velhonen froze. "As if they broke free and walked off."

Velhonen ran a frantic hand through his silver-blonde hair. "That's not possible! No-one should be able to undo the spell or use the blue re-entry stone even if they found it. It can only be used by the person who was chosen for it, and I *killed him*! It can't be re-assigned since no-one can get to the realm!"

He was pacing again. Ilene clutched her father's pendant, fighting to keep her breath and heart rate as slow as possible. If she could listen a little longer, she could learn something useful."

"Someone is mocking me.", Velhonen muttered. "Get the police on it. Take the list of my clients, install extra cameras near any of my statues anywhere in the world. Stop, search and arrest anyone trying to get near them."

"Whoever has been taking my prizes. I'm going to find them. I'll break them and find out where they learnt to set them free. If they are using the stone, I'll find a way to use it myself and start the attack on schedule. The elders won't stand a chance, even if they've got every Verndari soldier back and revived, they won't be able to stand against our numbers. I have the strength of their strongest in my body and their generals are my prisoners.", he gloated, vocalising his self-assurances, subconsciously looking to his right at the large oil painting standing against the bare brick wall.

"Why get them back *now*? And why is it even bothering you?", David quizzed, folding his arms. "After the attack they'll either be destroyed, or you can turn them back to stone."

"BECAUSE...", Velhonen exploded again, his arms bulking out, tearing the seams of his sleeves as claw protruded from his fingers. "Whoever is taking them is not only defying me but may have something in their possession which gives them the upper hand.

Only *I* should be in control. What was the point of spending *centuries* amassing this wealth and respect and getting control of the police, military, politicians and media in this and every other country if the people I'm targeting are just going to side-step it all?"

Ilene smiled. She tried not to think about how satisfying it was knowing she'd gotten under his skin. She used Mek'el's White Room concentration technique to keep her mind clear and present. She was only thinking of what was being said in the room below.

Velhonen was trying to breathe evenly, his body slowly returning to normal. He'd never been taught how to control his powers and emotions. The people who had tried to give him therapy of teach him to meditate usually wound up dead.

"The demons are growing in number thanks to the increasing fear, anger and despair in this world. I contribute, of course, by keeping the corrupt people in positions of power and sending those feelings out into the media. I keep the good people poor and feeling unable to change anything and the bad rich. If any good ones try to help, I distract the masses with fluff pieces, new diseases and mental segregation. I keep life just bearable enough to keep them from offing themselves, because if they do that, I don't get to benefit from their despair."

Ilene was trying not to react, to push down the feeling of utter horror and disgust building in her gut. It was utterly despicable. He was ruining lives to gain an army. But why? Humans would nuke, shoot and hunt him if he really tried anything. What could he take in this world that he didn't already have?

David chuckled and shook his head. "Sir, you are something else.", he acknowledged.

Velhonen was smiling now, and his Head of Security was grinning sadistically. They clasped forearms.

"After all these years of planning, my friend," David said, "Soon we will have enough soldiers."

Velhonen nodded, his irised swirling pools of yellow and red. "And then... I'll set right what was done to me... done to all of us, all those centuries ago."

Ilene froze. She couldn't read his mind clear enough, but he could feel his pain and anger. So much pain. It clawed at him on the inside like an animal, and Ilene felt every wave of it.

Velhonen and David let go of each-other's arms. David's eyes fell onto Velhonen's sleeves.

"We'd better get you changed again. You have a meeting with the Chief of Police and Mayor in thirty minutes. You can't walk in looking like you hulked out."

For the first time, Ilene heard Velhonen genuinely laugh. It sounded warm and lovely. The clawing pain lessened. She couldn't help feeling a little sad for him that she'd only seen him genuinely happy once in six months. Why was she feeling even the briefest of sympathy for a murderer was beyond her.

"O.K. Let's go.", he agreed, picking his phone off the floor from next to the pieces of shattered table. "I'll need to go shopping for a new table when this is all over. How about that place in Norway that I love?"

Ilene didn't hear the rest. The doors were already closing. She waited three minutes and then leant over the building's edge, watching her enemy leave with his entourage. She didn't need to follow him yet. She knew who he was meeting with and could get Charlotte to hack the reservation list for every high-end restaurant on this side of the planet. However, she was curious about this attack. But if her suspicions were correct, she needed what was behind that oil painting. She put in her earpiece (a gift from Charlotte) in and started to strip. There were no cameras on the roof which wasn't surprising. Why would a Verndari ever suspect him and why would one fly low enough to be seen from the ground? They'd have to be crazy. Thankfully, Ilene was just crazy enough.

"JJ?", Ilene called, looking into the room for cameras. There were none. She imagined there were cameras in the hallways and security in the building, patrolling every floor. Although to anyone's knowledge there was nothing in Victor's office of any real value except some antique furniture. But *they* hadn't known where to look.

"Yeah?", Jason answered. "Thank God! I was starting to worry."

"No, I'm good, just getting ready to go into the room. He just left with his Head of Security. They kept talking about an attack."

"Wait! Why are you going in? You have information."

"But I need to know more about the attack he has planned. Also... I think he's holding people, my people, on this level."

"Well, use your bird telescopic vision to see into the room. Come back another time with back-up.", Jason urged. He was getting more anxious, and she could hear it.

"I might not get a chance like this again. We need the numbers. He's building an army. He might move those prisoners because we keep releasing the others. He knows, by the way. And the way he was talking, it sounded like the attack was coming soon. Now are you going to let me use that big brain or yours or not?"

She heard Jason groan. "The building you're standing on is one of the first towers ever built in this city. The plans are so old, they're practically a national treasure. Everyone always focuses on the fact that it was the first in the country to have working elevator. Sounds like something an egomaniac would buy to show off."

"Flash git.", Ilene mumbled, through gritted teeth, tying up her hair.

"In the 19th century, there was an opening from the roof down to a fireplace that was really wide. No-one knew why Victor's ancestor wanted a large chimney on a skyscraper. They put it down to eccentricity but know we know why."

"It was a way to get back in the building for him and his group of deserters. Faster than making yourself look human, changing into all those clothes and entering at ground level through the front door." Ilene answered, nodding as she walked around looking for the entrance. She found it tucked to one side, rusted and unused. It was a large square chimney flu, eight feet by eight feet. It probably didn't do to be flying around in numbers especially after the invention of cameras. It would draw too much attention. That's why there were no cameras on the roof. He couldn't have footage of his true self on record in the building. There were no camera's facing upwards anywhere in the city, in fact, and no observatories in the city. It was probably something Velhonen helped implement a few decades ago.

She lifted it as gently as she was able. She wanted it to look like no-one had been there after she left.

She dropped her temperature further and started climbing down, after checking where the entrance was. Thankfully the fireplace hadn't been bricked up to give the room the air of an ancestral building that Velhonen had to give off.

She swung the hatch slowly so that she didn't blow any dust or soot into the room, making it obvious she'd broken in. She thought of all the creatures who stuck to walls and watched her fingers become an of reptile and insect imitation. At least she wouldn't leave clear DNA or fingerprints if the place was combed over.

She carefully and quietly worked her way through the dark, making sure not to touch any of the wall art. Now she was at the gold venetian frame of the oil painting. She scoffed at the arrogance of the face in the image. It was Velhonen but in baroque regalia, posed next to a sandstone column, a cornucopia of fruit and surrounded by beautiful European flowers. She recognised the types from every European oil painting she'd seen in trips to museums and galleries when she was younger. His eyes were even colder in this painting, and if you looked closely around the pupil there were hints of deep blue. This was probably painted not long after he had left the Verndari realm.

There was nothing on the wall to the right of the painting, so it was probably a sliding that moved left. But how would she open it without tripping any alarms? There was a bookcase to the left of the painting. Surely, he couldn't be that stereotypical of a villain, could he? She climbed near and surveyed his books, all old copies of literature about business, accounting and commerce, probably first editions he had purchased himself at the time it was originally published. But one stood out. It was old like the others, but she recognised it, because she had the exact same copy in her parents' library. It was a hardback copy of 'The Count of Monte Cristo' by Alexandre Dumas. It had a red woven cover, woven binding, and gold tooling. It was published in the 1920s.

It was on a shelf full of revenge stories. The reason it stood out is because unlike the other books 'Hamlet', 'Carrie' and 'True Grit', to name a few, it's the only story where the wronged hero doesn't kill the villain directly. Ilene ran her finger along the spines of the books, listening carefully, and sure enough, there was a small echo from the with the Dumas book and signs of the top of the spine being pressed down several times.

Ilene grabbed the top of the book and pulled it out at an angle. She grinned when she heard a click once the book wouldn't move any further. A loud rumbling sounded as a very old mechanism started to move and the painting glided to one side, stopping with a 'thunk'. This was just like the adventure stories she had read as a child.

Behind the painting was a solid door with no handle or lock, but Ilene recognised the style. It was metal with vines and rock textures carved into it, some of the vines spreading onto the nearby wall. Ilene inched nearer above and lifter her father's pendant to it. With a soft release of air pressure, like a whisper, the door's carvings began to move towards the centre of the door, freeing the wall from its grip. The vines also lowered the door into the secret room, like a drawbridge, before fully retreating and coiling into the door's centre.

Ilene swung herself into the room, noticing the stone floor, clearly old like the door mechanism. This room hadn't been updated in maybe 100 years. The men who designed the doorway were definitely dead, that is if they had been allowed to leave the building alive after their project was completed. So, Ilene was sure there would be no modern security measures in here.

She climbed down and placed one foot on the floor. No clicks, clunks, beeps or blaring alarms. Good. "I'm in.", she whispered.

"OK.", Jason answered, "Keeping talking to me."

In the dim light, Ilene could see the room was bigger than it looked. She looked by the doorway and found an old switch akin to a large hand-crank 19th century style one, that made her think of old Frankenstein movies.

'I really hope nothing comes to life and attacks me.', she thought as she grabbed the handle and pulled it up.

She heard a clank and a growing buzz. Several small spots of light appeared. The room lit up slowly as the whirring of an old generate coughed out dust.

"The room has an independent generator. It's smart. You don't want a room that shouldn't exist attached to a modern power grid. Questions would be asked.", Ilene mused, walked forward.

"Hmm.", Jason answered, trying to sound calm.

Ilene was about to comment on his efforts but then her vision picked up on what the room held. She gasped.

Efforts over, Jason went into full panic mode. "Ilene! What's wrong? What is it?"

Ilene could only whisper one word. "Prisoners."

In three lines were large stone pedestals and on each was a Verndari. Some still looked human and some were mid-transformation. Only their skin was stone, but they were still wearing the clothing, like someone had played dress-up with a statue. She saw clothing from every corner of the world: Incan, Pacific Polynesian, Japanese, aboriginal Australian, Arabic, Indian, English, Norwegian, Kenyan Masai and Namibian and Indigenous American to name a few. But Mek'el wasn't among them. Ilene's heart sunk a little. She was wondering why these people weren't sold, but then she remembered who did this. Velhonen was proud, vengeful and a show-off. Why wouldn't he have a trophy room for his most troublesome enemies, that couldn't best him now, walking among the inanimate faces, talking to and taunting them.

Well, that ended now.

Ilene sat in the centre of the room, cross-legged and held her father's pendant in her hand. She deepened her breathing and focusing on the hope in her mind. She thought about how much she and the world needed these seasoned warriors. She closed her eyes.

The room began to fill with a new light. Slowly as a small orb at first and then it burst around her, spreading in waves. Ilene opened her eyes as she began to hear heartbeats. Still focusing, she stood and slowly walked around the room, watching whoever was nearest to her have their skin turn from a textured grey to what it was before their imprisonment. Each person reacted the same when they saw her pendant and how young she looked, with shock and hesitant acceptance. She gave mental instructions as she passed, telling them to crawl along the wall to their right and escape through the fireplace.

Most of them knew where her parents' house was anyway. The feeling in the room was joy, confusion, apprehension and surprise. Some thought it was the eighteen-fifties, some the nineteen-seventies, and some thought the Great War was still going on. These were the oldest of Velhonen's prisoners. Maybe Velhonen ran out of storage space and just decided to sell his prisoners after the seventies. Ilene quickly got them up to speed, showing them images of the new world. They all wanted to hug and talk, but Ilene reminded them there would be time for that once they were safe at her house.

"JJ?", Ilene called, touching her ear.

"Yes?", Jason answered.

"Call your mum and Beatrice and let them know to expect company."

Jason missed a beat and then answered. "How much company?", he asked.

"Errr... about sixty.", Ilene said. It was a rough guess, but she was oddly certain.

Ilene strained her ear from inside the building as she listened to the phone call. She nodded when it was done and watched as these grateful warriors quietly escaped.

Just as Ilene was about to follow, she noticed another figure on his knees in the corner, still lithified and in a thick glass case wearing the thickest iron shackles she'd ever seen. Someone really didn't want him to get out. He only wore trousers which were threadbare and, for the most part, missing and torn. Some of his bones were clearly broken, his fingers deformed, and chunks of his flesh missing.

She looked at his face as she concentrated, the blue pendant glowing once more. He looked familiar. As his face transformed back into living skin, he took in a deep gasp of air, as if he'd been holding it the whole time. He toppled forward as his limbs returned to normal, his fingers and toes clicking and snapping back whole. The cuts on his upper body which slowly started closing up as he woke. He placed a shackled hand on the glass to steady himself.

He was weak. She had to help him.

'Oh well,', thought Ilene, 'In for a penny, in for a pound. Shattered glass wasn't going to make Velhonen any less pissed once he discovered someone had pillaged his dungeon.

The sounds of her mental voice made the man look up for its source. Ilene smiled back at him and waved while he just looked at her.

"Can you move away from the glass a bit, please?", she asked, sheepishly.

He sat back and far as he could as Ilene plated her fists with keratin, like a rhino's horn and pounded at the glass. The sound shook the walls, and Ilene was suddenly regretting the decision, thinking she may have been heard. But it was too late now. After about twenty seconds, she'd broken through. He looked up at her. He was probably about forty, dark hair and blue eyes. Ilene couldn't put her finger on it, but she had a strange feeling she'd met him before.

His mind as a swirling mass of sound. No words, no sentences, just images of torture, even though the evidence of it was disappearing from his skin with each passing second. However, as his body healed, so did his mind.

In an instant, his head snapped up and yellow filled his irises. 'Oh god!', he cried inside, 'Where am I? Is she safe? Have they found her?'

He looked at Ilene with a gaze so focused it nearly knocked her back. He stood and grabbed her by the shoulders. "Who are you?", he demanded. "Never mind. What year is it?"

Ilene took a step back as he heard the answer from her mind.

The sudden sadness and horror in his eyes were like a punch to her heart. She heard him scream but his mouth didn't move. The sound froze her. It took her a moment to come back to herself, before she realized she was alone, and he was exiting the room. He must have heard her plea to stick to the wall because he did so.

Ilene pulled the door closed and swung one wing towards the bookcase before she leapt at the fireplace, hearing the oil painting slide back into place. She clambered up the fireplace as quickly as she could so she could follow the last prisoner and take him to her home. She sealed the chimney flu and grabbed her clothes, leaping from the room, sprouting her wings before she started to plummet off the building's edge.

She touched her earpiece again. "Jason, clench up and close your eyes."

She could see the man; he was flying fast. She'd have to really work to keep up with him carrying the extra weight. Jason was standing at the edge of rooftop, obediently, with his eyes closed. Ilene swooped down and grabbed him with one arm. She tried to put her trousers on with the other arm, which, with the wind drag, was made extra difficult.

She kept the man in her sights while trying to hear his mind. She caught the odd word but no names or faces. He was in a blind panic but was somehow going in the right direction. The main thing she kept hearing was 'Hang on, baby. I'm coming home.'

Now Ilene was starting to panic, she was trying to put her boob tube back on with Jason holding onto her legs, meanwhile, things were starting to come together. His face. She knew where she'd been seen it before.

She kept her eyes forward, all the while thinking 'Oh god, I know who he is.'

They passed the village and were getting very near to the Manor.

Jason had gingerly opened his eyes after he sensed Ilene had stopped jostling with her clothes. He dared a quick look upwards and then looked at where they were and who they were pursuing.

"He's heading to the house. Did you tell him to go there?"

Ilene was still focused on his mind. "No.", she answered. They were about a minute away.

"That's weird ...but good I guess.", Jason responded, curiosity and his old distrusting tone returning.

Ilene could hear the other Verndarar minds. They had just landed a few seconds earlier. Ilene used her eagle eyes to see them. They were being welcomed and they were all hugging.

"I'm going to land behind the hedge and change back to normal. Your mum can't know about this or that you're involved. I don't feel like explaining all this to her.", Ilene informed.

The last prisoner did the same thing they were doing. He landed at the other side of the hedge that marked the edge of the long tree-shrouded driveway. His stance was wary.

He stepped out and headed toward the front door.

Jason set down, a little wobbly and Ilene dropped to the ground behind him, making her wings vanish before they walked as quickly as they could around the corner.

Ilene was stopped in her tracks, her heart in her neck, when she saw the prisoner walking to the house.

His wings were still out!

He was looking around from person to person and froze, just outside of the pool of Manor's light as he saw one particular person, blonde-grey hair pulled back in a braid. It was Amanda.

Ilene could hear the anxiety in the prisoner's mind, but she hoped he'd pick up on hers. She was screaming inside, knees weak with fear.

'No! NO! She can't know about our kind! Normalise, *NOW*!'

Amanda saw the silhouette as she turned around and smiled.

Ilene's nerves were replaced by something else. Amanda saw wings and didn't react. She *knew*! She knew about it all!

Amanda continued to smile. "Welcome. Come on in. We've got lots of food...."

As he stepped into the light, several things happened. Amanda stopped speaking, the blood drained from her face and Ilene heard her heartbeat slow right down for the briefest of moments and then pick back up so hard and fast, it hurt her ears.

The next thing that happened was the prisoner's mind went completely silent, however the feeling of peace and happiness in his mind was spreading from him like a mist.

Amanda began gasping to catch ragged breaths, her face contorted in pain and relief. She was trying to reach her hand forward but was shaking too hard. She took a step, faltered and started to fall forward, sobbing. The prisoner dropped too, catching her effortlessly. He stroked her hair as she cried what was left of her heart out onto his shoulder. Ilene could hear him crying too. Amanda eventually managed to lift her head and began tracing his facial features with her fingertips. She closed her eyes, muscle memory confirming that it was him and that this was real. He then kissed her with a feverish passion that shocked everyone. Some Verndarar laughed, some sighed, but almost everyone was smiling. All but two.

They eventually stood, laughing as he lifted her and swung her around before hugging her so tight, she had to remind him to be gentle.

He laughed. "You're still so beautiful.", he said, emotion almost choking his voice.

Amanda blushed, lowering her head, her face sad. "I'm old now."

The prisoner took her face in his hands. "No, just beautiful." His face fell and he almost started crying again. "I'm... I'm so sorry. We got captured...."

Amanda shook her head, trying to silence him. "You don't have to reassure me. I know you were trying to save your people. I know you'd never leave me."

"I was so stupid. I went on that mission promising I'd be back that night. You didn't want me to go, but I did anyway. I thought we had more time. I was proud, cocky and foolish. I should have stayed home and found out what it was you wanted to talk about so badly. I'd give anything to turn back time and do it over."

Jason had been watching this, detached, like it was a movie. He had to shake himself back into reality. This was *his* mother. He stepped forward into the light.

"Mom.... who is this man?", he asked, quietly.

Amanda looked at Jason, a little startled and pulled out of her joyous bubble. She looked back into the man's eyes and smiled, biting her bottom lip. She took the man's arm and turned him to face Jason.

"This...is what I was going to tell you.", she whispered, suddenly the sheepish girl she once was over twenty years ago.

Jason stared, dumbfounded. It was the first he was seeing this man's face, but it looked so similar... to *his*.

The prisoner looked from the boy's face back to his love's blue eyes. She nodded, tears falling down her cheeks. He looked back at the boy. Her eyes and nose but his jaw, hair and build.

He tried to steady his breath, but he couldn't and the next thing he knew tears were filling his eyes and that of his younger reflection's.

He stepped forward. Jason didn't move. His father lifted his hand and held Jason's face. "Oh my god!", he breathed, "*Look* at you!"

Jason was suddenly shaking, struggling to keep his tears at bay. "You didn't leave us.", he confirmed, unable to move or even think.

His father took him into a strong embrace. "My son, I would *never* leave you or your mother."

Years of rage, loneliness and sadness filled Jason. All his questions were now answered. Everything missing in him clicked into place in the arms of the man he'd been subconsciously looking and longing for his whole life. The knowledge that he wasn't abandoned recentred his whole world, giving him an inner peace he'd never felt before.

And there, in the middle of the driveway, two men cried quietly and held each-other fast. Ilene didn't know how long it had gone on for. In her opinion, no amount of time was long enough for this.

When they eventually pulled themselves away from a hug that had contained twenty-two years of hurt, Jason was aware of Ilene stood behind him. It gave him a small pang of embarrassment but also reminded him of all his new knowledge.

His next thought fell out of his mouth unfettered. "You're Verndari?"

Both of his parents started. Amanda's eyes went from soft to protective anger. "How do you know that word?"

Jason answered hesitantly, turning towards her. "Ilene told me. How about another question: why didn't *you*?"

Amanda looked briefly at Ilene with a blood-freezing glare and then she sighed, her face becoming soft once again. "Would you have believed me? Besides, it wasn't safe, what with all the disappearances. I didn't want to go looking for him and go missing too."

Jason's eyes shone with fresh tears, regret, pain and shame every part of him. He hung his head as he took Amanda's hand. "You were just trying to protect me.", he acknowledged. His bottom lip trembled as he hugged his mother so tight and suddenly, it knocked the air out of her. "Oh, mom. I'm so, so sorry. I thought you never told me about my dad because... I was the result of a one-night stand or something. Mom.... all these years! I'm so sorry!"

This time, he was crying, freely. The woman who'd raised him alone, receiving his hatred for over a decade while she waited for her love to come home the whole time. He regretted every selfish, angry second that he'd wasted. If only he'd known.

Once everyone had calmed down, Ilene stepped forward. "I'm sorry to interrupt, but we need to have a meeting. I have information that will help us to possibly end this."

Jason's father looked from her face to the pendant around her neck in a flash. "Siobhan?", he asked.

Ilene smiled at the sound of her mother's name. "No, but I get that a lot. I'm Ilene, her daughter."

He looked at her, almost afraid, for a moment, but then he read her mind and intentions, and he smiled. He stepped forward and hugged her suddenly. The surprise made her laugh. "You're the spitting image. Is she in the kitchen? Or the games room? It'll be good to whoop her butt at pool for the three-hundredth time."

He was marching towards the house, excitement in his steps. Ilene followed and grabbed his arm. Her face was sullen now. Jason saw his face drop. Ilene had a sad focus in her eyes. He stood frozen and Ilene shared her knowledge, her visions and the news.

His sadness became rage, and he began to growl. Amanda and Jason started as sounds of anguish and fury could be heard coming from the house. Ilene's message had reached everyone on the grounds. They could even hear Charlotte, who hadn't received images of her friends' deaths before. Ilene, in turn, was barraged with so many images, sounds and memories, she clutched her own head. They were all tinged with so much sadness, she almost couldn't bear it.

The eyes of the warrior stood in front of her glowed red and fresh tears filled his eyes. His fists were clenched. All this emotion was overwhelming him. He wasn't used to being allowed to feel this much. He almost wished he was outside the protection of the Manor, so he would have to bottle up all this pain. He trembled slightly as he forced himself to regain his composure.

He lifted a hand and held Ilene's. "Your parents were... by far, the greatest leaders, the fiercest soldiers and the best friends any of us ever knew. I'm so sorry that you never got to know them the way we did. Their loss is a blow to our kind, and I will miss them every single day." His eyes switched from aching to resolution slowly. " I promise you; we will avenge them and gain back our freedom and our world."

He stepped back and bowed low, folding his left arm across his chest to his shoulder. "My name is Gierozzo, but you can call me Gerry Dunney, and as I served your father, I will serve you, to my last breath."

Ilene felt a lump in her throat. She felt the weight of her family name and held it with pride. No-one had even sworn temporary friendship to her in her short life, but now an immortal man was swearing fealty to her till the day he died. It was a lot to handle. As Gerry stood, she stepped towards him and slowly hugged him. "Thank you.", she said.

Gerry turned to his family after Ilene released him and held out his hand. "Come, Jason. We have much to talk about."

Jason sighed and smiled. As he walked to his father, he stopped short. "Wait, how did you know my name?"

Gerry smiled. "It's my middle name, and I know your mom's mind works."

Jason chuckled and looked over his shoulder back at Ilene, shaking his head, bearing a dumb founded but intensely gleeful expression.

Ilene started to walk to the front door and was joined by Amanda. She took her hand, stopping them both. "I'm sorry, Amanda. I had to tell him. You're right. He's an inquisitive guy. He would have looked into it and maybe got hurt.", she whispered. "Maybe it would have been better for him if I'd never come here."

Amanda sighed, turned towards Ilene and squeezed her hand in response. "It's ok. I should thank you. It means that I have less lies to tell my son." She chuckled weakly, the weight of secrecy lifting and revealing how mentally exhausted she really was. Suddenly, her age showed in her face. "Besides, I had to protect you both from Velhonen."

After Ilene was done reeling from hearing this unassuming-looking human woman using terms she'd only heard other Verndarar used, her brow furrowed. "Both of us? Why?"

Amanda looked squarely and seriously into her eyes, just as her husband had done earlier, shaking Ilene with the look she gave.

"You're the first Verndari-born in five-hundred years and my son is the only 'half-breed' in history."

"You mean.... no other Verndari and human have ever...?", Ilene tried to ask, squirming with the awkwardness.

"No. They were banned from relationships and what would be the point of having children, it was even possible? If the children were more human, the parent would just live forever, watching their lovers and descendants grow old and...", Amanda explained, faltering. "It's sad and a little scary for humans, but it'd be worse for the Verndarar. And if the children were Verndarar, they'd be taken by the elders. So, they practise abstinence, which is easy considering the society and time periods lots of them come from. But Gerry and I... we just couldn't stay away from each-other. We fought it with everything we had. He lied saying he was already married, but I could tell something was off. So, I went digging for answers, almost getting myself into some dangerous situations. After he eventually admitted what he was, we agreed it'd never work and went our separate ways. But it hurt too much to bear. He literally flew back into my arms, just like today. And the rest is history. We had five glorious years together before he disappeared, and I regret none of it."

Amanda was smiling, but Ilene just wanted to cry. Ilene was thinking of the truth she'd been repressing about herself and what it'd mean for her family in London. One day they'd be gone, and she'd be stuck with the pain. She wasn't sure if she found the Dunneys' decision foolhardy or insanely brave.

Amanda hugged her and rubbed her back. Whether it was immortality or having your life restricted to one lifetime, it sucked. Mortality limited your potential, and immortality just lengthened any torturous emotions you felt and pain or horrors you witnessed.

Ilene was drained. She'd done way too much crying over the last few weeks, most of it in the privacy of her room. She couldn't imagine how the Dunneys felt, along with everyone else in the Manor.

The two women took a deep breath, together, and walked into the house, heading for the dining room.

It was time to discuss a plan.

*

Ilene stood at the head of her parents' dining table with Charlotte, Kuruk and Gerry flanking her. Over eighty pairs of eyes were staring warily and expectantly at her.

She thought of her father's leadership and her mother's strength and held them in her mind.

She looked at everyone with a sweeping gaze. "For the sake of the humans in the room, can I request that we speak aloud? They are part of this too, so it's only fair."

This was met with nods and grunts of agreement.

"Let's get this done. I've got a meeting at two.", Marcus grumbled, folding his arms from his seat in the corner.

"How can you be thinking about your job and money? We're kinda fugitives here.", Charlotte questioned, her brow furrowing, her incredulous expression mixed with exasperation. "And who the hell meets with an accountant at two in the morning?"

Marcus smirked, a lop-sided smirked forming on his face. "That's confidential.", he teased, tittering to himself.

Kuruk rolled his eyes at this normal scene of them fighting. Gerry cleared his throat, impatiently, before nodding at Ilene to continue.

Ilene smiled. "I can't imagine what you have all been through. I'm glad we've managed to free so many of our kind.", she started. "However, lots of our people haven't been as lucky. Some are still prisoners; some were sold as art pieces and others have been killed."

There were sad tears and faint growls around the room and Ilene was flooded with the memories of faces of Verndarar lost, including her own parents and Mek'el. But she held her emotions in check.

"When I spied on our enemy tonight, some things started to make sense. The demons have been appearing in greater numbers and although we managed to purify one or two of them, the rest of them disappeared."

"It's almost as if they were called somewhere more important.", Charlotte added, nodding.

"Velhonen said he's been building an army, growing his numbers. He plans to attack the elders, which he can't do because he can't get into the Verndari realm as he killed my Father and doesn't have this.", Ilene explained touching her pendant. "He said no-one can use it except the person it was assigned to."

"Or their descendant.", interjected a Maasai warrior, her beads moving as she gestured. Her skin was a red toned brown, dark and glowing, her hair scarlet short and braided into an intricate style.

"Remember that he got out of our realm using the other pendant, which belonged to his father."

"I don't know if I can use it fully, Naeku. I'm not powerful enough yet. Which I'm thankful for, at this moment. I was being taught by Mek'el how to use it, which is how I was able to reverse the spell, or Calling, over you all."

Marcus piped up. He had just lit a cigarette, lifting it up to his mouth as he started to talk. "Maybe you can't fully use it because you haven't accepted what you are yet.", he suggested, looking at the ceiling and smirking some more. "I mean, a few months ago, you were just a human, living thousands of miles away. You're new to this. You're not one of us, not really."

"Come off it, Marcellus! She found out she's an orphaned immortal non-human in the space of a few days. She's dealing with it *all* and at her own pace. She's doing incredibly well, everything considered." Charlotte retorted, protectively. "And put out that cigarette. You know Siobhan would have your head for that if she was here."

"Well, she's not. She'd died, twice, and I'm pretty sure she's not coming back.", Marcus answered, darkly and spitefully. But Charlotte's sudden snarl made him straighten up. "Fine. I'll smoke elsewhere. It's not like I need to be in the room to hear everything."

"You know exactly where the ashtrays are.", Amanda called out after him as he slunk out of the room.

Ilene smiled as Charlotte and Amanda smiled at each-other, trying not to dwell on Marcus' callous comments. Kuruk shook his head.

"There will be a smoking break later, I promise.", Ilene reassured, continuing to smile at the faces in the room.

This announcement was met with a surprisingly louder grateful sound. And why not? Smoking was part of a lot of their cultures' relaxation. What's more, they couldn't be harmed by it.

"So, he's trying to build an army to do what? Wipe out humans? Why? Without them he has no income and all those years of gaining power would be a waste.", mused Gerry.

"He could. He's crazy. Remember, this is the guy who killed his parents as a teen.", answered the Japanese warrior down the table, in a calm and authoritative voice. His eyes were dark and calmed with years of living, and his long hair, pulled back was even darker, seeming to absorb the light around it.

"He does seem crazed, Toshi. But this craziness has direction and planning. And he's full of rage.", Ilene answered, recalling what she felt coming from Velhonen's mind earlier that night."

"Why?", scoffed another Verndari woman, she looked Scandinavian, with similar bone structure to Mek'el. "He's a murderer. We wasted years hunting him to bring him to justice."

"But with the book of Callings in his hands there's no way you could have succeeded. Instead of wiping you out, he made you trophies. This was calculated, malicious and spiteful. Like he was evening a score." Ilene mused in a low voice, even though everyone heard it.

"Revenge...", Amanda mumbled to herself, staring into space. "Ilene what did he say when you saw him? Did he mention an intended target?"

"He said he'd set what was done to him right. In fact, he said 'what was done to all of us'."

"He's not targeting the humans. He could trap all Verndarar and wipe them out, but he's been keeping them. He lets despair build while he builds up an army." Amanda bit her lip and twiddled her fingers absent-mindedly as she thought. "Honey..."

274

Gerry smiled a smile that melted Ilene's heart. She heard him sigh mentally like a man finding an oasis after crawling through hundreds of miles of desert. "Yes, my love."

"What was that thing you once told me about Verndarar existence and human existence being tied together?"

Gerry's brow furrowed as he remembered the conversation. "Verndarar would waste away into nothing without a world of beings to protect, but if every Verndari died..."

"The human race would carry on with no-one to protect them.", Ilene finished.

Charlotte stood up suddenly. "He's going to wipe us out. Get revenge on the elders that banished him. Then he'll come back here and live... eternally young and wealthy. In complete control of this world."

Ilene shook her head again. "That speculation doesn't make sense. He could have wiped us out years ago. He just can never get through the Verndari realm so there'll be a part of his revenge he'll never get to complete."

Charlotte huffed decidedly. "Whatever his plan is, we have to stop it. We need to scour every inch of the city and look into his activities, find where's he's storing his army and dispatch them."

"We also need to arrange a mass strike so we can take the green pendant from Velhonen.", interjected a Polynesian warrior, his huge muscles decorated in some of the most intricate tattoos Ilene had ever seen. He obviously had no issues with pain, even as a human. "That way we can get back out and go back to how it was 500 years ago."

Ilene felt herself freeze. What would that mean for her? She was a forbidden child. Would they lock her up? Kill her? Send her away?

Charlotte felt Ilene's tension and put a hand on her shoulder. Ilene tried to smile and squeezed her hand. She was grateful to never be truly alone, especially with all the crazy things she was facing now.

"I'll take a look into Velhonen's businesses and properties. It'll take some time, but I can do it. Ilene and Bob can track his movements, so we know where he'll be when it's time to strike." Charlotte announced.

"Just try not to get arrested. I can't handle another of my friends getting falsely convicted then conveniently disappeared on transit to prison.", Toshi warned.

Jason raised an eyebrow. "Arrested? Well, don't get caught... hacking the servers of one of the most powerful men on earth then.", he mumbled. "I imagine the people who were around when these systems were *created* would have no issues avoiding detection."

Charlotte smiled wryly. "Honey, I was in Bletchley the computer's precursor was created."

Ilene couldn't help herself. Her mouth dropped open. Charlotte heard the questions in her mind and nodded in response to them all. If they made it through this, Ilene had a lot of pasts to see and ask about.

Jason was still frowning. "One thing I still can't wrap my head around, why kill some Verndarar and capture others? What did the murdered ones have in common?"

Ilene almost stood up as one word echoed mentally around the room as every Verndari thought of her father and Mek'el.

'General'.

"They were all Generals. There were selected by you all and had proved themselves over time but not just in battle. I've seen Mek'el's mind. It's like an iron fortress...wrapped in barbed wire and surrounded by a piranha-filled moat. They had to have extreme mental discipline, perhaps to protect something.", Ilene mused standing fully and beginning to pace along the wall. Then she stopped and looked at Charlotte. "Why didn't you tell me?"

Charlotte hung her head, apologies bouncing around her mind. Ilene could hear fear. "Due to your ability to see into our minds and how close you two were becoming, we were afraid you'd ask him the wrong question if you knew what to look for. You're young and that means being curious and rebellious. I didn't know or trust you well enough. I couldn't risk it."

Ilene's chest stung as she heard these words, and this feeling didn't make sense as they'd only known each-other for a few months. Maybe she was young and naive but what did they think she'd do: go straight to her parents' murderer and just share information that would topple the only group standing between the end of this nightmare and humanity's extinction? She wanted to yell, she wanted to cry but Mek'el's lessons had served her well. She just took in a slow deep breath until her eyes weren't burning anymore.

Charlotte smiled and stood. She opened her arms and hugged her tightly. "But this was before I saw how in control you were and how you've embraced who you truly are. You're one of us." Charlotte sighed, shakily. "All Generals have keener senses than us. There are many portals around the world, and they become active and inactive at different times to avoid patterns that could lead to us being caught. Most are inactive, like the one upstairs. Generals can sense the nearest active portal. Generals, if they are caught, are tortured and killed, normally. That's why Gerry was tortured. He was a General, but he stepped down years ago to live in the human world with Amanda."

Ilene looked over at Gerry watching the pain appear on Amanda's face as she felt her husband freeze under her hand. Ilene was doing everything possible to control her face, but Amanda looked at her before she fully achieved it. Ilene was mentally revisiting the state she'd found him in only a few hours ago.

Verndari or not, a person would have severe PTSD after something like that, and because he healed rapidly, the torture was extensive and ceaseless. But he never revealed anything because he knew nothing. Ilene saw memories of Velhonen leaving to find portals and then returning frustrated after finding it inactive and taking his ire out on Gerry.

Ilene shuddered and sighed. The others were right. Velhonen was more than just evil. He was a demon himself.

'You can talk to me any time, OK?', Charlotte reassured, not moving.

'Thank you.', Gerry answered, his face still and calm.

"Well, he got nothing from Gerry, but if Mek'el breaks and he manages to take me out, we're all screwed.", Ilene vocalised, still traumatised by Velhonen's level brutality.

"Well, this is a fight we can still win.", an English warrior stated. "We have numbers once more and experience as an advantage. We've faced Velhonen before. Plus, we have the first Verndari-born in 500 years on our side."

Ilene swallowed, suddenly feeling inadequate as everyone turned and looked at her.

Gerry cleared his throat. "Actually, we have two." He looked a little wary and sad, as he turned towards Jason.

Ilene ran to him immediately when she saw his face.

All the blood had drained from it. He was shaking and sweating a little, as his eyes stayed transfixed on nothing. No-one had noticed that Jason had been completely silent and still.

Amanda freaked out and grabbed his hand. "Sweetheart!", she shrieked. She turned to Gerry, tears in her eyes, breathing raggedly. "What's happening to him?"

Gerry was calm but the feeling of guilt was bursting from him. He felt responsible for so much of the pain his son had felt and even what was happening now. He knelt down in front of his son and placed a hand on Jason's knee. 'Son, ... can you hear me?', his mind called.

Almost immediately, Jason jumped at the sound of Gerry's voice. He locked eyes with his father and looked like a lost little boy. It made Ilene want to cry. He started panting. "Dad?"

The mixture of guilt, sadness and joy from hearing his son call to him almost emotionally broke of his parents. They both wrapped their arms around their son and squeezed him with all their might.

"We're here, Jason. I'm sorry. I wish that happened another way.", Gerry whispered, as he kissed Jason's forehead.

Jason sighed and his mind started moving again.

Ilene exhaled shakily. He'd heard or seen what Ilene had seen that night and what his father had experienced. Other things suddenly made sense.

"That voice... all this time... It was *you*?", Ilene gasped.

Gerry furrowed his brow. "What do you mean?"

Ilene had her hand over her mouth. For once, she was lost for words, but now she had to find some. Even her mind had stopped. "When I'm with Jason, I always hear what sounds like a radio turned all the way down, like, infuriating low background chatter."

Jason looked at her and nodded, moving. "You're always trying to turn the radio in my car down when it's already off. I thought you were just...weird."

Ilene laughed, feeling grateful she wasn't losing her mind after all. Questioning her own sanity didn't do much to help with the mental house of cards she'd been trying to keep stable all these months. "So, the person talking through the movie was you too?"

A woman with curly long auburn hair stood, moving cautiously over. "How is that possible, when we can't hear him?"

Ilene answered without taking her eyes off Jason. His mind was stretched to its limits and now he was hearing voices. He was hyperventilating a little, gripping the chair he was sitting on hard for stability. "According to Mek'el, I have a gift few Verndarar have. I can't just hear thoughts, I can see them as well and send images to other minds, as you all saw tonight. The night of my eighteenth birthday, I saw my parents' death through my mother's eyes. I think Verndari-born have a special link to their parents and to other Verndari-born people. Their minds are somehow... more powerful."

The woman raised an eyebrow and huffed. This didn't sit well with her. She didn't like the idea that she was no longer one of the most powerful creatures on earth. "She's just a child.", she mumbled, folding her arms. "Prove it. What am I picturing?"

Ilene's eyes briefly flashing red at the woman's demeaning tone. But she collected herself again and kept her eyes on Jason still.

"A pineapple.", she announced, then she paused and cocked her head to the side, a confused look on her face. The woman behind her stopped breathing. "A dog. A unicorn- are those real? Nixon naked? *Nixon*? Really? Ice-cream..."

The woman's arms unfolded, and she walked towards Ilene, her fury building and began growling in Irish Gaelic. One of the others stopped her. But Ilene kept going. She should never have belittled her, even mentally, in her own home.

Now Ilene turned and stood, folding her arms. "Handcuffs. Spray-cream. Black PVC."

The woman's eyes were glowing red now, as she heard everyone in the room giggling and gasping. Ilene held her gaze. "Are you going to test or insult me anymore? Or shall I reveal more, Niamh?"

The woman sighed and bowed a little. Then she smiled, extending her hand. Ilene hesitated, still pissed, but she eventually took it. They all needed to be united for the hell that was to come. "My apologies, young one. You're no fool. And, my god, you are so like your mother. She and I had our fair share of tussles back in the day. I guess I couldn't help myself."

Ilene smiled back. It's odd to be told over and over again that you're so similar to someone you don't remember meeting. But she found it oddly comforting.

There was a sound, too far off for ordinary ears to pick up from where they were but all heads in the manor, save one, turned as it reached them. The sound of a thousand screams coming from the city and its surrounding towns. There were sounds of heavy things slamming into the ground and wood splintering.

Amanda was frightened by the sudden united action.

Jason's eyes were scanning the room frantically. "What's happening? I can hear something. Is it real?", he whispered, still holding his mother's hand.

Ilene was now the one panicking. She was shaking and terror filled her eyes, irises gleaming yellow. "Attack...hundreds of them, happening all over the city, but it feels like it's coming from everywhere. People are dying."

Charlotte was frozen in place but turned to look at Ilene. "You mean this is worldwide?"

Ilene nodded slowly, still looking at the same spot in the air, eyes wide.

Kuruk strode into the hallway at a speed that didn't match his build. He leapt the stairs in a single bound, grabbing ancestral swords and other weapons from the walls and gloves of armoured suits.

He threw them to other Verndarar as they entered the hallways. Some stretched their muscles, gearing up and practising small skin changes they hadn't got to do in decades. Charlotte was handing some of the concealed weapons she had.

Ilene, Jason and Amanda followed them out to the front of the house as they all geared up and unfurled their wings, some feathered, some like butterflies and some leathery like Ilene's. Ilene had never seen so many of her kind battle-ready. It was beautiful. It filled her with awe and pride.

Gerry was about to do the same when Amanda grabbed him arm and pulled him back. Tears were already falling from her eyes. Gerry took her face in his hands. "It's my job.", he whispered.

Amanda grabbed him by the shirt and held him with all her might, shaking her head. Terror and anger blazed in her eyes. "I'm NOT having the same conversation with you again. The last time I did, you NEVER CAME HOME!"

She was suddenly crying so hard that the sound ached Ilene's heard and judging by the look on Gerry's face, it ached his too. She suddenly got so quiet, everyone looked at her face to check if she was still breathing. Instead, they heard a tiny voice. "I just got you back.", she whimpered.

Gerry sighed. He scooped his wife into his arms, who was still crying, and "put" his wings away, walking back into the house. Ilene touched his arm and they both nodded at each-other as he passed her. 'Thank you' was all Ilene could think.

She turned to Jason who also was rooted to the spot with terror, thinking that he was going to lose his father again. Ilene hugged him gently. But when he took in a breath and shakily exhaled, he hugged her back, putting his head on her shoulder. She could feel him trembling but after the hug, it subsided.

She let go and looked at his anxious eyes. She touched his face. "Go.", she urged. "Be with your parents."

They walked back into the hallway together. Jason gave her one more quick hug and walking into the Games Room. "Parents.", he repeated, chuckling.

Ilene turned and was almost about to "wing up" when Charlotte stepped in front of her with a stern look on her face. Ilene groaned and felt her stomach sink.

"Come on! Not again!", she whined. "We need everyone we can get tonight. I'm going to go crazy if I stay here."

Charlotte just stepped forward and hugged her. "I need you here. Protect the pendant. They can't get in.", she instructed, her voice so soft, it only unnerved Ilene more. "You think I won't be insane with worry if you're out their fighting?"

Now it was Ilene's turn to start crying. She hated how emotional she was these days. "But that's what we have *each-other* for! We're not just in the same army, we're *family*! There's no-one I'd rather risk my life for."

This time Charlotte's eyes welled up and she just about contained a sudden sob. 'You mother once said those exact same words to me.'

Ilene realised those words were the nail in the coffin. She sighed and rubbed her face. "O.K. I'll stay. No need to break my legs."

From the other room, Ilene heard Jason cry out. "*What*?!"

Ilene laughed, imagining the look on his face. Sounds like his acute hearing had fully kicked in.

Ilene hugged Charlotte even tighter. "Come back to me. O.K?"

Charlotte stepped back and stroked Ilene's face, endearingly. Then with a smile she turned and strode through the front door. "It's going to be a wild night.", she announced loudly, turning back and winking. "Just keep that healing crystal powered and ready for when we return. We might need it."

Then the front door slammed shut with a boom that felt like it echoed all over the house.

Ilene was focusing on her breathing, fighting to keep it even, so she would remain calm. She walked to the foot of the stairs, sat down and waited.

*

It had been two hours already. Ilene could smell smoke wafting in from everywhere. People would probably put tonight down to a large-scale terrorist attack, but the sinking and sickened feeling that kept hitting Ilene told her there was no way this was the work of humans. She sat nervously, listening, stretching her mind to hear anything. She got vague images but not much. It seemed manageable, not as bad as she'd thought. She tried to meditate, but she failed because she kept hearing distractions from inside and outside of the house.

She walked into the dojo to practise, venting her frustrations of not being out with the others at imaginary assailants. It was so quiet in the house. Too quiet. Even in the dojo. Ilene realised what sound was absent. The waterfall feature was off.

Ilene shrugged. It'd probably just have annoyed her anyway. Also, it wasn't like she could walk through and get help. Not being able to use her father's pendant was a blessing and a curse.

It was still too quiet, so Ilene decided to go back downstairs to look for the Dunneys. They were in the Games Room. Jason was sitting next to his father, smiling contentedly, while Amanda laid across the same sofa with her head resting in her husband's lap while he played with her hair.

Ilene stood in the doorway watching for a moment, basking in the waves of emotion coming from Jason and Gerry. She felt a pang of jealousy twisting in her chest. This scene was something she would never know.

Gerry must have felt her sadness, because he looked directly at her without needing to look for her. Ilene always found it unsettling how the Verndarar could do that.

She walked into the room and settled on the opposite sofa and watched them for a bit longer, listening to Amanda and Gerry talking about old memories, favourite haunts and things they intended to do, now thatthey'd found each-other again.

While the loving couple talked aloud, Gerry 'spoke' to Ilene about her father, sharing memories. Gerry's ability to mentally focus on and participate in two completely different conversations without showing any sign that he was doing so was amazing.

Ilene hugged her favourite cushion while she watched and listened.

'He was a great swordsman, with techniques only mastered by few people in this world. Even Verndarar couldn't best him. He was the finest warrior, a natural leader and a dear brother. I miss him so much it burns. Even being in this house, I feel like he and Siobhan will walk through that door any moment.' Gerry sighed in his mind. 'I feel sorry for you that couldn't know them. But at the same time, I'm glad you didn't because the pain you'd be feeling if you did would destabilize you.'

Then he broke his gaze from his wife's fall and looked at her.

'But don't be sad. We are the children and the memories we leave behind. As long as one person living remembers or descends from us, no-one is truly gone.'

Ilene now had tears stinging her eyes and was clenching her jaw, swallowing back her feelings to retain her composure.

There was one loud knock at the front door, just at that moment.

Gerry lifted up his wife's head up gently with one hand, standing slowly. "Back already?", he called, kissing Amanda's cheek, making her giggle. "I'll get it!"

As he walked out of the room, he pointed at Ilene, his voice echoing in the hallway. "Hey, Ilene, how about we go a few rounds in the dojo?"

Ilene grinned, craning her neck to throw her voice, although she didn't need to. He'd hear her if she whispered through the cushion in her hand. "You're on. I just came from there actually." Ilene answered, turning to Amanda. "By the way, why did you turn the waterfall off?"

Amanda's smile vanished, her breathing stopped, and Ilene heard her heart stutter.

Her eyes widened. Her mouth opened before she moved at all. "GERRY! DON'T!", she screamed, rising from her seat.

The front door handle clicked, as it was turned.

The next sound shook the house from the foundations to the roof. The heavy door exploded into the hallway, sending flames, dust and splinters in every direction.

Ilene saw Gerry's body zoom through the air, crash into and slightly through a wall at the foot of the stairs and land, limp, on the floor. He wasn't moving.

Ilene was up and in the hallway in seconds. She picked up two of the remaining swords throwing one to Jason, no looking back to check whether he caught it. There wasn't time.

Demons poured into the hallway eyes blazing, breaking the remains of the door off its hinges. Ilene heard a few windows shatter in the Games Room and kitchen. Ilene gripped her sword and leapt forward, trying to keep her eyes on her friends. She sliced and hacked at anything that came near her, throwing and reclaiming her blades, her anxiety upgrading itself into frustration-fuelled rage. She saw leaves, sparks, wood and splinters litter the air as all of her training kicked back in. Every demon that came near was attacked if they had personally taken her mentor. Finally, she let all her emotions flow through and power her.

She saw Jason, run to Gerry , his eyes watching Ilene dispatching their uninvited guests with feral energy.

'He's alive.' Ilene told him 'I can hear him breathing. I'll get him to safety. Take Amanda and hide in the garage.'

Jason nodded and looked for his mother. He expected her to be behind him like she was a moment ago, but they both turned at the sound of her feet running up the stairs.

"Mom! What the hell are you doing?" Jason cried, anger and panic in his voice.

They both heard her ragged breathing and terrified voice. "The barrier!"

Ilene's widened as she realised where she was heading. "The waterfall! It's been powering the barrier this whole time?!"

"I'll help her!", Jason called, looking at his father, fighting the urge to stay with him and then racing after her with long strong bounds. He was already at the top of the stairs as he finished his sentence.

Ilene smiled as she kept swinging, pieces of demon littering her hallway. His body was accepting what he was faster than hers had. 'O.K. Reach into my mind if you're not sure how to fight. I'll show you-'

As she 'said' this, she saw Jason's sword swing through his mind's eyes and a demon's head bounce off a wall in front of the dojo.

Ilene leapt off the back of demon while taken the arm off a second and landing her sword in another's chest as she hit the ground. 'Well, the offer still stands but it looks like you've got this.'

She heard Jason laugh, nervously. Ilene got hold of Gerry as he started to regain consciousness. As she tried to lift Gerry to his feet, a tree demon swiped at her side, taking a chunk out of her just below the ribs and she dropped him.

Gerry was suddenly alert. 'Where's my family?', his mind shouted, instantly.

'Dojo.', Ilene replied.

Gerry jumped up and leapt up the stairs, as Ilene heard more windows smash upstairs. The demons were following the Dunneys.

"I'll meet you there.", Ilene called as he disappeared, trying not to slip on her own blood and to ignore the pain in her torso. Part of her was mad that he just left her bleeding, but she understood. Plus, she was no weakling. Not anymore.

Gerry entered the dojo, sliding under the legs of a demon and slicing upwards with his clawed hands simultaneously. He reached his son, who was bruised and cut while he clutched his mother protectively to him. The relief that filled Jason's eyes when he saw him gave him strength.

Suddenly the demons surged forward into the room through the shattered sliding door and both Gerry and Jason felt a small pang of dread at the numbers, until they heard a small grunt from a voice they knew. Ilene burst through the hoard from their rear, blade singing through the air and eyes gleaming a bloodthirsty red. One slipped past her, but Jason spotted it.

Jason leapt in the demon's path and sliced off one of its legs before taking its head off in on swing.

Ilene saw a brief look of pride and surprise pass between Amanda and Gerry. Gerry was beaming, his irises glowing the most beautiful shade of aquamarine Ilene had ever seen.

More demons poured in through the window and Ilene and the Dunney lads went to work clearing a path to the waterfall. Rock demons started to come in through the windows, their weight splintering the sill frames. Ilene was starting to wish her parents had made the manor out of marble.

A tree demon swiped at her, caught her on her injured side again and clawing at her neck. She shrieked with pain, while it ran out of the door, just as Jason got clipped on the leg by a rock demon, breaking his femur neatly. Amanda was using the opportunity to duck under the carnage and edge nearer to the waterfall. The demons just ignored the weak and feeble human, so she used this advantage. The cry of her son froze her blood and she turned from her task instinctively. But she remembered the importance of her goal. If she made it, if she restarted the barrier, all this would stop. They'd be safe.

At this moment, David, dressed in his usual black suit, strode into the room the demons parting without looking as if he was one of them. He scanned the room in seconds and noticed Amanda about five seconds sooner than she'd have liked him to. Ilene noticed this and threw her sword at his head without thinking twice. He lifted the gun that was already in his right hand and pulled the trigger just as Ilene's blade hit his head, knocking his shades off.

The bullet flew in what felt like slow motion as Amanda reached the waterfall, entered her left shoulder, just next to her heart. She screamed in shock and pain, her eyes popping wide open.

The Verndarar froze as they saw her back arch in reaction and her grip on the wall that she was climbing, fail. She started to tumble downwards, turning towards them.

Amanda gasped and groaned. She felt strange. There was pain and numbness at the same time but she could feel warmth spreading down the front of her torso. She could see the look on Ilene's, Jason's and Gerry's slowly rising faces. They were clamouring to reach her, but she was surrounded. She had to save her family. It was her only thought as she dropped to the floor.

I have to protect my family.

Jason felt like he was frozen to his spot. He could feel and hear the despair and anger of his father and Ilene, but at the same time nothing else existed around him. Among the chaos around him, the world felt silent and still. All he could hear was his heart pounding in his ear, his heavy breaths and all he could see was him mom bleeding out on the floor.

Gerry and Jason started powering their way towards Amanda, their faces frozen in horror, while Ilene slew the enemies at the back, heading towards David. None of them could see Amanda suddenly and the panic that hit them made their swings wilder.

Suddenly a little hand rose from the edge of the fight and touched a vine at the side of the waterfall.

Ilene had reached David and she forgot about her weapon and started the pummelling his head and chest with her fists. Then she lifted a blade from the wall near her, driving it through his shoulder and into the wall, pinning him to it. His scream of pain was a satisfying sound. If that made Ilene a sick person, she didn't care.

Amanda pulled herself upright and reached for the Verndari emblem. She didn't have much time. She had to do this one thing. She climbed up on one of the stones and touched it. She went back in her mind to her last conversation with her friend and employer, Siobhan McCampbell. She'd taken her hand and told her something that no-one else knew except her husband, the words that would keep "the little ones safe". She never knew what that meant but now she did. She smiled as she said them, her body getting colder with each passing second.

At the moment Amanda started to speak, Gerry was surrounded, Jason was pinned down and the remaining demons had encircled Ilene and were about to grab at her.

"Domus nostra defendat. Praesidio nostri genere. Gaia Rogamus!"

291

With the last two words, the waterfall gushed into life, a faint blue light glinting off its surface and a beam of light of the same colour blasting out from the water as it hits the stones below it.

The blast shook the walls and blasted through all of the Tainted within its radius. The red glow in their eyes died and they all tumbled to the ground in pieces, becoming what they once were.

The house was still for a few seconds.

Then a scream shook it. Gerry stumbled forward to his wife, calling her name and already crying.

Ilene gasped as she looked at her pale limp body lying halfway in the waterfall's pool. Gerry lifted her torso out of the water, cradling her face, rocking her as he wept.

The strength in the waves of his pain were like a force-field, stopping her or Jason from moving. Ilene fought against the heaviness in her legs and moved forward. Jason moved even slower, transfixed by the scene, bile rising in his throat, every part of him trembling. His legs didn't even feel like they were connected to the floor. He didn't even notice the break in one of them. He was cursing his new-founded abilities. He could hear his mother's heart slowing.

The pool was already turning red. Some blood was on the wall and floor, the smell of it was everywhere. Ilene stumbled forward and almost fell at her side. She was trembling. She wanted to run but she couldn't. She clutched at her neck, looking for her father's pendant, but it wasn't there. "*No!*", she whimpered. "That Arboris!"

She took Amanda's cold hand and looked at Gerry. "I have to try..." was all she could manage to whisper.

Ilene tried to clear her mind. But all she kept thinking was how much she needed Charlotte and Mek'el or her parents, and why they weren't there. She was fighting the anger stirring and clawing away inside her, when she opened her eyes again, they were beams of bright blue light like the crystal, and the water started to shine in the same hue. She dropped her right hand into the pool and tried to focus. She called out with her mind, but it ended up coming out of her mouth instead.

"Please. Can anyone hear me? I don't have the strength. Help me save her, please!", she cried.

Jason was now openly sobbing. He knew what was coming.

"Please! Anyone! God! My *people*!", Ilene screamed, tears pouring down her face and her breath catching in her throat. "Give me your strength! *DO* SOMETHING!"

The next name that came out was called with such rage and despair that everyone looked at her.

She took her deepest breath and bellowed like she wanted the whole planet to hear. "*GAIAAAAAAA*! PLEASE!"

Ilene grunted and almost fell into the water, what was left of her strength completely spent, but still crying, too tired to move.

"Why isn't it working?", she whimpered, her lower lip trembling.

Gerry sighed, suddenly calmer. Acceptance had taken over, although she could feel him fighting for what was happening not to be so.

"The stone is made to heal Verndarar who are already healing. But....", he faltered, his emotions giving way, "...my angel is only human. And the wound is too extensive."

Ilene managed to lift herself onto her elbow, her head spinning like she had never felt. She looked at Amanda. Her beautiful face was smiling.

Gerry was rocking her in his arms again. Ilene could only just make out his next words. "Please stay with me.", he implored, "I'm so sorry. I have so much to say. So many regrets."

Ilene watched as Amanda used the remnants of her strength to squeeze her husband's hand. "Well, ... I have none. We had a beautiful son together, and he got to grow up... in peace.", she stated, in a voice almost too quiet to hear. "But...most importantly... we all got to be together again. And that is worth.... *everything* to me."

Jason and Gerry smiled the same smile, tears pouring from their eyes.

Amanda reached for Jason, and he took her hand. She smiled her normal large smile, her blue eyes slightly unfocused.

"Take care of each-other.", she whispered.

And with a sound like a sigh, she was still, and her eyes clouded over.

No-one moved.

For a few seconds, it felt like everyone had shared her fate.

With one shaky inhale the silence broke, and Gerry cried out with a sound so painful, it burned itself into Ilene's bones. He abandoned all his reservation and wept in the most uncontrolled and unrestrained way.

He was no longer a General, an immortal or a soldier. Today, he was just a man, a man who had lost his greatest treasure. Today, he was human again and it was the worst torture he'd endured, easily surpassing every wound that had been inflicted in his very long life.

Ilene sat up slowly and painfully, not because of her wounds but because of the tirade of mental pain coming from her right.

All she could hear was Gerry's voice screaming, saying it should have been him, calling for his wife and Jason repeating the phrase 'She's gone.' with no emotion attached. He was in shock and in Ilene's opinion he was the luckier of the two. She would have given anything not to be able to feel but she'd give even more to take away Gerry's pain.

Ilene moved to Jason as his brain began to process the scene. She could feel his emotions rushing forward like a tsunami, with him standing alone and unprotected against it. His breathing suddenly became faster, and tears began to fill his eyes. They danced about wildly before settling on Ilene's face. Then he broke, unable to catch his breath. He was backing away, terrified to even look at Amanda's body.

Ilene moved as fast as she could, wrapping her arm around him while he fought the onslaught of feelings hitting him, wave after wave.

Ilene couldn't say the usual phrase of "I know how you feel", but she could definitely say she knew what the Dunney men were feeling. She couldn't escape it.

Ilene had never felt so helpless. The anger and frustration were starting to rise again. This room contained three of the most powerful beings in existence and all they could do was sit and watch the woman who had loved and cared for them all just slip away.

What was the point in all their strength if they couldn't even protect their own?

At that moment Ilene heard a grunt and running. She turned quickly, tore a stone slab out of the dojo floor and flung it low before her captive reached the door.

David screamed as the blow snapped his shins.

Ilene gave Jason a few more seconds of her hugs, then she whispered, "I'll be right back."

She stood slowly and walked to Velhonen's right hand man, pulling the sword she'd trapped him with before out of the wall.

She grabbed him by the neck and lifted the squealing wreck off the floor. She turned him towards another wall and pushed the blade through his left shoulder and into the new wall, pinning him again. Her teeth were gritted but lengthening as her emotions started to be reflected in her appearance. Her top lip quivered as she struggled to contain herself.

But in her peripheral vision, she saw her father's statue laying on its side, surprisingly undamaged. She closed her eyes and exhaled.

She walked slowly to her father's likeness and stood him back up, in his rightful place, watching over her, as always.

She walked towards the dojo and paused in front of her prisoner. She couldn't even look at him for fear of losing control. "You're lucky what they say about the Verndari-born isn't true.", she informed, through still gritted teeth.

Through the pain, he was laughing. Ilene's eyes blazed a dull red, which was probably worse than bright and blazing. "You're weaker than I thought. You won't even kill me."

"I *protect* life! You and your Master just got hundreds or thousands of people killed tonight!", Ilene seethed, turning to him, her clawed hand inches from his eyes. "I'm not a monster. But I should kill you for your part in this!"

David smiled still, pleasure filling his cold blue eyes. But then Ilene's face became pensive, and she raised an eyebrow. "But Death is too easy. Too quick. Maybe I should take a page out of your Boss' book.", she mused, leaning towards his ear. "I know everything that Velhonen did to my friend in there."

Suddenly the colour drained from David's face. Ilene stood back, smiling darkly, and balled up her fists, landing one strong blow to his head and knocking him out.

As she walked back to the dojo, she heard the sound of air disturbed by wings and tensed. She grabbed the nearest weapons to her and began racing to the main hallway. She would fight all night if she had to. But she froze when she heard a voice calling her.

Charlotte was flying right into the front door, eyes bright yellow with panic, blood, soot and dirt smeared across her face and clothes. Ilene dropped her swords and began to cry immediately, almost tumbling down the stairs in pure relief. Charlotte swooped to her and caught her just in time.

Everyone arriving in the hallway gasped at the garbled and jumbled thoughts pouring from Ilene. Bob broke into a lupine run straight towards the dojo.

As the tears started to slow and Charlotte's arms loosened from around her, Ilene realised the hallways were filled with people with injuries, from dislocations to lengthy gashes with exposed bones. Her people needed her. This wasn't the time to focus on herself.

Ilene stood, leaving Charlotte's arms and walked towards the warriors. She asked to bring Jason down when she could, as he needed healing too. There was a lot to do, and she needed her strength and focus. She might not have the pendant anymore, but she felt it earlier: she still carried some of its power.

And so, she got to work.

*

In the hours that followed, the sun rose on a broken house and household.

Ilene had healed everyone physically and some had showered the blood and debris off them. But the house was quiet.

Charlotte's next task was tending to Amanda. They bathed her, dressed her in her favourite dress. They laid her in the room she slept in and surrounded her with flowers she had tended to. Even in death, she was still beautiful and youthful.

Everyone gathered downstairs in the dining room again while Gerry remained upstairs, still and quiet.

Ilene sat in the dining room watching her people's memories with her eyes closed, so she could focus. The common thought was that although there were casualties, the Tainted were defeated too easily. Now they knew why: Velhonen attacked an entire city to draw the Verndarar out, empty the Manor so a B-Team could enter and steal the pendant.

Ilene was clenching her fists so hard that everyone in the room could hear her bones cracking. Charlotte took her hands and crouched down to eye-level.

Ilene was shaking, silent tears rolling down her cheeks. She'd never felt this level of rage before, the kind that makes you motionless. "He has to be stopped. This *cannot* go on."

Charlotte sighed and nodded. "I know. But how? There are at least twenty portals in the country, and we don't have enough numbers even if the majority of us were in fit condition, to be at each one. And if Velhonen shows up and manages to get through we wouldn't reach that portal with enough of us to help. It's suicide. He'll just cut down each wave that comes."

"But he can't go through even with my pendant. He'd need me and I can't do it."

Toshi cradled his arm, which was beginning to set after Ilene's treatment. "I have a bad feeling. He wouldn't go ahead with such strategic attacks if he hadn't figured out a way to get what he wanted." He looked around him. "He's figured out a way through."

The Masai warrior was leaning against the wall as her leg was held straight with a large splint made from a piece of the front door, a large bandage on the left side of her head. She'd lost an ear and a chunk of her jaw during last night's fight. 'How many are injured? And how many did we lose?' she asked, wincing as she tried to move.

"I don't know.", Niamh answered, her red locks accented by patches of bloodstains. "This room feels emptier."

Bob's booming voice then filled the room. "Where is Marcellus?"

Ilene's face dropped. She hadn't seen him since the meeting the night before. She hadn't seen him leave for the battle or return.

"I heard him leave for his smoke break after he went upstairs for a bit. He must have used the toilet.", Charlotte answered.

Ilene's brain suddenly started working again. She realised she'd heard something Marcus had said earlier on the same day. "Oh god!", she groaned. "Charlotte, when did you meet Marcellus? I noticed he wasn't in any of the group photos or paintings."

Charlotte furrowed her brow. "He's been living in the human realm for centuries; he was a bit before my time. I met him twenty-five years ago. Why do you ask?"

Ilene let her mind run, watching Charlotte's face change from pensive to horror to anger.

'Roger met him first.', Charlotte explained, amidst a tirade of expletives. 'He had been poking around the house at the windows and doors. He claimed he'd been looking for your dad.'

Ilene saw a Marcellus from a different time in Charlotte's mind. He was, as usual, sharply dressed but in very dated fashion.

'You see, most Verndarar only used the ground or second floor of the house. Very few people ever went on the first floor. Even I have never been in the dojo. We trained outside in other private locations. Roger was experimenting at the time with the pill you took all your life. He was Dr Fischbeck's guinea pig. So, when he met Marcus at first, he couldn't read his mind and didn't trust him. Marcus said he'd stayed in the human world too long and wanted to re-join the fight, so he came looking for a General. Marcus seemed frustrated but I just thought it was because he was a bitter and miserable old bastard. Maybe it was because he couldn't "hear" your dad.'

Bob sat down slowly, looking aghast as he followed Ilene and Charlotte's train of thought. He began thinking of suspicious and unexplained moments he could remember.

'Mek'el gave him the benefit of the doubt and welcomed him.', Bob added, shaking his head. 'Amanda once said he used to look around the house a lot, at every wall, door and fitting, when he thought we weren't looking, claiming he was interested in architecture.'

Charlotte shrugged. 'I thought he was just inspecting everything and being his snobby usual self. He inspected and graded everything and everyone. It wouldn't surprise me if he actually created Yelp. It was just odd.'

Ilene looked inside her head. 'Aside from the snooping, why did you think he was odd?'

'Because every time we spoke about Velhonen, large scale attacks or Gaia, he'd start doing tax and profit margins calculations in his head. He also did it...'

Charlotte faltered, her jaw clenching and her hand slowly gripping her legs as she sat.

'When? When, Charlotte?', Ilene asked. Charlotte's mind suddenly sounds like a disturbed hive.

'Two days before your parents died, at a dinner meeting we had, where Roger told us he'd be away for a while, visiting the UK, and...' she answered slowly, struggling to keep her breathing and feelings even. '...last night, as he left for his cigarette break.'

'That's why he was extra grumpy and was about to light that cigarette in the house he knew he couldn't smoke in. He wanted to go and inform his client, his friend.' Ilene mused, her head in her hands. 'He started acting up the moment he arrived and saw who was here. The meeting at 2. I can't... *believe* it!'

Ilene didn't know whether to cry or smash the room to pieces, so she stood and started pacing instead. She had so much going in on inside of her, to be honest, that she just felt numb. She knew she should be exploding with fury, but nothing came.

Velhonen had a meeting at 2 last night. That *snake*! He was working with him the whole time. He was faking a friendship, gaining their trust and feeding their enemy information. He was advising him when to strike. But why? Why at those times? What did they know?

Ilene's head was spinning. She had to sit down again, so she went back to her chair and did so. She couldn't believe it. Someone under her own nose, the man who betrayed her parents had been socialising with her feeding information to their murderer from day one.

He had been trying to find out where the barrier was and how to disable it. He'd told Velhonen where to find her parents so he could fight them when they were alone and unprotected by their friends. *He'd* told Velhonen to strike last night, so he could remove both layers of the house's protection, so he could get to her and the pendant. The reasons for these plans and actions made no sense, but they didn't feel important at that moment. Because of Velhonen's greed and Marcus' lies, two people had lost parents.

'THAT BASTARD!' Charlotte all but screamed, her teeth grinding against each-other and hands shaking with rage. 'If I ever see him again, I'll *kill* him *MYSELF*!'

Niamh walked to Charlotte and hugged her, tears streaming from her green eyes, her uncharacteristically tender behaviour switching Charlotte's anger to bitter tears.

Could no-one be trusted anymore? How could so many of their kind take sides with this mad man and play a hand in the killing of their own people? They needed a plan.

Ilene was still frozen in place, staring at nothing. "He must be stopped. We have to figure out a way."

"There is a way.", Gerry said, stepping silently into the dining room. Everyone nodded in respect. Ilene looked at him, shocked. His eyes were dead. No light, no colour. There were no more emotional waves coming from him anymore. It was like he was a statue again.

"If I reinstate myself as a General, I will be able to sense the nearest active portal. We can make our stand there and finish him.", he answered.

Charlotte's face looked pained. If he did this, he'd make himself a target. Also, it was evidence that nothing in the human realm held him there anymore. As advantageous as this was, it was also heart-breaking.

Bob nodded and walked to him. "How do we do this?", he asked. "It's normally done by elders or another General."

Gerry turned to Ilene. "How about the only living descendant or our most Senior General?", he suggested.

Ilene almost felt like running away as everyone turned to look at her, yet again. She felt like they were expecting far too much, like she had no power or authority, not in the way they thought she did. She was not her father or her mother. She was just some girl from north London.

Gerry felt her mental recoil. 'It's OK. You can do this. You inherited his abilities and skills, and through his blood, his position. Also, there's something extra about you that I don't even think you've realised. You are beyond special.'

Charlotte nodded. No-one had ever thought of it that way. But then there had been no Verndari-born children who had been there to test this out before, or children born to Generals.

Ilene sighed. "How can you be so sure? I'm not my dad. I don't think I can do half of what he did."

Gerry smiled and pointed to his head. Ilene saw memories playing side by side, from the previous centuries, memories of her parents in battle and the others were from the night before. When Ilene focused, she noticed incredible similarities in stance, wrist flourishes, even facial expressions. No-one had shown her this before. All this time, Ilene thought genetics were the only thing that linked her to her parents. But now she saw things she'd been doing before she even turned eighteen. They'd always been a part of her. Maybe Gerry was right. Maybe this could work.

Ilene looked at Charlotte, as she smiled back. She was shaken to her core. She didn't know what she was capable of anymore, save healing a few wounds.

Ilene turned to Gerry. "What do I need to do?"

"There's a book in your father's office. In his safe. It has a black leather cover. There's a lot of handwritten Latin in it.", Gerry instructed. "Bring that and meet me by the tree in the back garden."

Ilene nodded and ran up the stairs as she listened to Gerry ask Charlotte to look into the dealings of Hillman Consolidated, especially the illegal ones.

She walked into the office and opened the safe using her real birthdate. She'd seen the book at the back before but never really paid attention to it. It was so old. It looked like it was written on papyrus. The leather cover on the spine was worn down to the woven cords that bounds its pages.

She took it gently and headed for the nearest window. Gerry was already halfway across the lawn. She could hear him doing breathing exercises, talking to himself and telling himself that he could do this, that he had to do this.

Ilene leapt out of the window with no wings. She walked up to the tree where Gerry stood, facing it. She placed a reassuring hand on his shoulder. She didn't know why she felt the need to ease his nerves, but she could feel his inner conflict.

He turned to her and forced a smile. "Sorry.", he muttered, sheepishly. "I just thought I wouldn't be doing this for at least a couple of centuries. I thought... your parents would always be here if ever this world faced a big threat."

He sighed and looked at the stars above him, like he was seeing them for the last time. "Oh well. Standing around and thinking won't save anyone. Let's do this."

Ilene nodded, opening the action book. "So, what am I looking for?", she asked.

The book was full of ink drawings, inscriptions, seal stamps and entries in languages she'd never seen.

Gerry stood next to her. "Look for something called 'Sacramentum imperatore', it should be right after 'Seniorem foedus'."

As Ilene was thumbing through, she was aware of feet crossing the lawn. The house had emptied and everyone, including Jason, drew closer, ending up standing in a semi-circle, near them.

'I'm not a good public speaker. I hope this sounds ok.' Ilene apologised, just as she found the page.

Gerry smiled and nodded slightly. 'You'll do fine. Let's do this in English. Latin is trickier.'

Ilene looked through the instructions and placed her right hand on Gerry's chest, just over his heart.

"Gierozzo Dunney.", she began in a calm and clear voice. "You stand here today to reclaim, your position as general. Will you promise to protect the human realm?"

Gerry inhaled, his eyes starting to shine with fresh tears, the full realisation of what he was doing hitting him all at once. "I will."

Ilene could feel him struggling to box up his emotions, for his own protection, as he had been for the last few hours.

"Will you lead and protect your people, making the optimum decisions to keep them and our realm safe?", Ilene continued.

305

"I will."

"Are you willing to lay down your life for the sake of humanity, even if it means the loss of your kin?"

Gerry's eyes were brimming now. "I am.", he replied hoarsely. Ilene could see memories of Amanda flowing through his mind. They were a comfort now, strengthening him, making him ready to face what would be coming.

"Do you swear to avenge all who we have lost, and stop those who to destroy all that we love, whatever the cost?", Ilene asked, affirming to herself as much as seeking affirmation from Gerry. Her emotions were making her eyes burn.

Ilene didn't realise it, but her eyes were glowing the colour of the pendant's gem again, as was the hand that was pressed against Gerry's heart.

"I swear it.", Gerry replied through gritted teeth, swallowing the ball in his throat.

Ilene nodded. As she spoke her last words, the group around them echoed the same words. "Nos sequamur, imperatore."

The light under her hand shot into Gerry's chest and lit up the surface of his skin. Gerry felt a weight lift in his mind, like a veil, and his thoughts became slightly clearer.

All Verndarar in attendance balled their right hands into a fist and touched that fist to the left side of their chest, all bowing to their General. There hadn't been in Imperatore ceremony in many hundred years, but they remembered it like it had happened yesterday. This took them back to those days where they were stronger, freer and less fractured as a people. It made them long for it again, and they would get there, one way or another.

Charlotte walked forward smiling. She wrapped her arms around Gerry's shoulders in a stronger hug. "It's good to have you back, General.", she greeted.

Gerry smiled, only slightly, and nodded.

Toshi stepped forward and bowed, his good hand resting on the hilt of his family sword. "So, what is our next move?"

"I'm planning to find the nearest active portal and get there as soon as possible. If he's already there, we cut him off and take him down. If we beat him there, we form a blockade and keep him out. Either way, we'll make sure he gets nowhere near the portal since we don't know what his plan is.", Gerry explained.

Ilene looked around at the bandaged warriors stood around her, already mentally preparing to fight.

Jason's voice filled her ears, surprising her but making her smile.

'Ilene, you're sad. Why?', he asked, his eyebrows furrowing slightly with concern.

Ilene sighed. "I just don't want anyone here to die. He has the only weapon that can kill our kind.", she replied, aloud.

Every Verndari was looking at her now. Resolution and fondness were coming at her in waves. Some were surprised at her concern. Some were proud of her inner strength.

Ilene held their gazes. She didn't look away. And she wasn't going to run. "Are you sure?", she asked one last time.

Gerry stepped closer. "You forget, I haven't lived in over twenty years. And most of us, lithified or not, would say the same. We're tired of hiding, tired of living in fear...", he answered, gritting his teeth again, another lump coming to his throat. "...tired of losing family."

When he said "family", so many faces flushed across the collective minds nearby.

"We've been doing this for centuries. It's our duty, and we'd have it no other way.", Gerry continued, reaching his hand out for his son. Jason walked nearer to them both. "But you two, you've lost enough for people so young. You don't have to fight. You can sit this out. My question to you both is: are *you* sure you want what comes with fighting with us?"

Jason and Ilene exchanged glances. No thoughts passed between them, but their expressions said everything.

Ilene turned to her people. "No more hiding. No more waiting for my friends to come home.", she declared, shaking her head. "Look into my mind. I have been alone and afraid and unaccepted for as long as I can remember. I was never happy with who I was. I felt like I was living someone else's life. And then I came here, and I found out that my life could be more than I ever dreamed."

Charlotte was grinning, brimming with motherly pride. Kuruk was welling up, proud and happy. Ilene could feel everyone releasing their emotions, so she let her emotions go too.

"Velhonen has been unchecked for too long. Thanks to him, we have lost friends, our freedom and the lives we should have had. But we *will* take it all back.", Ilene was bristling now, her skin changing, the changes coming faster and faster with each wave of her own feelings. "I came here not knowing what I was really looking for, and I found purpose, patience, support, love and family that is more beautiful than anything I've ever known, made up of the greatest warriors this world has ever produced."

Ilene unsheathed her father's sword, looking at her home and her comrades. "I'll be damned if I'm giving that up.", she stated quietly, her fist clenched around her weapon. She turned back to Gerry whose eyes were watery too. "No more hiding. No more suffering. We will be free."

Gerry's grin took her by surprise. A burst of laughter came from him, his face crumpling with emotion and a look of yearning. He put his right fist over his heart and bowed.

"There's my General.", he gushed, his chest puffed out with pride, joy and relief emanating from him like the gentle warmth of the sun, as he stood straight again. "Your parents never left."

Ilene smiled and bowed back as Gerry turned to address their small army, some who were wiping their eyes. "We'll free this world and free ourselves in the process. Let's get ready."

They all turned and headed back into the house, some bumping fists, some with arms around each-other's backs. Most of them headed to the armoury on the second floor. Ilene, Gerry and Jason went into Roger's personal office and found some weapons. Ilene put the black book back into the safe. Then she walked to the corner cabinet, opened it and looked at her parents' armour. She hadn't looked at it properly before, but it was made simply to guard the front of the torso and leave the back exposed. It was also a collection of concealed weapons. It was matte black and covered in straps and links to accommodate a constantly changing body. The boots, which on her father's armour were more like shin-guards with detachable soles, were a mixture of leather and metal components. Her mother's boots sported spikes on the front and a sharpened heel. She called Jason over mentally and took out her father's armour.

Jason stepped back, a look of fear on his face and a sense of low self-esteem coming from his mind. "I can't.", he protested, "It was your Dad's."

Ilene smiled. "I know. But it's mine now. And I can think of no-one else I'd rather have wear it."

Jason was still shaking his head. Ilene laid it down on the nearby desk and took his hand.

"I feel like he would have liked you. You're strong, you can handle yourself and have protected and maintained his home for years, even though you didn't want to. I know this seems like a lot right now, but I just know that once you have been trained, you'll be the kind of warrior and man that would make both of our fathers proud."

Jason smiled. "How can you be so sure?", he asked, his nerves lessening but still tangible.

"I knew it before I could hear inside your head. And if in doubt, stick by your dad or any of the other ancients.", Ilene advised, reaching for her mother's armour.

"Hey! Did you forget? Super-hearing.", Gerry mumbled from across the office, checking a very large crossbow and strapping it to his front.

Jason and Ilene laughed. Jason looked straight at Ilene and held her gaze. 'OK, I'll wear it.', he conceded. 'But I'll stay by *you*."

Ilene smiled and felt her skin go warm. Around the centre of his irises, there was a tinge of pink, mixing with his natural blue. Just as quickly as she saw it, it was gone.

Ilene tapped him on the shoulder with a light, playful punch. "I'm going to change. I'll meet you back here in a few minutes."

Ilene found a halter top and black cropped leggings to wear under her mother's armour. Then she pulled her thick curls into a puff ponytail to keep it out of the way and looked in the long mirror in her bedroom. She pictured her parents getting ready for their missions. They were experienced and had each-other's backs. Ilene was wondering if she could match up to what they were. She knew she couldn't. She could only be herself and do things her way, being better than she was yesterday. And she wasn't alone either. Like them, she had an army of friends.

Ilene wasn't religious but she said her own version of a prayer. She asked her parents for their strength and the fragments of their memories she had within her to stay with her, tonight most of all.

She sat down in front of her laptop and sent a quick email to her family in London, telling them how much she loved them and missed them. She tried to keep her mind clear of the thought that it could be her last communication with them. She couldn't think about anything but her mission.

Ilene walked back into her father's office. Gerry was sitting next to Jason, 'talking'. Gerry was telling him how proud of Jason he felt and how proud but nervous his mother would be.

'She'd tell you to fight as dirty as possible so you can come home.', Gerry instructed, smiling at the memory of her face.

'Did she fight dirty?', Jason asked, trying to picture her having this stressful conversation.

'Yes.' Gerry answered, laughing aloud. 'She used to wrestle and win, even against me. She used my love for her to her advantage. She was amazing, feisty and at times terrifying.'

'But you've fought demons!', Jason responded, furrowing his brow.

Gerry raised one eyebrow. 'Women, even the human ones are scarier. Trust me. I'd rather take on ten demons instead of your mother when she was mad at me or not letting something go.'

Jason nodded. 'True.'

Ilene laughed and they both looked up.

Gerry smiled. 'Speaking of which, here's a she-devil now. I'll meet you both downstairs.' He ruffled Jason's hair in a fatherly gesture, while Ilene could still hear that it still freaked Jason out a little as well as filling him with joy. Gerry stood and helped his son up as he started to stand too. He hugged his son again and then winked at Ilene as he walked out of the room.

Jason sighed. "I always pictured what my dad would be like. I have to say, this...*he* is cooler than anything I could have imagined. I can't believe I feel so sure and strongly about him already."

"Well,", Ilene said, leaning against the doorway, "Being able to see into someone's head speeds up relationships. I'm the most distrusting person I know, but in less than a year, I've met a bunch of people who I'd happily trust with my life."

"It's bizarre.", Jason commented, shaking his head.

"Absolutely.", Ilene agreed. She shook herself out of her thoughts and stepped in front of Jason, looking at him properly. "You look good."

Jason grinned. "Really? Thanks. It feels lighter than I thought it would, Also, did you know there's a patch of tartan on the inside?"

Ilene's eyes widened a little. "Oh cool! To be fair, I found a kilt ad sporran in my dad's closet. I like that there's a bit of him in each thing I find in this house."

Ilene started walking out of the room into the hallway and Jason followed.

"What part's your mom?", he asked.

Ilene smiled, devilishly, descending the stairs. "The African sculptures, some of the décor, a few cooking utensils I've seen at African market stalls and houses before, and most of the weapons.", she said, proudly. "Also, this Kente-cloth inside my armour."

Jason leaned over while they walked. "Oh, nice. That's pretty."

Ilene smiled, rubbing the patch stuck to the inside of her breastplate. "Yeah.", she agreed. "Like her: vibrant and beautiful."

Jason and Ilene were descending the main stairway together, readying themselves. They become acutely aware of a sudden silence as the rounded the corner into the last part of the staircase which led directly to the hallway.

They stopped walking.

Every eye was on them. Ilene heard no mental chatter at all which freaked her out. She was suddenly worried if they'd be upset at what they were seeing but the feeling that came from them all simultaneously, it was relief. They felt comforted. It was like seeing their old friends again. Charlotte was already crying and oddly enough, so were Toshio and a couple of others.

Ilene could hear how much they missed her parents and the incredible pride filling their hearts.

As one, the older generation bowed to Ilene and Jason as they continued walking down the stairs.

Kuruk walked to Ilene and hugged her. "You look incredible, Ilene.", his deep voice rang, even though he was speaking softly.

Gerry was staring at his son, dumbstruck. "It's like it was made for you.", he breathed, smiling gently.

Charlotte squeezed Ilene again, collecting herself and not allowing herself to speak aloud as she did so.

A dark-haired woman with blue eyes and lots of tattoos, who Ilene knew as Skögul, laughed. "What do you expect? They come from fine warrior blood."

Jason's eyebrows lifted and found himself laughing nervously. Ilene heard him "say" 'Me?'. Ilene patted his back.

'Yes, you.', she confirmed, showing him memories of him fighting. Jason suddenly smiled and stood a little straighter.

She noticed that the others were watching her, and Jason's interactions fascinated how his demeanour changed so much from their mental conversations and shared images. They had never seen it before because none of their children were seen in each-other's company after they "came into" their powers. Ilene could hear the anticipation of how well they could fight together in the upcoming battle.

Jason heard some of these thoughts too. His mind was becoming stronger, hearing more and more of the voices around him. He looked over his shoulder at Ilene and shrugged, making a face that made Ilene suddenly giggle. He looked so dumbfounded and awkward. 'Maybe we should try and be as linked as possible when the fighting starts.', he suggested.

Ilene nodded.

As one they all started filing out of the front doorway and turning left to go to the back garden. Everyone did a last check to make sure they had as many weapons as they could carry.

Gerry stepped ahead of them, to their front, and faced them all.

Every warrior in the garden formed three lines, each person standing around six square metres apart from each-other.

The unfurled their wings and looked to Gerry for directions.

Again, another beautiful sight. If it wasn't in bad taste and their existence wasn't a secret, Ilene would take a picture of this. Instead, she burned every detail into her mind.

Jason stepped at the front of the formation and looked to Ilene, who stepped up to him and wrapped her arm around his waist.

'I can't wait to be able to do that,', Jason thought, as he watched Ilene unfold her large wings.

He flinched a little, being lost in his own thoughts and forgetting that she could hear, as Ilene replied. 'Soon, J. If we live through tonight, we'll train together, fight together and fly together.'

Jason smiled. 'I look forward to it.', he responded, quietly. 'So, let's survive.'

Gerry exhaled slowly, stretched his neck on each side, rolling his shoulders and unfurled his wings, which somehow seemed bigger.

He jumped from his position and took to the air, his little army following him, rising slowly from the grass. The nearby trees danced in the wake of the movement of their wings. He closed his eyes until he could feel a tingling sensation coming towards him. It felt like static, but stronger. He knew where to go. It was coming from the North-East.

Gerry inhaled and brought his wings down, moving forward so fast that Ilene and Jason's jaws dropped. The rest of them soon caught up, keeping him in their sights and but not wearing themselves out in an attempt to stay right by him.

They passed over towns and villages, looking at the damage done to them by the previous night's attacks. Ilene hadn't watched on TV in the last day but the scale of the attacks she saw from everyone's minds were enormous and couldn't be passed of anything but supernatural. It would be almost impossible for Charlotte and her team to convince the general population that it had been natural disaster, if the same thing had happened everywhere around the world. Trees, rock and water can't move that way and be rationally explained as terrorists in costumes. They would have a lot to deal with after tonight. Their anonymity was more important than almost anything now. They would either have to stay in the Verndari realm, if they were successful, or live as human until this calmed down.

The whole thing could turn into a world-wide witch-hunt.

Ilene didn't need to worry about that now. They were above the cloud line now, out of sight.

Thankfully, they didn't need to travel far. Gerry's senses took them to Helmcken Falls in Wells Gray Procivincial Park, still within the province they lived in.

As they looked down, preparing to land, they saw what was awaiting them. In front of the waterfall, laying on the floor and tied together, looking filthy and almost dead, was Mek'el and two other people, male and female.

Ilene's heart leapt at her first glimpse of her mentor in over a month, but she managed to keep her emotions in check, even as she took in the rest of their surroundings. The waterfall was glowing, the same colour as her pendant and she could see the Verndari realm through it, like in her dojo. However, the feelings she was sensing from her comrades told her this wasn't just an image, as it had been so many times before.

In front of the waterfall, a small force of the Tainted were waiting to delay and diminish their ranks.

Ilene took out her father's sword. They would not succeed. All they would accomplish would be serving as a nice warm-up for them all.

Jason looked at her and nodded.

'Ilene, let's stay linked now until it's all done.', he thought, tightening his grip on the double-headed axe he was carrying.

'OK.', Ilene agreed, somehow instinctively holding open their mental channel and opening her mind more than she ever had, so that they could see through each-other's eyes, like they had in the house accidentally, the night before.

Ilene dropped Jason down on the floor and landed a few metres in front of him.

And then it began.

Seemingly harmless parts of their landscape stood up, some of the water from the base of the waterfall sprang out and trees shattered, splintered and regrouped into their tainted humanoid and animal forms. It was a sea of red eyes and malice.

So, they all went to work. Swords, Sais, axes, serrated chains, shields, daggers, maces and spears soared through the air and stumbling the first wave. No-one got in anyone's way because everyone knew precisely where their friends were. The most skilled powered through, taking out limbs, heads and vital points with barely a sign of strain even though they were sometimes cutting through stone and century-old bark.

Ilene worked her way through the middle, dispatching some and calming whichever of the Tainted that she could, and returning them to their normal state.

She and Jason protected each-other, Jason doing most of it when Ilene was using all her energy on purification and Ilene doing it when Jason didn't notice something in his surroundings. They left a circle around their path of dead elements and squirming parts.

Every now and then Jason's mind would slip to fear or missing his mom. When that happened Ilene would mentally comfort him and pick up the slack.

In a matter of a few minutes, the force that had awaited them had been obliterated.

Gerry found his son quickly, amazed to find him with barely a scratch. He looked between Ilene and Jason. He didn't know whether to thank her and praised them both.

He could find no words, so he had said none. He nodded to them both.

Ilene ruffled Jason's hair before flying herself over to Mek'el and the other captives. There was no heartbeat or body heat coming from the man he was tied to, and the woman was barely breathing. They both looked so gaunt and weak. Seeing Mek'el like this made Ilene tremble with fury. Ilene closed her eyes and stilled her pounding heart. She took deep breaths and concentrated. Ilene mentally detached from Jason, sitting herself down in front of them. Her hair and eyes began to glow after a few seconds.

Gerry heard her grunt, turned toward the sound and walked hurriedly towards her. "Ilene, stop!", he cried. "I remember what this did to you when..." He faltered, pushing back the memory his brain was instantly bringing up. "We need you."

Ilene smiled, her glowing eyes creasing in the corners. "No.", she answered a slight echo in her voice that Gerry had never heard before. "You need Generals, experienced strong soldiers. I'm already a little depleted, I won't be as much help as these two will be."

Jason charged forward after hearing the conversation and the thoughts in his father's mind. "No!", he called out, but Gerry's arm blocked him.

He looked at his father's face. It looked a little pained. "She's right, son.", he explained. "Strategically, her idea is valid."

He looked over her shoulder. "And an unexpected smart, level-headed and giving decision for someone so young."

Ilene laughed, despite knowing what the outcome could be. Her personal revenge might have to wait or might not happen by her hands. She grunted again she felt her energy level dropping. It was getting harder to hold herself up, but as she looked in front of her, she saw the two-figures filling out and starting to stir.

Gerry sighed. 'It's working.', they all thought as one.

Mek'el and the woman who was East Asian, opened their eyes simultaneously and sat up like marionettes as the shock of new energy hit them.

Ilene's glow dimmed and then disappeared, and she slumped back into Jason's arms, who Gerry hadn't even seen slip past him.

Ilene was breathing slower than normal, and her skin was cold to the touch, but as Jason held her, asking mentally if she was OK, her vitals picked up. She opened her eyes and smiled at him. Jason sighed and squeezed her tight in his arms.

The older Verndarar all breathed a sigh of relief with Jason. Some of them tended to Mek'el and the woman, named Mei, who were both light-headed but well.

Niamh spoke up suddenly. "I've been meaning to ask, how the hell can she heal us without the pendant?"

Ilene sat up slowly and tried to stand. She didn't do well and slumped back down. "The same way I can tell you that the pendant is through that.", she answered, lifting her chin towards the waterfall. "And that once I'm near it again, I'll get my strength back."

Mek'el spoke for the first time. "She's connected to it, the way Roger was."

Ilene let out a little laugh of relief. "Hi.", she said softly, her eyes glistening with happy tears.

Mek'el slid himself along the ground next to her and she leant herself against his shoulder. "Hello, you.", he answered. They were both smiling. "I missed you too."

Ilene was so done with being an emotional wreck these days, but even she couldn't stop the one tear that fell when she heard that.

All the soldiers retrieved their weapons and headed towards the waterfall. Jason put Ilene onto his back. She had protested as wildly as she was able, but he silenced her with two words.

"Hush. Rest."

Gerry and Ilene's eyebrows shot up. Mek'el laughed. The fact that anyone other than Charlotte could even try to tell Ilene what to do was amazing. Ilene grumbled but held onto his neck and wrapped his hands through her knees, in a piggy-back carry.

Mek'el and Gerry had a quick hug, wishing they had time for it to be longer and make up for the twenty-plus years apart, but it would have to wait.

They stood in front of the gateway, ready to work.

'Are we too late?', asked Toshio.

'We'd know if we were. This forest would be trying to kill everyone.', Skögul deduced.

320

'True.', Gerry said. He looked at Mek'el. 'Are you ready to go home?'

Mek'el sighed, forgetting himself and speaking aloud. "My friend, I've been ready for centuries.

Gerry patted his back, reassuringly. 'I'll go first.', he told everyone, 'I'll observe what's happening and send you the plan. Agreed?'

'Yes, General.', everyone replied but two. Mek'el and Mei were stunned for a moment. Ilene sent them both a quick update and watched their faces fall. Mek'el's eyes brimmed with tears, but in a breath and with the gripping of his sword, they vanished. There was no time for it yet.

Jason heard her and tapped her leg, tutting. 'Rest.', he reminded her.

Ilene rolled her eyes. 'Are you ready?'

Jason looked at the image in front of them. 'Nope.', he replied. 'But we never truly are, are we.'

Ilene shook her head and spread her wings, slower than usual, shielding them both as everyone else did the same.

They stepped into the pool and advance steadily, the water tumbling onto them, heavy and deafening.

And then there was light.

STONE

Chapter 18

The Portal

The first thing to hit Ilene's senses was taste and smell. The air was so clean, it made her wish her lungs were bigger. The place smelt of fragrant flowers, some she knew and some she'd never smelled but the scents were addictive.

It always seemed to be daylight there. The floor was a carpet of soft moss that covered every space between the realm's gargantuan trees.

But no sound of life. This was a peaceful place, but Ilene doubted it was meant to be this quiet.

The next sound made them all jump. There was a thump like a roll of thunder and the biggest Tertis Ilene had ever seen crashed through trees that broke and regrouped into a large Arboris. Vines snaked up the Arboris' body and reached for Ilene and company.

They didn't have enough time to raise their weapons. Some were knocked flying, other were bound before they could dodge the vines.

Ilene was knocked from Jason's back landing on her wings and breaking one before she could "put it away", as Jason was struck in the ribs by the large Tertis. An Arboris wrapped itself around her and held her to the floor.

Gerry heard the impact on his son's bones along with the sound of the air being knocked out of him and turned to run to him, but another Arboris grabbed him covering his mouth.

Velhonen stepped out from the wake of the Tertis' destruction, smiling. He was holding the Mwisho, the deadly sword, and it was already soiled with Verndari blood.

The mystery and dread as to the owner of the blood made the captured Verndarar furious and even though they couldn't free themselves, they struggled with all of their might, some hurting themselves in the process, not caring about the pain.

As they did this, Velhonen stood looking at nothing in particular and listened. Then he heard something that made him smile. He turned to his left and looked up towards Gerry.

"Welcome back, ... General.", he cooed. "Such a shame about your wife. Amanda, was it?"

Gerry let out an angry scream that startled everyone around him. His skin and size changed over and over, cutting some of the vines holding him but new vines replaced them soon enough. He got worse as David and Marcus walked up behind Velhonen. Marcus was out of his normal suits and wearing some blood-stained Verndari armour which made the sight of him worse.

Now Charlotte was becoming increasingly enraged, spitting curses in languages that Ilene hadn't known anyone still spoke.

"MARCELUUS, YOU *BASTARD*! I WILL BREAK YOUR BONES ONE AT A TIME IF IT'S THE LAST THING I DO ON THIS EARTH!", she screamed, spit and sweat flying as she did.

"WHY?", bellowed Kuruk, "We *trusted* you! Roger trusted you! How can you *betray* us like this?!"

Marcus frowned, his eyes closed and sighed. "I do regret having to hurt some of you.", he confessed.

"HURT?", Toshio shouted, incredulity creasing his timeless features. "Our friends *DIED*! You're wearing a dead man's armour *right now*!"

"Some things are more important!", Marcus exploded, silencing the group. "I'm tired of Gaia and the elders controlling us and taking what is rightfully ours!" He looked at Velhonen as he said this. Velhonen lowered his head.

Marcus smiled at the confusion on the faces around him. "All will be revealed shortly.", he promised. He turned and started walking back in the direction he had appeared from.

Velhonen's faced became focused as he raised his head again. "Take them to the temple."

The Verndarar struggled as they were carried or dragged through the shattered forest. They were bruised and bleeding, but their bodies simply healed again. Ilene could feel that they were wary of the blade in Velhonen's right hand but none of them were scared to die. They'd been there, done that. They were more afraid of failure and leaving their friends to suffer.

The trees suddenly fell away, and they came into a large clearing.

Another smell reached them, and it changed the mood completely.

Blood.

On the right of the clearing was the spot where meetings and ceremonies were held.

They could all see a few dead Verndarar on the floor, their irises grey and pupils large. Their blood was staining the ground, reflecting light as it coated the stones of what Roger had once called the Amphitheatre because of its design. It was a few descending rows of stone benches carves in a semi-circle around the level speaker's ground in the middle.

The Verndarar that remained were bound and held by some of the

Tainted outside of the meetings grounds around. They were either laying, some were awkwardly standing, and others were held over the ground by vines. Ilene and her group were lifted and carried with them in the same direction, some of them staring hard at her trying to figure out who she was.

Ilene noticed some holes in the ground. Velhonen had obviously tainted some of the trees in the realm after his arrival to add to his ranks.

Down at the speaker's level of the Amphitheatre were the three remaining elders, as young-looking as the others but wearing robes in the same colours as the stones. They were tied together and held captive by a group of Arboris.

With a gesture of Velhonen's arms, they were lifted and carried ahead of them, behind Velhonen and Marcus.

This strange procession of conquerors, captives and elementals final reached the centre of the clearing. There was a paved section of the floor with stones laid out in a circle about twenty metres in radius with a large notch missing from the centre stone, and in front of that was a building that was clearly ancient. It looked like a mixture of an ancient Chinese palace and a Nordic Hall. Vines and moss grew and snaked up its columns which were decorated with carving of animals and flowers.

Ilene didn't know how a building could look so humble and grandiose at the same time, but the Temple achieved it. This was the place Mek'el had told her about, the place where the other Verndari children were taken after they came into their powers. It suddenly terrified her. Maybe she would be sent there after this was all over.

Velhonen stopped and looked at the building with disgust. Then he turned to face his prisoners.

Everyone halted just behind him, still bound.

"I have brought you all here...", he announced, "To learn the truth."

The mouths of all Verndarar became uncovered, instantly followed by a flurry of anger and cursing.

Velhonen just spoke over them ignoring them. "I hear what is in your minds. It is true what I intend to do. I will lay waste to the Human World."

The struggling and protesting picked up from all of them. Ilene popped a few joints trying to get free, thinking of her adopted family. All she could see was London burning and bodies everywhere, just like in the dreams she'd had over the past few months. It was all about to happen, and she was weak and powerless. She felt the frustration coming from everyone around her. Their rage was shaking the trees.

After they had worn themselves out trying to break free, some now crying quietly, Velhonen spoke again. "But you are my people, as much as I've tried to deny it, so you deserve to know why."

Marcus stepped forward. "You all know me and my real name. But I am not as young as all of you."

Ilene frowned when she heard Marcus describe the individuals around her as young. What the hell was going on?

"I...am the *first* Verndari.", Marcus explained. He stopped in front of them all and began his explanation. "In the beginning, Gaia used regular humans who were strong, selfless and brave, like everyone here. But without the abilities we now have, all but me died fighting the Tainted. I was the first to be given the ability to use the skills and defensive traits of the world's creatures. We talked endlessly and she taught me about this realm and the things she could do. I began writing them down as I figured them out, over the years. All our ceremonies and "promotion" rites were penned... by me!"

The last word burst out of him like a gunshot. His teeth were gritted, his eyes flashed red and then the colour died into a dull, deep blue. "I would have done anything for her. I wrote the Book of Calling in secret, using my understanding of our worlds and Gaia's powers to try and guide the humans. They were headed down a path of bloodshed and destruction. But with my leadership they could have reached their potential and the Tainted wouldn't have appeared at all. We would have been guides and teachers instead of protectors, breaking ourselves over and over for millennia for the sake of beings who just... don't deserve us."

He sighed. "Gaia got upset. She was too forgiving of humanity's flaws. She had hoped that they'd become better on their own. She said it wasn't our place to interfere or she'd have simply wiped them out with poison or disease years ago.", he stated, Gaia's quotes said in a mocking voice, like a child angry at their mother.

"So, she cast me out into the Human World and closed all the portals to this one.", Marcus sat down on a nearby stone. "She took some of my abilities, changing her powers so your average Verndari couldn't use the book of calling. I wondered the earth alone for centuries. I was angry, bored, ...and I couldn't die.", he continued, his voice breaking with sadness. "...no matter which ways I tried."

Ilene suddenly felt his sadness, despite his betrayal.

"But around half a millennium ago, I heard tell of a young man, ruthless, intelligent and no-one knew where he had come from. I became interested in something for the first time in I don't know how long. So, I found him. The moment I got near him, since we were in the same circles, both of us having amassed a substantial amount of wealth, I heard his mind and realised he was like me. I told him about the Book of Calling and taught him how to use it. And lo and behold, he was the loophole I'd needed. He was no ordinary Verndari. He was *born* of Verndarar. So, we amassed a small force of defectors and deputized our power and influence between them, so

329

we had control of groups, governments and sectors all over the world. He told me what had happened here and that no-one had seen Gaia for more than a century before he'd left. Which means that these cretins have her imprisoned somewhere.", Marcus stood and walked over to the elders as he got to his last few sentences, striking one of the elders on the head.

Ilene could hear the mental susurrus of the group protesting and crying out that the elders wouldn't do that to Gaia, that they served her, as they all did. But the doubts and nervousness were appearing in their minds.

Marcus nodded. "I hear you.", he acknowledged. "Well, that's why you need to listen to this young man so you can understand why we're here right now."

Again, the bound Verndarar stated seething. "Murderer!", some screamed, their faces changing and skin rippling.

Velhonen stepped forward looking at the anger surrounding him. "YES!", he shouted silencing everyone. "I am a murderer... but not in the way you believe and everything I have done for the last few centuries is so that I could get back here."

The other Verndarar looked at each-other, puzzled but still angry.

"As Marcellus explained, he was exiled, and Gaia revived more brave souls and out of these first few she selected four and made them the Elders. They were chosen to manage the Verndarar that came after, lead them and monitor missions, reporting back to her. One of them was my father. Verndari couples began to fall in love and have children. In this realm, there are few things that are almost as powerful as Gaia. Elder are one but surprisingly there is another that is even more powerful than them. That is a young Verndari-born on the first day of their eighteenth year. Their raw energy and power made them more connected to Gaia and the human realm. They saw visions and because they could literally see into each-other's minds, they were a powerful hive mind, and they would move into the temple to use their connection to allocate missions and help the Elders see the battles as they were happening."

Skögul growled. "We already *know* this."

Velhonen's eyes suddenly became sad. "But this is what you didn't know.", he countered.

Velhonen sat on the knee of his giant Tertis and sighed. Ilene saw an image pull itself reluctantly to the front of his mind like a file being retrieved from the back of a basement.

"You have been lied to, my people. What did your Elders tell you? That I lost control? Flew into a rage?", Velhonen laughed a soulless, pained laugh. Ilene could feel him shaking. He exhaled and focus. He began "broadcasting". "Here we go.", he muttered to himself.

Sound filled the mind of every Verndari, but Ilene and Jason got more than they bargained for. They saw a little blonde boy inside a house, near to where they currently sat or stood, in this realm. He was in a basement looking longingly from the window at other children playing. Ilene recognised the face of the boy instantly in the window's reflection. It was Velhonen.

"I was born and hidden in my father's house for the first eighteen years of my life. My mother told me it wasn't safe to go outside.", he explained.

Ilene trying to shut out the images. Seeing young Velhonen innocent and happy was so disarming.

"She loved me so much. I now understand how my loneliness and frustration hurt her, but the consequences of giving in to my wishes would have been worse." Ilene saw him trying to go upstairs and his mother reassuring and denying him with sad blue irises. She was beautiful, long auburn hair, green eyes, her young face dusted with

331

freckles.

Velhonen had tears steaming silently from his face as the longing for his mother's arms filled his chest. Jason was crying too, and they looked at each-other in understanding.

"My Father taught me self-control and strategy, honour and how to fight. I was lonely, but the two of them were all I ever needed. So, I pushed my loneliness aside for years."

Then Velhonen's face became still. "One day, when my father was certain I had control, he told me the truth, why no-one could know I existed until after I turned eighteen, maybe nineteen."

Everyone was so engrossed that they didn't speak anymore.

"Gaia gave the Elders a sword so that if there was a Marcellus incident again, it could be contained. We're too powerful to be let loose.", Velhonen recounted, his brow creased. "It is true that an eighteen-year-old did lose control of his emotions once. He had been missing his mother. An Elder grabbed this sword warn him, hoping the threat of it would make the young one sees reason and calm down but, in the struggle, the young one fell on the sword, dying. His name had been Darius."

There was a cry and then a sob from one of the captives. The mother of this man began to weep, images of a young happy man with dark curls and a beautiful light brown skin mixing with Velhonen's thoughts.

"Then something happened that changed everything.", Velhonen continued, looking into the skin, a tone of mock wonder in his voice. "The boy's power flowed into the nearest Verndari, namely him."

Velhonen pointed at the Asian elder in the green embroidered robes. Ilene heard from the others that his name was Malik. Malik didn't move or speak but he closed his eyes, his face twisted in fury at having been captured by this exile.

"This increased his powers and ability to change his physical appearance. They had been alive a long time and were unhappy with taking orders. Tired of the facade that covered their rage and frustration. There were close to gods. Why not get closer? Who needed Gaia? So, these three took turns calling the young ones into a private room...", Velhonen's voice shook. "...and killed them *all*."

A stunned silence filled the clearing, and no-one moved. The warriors were in such shock, they didn't even realise the Tainted had released them all from their confining grip.

They all looked to their Elders for at least some denial, a protest, a laugh to say it was a joke.

"Oh, I forgot to say. I used the Book of Calling and some substances my company cooked up to stop them from lying or being able to control their minds. So, if you don't believe me, read away.", Velhonen added, a devilish smile on his face. He leant down and whispered, "What's eighteen plus three?".

They all gave the answer immediately without moving their mouths.

Toshio stumbled forward. "Please Malik,...tell us it's a lie, that you wouldn't-"

But as these words left his mouth, the sound of screams from memories long buried filled all the minds in the clearing. Children called out in pain only to be abruptly silenced.

Eyes widened as some recognised these voices.

Then everyone fell apart.

Some were sobbing, some were screaming, and some didn't move. The pain was worse than anything Ilene had ever felt. It was like someone was setting fire to her lungs and skin. She was laying on the floor writhing, changing subconsciously, clawing at the ground as she heard the trees creak and the ground shift. She couldn't even draw in breath due to the pain. Ilene and Jason were barraged with memories of frightened faces and blood spurting, pouring and splattering across very nearby surface.

Velhonen was now sobbing, seeming oblivious to the chaos he was causing, lost in his own memories.

"I was a fool!", he cried. "I should never have snuck out! My Father told me we would escape the realm together, but I became impatient, knowing I'd be free soon. I wanted to taste freedom on my own terms, not because my parents said I could. I managed to get outside, and someone saw me, so I became afraid and rushed back home. I was stupid, *stupid, STUPID*!"

Everyone quietened down. "The next day these.... MONSTERS came to my home and broke down the door. My Father begged them, tried to reason with them and eventually fought them when they wouldn't listen."

They all heard his Father, an older heavier-built version of Velhonen step forward. "I won't let you do to him what you did to the other children. I won't let him die."

And then, the voices of their beloved Elders in a tone their didn't recognise. "We will have his power. It is the only way to keep her subdued. Hand him over or we will take him."

There were sounds of a struggle, Velhonen's father crying out and a thud as two things hit the floor.

Ilene was still in agony, groaning and crying out, with the pain and Velhonen's pain added to it.

"Next my mother took a weapon to try and save me.", Velhonen continued, reluctantly.

Ilene didn't know why she closed her eyes, as if it would stop the images. With their advanced knowledge, they saw what she was planning to do, despite her keeping her mind clear. The blue Elder, a Caucasian woman called Serilda, broke her arm and spun her right into the one green Elder, Malik, who was holding the sword. She gasped and then cried out in pain looking down at the blade that had entered her chest, feeling it scrape her spine and ribs as she pulled herself back and fell onto the floor. She scrambled towards her son, who was crouched against the wall where she'd left him, shaking all over, wide-eyed and panting.

Her breathing was becoming more and more shallow as she dragged herself on her one working arm towards her terrified child. "Ru-...run." she wheezed. Her body slumped to the ground with a sigh and her eyes glazed over, irises turning grey.

Velhonen could be heard gasping and calling for her. A few seconds later, a glow like moonlight lifted itself out of his parents' bodies and moved towards and into Velhonen, disappearing and darkening the room again. He took in a large breath and sat up straight. He felt himself grow strong, even stronger than he'd felt a few days before when he'd turned eighteen.

He looked at the Elders as they readied themselves to take him. Malik, in black robes at the time and standing over his father's body, was reaching for his pendant, the stone that matched his blood-stained robes.

In a movement almost too fast to see, Velhonen charged forward up the walls of the basement that had been his world until yesterday. He landed behind the first of the two elders, Ekong, in the red robes, and landed a blow with one arm that broke his spine almost neatly. He grabbed Serilda by the arms and pulled until he heard a sound. He smiled. Malik, who appeared to be in charge of the other two, clearly looked less confident than he was a moment ago, gripping his sword nervously.

Velhonen smiled and ran up to him, stopping right in front of him. The Elder made the mistake of raising his right arm out to the side to swing and the left balance his stance. As he approached, Velhonen wrapped his arms around him. The Elder's face wrinkled in confusion. Then Velhonen turned his right-hand's palm-side out and interlocked his hands into an S-grip. He clenched his jaw and began to squeeze. The Elder tried squirming, but it was no use. The sounds that followed made all listeners flinch over and over, and Malik, who had received the injuries so long ago, yelp anew as if it were happening again.

Ilene and Jason were attempting to stand, traumatised by the wave of images and forgetting how to breath normally.

They saw Velhonen looking out of his window for the nearest portal and how to get there. He took up the Elders' precious sword and gently removed his father's pendant, kissing his forehead one last time.

He went to his first forbidden portal, the front door of his house and ran through it.

STONE

He heard people cry out around him, as he ran and jumped as fast as he could, his breath burning his chest. He could somehow hear someone discovering the bodies and calling everyone to arms.

The Verndarar rewatching this for only the second time felt sad suddenly. All they had seen was a boy running out of one of their Elder's homes carrying a blood-stained sword.

The emotions among the group were growing again but it was pure hatred and disbelief toward their leaders.

The memories continued as Velhonen found a waterfall at the edge of the forest, the one Ilene and the others had just come through.

He heard voices approaching, and his tear-stained face turned towards the noise. There they were, several Generals and quite a few other warriors. Among them were Ilene's parents and the faces she now knew, all except Marcus, of course, as he was already in the Human World.

The portal glowed, sensing his power and fear, and Velhonen saw another landscape through it. He didn't even hesitate, he simply leapt through.

Within seconds he was out, somewhere in Norway, the land of his Father had come from. He ran, accidentally sprouting wings in his panic. He teetered through the air like a baby bird. He realised that he could see heat signatures of animals and people below, so he headed for the nearest fjord and crashed himself into the snow, burying himself as far as he could.

There he waited, curled into a ball and shivering for hours, until the sun came up and there were no sounds nearby. He slowly climbed out of the ice and into the sun, looking around him. The coast was clear. He slumped down and cried bitterly, longing for his parents, remembering their love and seeing their bodies in his mind no matter what he did.

Then the anger took over. He shouldn't have left those Elders alive. They'd just keep hurting more people like him. "I'm sorry, Mother.", he apologised, wiping his tears away. "But I can't run. I just can't."

Then the memory melted away and Ilene and Jason found themselves back in the clearing. Velhonen raised his head. In his eyes, Ilene saw the boy he'd once been. Then in a movement of his hand, a clench, he was gone and replaced by the man she'd learned to fear.

"I vowed I would come back to expose the truth about them, in front of everyone so they couldn't hide or deny it. And everyone.... EVERYONE would know what they did to my family! And so many other families."

Ilene rolled onto her knees. "Velhonen.", she called.

Velhonen turned at the sound. He hadn't heard a woman use his given name like that since he last heard his mother's voice.

He tried to keep his heart cold, but that sound had softened him, momentarily. "You must be Ilene.", he replied, his chin lifted as he tried to appear unaffected by her. "Marcus told me about you. The Secret Child. Your mother accidentally thought your name before she died."

Ilene suddenly looked angry despite her weakened state. "Why?", she asked. It was all she could think of at the moment. Her original question had left her mind at the mention of her mother.

"Why did I kill your parents? New information.", Velhonen answered, turning to face Ilene. "Marcellus had told me that the gems wouldn't work for anyone else but the person they'd been assigned to, hence why my father's pendant works for me. But them Marcellus told me

338

about the Book of Calling and something he hadn't figured out before, but I'll get to that in a moment. I went after him, and I was told he and his wife were leaving the country alone. No escort, no friends. I could get to them on my own and take the pendant myself. All other attempts by people I'd sent in the past had failed and I didn't know how to control the Tainted yet, only how to encourage their creation." Velhonen looked impressed for a moment. "They fought well. They took down a small army that I created right where I found them, but they didn't manage for long. As I approached them, I realised they didn't have the pendant. I killed her as punishment for not telling me where it was and them, I killed him because...well, I didn't need him."

He shrugged nonchalantly and few Verndarar flashed fangs and claws. Velhonen rolled his eyes, motioning to the Tainted with his free hand. In seconds, everyone was bound again. He chuckled and continued.

"Do you know the only thing more powerful than a General assigned to a stone? More powerful than even a young Verndari at the height of their abilities?", Velhonen asked, excitedly, like a sordid Game-show host.

No-one answered, so he tutted and stood. "Generals in a state of extreme emotional compromise.", he answered, walked to the Elders and stood over them. "That's how I got through your portal and that's how I control my armies."

Ilene struggled and protested. "You've done what you came to do. What now? Kill them? Kill us all?"

Velhonen's face twisted into a sickening smile that instantly made Ilene's heart sink. "This spot...", he announced pointing to the notch in the central paving stone. "...is a direct link to the entire Human World, if you use this sword as a conduit."

Everyone looked at each-other, confused and wondering why they had never been told or warned of this. The confirmation they needed came when all three Elders cried out in desperate protest.

"I can either heal that world or raise every Tainted creature possible and wipe it out. I and only I can do it, because these Elders do not have the power and neither does anyone less than an Elder, because they would not likely survive the energy that would be taken by doing this. I will weaken and it may kill me, but I don't intend to die today."

"Good luck with that.", Jason and Ilene answered as one.

Velhonen laughed, looking amused at their bravery and futile struggles. He walked over to them casually. "So, I will need a little juice. Three Generals should do it. And since I'm one short thanks to that....", he waved a hand dismissively and irritably. "...portal business, you will do."

Jason and Ilene almost sobbed as Velhonen pointed at Gerry, a malicious smile on his face.

Gerry growled angrily trying to keep his mind clear and his eyes on Velhonen.

Everyone was already emotionally compromised and the fear of what was coming made it more of a strenuous effort to pull back and box in those feelings.

"I've missed you, my pet.", Velhonen cooed. "Come back to me, or..."

Velhonen swung his sword, stopping it just short of Jason's throat. "...I'll kill your son.", he hissed.

Gerry froze, a sudden wave of terror coming from his mind. He was revisiting his wife's death subconsciously and had stopped breathing as he struggled to gain control of himself. "If he dies here, Gaia can't revive him, can she? It would be a shame for you to lose...everything in two days."

Gerry was now crying angry tears, his whole body shaking as he looked at his son.

Jason swallowed and kept still. Despite the threat and the fact that he was shaking so hard, he managed to speak. "G-go ahead. I'm...not more important than every person on earth."

Ilene couldn't breathe. What the hell was he saying? He must have been crazy. Now was not the time to play hero.

Velhonen paused, tilting his head as he thought. "Hmm. No... I've changed my mind. If I kill you, your father will go numb.", he mused, moving his sword away, but sending a swift kick to Jason's ribs when he tried to charge at him. "I need emotion....and nothing works like a constant state of fear."

Velhonen lifted his left hand and mumbled some words. Jason cried out tumbling to the floor.

Ilene moved her legs with all her might to run to Jason, the ground cracking with her effort. But she was held and soon trapped by an Aquatis. She tried to fight but she was suspended by water and every move she made was adapted to, holding her away from him.

She watched as his legs turned grey and stopped moving. He called out in terror as he started to lose feeling in his limbs and lungs. He cried out to his Father, who writhed in vain to try and get to him, tears pouring from both of their faces.

Then he was still and silent, frozen in a position of pleading and a look of horror, his hand reaching out to his father.

Velhonen walked to Jason's figure and lifted his right hand, holding the sword over him again. There were no brave words from Jason now. He was helpless. Velhonen looked at Gerry as he took a breath and prepared to swing downwards.

Gerry screamed in a voice that took everyone by surprise. "NO! *NO! PLEASE!! PLEASE*...DON'T!"

Now he was sobbing. He'd failed. He had only two responsibilities: protect his people and protect humanity. He had failed at both. Gerry's frame changed, his back craning over his knees, all his strength sapped away. He couldn't fight any more.

Velhonen laughed, a laugh so joyful and out of place, it only enraged Ilene more.

But as her rage swelled, she ran out of air, remembering too late how to grow gills, and she began to pass out. The scene in front of her began to darken as her body shut down.

*

Ilene felt before she saw. Her lungs were burning, and her limbs felt like noodles. She coughed and spluttered, heaving liquid from her body. As she took in a breath, she opened her eyes. It was so dark that she thought she hadn't opened her eyes at all, even though she'd felt it happen. She thought about owls and her vision became clear, her surroundings lightening as if a candle had been lit in every corner.

She saw Kuruk shackled nearby looked at her, as he attempted to break free, straining. The shackles didn't look particularly strong, but the engravings on them told her they were Verndarar-make, so he'd be struggling for quite a while.

"You're awake.", Charlotte confirmed, relief in her voice. Ilene realised she was laying with her head across Charlotte's lap and

342

Charlotte was now stroking her shoulder. Ilene's face and side were the only places on her body that were warm.

Ilene sat up slowly and everything was still stinging. Everyone's despair had left its mark.

She looked around with her temporary eyes. "Where...?", she asked, but as she did, she got her answer. "I know this room."

She'd seen her new prison recently. In a twisted sense of poetic justice, she'd been imprisoned in the room that had been Velhonen's limited childhood world. She was his drawings, toys, books and bed. This room made her sad but not because she and her friends were trapped in it.

As she scanned the room, she saw something and cried out. She half-crawled, half-dragged herself to the motionless figure lying in the corner. She hadn't spotted him at first because she was looking for body heat. Jason had been put in there with them. He didn't appear to be damaged or missing anything.

She began to cry as she cradled his head. "I'm sorry... I'm sorry!", she whimpered. "It's all my fault. I should *never* have got you mixed up with all of this. I brought this on all of you. I should have just stayed in England."

Charlotte was heading towards her, trying to comfort her. "It's not your-", she began.

But Ilene was spiralling. She couldn't hear sense. All she could see was her part in the pain. "Mek'el wouldn't have gone looking for Velhonen. Marcus wouldn't have sent those monsters to the house. Amanda's gone because I came back. Mek'el got captured. And Jason...We're going to *lose!* The world will die and it's *all my fault!*"

Ilene sobbed until she ached but kept sobbing anyway because it was the only thing her body still had the strength to do.

Charlotte wrapped her arms around Ilene, despite her wrists being bound together. "Mek'el would have been found eventually, with or without your appearance. They'd have got through to this realm without the stone. The house could have been attacked twenty years ago. You gave us our purpose back; *you* found out where Velhonen was hiding and what he was planning. You reunited a family. You gave us our friends back."

Ilene was still crying. Charlotte kissed her forehead. "Why do we fight?", Ilene whined. "We fight monsters that spring back up like *weeds*. There's more despair and evil among people than there ever was. Yeah, people are more aware and try to change things but the real ones who make the horrors happen don't change or even stop! The Verndarar are literally here because of the *worst* qualities of humanity."

Charlotte nodded. "It's true. We have a continuous struggle. People have a great capacity for evil. We've all died *and* lived through it. But things are actually *better* than they have been. We've seen their horrors and sins, but I've also seen amazing things. I've helped with relief efforts, watched nurses work thanklessly through plagues, wars and crises, seen people give to strangers, invent life-saving things and fight for other people's rights to be free and considered."

Ilene turned to look at Charlotte's face, focusing through her own sadness to get glimpses of her memories. Charlotte looked down at her and smiled gently, pink tingeing her blue irises. "There will always be evil and despair in places. But if humans can achieve so much good in five-hundred years, what do you think they can achieve over the *next* five hundred?", she mused. "That's what *I* fight for. The good. The possibilities. The potential."

Ilene looked from Charlotte to Kuruk, who was nodding. Then she looked at Jason's frozen face. The other's had lived through this for years, whereas she'd only has to handle it for less than one. They'd lost friends to death and lithification too but kept going. They never gave up. No matter how much ugly reality was thrown in their faces, they brushed it off and kept moving forward. Ilene realised she couldn't stay defeated. If they quit now, then over five hundred years of struggle and loss would have been for nothing.

No. Not on her watch.

Ilene furrowed her brows. "Why are only *we* in here?", she questioned.

Kuruk chuckled. "Good behaviour."

Charlotte looked a mixture of proud and ashamed as she spoke. She was only ashamed of having to say it aloud, but not of the action when it had happened. "We...er...kind of kicked off after you drowned."

Ilene laughed and then immediately shuddered. "Yeah, I'm not going near my pool for a while."

Ilene stood slowly, being careful not to jostle Jason at all. She didn't need to look for the window from Velhonen's memories. She found it immediately. The others were still where they were before she "passed out". Velhonen had Mei, Mek'el and Gerry suspended above him, being held by vines against the giant Tertis standing behind him, so they couldn't wriggle much, if they ever found the will to try. Velhonen had all three pendants around his neck.

As Ilene was watching, Marcellus sat down in front of the captives, facing Velhonen. Once he was sat comfortably, Velhonen pulled out the Book of Calling and began reading. Mek'el groaned. Ilene could see a pale light leaving from the three Generals' chests and drifting into Velhonen's.

It has begun. He was draining them.

Ilene turned around and walked to Kuruk, taking hold of his shackles. He protested as she gripped hard and began to pull. Charlotte joined his protest as they all heard Ilene's wrists and knuckle joints creaking. Ilene ignored them as her middle finger snapped along with part of K's left shackle.

"I have a plan.", she grunted, as the shackle completely broke with two more of her fingers. "Kuruk, please free Charlotte."

Kuruk and Charlotte looked at each-other and then watched Ilene move back over to Jason's body, her fingers healing themselves quickly with quiet click and crack sounds. She sat down cross-legged and scooped Jason into her arms.

'What's the plan?', Charlotte communed, as Kuruk worked on her shackles in the same quiet way Ilene had.

'Kuruk and Charlotte, I need you to free the others. There's a window upstairs that goes directly to the trees. Bust through and sneak round in camouflage. On my signal, everyone needs to take out the Tainted. Charlotte, you handle Marcus.' Ilene was slowing her breathing and closing her eyes.

'What's the signal?', Charlotte asked.

Ilene opened her eyes. They were glowing and her coils were snaking around her face in a non-existent wind. 'When we walk out of this house and attack Velhonen.'

Kuruk frowned. 'We?'

Ilene breathed carefully and placed her hand on Jason's shoulder. Her mental voice was suddenly loud and echoing, accompanied by a sound like glass scraping against itself. 'Jason, your dad needs you. Let's fight. And let's win.', she called.

A blue glow started at Jason's toes and moved up his body. The glow got so bright that Kuruk ran to the window to cover it, so the element of surprise wasn't lost, and they didn't draw any attention to their prison.

Ilene smiled. The glow died and there Jason lay, as if dozing. Then his hand twitched, and he took in a deep and loud breath. He coughed, his eyes fluttered open and his pushed his torso off the ground.

Ilene went to reach for him but then his body jerked and his back arched. His skin began to goose-pimple. Ilene could hear his bones shifting. Ilene smiled. She knew what was happening. Kuruk and Charlotte were instinctively moving to help him, but Ilene held up a hand.

'Stay back', she cautioned. 'You're about to see something you haven't in a while.'

Jason's hands contorted and then changed. They became claws and his skin grew thick, then furry and then disappeared altogether. Jason was grunting and fighting against what he was feeling. He hadn't even looked down at himself yet. He was still dazed from being turned to stone and then back again.

Ilene moved to his face and looked into his eyes. 'Jason, look at me. I'm here.', she called, focusing her thoughts.

Jason opened his eyes. He'd squeezed them shut when it had started. 'Ilene? What happened? What's happening to me?'

'I'll explain later.', Ilene reassured. 'But right now, you need to breathe and focus.'

Jason finally looked down at his hands and his breathing stopped short. 'I'm....', he faltered.

Ilene nodded. 'Like me. Breathe, Jason.'

Then Jason did something no-one expected. He smiled, a smile bright as noon sunlight. "Ha!", he cried, almost too loudly. With that sound, a pair of wings, feathered and large, like Gerry's burst through his T-shirt. Jason felt it and turned, trying to see them. He gasped. He stepped to Ilene. Ilene saw something she hadn't before. She saw a daydream, not a memory, as the edges of it were softened like an old movie. In it, Jason, Ilene and Gerry were all flying together. Jason was feeling so happy, touched and excited by the thought. There were small tears in his eyes. His life had gone from empty and painful to full of promise and hope in what seemed like a single moment.

Ilene smiled and then giggled. 'Soon. But now we have work to do.', she agreed. 'Put them away for now. You can call them back whenever you want. But now we need to save the others. Velhonen's draining the Generals right now.'

Jason's irises flashed piercing shades of yellow and deep blue. 'Dad!', he cried, mentally.

Ilene turned to Kuruk and Charlotte, who were staring at them, dumb founded. They didn't have time for words, but Ilene heard their rapid thoughts. K was stunned by Jason's transformation and control. Charlotte was shocked by the same thing but also that Ilene had brought him back and given him his birthright and abilities without being drained herself. Charlotte quietly concluded it was because the stone was nearby and in the place where it was created. Charlotte was now more confident that they could succeed.

A sound like rolling thunder overwhelmed their ears and the ground shook. Ilene looked out of the window. Velhonen had his sword in the ground and had started the process. He was visibly being depleted, pouring all his despair, malice and rage into the earth.

"We have to move. Now!", Ilene announced.

Kuruk flew straight up through the floor, sending earth and dust around him in a ferocious cloud, and Charlotte followed close

348

behind, in the wake of his movement. Ilene watched through their heat signatures as their legs turned lupine as they raced around the treeline to their friends. Ilene and Jason climbed up through the hole Kuruk had made and jogged to the front door. Jason grabbed a sword mounted on a wall next to the front door.

Ilene found another sword, slightly bigger than Jason's. Ideally, she wanted her father's sword, but this one would have to do. 'Jason', she called privately, re-establishing their connection.

'Yes?', he replied instantly. His voice was clearer and louder than before. 'Wow, this feels different.'

Ilene smiled. 'No matter what happens, your focus is to free your father and keep Velhonen down. Nothing will distract you. Do you understand?'

Jason's brow furrowed. A section of her mind was dark and was being kept that way. 'What are you planning on doing?'

Ilene turned to the front door. 'Setting everything right.'

Jason placed his hand on the furthest side of her head and brought the side of their heads together. Ilene could hear his worry, so she just repeated. 'Nothing will distract you.'

Ilene gripped the front door's handle and pushed, a little too hard, but she meant to do that. The door cracked, its thick timber buckling and shaking.

The sound made Velhonen turn his head, slightly slower than normal. Ilene kicked it wide open, shattering it from the crack outwards. Velhonen shouted angrily, not moving from his spot but standing a little straighter.

Ilene stepped out, swinging the sword she was holding over and resting it on her shoulder. Velhonen's eyes widened as he saw it, tears appearing in them, but then he began to shake, his teeth clenching and his eyes going from specks of red to beacons of pure hatred.

As Ilene watched Kuruk and Charlotte move nearer to the clearing, she noticed something new. Whatever Velhonen was doing, it was making even the trees and rocks of this realm stir. The thought of what was happening in the Human World as that very moment focused her mind even further.

"Well, that's got his attention.", she confirmed to herself.

Velhonen was breathing hard. He screamed at her, spitting as he did. "GIVE ME MY FATHER'S SWORD, *NOW*!"

Ilene cocked an eyebrow not moving other than that. "I believe the world you meant is 'please'.", she corrected. "Give me my father's pendant."

Velhonen shook his head, looking at the sword in his grip, light flooding down through it and into the floor. "Can't you see what's happening?"

Ilene couldn't deny it. His plan was working. She was being hit with wave after nauseating wave coming from every direction, but she focused like Mek'el had taught her to. She kept herself in the White Room.

Velhonen grinned, blood in his teeth. "You know that I can't do what you ask."

Ilene started to walk forward. "Then you're not getting shit, and I will *take* it.", she hissed through her teeth.

As she walked, she heard Gerry begging her not to antagonize Velhonen, thinking of Jason. But as he did, Jason stepped out. Velhonen's fury only grew, a confounded looking passing briefly over his face.

Jason smiled darkly at Velhonen and ran towards him, Ilene keeping up with him.

Ilene and Jason flanked Velhonen and attacked him from both sides, pounding him with attack after attack as Velhonen tried to fight with only one arm, sending beams of burning light out up his body and out of his hand. They burned whatever they touched leaving etched out circles with glowing ember edges where they had missed their intended targets.

Jason laughed. He was fast, maybe even faster than Ilene. He let his rage focus his mind and fuel his muscles. He leapt and somersaulted off trees and rocks, almost flying over them without needing his wings.

Velhonen held them off but barely. Noticing too late, that the other Verndarar were being freed and were taking on his Tainted army again. He snarled and screamed in fury, attacking more wildly now, less focused and deliberate.

Jason and Ilene's synchronicity was tighter than ever before. They didn't have to think about it. It was as if they were one being that had been temporarily split in half. Velhonen was being cut and hit every time there was an opening. He was visibly being worn down, now on one knee.

Velhonen then got the idea to use the Book of Calling and as he lifted the book from his pocket, Ilene sped in from his left and broke his free arm in three places, so fast that even Charlotte didn't see it. Velhonen shrieked but that was cut short as Jason came from his right and hit him in the head.

Velhonen dropped onto both knees, still holding the sword. His mouth wasn't moving right.

Jason slowed down to normal speed and walked up to Velhonen, taking hold of his good arm. "Can't turn anyone to stone if your jaw's broken, right?"

Velhonen looked into the young man's face and attempted to fight him, but soon his good arm was a good arm no longer. Velhonen raged as Jason lifted him from the floor and pulled him away from the centre of the clearing. Jason held him still while Ilene took the three pendants from Velhonen's neck.

Ilene didn't like to be childish, but she couldn't help it. This moment just felt too good. She leant into his face and sneered. "I told you I'd take it."

Velhonen's jaw was starting to heal. "You haven't won yet.", he eventually cried, trying to smile but causing himself pain in the attempt. "The whole world is Tainted. You don't have enough warriors to put them all down."

Ilene nodded and then looked past him to Jason. "They won't need to.", she confirmed.

The others were still fighting the Tainted army, and it was going in circles. No clear advantage or winner was visible. Charlotte was busy flying around Marcus, hitting with everything she had, gaining tangible satisfaction from every blow that landed. His thousands of years of experience didn't have a prayer against an enraged woman with a solitary focus in mind. He tried to counter her, but she was too fast and getting faster. She used her sword to cut the armour off his body. In a blur of colour and angry screams, he began to cry out himself as countless blows hit every bone in his body, and he began folding towards the floor. Charlotte stopped in front of him and picked him off the floor with both hands, holding him by the shirt he was wearing. She looked him in the eyes, tears building, and jaw clenched. She took one deep breath and brought her knee forward onto his head, hard. The crack and crunch sound this blow made seemed to echo. She dropped him to the ground, looked him one more time before spitting on him for good measure. Then she turned and walked away to re-join the fight.

Gerry, Mei and Mek'el had broken free thanks to another Tertis who had crashed into their restraints and Mei had joined the fight. Gerry had started by finding David, as his son didn't need his help. That was a short battle, but David was only human, so he didn't last long. David managed to fire three shots, but they all missed. Gerry struck him on his shoulders, which has only been partially healed by the book of calling. Then he took his sword and avenged his wife. He hated having to do it, as David was a human, but he couldn't be allowed to live after what he'd done and the knowledge he had of their world. He dropped to the floor in a heap. Gerry stood with his head tipped back and his eyes closed and let a few tears escape his eyes. It was done.

He turned towards the clearing and went to carry on fighting.

Mek'el and Gerry were running over, tears of relief in both their eyes.

Ilene nodded to Mek'el as she turned and walked towards him. But then she walked past him. Mek'el's brows almost knitted themselves together with confusion.

"Ilene, what are you doing?", he called following her.

"What only I can.", she answered, walking to the sword.

Mek'el got to her just before she touched the sword and grabbed her by the shoulder, but she simply twisted away, touching the swords hilt with one hand and putting the pendants on at the same time. She gasped and her stance faltered but she pulled herself upright again.

353

"DON'T!", Mek'el cried, trying to take her hand from the sword but recoiling as he felt all the strength in that hand leave it, like when he had been drained. It was as if the sword wanted to make it impossible to separate her from it.

Ilene placed both hands on the hilt. She grunted softly, light leaving her body and pouring into the floor, like it was leaking from her pores. She looked around. The trees were still squirming, the ground still quaked and the army was still standing.

Mek'el was beside himself. All his efforts to protect her, teach her and now he couldn't even touch her and still have strength to pull her to safety. He begged Roger's forgiveness, wherever he was. He was failing. He should be the one saving her, not the other way around. Mek'el looked at her, powerless. "Why you?", he asked, his quiet sad voice still heard over the tremors and noise.

"Who else could?", Ilene answered, genuinely terrified but letting out a weak chuckle. "I'm still eighteen. I'm bonded with a gem. And I'm the illegal child of two of the greatest warriors that ever lived. I'm the only one aside from Velhonen who can. It's like... I was brought into the world for this moment."

Mek'el had tears streaming down his face despite knowing the danger releasing his emotions could do at this moment. "But you'll..."

Ilene's hair was glowing and so were her eyes, blue light was almost coming from her pores again. The light changed into the colours of the three gems but then slowed blended and became bright white.

"I wish I could give you my strength.", Mek'el sobbed as he looked at her. He didn't know what to do with himself. He kept reaching forward, out of instinct, only to give up and start doing it again.

Ilene smiled, as brightly as she glowed in that moment. "But you did. You all did.", she answered. "And for all of you, I have to do this. Let someone else give for *you* for a change."

"O.K.", he conceded. Mek'el nodded and wiped his eyes. He could guide her one more time. He regained control, but barely. "Obliterate the White Room, Ilene. You don't need it anymore.... Let it all in."

Ilene nodded and closed her eyes. The glow grew brighter as she let her emotions go completely. She revisited every memory, good and bad but she focused on the good ones. She saw her families, adopted, chosen and biological. She saw their smiles, their lessons and heard their voices.

The ground slowly stopped shaking and trees began to stand still. The water stopped roiling and rocks fell back to the earth.

The Tainted army tumbled to the ground, littering the realm with debris and dust.

The Verndarar looked around, dumbfounded. They headed back to the clearing, moving to the Light which was so bright now that they couldn't see that someone was standing at its centre.

Charlotte ran forward when she noticed Mek'el there and could hear Ilene's name circling around in his mind. He heard her coming and spun to stop her, wrapping her in a submission hold that she would normally have been able to evade if she hadn't been so full of emotion and focused on Ilene. They tumbled to the floor together.

"*No!*", she cried, "Let me go! *Damn* you, Mek'el."

Mek'el was like stone again. He wouldn't budge. "She has to, or no humans will survive the night. And we will all die."

"I don't care.", Charlotte screamed, clawing at her oldest friend. "I *won't* lose another *child!*"

Mek'el eyes widened in surprise at her words and the narrowed in pity and pain. "I love her too, Charlotte. But only she can do this."

Charlotte began to sob, and Kuruk walked up and placed a hand on her shoulder. He was struggling to hold it together too.

"Charlotte, be calm. The more we lose control, the harder we make it for her to do what she has to."

Jason could hear all of these conversations while he and his father were holding Velhonen. Toshio walked up with Skogul and the others.

Niamh pushed Jason off Velhonen and forward, taking his place and holding Velhonen down. "Go to her.", she urged, slight annoyance in her tone, mainly because he wasn't moving fast enough.

Jason walked forward, as if in a dream and then he started to run straight for the light, past everyone. He vaguely heard Mek'el's warning not to touch her.

There she was, almost too bright to see, as there weren't any shadows to pick out her features. She saw him as he slowed back to a walk. His eyes adjusted and he could suddenly see her face, but she looked horrific. Her face was so thin, she was already looking skeletal.

He reached to touch the sword but heard a weak grunt and got blasted back.

"Let me help!", he cried, "Please, I owe you everything."

Ilene shook her head in a tiny motion. 'No', a smaller version of her voice answered. 'I'm almost done. I'm not just fixing two realms here. You have a life to live. You have an eternity...so take it. My second unintentional gift to you. Put the world back together with our family.'

'Where's that book?', Jason thought, looking around frantically.

Ilene's voice came through stronger suddenly, fury darkening it. 'DON'T YOU DARE!'

Jason looked at her face as she slumped down, weakened by her outburst. 'I won't take life, not even if it's given willingly. This is for me to do, for all of us.'

Jason was struggling not to cry now. He didn't want to bury two women in his life. He couldn't bear it.

Ilene was sitting with her front against the sword and her hands still wrapped around its hilt. He could barely hear her breathing. Jason sat beside her slowly and laid his head against her leg, even though her skin burned his cheek. He didn't care. He just wanted to stay close to her.

'You told me we'd train together.', he whispered.

Ilene sighed. 'I know.'

'You said we'd fly together.', he protested.

Ilene was in agony. It felt like someone was branding her muscles, clawing at her bones and pouring lava into her head through her eyes. She couldn't stop it. She was too weak to let go of the sword, even if she'd wanted to. But she didn't. She was almost done. Everyone would be safe.

Almost done.....

Almost......

Ilene was silent. Jason looked up. She was motionless a silent tear running down her cheek.

Jason's face wrinkled in pain. They didn't have long, and her light was literally fading.

Charlotte was standing, holding onto Kuruk and Mek'el's arms for support. She felt a wave of nausea hit her, but she shouldn't have.

One of the Verndarar who hadn't left the realm in decades came running through the trees. He was Aboriginal Australian and shifted out of a lupine figure to standing.

"I just took a look through the portals. They're all open. Most of the Tainted are gone but she *has* to keep going."

Charlotte's face fell. "She won't manage much longer." She turned to Mek'el. "What can we do?"

As she asked this, the ground moved slightly and a nearby body of water, shifted unnaturally.

Kuruk took out his sword, preparing to fight again.

Charlotte's face fell into her hands. "No, no, no, *nooooo*!", she groaned.

Then Mek'el froze in and place and took her hand, hard. "*Look!*", he gasped.

Charlotte lifted her head and her mouth fell open.

Some of the previously Tainted debris reformed, moving towards Ilene, but not in the form they'd all been fighting.

The bark climbed up into a full and curvy female humanoid frame, walking slowly, and vines wound up around the back, weaving themselves into a glowing green robe that trailed about a meter behind, flowers in its 'hem' and down the back. Water flowed up its centre and poured from the top of the form like flowing locks. Every step the figure took, flowers and dew formed in the impressions of its feet.

A woman now walked across the clearing and was almost in front of Ilene's flickering glow.

'Gaia?', Charlotte called.

Everyone who could dropped to their knees in shock and their familiar respectful gesture.

Jason heard movement in front of them and opened his eyes. What he saw made him sit up straight before he'd realised he had done it. A woman made of wood, greenery and water with glowing precious stones for eyes was in front of them. He found himself on his feet, moving away, but he moved back instantly when he saw who she was heading for.

The woman paused, seeing the wariness in the young man's face. Her face moved into a gentle smile.

'Jason', she greeted, her voice echoing just like Ilene's had done when she used her father's pendant.

This made him jump. His heart was racing. She knew his name.

'I have to help her, or she won't survive.', she explained.

Jason frame sagged and his eyes filled with tears. '*Please* save her.',

359

he begged.

Gaia smiled again, light reflecting in her gem eyes, and she nodded. 'I will. Because she is strong, the strongest of us. And also, she saved *me*.'

Gaia knelt down in front of Ilene and touched her face. 'Child, you've done well. Wake up now. Feel my strength. The task is almost done.', she cooed.

Ilene inhaled; her eyes still closed. She began breathing faster, colour returning to her cheeks with each breath, and her glow returning. Soon, she was hard to see again.

Suddenly Ilene's eyes snapped open, as Green as the exit crystal and she gasped. Light exploded from her body with a sound like a cracking stone. 'I see.', she whispered, staring up at nothing, her eyes flitting frantically in all directions.

Jason was on the floor looking up at her. The blast of light had sent out a shockwave from her that knocked everyone and the temple completely flat.

Gaia walked to Ilene's right and placed a hand on her right shoulder. 'Please. Save the Human World.'

Ilene turned to Gaia and smiled. She took in a deep breath and held it. The light began to pulse like a heartbeat, then it gradually picked up speed, resembling strobe lighting at its fastest. With a grunt and a shout, Ilene let loose one last shockwave, and everything went white.

There was dust and pollen everywhere. The air was thick with it, and everyone was picking themselves off the floor.

Kuruk coughed. 'I feel like I've spent the last day either tied up or falling onto my butt.', he grumbled.

Charlotte coughed in reply and chuckled. 'Ah, I wondered why the ground kept shaking.'

They all walked forward as the air cleared. Ilene and Jason were standing in each-other arms and a tight hug. It wasn't clear which one of them was crying but someone was.

Charlotte ran forward and joined the hug. Everyone could definitely tell she was crying. She pulled Ilene from Jason, a little too vigorously in her excitement, and took her face in her hands. "I don't care what apocalypse comes in the future, don't you *ever* do something that reckless again or.... or...."

Ilene just stared at her, dazed. "You'll break my legs?", she completed.

Charlotte laughed. "Don't tempt me."

Mek'el walked up, giving Charlotte a disapproving look and shaking his head. "Woman, you love waaaaay too hard. Chill out.", he reprimanded.

Charlotte laughed again and elbowed his side, making him wince. "Not in my nature.", she teased. She started looking around. "Where's Gaia?"

Jason suddenly spoke up. "Where's...?"

Ilene quickly pulled the sword from its groove in the clearing. "This night isn't over yet."

*

Scape. Pant.

Scrape. Pant

Velhonen was exhausted and fuming.

And now he was trying to escape, bleeding, his skin and joints burning with the pain, while he was dragging his mentor's unconscious and bloody body to the nearest portal.

Maybe he could salvage this, regroup and find another way. He had a scan of the Book of Calling in his office. Maybe, if Marcus survived, they could find another way to win in its pages.

'I can still do this.', he thought, attempting to focus past the pain. 'They will still pay. All of them.'

The portal was in sight. He couldn't see where it opened to. He didn't care. He just had to get away. Ilene and Jason had done a number on him, and he couldn't remember clearly but he was pretty certain Ilene had used the Mwisho sword on him because the gashes in his leg and side weren't healing.

He wasn't used to this. It was frustrating and truly irritating. He couldn't even unfurl his wings, not that he had done it much in the last century. But his strength was almost gone.

Out of his peripheral, he could see movement in the greenery. He didn't bother to turn. He just focused on the portal in front of him. But it was too late. He growled in frustration as the vines and branches that had been flanking him beat him to his destination and wove themselves into a barrier in front of him.

He dropped Marcus and screamed angrily, using the last of his strength to change his hands and claw at the blockage, sending pieces flying every in rhythm with his frantic motions.

The sensation of being dropped made Marcus stir and slowly wake up.

Velhonen turned as Marcus sat up, nursing the first wound he could reach. They both look up in the direction they had come from and cursed in unison.

Gaia approached, seemingly floating towards them as more vines and branches moves her forward on a living platform, which moved as an extension of her.

Velhonen slumped on the floor. Marcus touched his shoulder in a consoling gesture and begrudgingly looked into the eyes of the being he had loved for over a millennium. Her face was wracked with pain and pity. His heart changed from being full of reluctant longing to seething hot rage. How dare she look at him with pity after what she'd done to him, as if there was any regret in her heart about what she was going to do next! The gall of this... creature!

Ilene was looking at Gaia too and wondering if she processed emotions the same way they did. She was the physical representation of a planet after all. Did she feel it the same or less, the emotions now dulled over time? Or worse, did she feel more? What would happen if *she* lost control of her emotions? The planet would eat itself alive, devouring everything around it, most likely.

Gaia felt her eyes and probably heard her thoughts too. She turned to her briefly and smiled, her eyes still sad.

She looked down at her first warrior, her heart, or a semblance of a heart, aching, thinking of how things had been in the beginning and seeing his mind now. The anger, the disgust, the righteous indignation.

"Marcellus...", she began, but he cut her off.

"Save your false piety.", he spat, his eyes glistening with the beginnings of tears. "Just kill us and get it over with."

Gaia closed her eyes and shook her head.

Marcellus huffed. "You won't. You won't get your hands dirty, will you.", he jeered. "Got to keep your image clean, right? You just make creatures to do your work for you and clean up your mess."

Gaia opened her eyes suddenly, her hands clenched into fists. The ground of the entire realm vibrated, gently at first but then violently, making Jason and Ilene reach for the nearest thing to stabilise themselves against.

Ilene looked up at Gaia once she felt safer and didn't even recognise her. Her gown was now peppered with large protruding thorns and the layers of her bark-like skin lifted up like quills on a porcupine.

She was walking towards Marcus now, looking over him. Ilene didn't know what her face looked like, but it was enough to make a two-thousand-year-old soldier recoil and shrink into himself suddenly.

Ilene didn't envy him at this point.

"I 'made' my warriors because I can't be everywhere at once. Because the world need protecting. Because I couldn't, in good conscience, wipe out every human even though the powerful ones ruin EVERYTHING THEY TOUCH!", Gaia stormed, her voice growing louder and the realm quaking like a snow globe in the hands of a giant. By now, Ilene had grown claws and dug into the nearest tree. She looked around and she saw leaves, flowers and stones rolling around or falling to the ground. This little display was littering the already messy realm with more debris. If this didn't stop soon, she'd probably be the first person to puke in front of Gaia.

The quaking suddenly died down and Ilene looked forward and saw Gaia looking like her usual self. Ilene put her feet back onto the ground. She hadn't even realised she'd pulled her legs up.

She looked for Jason. He was coughing and gagging. They exchanged a glance. Jason mouthed the words 'Holy shit.' Ilene laughed quietly by huffing through her nostrils, and then reminded him he could have just said it, since everyone there could probably hear their thoughts anyway.

Ilene turned her head back towards the portal as Gaia stopped moving entirely. Marcellus was no longer in a recoiling and shrinking stance. He was looking up at her, puzzled.

Gaia blinked and opened her eyes to look sadly at him again. "I 'made' *them* because you broke my trust and...you let me down.", she groaned, her posture sagging and then straightening again. "And I needed someone to be better than that. And now you've returned, leading an army to destroy everything we built together?"

Marcellus had a ball in his throat. He swallowed it back and answered anyway. "Yes.", he responded.

"To kill what we have protected for all these years?", she asked again, making her face level with his.

The conflict in Marcellus' face was screaming from his features. The pain, the anger and the unbearable love, all jostling for power in his eyes, lips, neck muscles and brow.

"Yes.", he all but whispered.

They both quietly cleared their throats simultaneously as Gaia stood up again and took a step back, turning to face Ilene, one cheek wet from a rogue tear.

Gaia's voice was even. "Ilene, I have heard the desires in your mind."

Ilene froze a little. Which ones? That was never a good sentence to hear. The remaining Verndarar were now walking quickly towards them. The realm had been cleared of the Tainted and their curiosity about the quaking had moved them to find out what was happening.

"I have seen what has been taken from you, what you have suffered and what you have had to sacrifice to get here. And I appreciate all you have done for our people. So, I will give you the opportunity to choose what happens to these men."

A wave of growls and angry thoughts rose from behind Ilene, the loudest being Me'kel's, Gerry's and Charlotte's.

Gaia's head snapped towards the rest of her 'children'.

'She and she alone can choose. Do not influence her decision.', she commanded in a clipped and stern voice.

The growling, cursing and thoughts subsided, in obedience, to near silence.

Ilene didn't turn around. She was thinking. She could feel everyone's eyes on her, pressing into her head and shoulder blades like invisible fingertips. She was playing a mixture of memories in her head. Amanda's death, the pain of her people's faces when they were released from their stony prisons, the civilians injured or killed by the Tainted, the draining of the Generals, Jason's lithification, the despair spread and last, but not least, the first vision she'd had of her parents being killed. Their screams rang in her ears.

Ilene picked up the sword that had taken so many Verndari lives and strode to Velhonen. He held her gaze as she grabbed him by the back of his neck, pulled him to his feet, brought up the sword and poised it at his throat. He wasn't afraid, apologetic or resistant. He'd done the main parts of what he'd set out to do. The Human World lived but the Verndari world as they had known it was fractured and weakened. All its secrets were laid bare, all power structures were toppled and maybe all faith in their cause had been broken.

Velhonen closed his eyes, thinking of his parents and smiled. He didn't believe in an afterlife for Verndarar but he liked to think that maybe he'd get to see his parents again.

The blade pressed against his neck, nicked his throat and the pressure lessened. Then it disappeared altogether.

Velhonen opened his eyes, confused. He looked at the girl standing in front of him. Her face was blank, but her irises had flashes of red and then deep blue swirling in them.

He touched his neck and looked at the blood on his fingers as he lifted his hand in front of his face.

He felt anger growing in his stomach and chest. He could have finally rested and known peace for the first time in five centuries. He began panting as his anger grew faster and faster.

"WHY?!", he bellowed.

Ilene's face didn't change. "Because first of all, you shouldn't get off that easily. Death is too quick and good for you.", she explained, her face twisting in anger at the last word. "Granted, you were wronged and hurt. You lost and you suffered."

Velhonen's face became pitiful for a moment. The momentary compassion in her voice almost broke him. He knew he didn't deserve it and yet she kept displaying it.

"But that doesn't excuse torture, imprisonment, manipulation and mass genocide." Ilene found that she was almost shouting. "Secondly, because I refuse to be you."

Velhonen looked away. For some reason, this hurt him, and he was finding the look in her eyes unbearable.

"I lost my parents, the world I should have known and the life I should have had, just like you. And I spent years trying to figure out why I never felt like I belonged anywhere or with anyone.", Ilene confessed, not caring who heard. "But the people who raised me taught me kindness and compassion, just like yours did. And the people who created me risked their lives to protect both worlds, just like yours did."

Velhonen's head was hanging now. He couldn't look at anyone. Angry tears were in his eyes.

"You chose hatred, but I chose love. You chose revenge, I chose to continue my parents' mission. You chose murder, …. I chose and will *always* chose life!"

Ilene put the sword blade-first into the ground next to where Gaia was standing and walked away from it. "We were both raised by people who Gaia thought worthy enough to bring back so life could be protected, and yet you became…. this.", Ilene gestured with an almost dismissive handwave, disgust turning the corners of her mouth.

Velhonen suddenly found strength again. He raised his head and charged blindly towards her voice, but before he got to take more than two steps, she was in front of him, nose to nose. She struck him in the gut and then the neck, winding him. He dropped to the ground, clutching at himself and gasping amidst angry grunts.

Ilene shook her head. "They would be so disappointed in you, Velhonen. You betrayed everything they stood for and fought for. They saved your life with their own, only for you to spend *centuries* taking others."

Velhonen had tears welling in his eyes again, but Ilene felt no compassion, no remorse and no sadness at the feelings coming from him.

She turned to Gaia. "We won't kill them.", she announced, smiling at Charlotte's groan of disappointment. "But I want them to suffer. I want them turned to stone but not just once."

Gaia looked confused. "I don't understand."

Ilene looked around. "I've seen and felt the memories of everyone who had it done to them. It hurt, like being branded or dipped in molten metal, foot first.

Those who had experienced it shuddered and that now included Jason. Ilene managed to keep her reaction at bay and Charlotte looked like she wanted to cry or fight, remembering Ilene thrashing as she felt it happen to Mek'el. Mek'el placed a comforting hand on Charlotte's, horror on his face as he'd not been aware of this before now.

"I would like their mouths to stay as stone, always, but they're limbs to lithify and revert randomly, one at a time.", Ilene declared, "So they will feel a semblance of the pain they have caused others...only they won't be able to scream."

Gaia nodded as the sound of concurrence echoed around those gathered. Ilene swore she heard a high-five behind her and Charlotte's mind shout 'That's my girl!'.

Gaia stepped closer to her. "Are you sure this is what you want?"

Ilene was starting to second guess her decision as she heard Gaia's voice but then she thought of all the lives that were cut short, the pain dealt by the guilty parties' own hands, and she realised her punishment was actually kind. Ilene looked into her eyes and chuckled. "Hey, this is me being merciful. Someone was opting for eternal amputations."

Marcellus swallowed nervously and the colour drained completely from his normally olive complexion.

Ilene's smile faded to a straight face again. "But, yes, this is what I want... for all five of them."

Gaia nodded. "Ah, yes."

The realisation came to all in the clearing, including the Three Elders that had just been spoken of. They began to beg, and one tried to run. No-one knows why. He must have panicked and moved out of instinct. With a gesture of Gaia's hand, vines snaked through the air and Malik, Ekong, Serilda, Marcellus and Velhonen were bound. Then, they were lifted and carried away by some of the Verndarar like they weighed no more than a plank of wood. Ilene knew the Elders might receive some injuries if they struggled. Hell, they might receive some if they didn't. Especially, considering the people carrying at that moment had all been parents to some of the children they had harvested.

All five of them looked at her as they were taken away. Some eyes were beseeching, and some were livid. But one pair of eyes stood out the most. Velhonen's eyes were slightly sad but also filled with...Ilene couldn't tell if it was respect or admiration. This disturbed her slightly.

And then the five were gone.

The remaining Verndarar were heading back to the Temple's old site to begin to clean up. Gaia watched them leave and spoke to Ilene and Jason. Ilene smiled at her, relaxing visibly. It was all over. They were free.

"This is so weird.", Ilene commented, looking between them both. "About a year ago, I didn't know what my future would be, and I was a lonely teen in London. Now, I have friends, family and I'm standing in front of someone I've only seen in paintings."

Gaia laughed. "People paint me?", she asked, amused.

Jason nodded. "And you've been in cartoons and films.", he confirmed.

"Can you visit the Human World? I could show you around some time.", Ilene offered.

Jason's head whipped round in shock. A big green woman would be noticed.

Gaia laughed at his response. "I'll grow a disguise, Jason. Don't worry. But, yes, I'd like that. I think it's been a few thousand years, but I'd like to see what you just saved."

Ilene's brow furrowed. "You mean 'we', right?", she challenged.

"No, Ilene. *You.* I can't channel myself through the sword as I'm not a product of both worlds. Only a Verndari-born could have done what you did. That's why it only worked for you and Velhonen. It could have worked with Jason in time, once he'd trained.

Jason's eyebrows raised. He'd never need to do what Ilene did, but it was a hell of a thought. He patted Ilene on the back. "You hear that, Ilene?", he asked. "You saved the world."

Ilene cringed a little but smiled, her brow and nose wrinkled like she was smelling vinegar. "My god, that sounds unreal. I didn't think that sentence could ever be said seriously.", she replied, giggling.

Gaia laughed again at the expression on Ilene's face. "Well, it was, and you did it. Now, go home.", she advised, gesturing her hand towards the nearest portal. She held out the other hand and Ilene gave her the other two pendants before placing her father's pendant around her neck. "You've earned a rest. I'll send some of the others around to fix the house. We'll sort things here."

Ilene nodded and watched with wonder in her heart as Gaia walked away, her weft of flora drifting across the ground and the sun glinting off her streams of liquid locks.

Ilene started breathing normally again. She turned to Jason who had been watching her go too.

They looked at each-other and grinned. Jason started laughing. He scooped Ilene in her arms and swung her around, whooping and cheering.

When he put her down, he almost dropped her.

'We survived!', his mind was shouting. 'Dad's alive, you're alive and the world survived!'

Ilene was about to speak but then he hugged her and buried his face into her shoulder. She felt him shudder. Now it was over, they'd have to go home and deal with everything that happened, including how close they came to more loss. He didn't want to go back to his mom's apartment. He couldn't bear it.

"You don't have to.", Ilene reassured squeezing her arms as they wrapped around his back. "Stay with me."

Jason nodded and eventually stepped back, not quite meeting her eyes straightaway. "O.K."

Ilene held his face gently in her hands. "We'll get everything sorted. We have team of friends who can sort everything for us and with us. We'll handle it together.", she reassured him, confidence in her voice.

Jason nodded again. Still feeling the pull of the sadness linked with his thoughts.

Ilene leant into his ear. "Go and get your Dad.", she whispered.

Jason stood back, wondering why she was whispering.

Ilene headed towards the portal, her back turned. "We're flying home.", she announced. She paused and looked over her shoulder. "And this time, I may not have to carry you."

Jason's eyes lit up and he turned, running at an alarming speed to find Gerry.

Ilene shook her head with an incredulous look on her face and laughed, sitting her tired body down on a boulder next to the portal. She watched the Human World through it, now existing without the old threats.

She smiled. Everything was going to be alright.

I J FERRESTONE

STONE

Chapter 19

Family Visit

Ilene stepped through the Duty-Free shopping area.

It had been a month since the Quasi-Apocalypse. The last few weeks had been insanely busy. The house and the Verndari realm were finally repaired and tidied. Everyone was involved with several relief efforts following all the destruction.

Ilene had given the Book of Calling to Gaia and Charlotte had wasted no time hacking Hillman consolidated and stealing or wiping a lot of Velhonen's personal files including every digital copy of the Book of Calling in existence.

Due to all the sightings and online buzz to do with the Tainted, all Verndarar had to face a tough decision: either they stayed in the Verndari realm for a century or so until things died down, or they lived a normal human lifetime in the Human World. They could use their will power and not change or do any missions, as there wouldn't be any for quite some time. However, some who didn't want to risk accidentally outing themselves opted to take the pills Ilene had grown up taking.

Toshio and Skogul decided to stay in the Human World, as they were free to love each-other and be together, something they had effectively hidden from their friends for centuries. Ilene had belly-laughed at the look on Kuruk's and Mek'el's faces when it was revealed.

Those who decided they wanted to have children again stayed in the Verndari realm where they could raise and train their children without fear of being discovered by humans or harmed by their Elders or other defectors who hadn't been caught yet.

Kuruk stayed just because he felt he needed a break from the Human World for a bit. Of course, Charlotte stayed in the Human World. There was no way she'd be away for Ilene again.

The hardest part of it all, though, was registering Amanda's death after calling the police and declaring her missing. They had to place her body in an alley in a dangerous neighbourhood and unseal her wound, which Gerry and Charlotte had had the foresight to seal just after her death. They had done this before for human friends lost. Thankfully, there was a Verndari in the forensic department of the Vancouver police force who could assure that the true location and nature of Amanda's death would never be discovered or looked into.

Gerry couldn't be there. He had to play the role Jason had assumed of him his whole life: the absentee father. He would now show up after the police had "found" Amanda's body and Jason would have to act resentful and indifferent in front of them.

Amanda's funeral was beautiful. White Cala Lilies were everywhere. And everyone finally got to mourn over everything that had passed over the last few centuries. The wake was held at the McCampbell's house, which meant that everyone could let their emotions out without fear of affecting the elements. It felt good to let it all out.

Now everyone was free to move around the world without fear of death of capture, some moved to where their non-Verndari skills were needed.

Mek'el moved around, performing complex surgeries on those injured during the attacks.

Charlotte helped governments get their systems back online and working efficiently. Toshio, who's job over the last century had been carpentry and property development repaired homes and hospitals, and Skogul, who was a trained physiotherapists worked in physical rehab clinics with people who received long-term and more serious injuries.

Everyone had a lot on their plate.

Gerry took over Ilene's training while Mek'el was away and he also trained Jason alongside her, which made them both tangeably happy. Jason learned incredibly fast and reached close to Ilene's level very soon. Ilene was quicker and stronger now. She could read Verndarar minds further away than ever before. And she could now summon the strength to open portals to the Verndari realm.

It had happened randomly one day while she was in the dojo. She was thinking about when she had sent her energy through the sword, the sensations she'd felt, and then she was aware of glowing. She didn't open her eyes immediately, as the water feature usually glowed when she was near it, but there was a feeling like someone was waiting for her to do something. When she opened her eyes, she almost screamed. One of the other Verndari was staring at her with their mouth open.

She called Jason and Gerry. They celebrated together before composing themselves, testing it by throwing a spear through the portal and then all stepping through. It had changed everything. Life got easier from then on, knowing they could come and go when they wanted.

They'd go to the realm from time to time, checking on the progress there. The realm was looking lusher and healthier than ever.

Ilene would sit and talk with Gaia for hours. Asking about her parents, Verndari history or anything she could think of, and Gaia always obliged. She was unendingly patient. She had her control back after her brief slip with Marcellus.

Jason and Ilene would fly in the Verndari realm a lot, as they couldn't

do it in the Human World. Jason asked to do that almost every time.
He loved the feeling. Ilene could hear his mind and how happy he
was that they got to do what they had planned to. Ilene had never
felt his mind so at peace. It was lovely.

'Hey! Where'd you go?', Jason asked, stepping forward and grabbing
their suitcases. They were in Gatwick airport now.

Ilene snapped out of her thoughts and the chatter and noise of the
airport flooded her ears. Keeping under the radar was why she had
to sit in a tin can for hours breathing in people's air when she could
have flown it herself in about 4 hours. Oh well. It had to be done.

'Just thinking about the last few weeks.', she confessed.

Jason didn't nod, although he wanted to. 'Yeah. It's been…. it's
certainly been a time.'

They turned and headed for the exit. Ilene sighed. 'Well, I don't have
to think about it for a while. It's more or less over.'

Jason nodded and smiled as he spotted something in the distance.
'Well, this should make you feel better'.

Ilene followed Jason's gaze and almost immediately started crying.
There were the Blackman's, standing at the arrivals gate calling out
and cheering. Ilene hadn't realised how much she'd missed them
until she saw all their faces again. Billy was holding a sign he'd made
saying "Welcome home, Tess!"

Diane was beaming so hard it stretched her face out and Fred was
clearly trying to keep his emotions in check. But Simeon didn't even
bother trying. He jogged to meet her, picking her up and squeezing in
a hug that would have hurt her several months ago.

Jason's eyes popped at this display. He'd never seem siblings act like this.

Ilene laughed and playfully punched her brother's arm, being careful not to display any excess strength.

Simeon's brow furrowed, regardless. "Wow!", he said, "Look at you. You're...perkier."

Ilene laughed. He was right. She'd been a gloomy shut-in when she'd left. Now she hardly recognised herself.

Simeon's eyes did a quick sweep of her body. "And you're much more buff."

Ilene squinted and laughed. "No, I'm not. You've just probably stopped hitting the gym yourself. I'm pretty much the same." She couldn't say this for sure. She didn't look at her body often, although she did notice she was more toned thanks to the training.

Simeon wasn't convinced but in the grand scheme of things, it didn't matter. His sister was home, and he was so happy to see her. It'd had been so dull without her, and Billy had been driving him nuts. So, he just smiled and hugged her again. This was soon interrupted by a pair of hands trying to prise them apart.

"O.K. Enough, enough. Move away.", Diane instructed, "Let me hug my baby girl."

"Hi, Mummy.", Ilene gushed, giving her Mum the hardest squeeze she could, not holding back as much as she had with Simeon. As she pulled away from her, Diane looked at her with a surprised expression which became an impressed and proud look. Ilene felt like her heart was about to explode.

Diane nodded and squeezed her hand.

"They'd be proud.", she whispered in the quietest voice possible, barely moving her lips.

Ilene responding grin made Diana smile more, as it confirmed what she'd already guessed.

Billy stepped forward and latched onto her legs. His sign had been passed to Fred without a word. His face was buried into her side.

"I missed you.", he confessed, his voice muffled by Ilene's hoodie.

"I missed you too.", Ilene answered, putting her arm around his shoulder and giving him a little squeeze.

Fred walked up, smiling, placed his hand on Ilene's head and planted a tender kiss on her forehead. "Hello, bubs.", he cooed.

"Hi, Dad.", Ilene responded. She was complete. They were all there.

There was about a beat of silence.

Without looking up, Ilene called out.

"Come over, Jason.", she summoned. "They don't bite."

"But their hugs may crush you to death.", added Billy's muffled voice from within the hug. He made a faint trapped grunt, and everyone laughed gently and separated.

Ilene turned to Jason as he came nearer. "This is Jason. He and his family run my parents' house in British Columbia."

Diane smiled hard again and went straight in for a hug. Jason looked startled at first but then sank willingly into the Mum hug. Ilene could feel his heartbreak mixed with his contentment.

Billy had obviously been told about Ilene's adoption as he asked no questions when he heard the words "my parents".

He met everyone and shook hands with boys. Billy ran over to Ilene and asked in a whisper if Jason was her boyfriend. Ilene heard Jason laugh mentally at his cute and innocent question as he unintentionally eavesdropped. Ilene shook her head. Billy said that was dumb because he seemed nice. Jason smiled at her, and Ilene rolled her eyes while facing Billy, but also for Jason's eyes too.

'You'll get used to it. He's hyperactive and nosey.', Ilene explained.

'He's sweet.', Jason responded, smiling at the boy.

They all went off to the car and made their way to the Blackman's home. They made and ate their dinner together. Ilene and Jason told a human-safe version of the happenings in Canada. They explained that Ilene had done some digging into her family's history, met some of their friends and got a job. However, Ilene had left the job when one of her friends went missing and then some under-handed dealing within the company were made public. The friend thankfully turned up later but then Jason's mother passed away, so she didn't return to work until recently, now working at one of her parents' friends' surgeries.

A few looks passed between Fred and Diane, which Simeon pretended not to notice. He would ask them later. The family was aware of some of the small day to day events due to Ilene's emails, like the meeting of her parents' friends, Ilene staying home due to being "ill" and the new job. But the wider story hadn't been fully explained until now.

Once dinner was done and the boys were in the living room, while Billy showed Jason his video games and talked about films, Ilene wandered off to her old room.

She opened the door hesitantly and peeked in. It looked so foreign to her now, like the person who owned it was much younger than the person standing in there now. She sat on the edge of her bed and looked around.

Could she ever come back to this home? To this life?

A gentle knocking halted her racing thoughts.

Diane was standing in her doorway, holding a mug of tea by the handle.

"Hey.", she greeted.

"Hi.", Ilene replied, smiling. Seeing her there, it was almost like the last few months never happened.

Diane passed her the tea and Ilene took it, absent-mindedly, still looking at her belongings on the shelves and cabinets. Diane sat down next to her daughter.

"What's it like being home?", Diane asked.

"It's...odd.", Ilene responded, shrugging. "It feels alien to me now."

Diane smiled sadly and patted her back.

"We missed you, darling.", she stated quietly, her voice breaking. "So much. I was so worried about what you'd find. If you were safe. Were you safe?"

Ilene turned and was met with worried but knowing eyes. She smiled. She didn't need to worry her needlessly. Maybe one day she'd tell her the truth. "I was fine. A lot has changed about me."

Diane nodded and looked down slightly. "Like the fact that you're holding a scalding hot mug by the sides and not the handle, and don't seem to feel it?"

Ilene lowered her eyes and changed the placement of her hands immediately. "Oh!", she cried, feeling the skin on her palms go thin again as she moved them away from the mug's sides.

Diane giggled. She placed a reassuring hand on Ilene's leg. "Don't worry. I won't spill the beans.", she consoled. "It's good that you know and that you're comfortable with yourself. I wasn't sure how you'd handle it."

Ilene smiled. Her contact lenses were itching, and she wanted to remove them now that she didn't have to hide from her parents, but there were still her brothers to consider.

"Your mum, Siobhan, saved Fred's life once and I was studying as a nurse at the time. We weren't even married yet.", Diane reminisced, pulling out a photo. In it, there sat all of Ilene's parents out for dinner somewhere in Central London twenty or so years ago, smiling and care-free.

"So, Fred he'd help in any way possible. We helped them with information they needed, something your dad could do because of his government job, and I set up the distribution of your pills all over the world for...people like you."

Ilene was immersed in this story. One day, she'd ask her Dad about the day her mother saved his life.

"Then one day, they arrived in a hurry. We checked the schedules, there had been no flights from Canada that had landed within the last twenty-four hours, but they said they'd just landed. They said they had a favour to ask, something that was bigger than anything they'd ever asked before." Diane turned to Ilene and squeezed her leg again.

"Then they handed you a box... and a new-born baby.", Ilene finished, nodding.

"Yes.", Diane confirmed. "You were this beautiful sleeping bundle.

The look that was in your mother's eyes... I knew that there was real danger this time and they might not come back. The last thing she said to me was 'Look after her. Tell her I love her. She's my dream come true.'"

Ilene couldn't breathe. It was like she was watching it all from the hallway downstairs. She could picture it all. She's never heard her mother's side of that night. She could only imagine the pain of having to leave your only child.

"The wind must have picked up; I remember it because the noise was deafening. All the trees and bushes started moving a bit. The rustling and creaking. But it was weird:: I don't remember feeling a breeze. Your Dad sent your Mum off ahead of him while he did something outside the house and then came back to put that necklace in the box that he'd given us." Diane reminisced, her brow furrowing, and her head tilted back a little as she looked aimlessly at the ceiling. She briefly turned and pointed at the pendant around Ilene's neck. "When it shut, it sealed itself. We tried opening it over the years. So, you'll understand how shocked we were that you'd managed to, and on your birthday too. What are the odds?"

Diane sighed. "I don't know the full details of your people or what you will be doing, but I know it's a good thing."

Ilene nodded. "Yes. I save lives.... just like my Mums."

Diane smiled and bit her lip. Her eyes were streaming with tears before she knew what to do with herself. Ilene put her mug on the floor and wrapped her around Diane as she went wipe her eyes.

"Thank you.", she whispered. "Thank you for raising me, for teaching me and for loving me. You didn't have to, but you did it, which makes it mean so much more."

Diane was wiping her eyes again.

Ilene lifted her head and planted an adoring kiss on her Mum's cheek. "You're my hero, Mummy. You were the first to teach me about hard work and self-sacrifice. I'm glad I was taken here. If you need anything, tell me. I'll be here faster than humanly possible."

Diane nodded. "Oh, I know you will. Thank you, my darling."

"I'll visit as often as I can. I think I'll swim here next time. I hate planes.", Ilene said, her nose wrinkling during the last sentence.

Diane tilted her body away and looked amused and surprised at how comfortably Ilene mention this. They laughed until Diane had a little coughing fit and then hugged again.

They stood up together and moved towards the door. Ilene pivoted on the spot and darted back into the room, grabbing a family picture from on top of her chest of drawers.

She waved it in her hand as she walked to her Mum at the top of the stairs. "A little piece of home to take with me."

"Cool. I'll send over anything else that you want to have.", Diane said, as they descended the staircase.

"Brilliant. How about my medals?", Ilene asked.

Diane gasped. "Absolutely not!", she reeled. "I took ages setting that display cabinet up. Everything has its place."

Ilene shook her head. "Mum, I think you might be prouder of all the medals than I am.", she commented, laughing. "It's almost like *you* won them."

Diane smiled, her chin a little higher. "No, but I'm proud of my little girl and I want to be reminded of how amazing she is."

Ilene giggled. "O.K, Mum. I was only kidding."

There was a crash in the living room. Ilene could hear Billy and Simeon grunting.

Diane threw her hands in the air. "Lord, help me with those boys."

They ambled into the living room together and engaged in damage control before spending the rest of the evening swapping stories, eating and enjoying everyone being together again.

I J FERRESTONE

Chapter 20

Honoured

It was the start of the new year. Ilene was nineteen now and Charlotte had thrown a huge party at the house which ended in some sparring on the lawn under the influence of some serious drinks.

The quasi-Armageddon seemed almost forgotten by the general public, who simply went on with their day-to-day tasks. There were some, though, who weren't willing to go along with the collective assumption that a worldwide attack involving a simulated earthquake and airborne hallucinogens had been carried out by an unknown terrorist group or secret society of radicals. They would be monitored by the more tech savvy Verndarar.

But everyone was moving forward, especially the Verndarar. Everything they had known had changed. Some pregnancies had been announced and the remains of the temple had been cleared away.

Gaia was living in one of the newly built houses, among the Verndarar. She was tired of the lofty, revered role she had gone along with for centuries. She just wanted to be with her "children". People were no longer dropping to one knee every time they saw her. A small bow of the upper body was becoming the norm now.

Everything was going well.

Ilene sat in the bedroom of her Verndari home. It was built inside and around a hollowed-out redwood and used to belong to her mother before she married her father. She had pulled some of her curls back with a few shorter ones framing her face.

Charlotte walked in, sifting through the flowers in her hand. She'd picked some British wild ones, a mixture of Zebra blue primroses, wood anemone and blue cornflowers.

Ilene smiled, looking at herself in the mirror as Charlotte began carefully placing the flowers in her hair. "I'm nervous.", she admitted, her breathing slightly shaky.

Charlotte nodded, still focused on her task. "I know.", she acknowledged. "But you'll be fine. It's just a little Thank You ceremony."

"I've received trophies but never big 'Thank You's.", Ilene said. "But the crowds were never that big and...everyone in the room was human. It'll be my first time doing this around immortals and an anthropomorphic elemental."

They both laughed. Ilene stood and looked at her dress. It was white with some embroidered shapes of flowers and butterflies at the neckline and bottom hem. It had been made by some of the Verndarar, woven in a traditional method as old as the loom itself. It was a beautiful simple medieval gown that flared from the waist and had a small train at the back.

Ilene felt beautiful. Charlotte walked to her, and they looked in the mirror together. It was quite a change from their and other usual clothes. And they both preferred this look. Charlotte squeezed Ilene's hand.

"Let's go.", she urged, gently.

Ilene exhaled nervously and then smiled. They turned around and headed out of Ilene's front door.

STONE

Gaia had definitely decorated. Every surface had moss and flowers on it. Vines wreathed in flowers from all over the world hung and were festooned between trees, buildings and other plants. It looked like Bloemencorso Bollenstreek and Diwali all in one.

Everyone was in the realm, dressed in their finery from their times and cultures, some were standing in the clearing, and some were sitting on rocks and trees. The landscape looked like a busy renaissance painting with hundreds of people and angels in it.

The sun was brighter than Ilene had ever seen it. Every colour was heightened and clear, vivid and breath-taking.

As she walked forward, everyone standing in the clearing parted.

There stood Gaia, a crown of flowers in her hair and wearing a more modern-looking dress rather than her usual verdant gown. It was still decorated with flowers, but the fabric looked like a leaf when it is stripped of its chlorophyll, clear and marked with vein like lines like a dragonfly's wing.

Standing slightly in front of her but at her sides were Gerry and Mek'el. They wore long tunics of a similar colour to Ilene's, with different details woven in, trees and birds. They were healed and looked the best she'd ever seen them. They had flowers from their homelands pinned to the left side of their chests. They grinned at her as she reached them.

Gaia smiled at all three of them, her eyes resting on Ilene the longest. She tilted her chin up and scanned the area, seeing the expectant faces. When she spoke, her voice was loud and clear.

"We've come together today to honour our people. Those we're lost in the fight for our worlds and those who are here today, who continued to fight and never gave up."

Ilene looked out at her friends. Jason and Charlotte were smiling at her, and Kuruk was positively glowing with pride.

"But most of all I want to honour these three. Gierozzo, for his strength and leadership even in the face of torment and loss."

Gerry bowed deeply; his right arm tucked across his chest.

"Mek'el for continuing to lead those of you trapped in the Human World regardless of the possibility of a second death and for training the next generation, though he could have been punished for it at the time. You took on the role of parent and teacher and did it well."

Mek'el laughed, quick and joyful. Ilene had never seen him smile so hard. Ilene reached across and squeezed his hand as he placed on her shoulder.

Gaia's tone came down a little, but everyone could hear her, regardless.

"And to Ilene McCampbell, who faced terror, a new world and anguish. You cast off your old name and your old life. Your life was turned upside-down and you simply adapted. You learnt and accepted our history and our mission. You put the world before yourself and by doing that, you saved us all. Even me."

Gaia leant forward, reaching out. Ilene moved as she saw this, and Gaia took Ilene's hands in her own, holding them gently. "We owe you everything. You have made us all so proud. Your parents would be beside themselves with joy."

Ilene smiled widely as she pictured her parents there with them all. She held her emotions in check as usual. Charlotte's sniffles heard from behind her didn't help but she managed.

Gaia stepped back and addressed her "children". "You have been through much and although we have a few generals, we have no other leadership in place in case of something else happening in the future.", she began.

Ilene's brows furrowed and she looked at Jason with slight worry and confusion in her mind. Jason just shrugged.

"We are stepping into a new way of being and living and I feel that this require a new way of leading. I would like to suggest that Ilene be appointed as a General, like her father and remain the guardian of the Topaz pendant."

Ilene's mouth fell open with a pop. She was so stunned she barely comprehended what came next.

"And also, that Mek'el becomes guardian of the Ruby pendant, with Gierozzo as the guardian of the Emerald pendant."

Ilene looked to her right. Mek'el was looking at Gaia with the same stunned expression as her. Gaia giggled at the looks on their faces. It sounded like wind chimes.

"Does anyone object to the proposition?"

The clearing was completely silent. The resounding pleasure in the minds of everyone in the realm, though, was deafening.

Ilene felt so touched. Who was she to lead? She was too young. She still had so much to learn before she could earn something like this.

Gaia shook her head and smiled. "You already have earned it. Many times over.", she reassured. "Please repeat after me."

The next part was a blur. Even though Ilene didn't have the Book of Calling anymore, she remembered the words to the Sacramentum imperatore. She felt a tingle in her chest that spread to her toes and fingertips. She felt more alert. She could hear and feel everything. And there was a feeling, like an itch on her skin that resided in every part of her body facing a portal.

It had happened. She was a General. She would serve the Human World and her fellow Verndarar for the rest of her life....and she'd never felt better. She finally felt complete.

The clearing erupted in tumultuous celebration. Some took to the sky and wheeled and arced in the air. Some danced, some clapped and some like Charlotte and Mek'el just cried and crushed Ilene in a hug to end all hugs. Everyone gathered for the traditional post mission celebratory group photo. The tripod had to be set up very far away, since the picture had to include everyone there. But the picture came out beautifully. Everyone looked so happy.

And they danced and ate and drank for the rest of the day, free strong, hopeful and united with a view to the future.

And on the edge of the clearing, a solitary and small pink bud that no-one had noticed amongst the millions of flowers that day, bloomed on the once barren tree of New Life.

THE END

Printed in Great Britain
by Amazon

63221323R00221